PRETTY ENOUGH FOR YOU

D1714987

PRETTY ENOUGH FOR YOU

Cliff Hudder

Texas Review Press
Huntsville, Texas

Copyright @ 2015 by Cliff Hudder
All rights reserved
Printed in the United States of America

FIRST EDITION

Requests for permission to acknowledge material from the work should be sent to:

Permissions
Texas Review Press
English Department
Sam Houston State University
Huntsville, TX 77341-2146

Acknowledgements: See Page 354

Pretty Enough for You is a work of fiction. Names, places, incidents and characters are a product of the author's imagination or are used fictionally, and any resemblance to actual persons, living or dead, is entirely coincidental. Portions of this work have previously appeared in short story form: "Inappropriate Love," *The Cream City Review* 22:1 (1997) 78-88, and "Misplacement," *The Kenyon Review* 19:1 (1997) 105-117.

Cover design by Nancy Parsons, Graphic Design Group

Library of Congress Cataloging-in-Publication Data

Hudder, Cliff, 1957- author.

 Pretty enough for you / Cliff Hudder. -- Edition: First.

   pages cm

  ISBN 978-1-68003-038-9 (pbk. : alk. paper)

 1. Attorney and client--Fiction. 2. Fathers and sons--Fiction. 3. Parents of autistic children--Fiction. I. Title.

 PS3608.U3P74 2015

 813'.6--dc23

                2015003440

For Dyl

PRETTY ENOUGH FOR YOU

And I feel pretty, pretty enough for you
I felt so ugly before, I didn't know what to do

Eliot Smith "Pretty (Ugly Before)"

Part I

October for Sure

i.

I know myself. That's the good news. That's also the bad news. For example, I knew I was not equipped to deal with the Leudecke case. I also knew I wouldn't turn it down or hand it off to somebody better suited. But, seriously, what background did I have in eminent domain? Or with Mexican drug dealers? Or dead Mexican drug dealers? None. And I knew it.

I know October, too. October is the month of change. Maybe not for most, but for me, that's how it is. Or that's how it was last October because in that month, I was put in charge of the Leudecke case, I was hounded by a crazy pyro ghost giant, I got assaulted in Mexico, solved a couple of murders (of dead Mexican drug dealers), and . . . let's see . . . there was a witch involved . . . but most important, the biggest thing, was that I ended up very close to asking this girl, this young girl, to run away with me forever. I was very nearly about to propose to her that we begin a profound and enduring and meaningful relationship of reciprocal love, right there, from scratch: let's go. And it was in the middle of her wedding, too. Or her reception, at least. I came very close.

Then Henry—my son Henry—he touched his foot to home base and scored the last go-ahead run in the bottom of the seventh inning (there were only seven innings), the last run of the season, in a series championship game, although that, of course, was summertime. But his big moment came about because of what happened last October, too, because of how I tried the best I could to win the Leudecke case in that month, but failed miserably and lost my job. You can't have a month like that and keep a job. You'd probably get thrown out of a wedding reception by guys in green jackets, too, like I did, plus get fired—but maybe that, the loss of my job, is not what's important. It's not as important as the young girl thing, anyway, at least not in my mind.

And, now that I think it over, it's possible I might have given the wrong impression, because I need to clarify. Really this is one week in October I'm talking about. Or one week and two days, to be precise.

October in Houston is a bitch.

Even before all that, when I was with Alice—her sprawled on the high, king-sized mattress in her thong, her FBI T-shirt, her brown vinyl jacket—I'm pretty sure I already knew about her, too. I knew what I was about to do to her. I didn't know I'd do it twice, or lose Chloe, or lose my job, or that Henry would score the winning run of the championship season, or that I'd end up here. No. I knew what I was going to do to Alice, but there were plenty of other things I did not know.

ii.

This part happened in Austin, where, face down, Alice was spread like a skydiver, one pale, veined leg spilled over the edge of the big bed. Good old Austin, at the Sheraton by the convention center, at four o'clock in the morning. I already had the Leudecke case to deal with then, I just didn't know it.

I could, when I squinted to the right, look into Alice's dry knee, and if I turned a bit I could even see how her scalp showed through the places where her coarse black hair had thinned. It was funny how I always forgot about her thinning hair. Maybe the shiny dome of the chef on the cooking show I tried to watch on TV rather than listen to her excessive complaining called attention to it. Also, and I hate to mention this, but there it is: I could smell her. Especially her feet. I couldn't remember if Alice had taken a shower since we'd gotten to Austin, and we'd gotten to Austin four (or five) days before.

"I'm a failure as an adulteress," she said.

"Technically," I pointed out, "I'm the adulterer here." I still didn't look directly at her. "But if you think we should take some time off. . . . "

"So inefficient when it comes to cheating. Alton was good at it. Alton was incredibly versatile."

Yeah, yeah.

"Alton and I had that amazing Christmas in Cabo."

Fuck Alton. But she and I had snuck out of town for a few days, played hooky, holed up in this Sheraton in Austin, and it dawned on me—at four in the morning—that despite her relentless talk during those days, non-stop pretty much, I'd missed something about Alice that had to do with Christmas. She'd brought up the holiday in various annoying contexts five times in the past hour. But did she want to spend next Christmas with me? Why? Was there some big deal about it? And was there anything I could do to stop her from telling me?

Christmas? Hell, it was only October.

Alice and I had been up for hours in the hotel room. We had hashed out our relationship. We had hashed out the drawbacks of Sheraton room service. Although, really, she had hashed, and I had tried to watch cable TV. At that point I wanted to listen to anything except Alice and her words.

"I'm caught in a vexation spiral," she went on. "When I can't reach you, I'm lost. Then I can't call and tell you about being lost. And Christmas is coming."

"I won't lie to you," said this bald guy, Brad, on the 57" Sheraton TV screen. Brad called himself the Casual Chef. It was, in fact, the sixth consecutive episode of *The Casual Chef* that I'd watched trying to avoid dealing with Alice. It was a late-night Food Channel *Casual Chef* marathon. I kept watching these episodes and tried to ignore Alice, though I sat right beside her in a chair next to the bed where she sprawled, there in a fairly tiny hotel room in the early hours of morning. "It's true," Brad said. "Ladling crème gravy over the top will boost the cholesterol content." He was making an *étouffée* sub.

"And nobody knows how I feel. Nobody can."

"Probably, we should head back to town," I said, but rubbed my temples. I knew two more hours of this in the car would kill me. And not kill me metaphorically, either, because I'd begun, lately, to feel vulnerable. Fragile. Things didn't roll off me like they used to. My shoulder was a problem, and the pills didn't work on the pain any more. Really, the pills didn't work on anything any more, plus my "doctor" said I had vitamin deficiencies, especially D, but I kept forgetting to take the capsules. Shit, did I have memory deficiencies, too? I had done well. I had stretched my nineteenth year pretty far. I had stretched it right up to my forty-fifth year, some might say, but now I was forty-eight.

And I felt forty-eight.

"I don't blame you," Alice said. "Although it is your fault."

"That makes sense."

"But can't we stay one more night? God, it would hurt to lose you, especially now."

"I don't know. We've been gone for. . . ." I really wasn't sure. "Some amount of time."

"And you'll be with *you know who* for the holidays."

I'd spend the holidays with my wife, her sister we'd brought from the Philippines as an *au pair*, her brother we'd brought over for no purpose I could name (he was supposed to be our cook, but it was more reasonable to call him our poisoner), and with my son, of course, Henry.

"I need a shower, and/or bath." Alice dropped off the side of the mattress, removed her vinyl jacket, and drew her FBI T-shirt over her head. She wasn't in the FBI, she just admired it. This was because of Alton, an agent she knew at the Dallas office, this guy who rocked her world. Alice grasped the thin elastic bands of her thong at both of her hips between thumb and forefinger, pinkies extended, and daintily tugged it down her legs, then kicked the miniscule leopard-skin triangle onto a pillow. She laughed. She had a great laugh, a great smile. She was beautiful in a way, despite her coarse yet thinning hair and her inflexible possessiveness. It had been good between us at times, bad at others.

Court order bad.

I know myself. I knew I should not be in Austin with Alice. I knew it was my fault I was in Austin with Alice.

"If that's okay with you," she said.

"Sorry?"

"A shower."

Alice came towards me, dipped her naked hips in a dance that would have been incredibly attractive were there not a reddish elastic thong-mark pressed into her flab, and were I capable of being attracted to her at that moment. She leaned on me, and pressed her right nipple into my cheek. It was erect, and goose-bump-y. "Will you be ready when I get back?"

"Will I."

Then: "Bent, do you love me?"

My head throbbed. Light from outside flickered on the wall behind her: streetlamps, or a spotlight out there that rotated through the sky and drummed up excitement for an event at the Convention Center across the street. It was a weird time to shine a spotlight, though.

Alice took my head in her hands, forced my eyes from the light and *The Casual Chef*.

"Braised, roasted, grilled, fried," Brad said. "It doesn't matter once it's dipped in this."

"Just tell me. If it's more than her."

"Marisel?"

Alice pressed her fingers to my lips. She sat on my lap. Heavy girl. I wasn't supposed to say the name.

"So, what's your response, counselor? Her more? Or me?"

It was time for my tried and true answer to all such questions, no matter the audience or context.

"Why would you even ask such a thing?"

Alice, naked, bulging, pale—not fooled—rose from my lap and sighed. "Harrison Bent, why are you so incapable of love?"

I watched her saggy, rippled ass jiggle to the bathroom. The mini-fridge began to whine. It had struck me, in fact, that the Sheraton's mini-fridge let out a gasping wheeze for twelve out of every ninety seconds—not the kind of knowledge one acquires when happy. The 57" TV cut over to a commercial I'd seen many times in the past hours: a waffle maker of a "special" kind presented as a "special" offer. It was a deal in heavy rotation during the *Casual Chef* marathon. I stood, rubbed my right shoulder, and considered a Vicodin or muscle relaxer, but it was so late. Or so early. I tugged at my hair a little, then grew calmer after I heard the drum of the shower on linoleum, a peppering snap that meant I'd have several minutes, at least, of not having to listen to Alice. At the window I ran a finger down the heavy curtains and pulled them apart. Outside there should have been darkness, the early morning world, but instead, the street below glowed. I touched my cheek. I felt a wave of heat on my face, and on my eyebrows. A hot glare from below rose upwards towards me; not from streetlamps, not from the sun or a spotlight, but from a fire. There was a big fucking fire down there.

I turned to look inside the room. "Uhm," I said to no one in particular.

We were on the sixth floor, maybe seventh, so I turned back, gazed down on it, this burning onion dome of out-reaching flame.

"Fire?" I said, a little more forcefully.

It was at the curb across the street, on the Convention Center side of the hotel. And under this brightness—inside it—was a silver sedan. It was a car wrapped in flame, like a boat in a fire bottle, the whole interior of it orange and burning, wavering in the heat. Paint blistered along the doors and bubbled across the flat trunk. I thought I could hear the windshield shatter and break, and the crackle of the flames themselves, but that didn't seem possible from so far away, plus through the hotel window glass. Yet I felt sure I could feel the blast of the heat.

It looked like a BMW. Something in the M Series, maybe.

"Alice?"

No other cars were parked near the place where the sedan burned. None drove past. There was only the empty sidewalk, shadows of weeds cast by the fierce light, and flames in sheets that shot out of the top of the car. A chain-link fence behind it cast elongated checkerboard patterns into an empty parking lot. I watched the agitated shadows. Where was the fire department? First responders? In either direction, I could see nothing along the street. I got up close to the window glass, craned my neck to the right. On a nearby corner a stoplight cycled through its three silent eyes that opened and closed. Yellow eye. Red eye. Green. There was no one to see the burning car. Of course, it was four in the morning.

Was I the first person to notice this thing?

Should I tell?

I leaned on the windowsill, squinted, and, below, in the driver's seat of that car, a headless torso bent forward into the orange swirl—and I realized something. Something fell into place for me. But no . . . it wasn't a torso at all, it was just the seat itself. I'm pretty sure it was just the seat. Its headrest pulled ribbons of fire and smoke down as it curled and bowed into the oven heat. Flame spilled onto the pavement in weird patches after that: liquid fire. Both tires on the side I could see caught and burned like fat candles. The flames along their tops licked up into the wheel wells. The stoplight at the corner went from green to yellow. The shower sound came from the bathroom. I couldn't stand there and watch a car burn forever.

Then I saw the man. Had he been there the whole time? With the weird glow of the flames he had disappeared into the background, almost, but he was there alright. He leaned on the chain-link, one leg raised against the fence. His hands were thrust into the pockets of his blue sports coat. When the car threw an occasional flickering yellow wash across him, I could see his face for an instant, or some semblance of a face. He was pretty far away. It was a white guy, I was sure. He was not at all Vietnamese-looking. (I'd been having Vietnamese-related issues.) He had the kind of eyebrows that are really just one long eyebrow—or maybe that was a trick of the flames, a shadow under his forehead. He didn't look at the burning car. If I were some guy, and I stood there, not twenty yards from a BMW inferno, I would definitely have looked at it, but it seemed, instead, he looked up at me.

He raised a hand. Waved.

I stood there, on the sixth (or seventh) floor. I felt trapped. Suspended. My feet seemed too far from the pavement. His wave was turned inward, as if directed at his own chest. It was the same sort of wave Henry, my son, after much coaxing, would sometimes agree to give people when it was time to say good-bye. Or when it was time to say hello.

I raised my hand as I often would at home when I said good-bye to Henry. I turned it towards my own chest. I waved back.

Of course, Alice really ought to have seen this burning car and this bizarre man, but I didn't want her to. That was my realization. That was the epiphany I'd had when I watched the seat bend down into the flames. I didn't want Alice to even know about this wonderful burning car with the man who gestured as he stood beside it. I wanted someone else to know.

I went quickly to the bed stand, picked up my phone, and returned to the window. The car still burned but the man was gone. Shit! Again I placed my cheek against the window glass to examine the street in both directions. Nothing. Had the man been there at all? Had he been a trick of all the shimmering light? I rubbed my eyes. The chain-link fence showed nothing but diamond-shaped wires and shadows that moved beyond.

"Look at these brown fluffies," said the waffle commercial.

I snapped a picture. I held my hand up to my chest again.

I picked up the room phone and partly didn't believe anyone would answer when I called the front desk at that hour, but a clerk responded on the second ring. His voice was calm. I could hear other voices in the background, too, but caught no sense of urgency.

They didn't know.

"Yes, Mr. Bent."

I hesitated, listened for shouts and sirens. "I'm leaving," I said. "Checking out."

"Yes, sir." All efficiency. It appeared there was nothing strange in my request.

I arranged for them to print the bill, asked to have the Hyundai brought around, hung up quietly, stuffed my clothes into one of the hotel's plastic dry cleaning bags—neither Alice nor I had arrived with luggage—and in less than eight minutes I was out of there. The shower was still running as I carefully closed the room door and headed for the elevators.

I thanked the ignorant fools at the front desk. I tipped the friendly, clueless car valet. They had no idea. The conflagration was on the other side of the hotel. At the big semi-circular drive with its three giant flags at the main Sheraton entrance, all was quiet and predawn morning.

I knew I could drive around to the other side of the hotel and check it out. I could see the fire. I could look for the man who'd seen me (had he?) and waved. I felt like there'd been a smirk on that face, below the unibrow. Or did any of it exist at all? It seemed like a warning. From Ngo Dinh Duc? From the universe? I'll admit it occurred to me in a kind of fantasy that it really was Henry out there. The man had, momentarily, at least in my memory, smiled in a way that seemed to hide a secret, the way my Henry often smiled. Alright, obviously it could not have been Henry, who was sixteen, but maybe some Future Henry. A Henry I would never live to see, but who had fallen through a rip in the years, come to haunt my time, show me what he'd be like when he was fully grown and big enough to lean on fences, wear sports coats, set BMWs on fire.

Either way, the whole thing had the earmarks of some kind of otherworldly sign. A sign that read: *Escape.*

I didn't bother to check out the burning car again, but drove away from the hotel. I stopped at the feeder to I-35, paused to dig out my phone, and messaged the picture to Chloe.

Then I hit the southbound on-ramp. I drove through the darkness. *Escape and warn the others.*

iii.

As I drove out of Austin, I felt a little dizzy and checked to see if anything remained in the wine bottle that was rolling on the floorboard. It was the bottle Alice and I had handed back and forth as we drove in the Friday before. But no. Too bad, because I needed to clear my head, plus I needed to wash down a Vicodin. Or a Xanax. Or possibly a Soma. So I dry-swallowed one of each, then found half a plastic bag of pretzel sticks we must have opened four (or five) days before, and nibbled those. I tried to recall something Yvonne had said to me, and what it had to do with Chloe, and I tried to figure out why I might have thoughts of Chloe at that moment. I couldn't quite understand why a burning car would bring her to mind. Chloe was this young girl I knew. *The* young girl. She was a paralegal at the firm where I worked. But what was it Yvonne had told me?

Yvonne was my therapist. I paid her one hundred twenty-five dollars twice a week for forty-five minutes of soul searching and advice. Although, really, in those days I didn't want to admit to Yvonne how bad my life had become, so it was more like I paid one hundred twenty-five dollars twice a week for forty-five minutes of evasion and advice.

I was also trying, I'll admit, to recall what day it was. What would be on Henry's schedule today? I'd miss it, whatever it was, but I liked to know.

I flew down the highway. When I passed a car, I stared at the passengers inside. "Take a look at me now," I said to them. I was a bit loopy. I noticed a strange noise in the car, and then realized it was the sound of Alice *not talking*. My hearing had been stunned, traumatized by her constant analysis of our relationship, and her oversharing when it came to her other relationships, but mainly I was sick to hammered shit of those Alton stories. I might hear about him from Alice at any moment: his style in clothes and how it eclipsed mine, his taste in fine food, fine wine, *what-evah* (as Chloe would say; young girls have all these phrases and variations on phrases these days). But definitely I heard about him during sex—or just after—because Alton was the guy who really did it for Alice. "The best in the sack," as she said. "The cockmaster." He'd been, as a young man—before his law enforcement days—quite the ladies' escort. Nearly a gigolo. "He studied sex," Alice told me, time and again. "Made a study of it."

"Yes," I would say, "in Thailand."

"In Thailand." She rarely listened to me. "And learned a lot about technique."

"I myself have no technique."

"Which you have never, ever bothered to acquire, have you? Do you remember when we did it at the San Jacinto Monument, Bent?"

Alice was outdoorsy. We'd "done it" in several open-air locales. There'd been that *faux* Japanese garden. There'd been two apartment swimming pools, three State Parks, and the breezeway of a historical log cabin restoration. Once we'd had sex on the hillside above a darkened outdoor theater while performers onstage walked through a dress rehearsal of *Coriolanus*. She explained to me that the sex we'd had at the San Jacinto Monument, however, in one of the picnic areas, in broad daylight, was the very, very best we ever had.

"By which I mean about one-third as good as Alton's worst," Alice said. This particular conversation had taken place at a seafood restaurant following an afternoon of, as she called it, "consummation." Energized, she cracked crab legs with a wooden mallet while she hammered my male prowess. "Alton would come to me like a waiter, ask what I wanted, what I desired that evening. I could take my pick." Bang, bang, bang on the shellfish claw. "Alton would have a standard 'menu,' but he'd also have featured specials." She waved her mallet around the Crab Shack at various young men in striped aprons. "Like any good server."

Once Alton had brought along another man, which I'd

heard about many times. "My only threesome. But that was a lot of attention to be getting, Bent. Too much. I mean, they were giving me the kind of attention you'd give a snake bite."

I watched her tear into the crabs like a she-bear. "Why do you bother with me at all when Alton remains alive in the universe?"

"You remind me of him. Kind of sickly looking. Besides, sometimes a girl doesn't want to deal with a big cock."

At dawn, in Bastrop, since there was nothing to eat or drink in the car, I pulled over, decided to grab a bite at my favorite mega-convenience store: Lumpy's. This was the chain with the enormous inflated squirrel mascot that wobbled in the wind, the several air-conditioned acres inside, all the junk regular convenience stores have: pork rinds, nuts, cupcakes, novelty butane lighters—plus Lumpy's' own brand of preserves, cheese dips, salsa (six kinds), turkey sticks, and what have you. I filled the tank, then went to dig my baseball cap out of the plastic Sheraton dry cleaning bag to keep the hair out of my eyes while I drove. It was sultry, Texas October, but the Hyundai's AC hadn't worked in a while, so I had the windows down. I couldn't find the cap, but, as I groped for it, my knuckles brushed against the silk-like smoothness of multi-folded articles in the bottom of the bag. I pulled out a blouse. Then a skirt and bra. Alice must have dumped all she'd worn for the past few days into the bag, and I hadn't noticed as I'd left in such a hurry. I probed deeper. It seemed all of her clothes were in there.

I thought about going back, but I remembered Alice's brown vinyl jacket, her FBI T-shirt, her leopard-skin thong on the pillow where she'd kicked it when she'd headed to the shower.

Alice was a patent attorney. She'd make do.

Inside Lumpy's, food-wise, nothing looked good. The display case of fresh-baked kolaches and éclairs turned my stomach. It was the same for the sandwich bar and the ice cream counter (vanilla sprinkled with pickled jalapeño a featured weekly favorite). I wandered through a sizeable selection of Texas memorabilia—mugs, T-shirts, large silver-starred buckles. Most of it featured grinning squirrels. All of it was made in China. I tucked my hair up into a Lumpy's baseball cap. The price tag tickled the back of my neck. Then I turned and . . . amazing, against all reason, what did I find against the back wall but a large cooler with a very decent selection of foreign beer.

These were not the everyday usual kinds of foreign beers. Not Amstel or Heineken. I pulled on the glass door and in a blast of cold air plucked a six-pack of Dutch micro-brew off the metal rack, unable to believe my eyes. Made by Trappist monks, I recalled. I hadn't had any since Amsterdam, yet there it was in Bastrop, Texas. Oh, world. The cooler was near a wide opening that led into some kind of back storage area. Hanging plastic slats separated the customer space from this back room, and through the slats I could see another large garage door that opened onto the outside world beyond, where a hazy reddish sunrise lit up the scrub prairie behind the building. And there was a loud conversation going on in that back service area. It was just a space full of boxes, shelves, junk, but I could see there also, through the hanging slats, strangely, a three-foot-tall wire cage. And in this cage there was something—some animal—and it looked like it was going crazy.

"This is some fucking shit," a guy was saying. I could only see his skinny back in the pink glare of the sun through the weave of the plastic door divider slats. "I can't believe this fucking shit." His voice was urgent, but nasal, high like a girl's voice, and wasn't really selling the content of his words. "Get me the manager," he said, though without any great conviction.

After the Vicodin, the Soma, the Xanax, that tug or urge I'd had to escape and run after my experience with the burning car had dialed back, leveled out. I could afford a side trip, I thought, so slid my body through the slats, left arm first, and walked into the back area. The smell of the caged animal was thick and rank.

A small Hispanic kid in a white shirt and a paper hat, the kind the workers behind the Lumpy's ice cream counter wore, stood beside the thin man. "I am the manager," the kid said. "I keep telling you."

"What's going on here?" I asked. Which was the wrong thing. I always ask the wrong thing.

The skinny guy turned on me. He had large-framed

glasses—the Buddy Holly kind—and was red-faced, varnished with sweat. His cheeks were smooth but under his lip he'd grown—or almost grown—one of those unshaved soul patches that I guess are hip, except I'd heard my friend call his a "flavor saver" one time—since it was in such a good position to soak up spilled soup and such—so seeing those always made me giggle.

I giggled.

"You!" said this guy. He pointed at me. "Okay. Okay." He circled me. His track shoes scraped the concrete as he walked around me. His arms were thin and veiny. He had tattoos that were vaguely Polynesian, ringed around both elbows like targets, and a T-shirt that featured a large bald eagle with an accusatory look in its eye. "What the fuck do you think you're doing?" he asked me.

I lifted the beers. "I had them in Amsterdam."

"You've got a travesty here." He turned on the Hispanic kid again, then me. I had the definite feeling he did not want to be making these statements, and for that matter he didn't even want to be there. It was an odd impression: like he'd been sent by somebody. "What the . . . *fuck's* up with having a travesty?" he tried.

The sun streamed in through a big open delivery door where a damp concrete ramp led to a back lot. A breeze came in warm off the gray plain behind the place. Just outside, past the end of the ramp, was the dark-brown wound of a plowed field, staked and rebarred, ready for cement mixers, no doubt to provide additional parking. I stood with my Trappist microbrew and tried to adjust my eyes to the light. The animal looked to be a large-boned puppy that had been half-starved. It was small, fur-matted, with blood in patches on its skin. It paced in the wire cage, except you couldn't really call it a "pace." There was no room for that. In fact, I had never seen any creature move in such a panic. It careened nonstop, threw itself against one side of the enclosure as if the wire weren't there, like it expected to fly through. Then, it turned and attempted the same hopeless move against the opposite side of the cage. The hard sun showed the sheen and dampness of its fur and the threads of slobber that hung off its chin.

"I cannot believe this fucking shit," the skinny guy said to me. "I cannot believe you people." His eyes, however, shifted towards the door, the hanging plastic slats.

"It's come down from corporate," said the kid/manager. "There's going to be a petting zoo."

"You're gonna pet the fucking coyote?" He got in my face. He whispered. "Give it to me." It was like we were conspirators, and this, my handing over of what I only then realized to be a coyote, would solve everything. It was the Lumpy's baseball cap I'd put on. He couldn't accept that the manager was the Hispanic kid, though that guy obviously had more authority than me. He even had a name badge. HI, it said, MY NAME IS CHRISTOPHER. If you want authority, find people with name badges, not people with baseball caps. I reached behind my neck, tugged at the price tag to try to show it to the skinny dude with the flavor saver.

But then more people came through the hanging plastic slats: a man and a woman, both tousled and grimy, like they'd been camped out for the weekend. This man's T-shirt also featured wildlife, in his case a forlorn buffalo on broad grassland looking noble and endangered. The girl had a handkerchief wrapped around her head like a Japanese dive-bomber. "What's going on, Walter?" she asked.

"Sell me the fucking coyote, then." Walter poked a thumb into my shoulder.

"Owww." I really was having trouble with my shoulder.

"We, the Sparrow Clan, are buying this coyote and taking it the fuck out of here."

"It's not for sale," said Christopher.

"Oh, really," said the other male Sparrow Clansman, the one with the buffalo shirt. He carried a package of white bread under his arm, held an open peanut butter jar in one hand, a slice of bread in the other. He occasionally scooped the peanut butter out of the jar with a slice of the bread. He got in my face, too, and blew peanut breath, but could barely talk as he chewed. "Net for sell, you sey?"

"I'm an immigration attorney," I told him.

"You people need to go back inside." Christopher waved his arms and shooed us all towards the plastic slats.

"Walter is right," said the woman. She was burnt and red-faced, but with pale, wrinkled legs. She pointed at the coyote, looked at me with fury. She had a half-eaten Snickers and a Slurpee, extra mega-sized.

"This is no way to enter the world," Walter said. He held out his palms, as if to refuse the reality of the scene. "We can't come down from where we were and end up here, not like this." He shook his head at the cage. "Not like this."

The buffalo T-shirt guy dipped more bread into his peanut butter. "Walter," he said, like he'd seen pointless protest from the skinny guy one time too many. "They don't want to sell it, man."

"What are you people on?" I asked.

"Fuck you!" said the woman in a high squeal—nearly as high as Walter's, in fact.

"He said you were coming down." I was no fan of putting coyotes in cages, or anything else in cages for that matter, but these types rubbed me the wrong way.

"I am sick of people making fun of the Clan and the lodge," Walter said. "We've been sweating. In a sweat lodge. In touch with the spirit."

"What does that even mean?" asked the little manager. He cracked up, laughed. "Get out of here. I'm calling the sheriff."

Oh man, I didn't want to see any sheriff. I did just need to get out of there, like the manager, Christopher, had so authoritatively suggested. I needed to move on down the road.

"It's a purifying ritual," said the Buffalo-T.

"With peanut butter and Slurpees?" I couldn't seem to pull away.

"You make fun of the lodge, you make fun of the Creator," said the angry, chunky woman.

"We're taking the coyote with us, oh my relatives," said Walter. His eyes were closed.

"No, Walter," from Buffalo-T.

"Make fun of the lodge," said the woman, "you make fun of the Earth our Mother."

Obviously, no one needs trouble with the Earth our Mother—nor was this any of my business. But I still didn't leave.

"Really, too many in the SUV already, Walter." The second guy dislodged his tongue from the thick Jiffy. "I'm not sure Sam and Sarah should ride with a wild animal."

"We'll set it free!" said Walter.

"You think you can own a coyote?" the blotchy, angry woman asked me. She glared.

"It came from corporate," said Christopher.

The plastic slats parted yet again, so I turned to see whoever was coming next to add to this confusion. But the woman and the guy with the peanut butter didn't look towards the sound. Oddly, they turned away. Walter shrugged and faltered in his pacing and gesticulating, like he'd been caught at something. Some new current had entered the space, I could tell.

I had a strange experience then.

It's like when, from time to time, you walk through a museum and look at the paintings, or you're on the computer, or walking through an adult bookstore, and you flip through the pages of this or that periodical. You turn the pages, innocently, but then stop, because you encounter some picture, or image. One that gives you pause? And it's not because it's particularly shocking, repulsive, or unseemly. Not that. You just sort of lose all sensory input. The experience becomes "anesthetic" rather than "aesthetic." Like those pictures where the contortions, the twists, bends, placement of feet, arches of backs . . . elbow arrangements . . . it's just that it doesn't look like people right off. You have to sort of do "the lady or the duck" game in your mind for a second before you go: oh, that! When I turned I saw a woman who approached in a black leather jacket and cowboy boots. It was a human woman, tan, with very black hair. A woman, that is, as opposed to a balled-up fist, sedimentary rock formation, eggplant soufflé. But her detail was so dense.

I heard vague scratching sounds. It took me a moment to identify them, to separate them from the Sparrow Clan and its chatter. It was the coyote's nails against the floor of the metal cage, which I could hear more distinctly now because I was much closer to them.

I was flat on my back.

iv.

I opened my eyes and looked into crossed girders, the topmost racks of metal storage shelves, some kind of unhealthy-looking sprayed insulation that clung to the metal ceiling. I was lying on the hard concrete floor with low sunrays crossing my face from the big back door.

"Dude." Christopher's face loomed over me. "You went *down*."

"Oh," I said.

I had passed out in the back storage area of a Lumpy's mega-convenience store.

I closed my eyes again. The voice I heard next—I didn't have to see to know—came from the woman who'd just walked in. I didn't really have to have her identified, either. It was obvious; they'd brought her with them. To Lumpy's.

The Earth Our Mother.

I felt she was near me, tending me. Had been tending to me for a while, in fact. Years, possibly. Yet her voice was not nurturing, but hard and creased like it had been injured in a fire. The kind of fire you get when expensive shit is burned. It was a voice that had been scorched in a burning mansion or something. Each syllable resonated, echoed in that back room, or possibly in my skull. This was impressive, also, because, really, when it came down to the syllables she uttered, there were only three.

"I'm sorry," she said.

They took me back a little, her words. Both of them. For one, it sounded like she meant it. There was a sincerity in this woman. I could understand—just from the few sounds she'd uttered—how the Sparrow Clan would indeed revere her; how even I could look up to her if I gave it a try. I was kind of an expert when it came to that phrase, by the way. "I'm sorry." I used it a lot. I used it thoughtfully, strategically, and—if I say so myself—with a certain level of flair. But I don't believe I'd ever used it the way she had. There was something unordinary about her "I'm sorry." And why say it at all? Was it her fault I'd passed out on the floor?

Was it?

I squeezed my eyes shut, thought about glancing at her, but couldn't bring myself to try it. I needed a moment. Her words were an apology of a kind, yes, but not the kind you hear every day. It was like the way you sometimes feel you have to apologize for your kid's howling meltdown at Burger King. Or, better, like on a tour of the Coliseum in Rome, when some American assholes in the group won't shut up—they insult the ruins, talk loud on their cell phones as the guide attempts to explain how many Christians were slaughtered—and they make you feel you have to apologize to the guide and all of Rome and to a lot of dead Christians, too, and not just for the assholes or their behavior or even for yourself, but for your whole country: maybe your way of life. It was that kind of "I'm sorry" she'd said to me. Nice. It was an apology not just to me, but to *all* of me—every part of my body, sprawled helpless on the concrete floor in that back service area. Plus it seemed possibly everyone in the store, the parking lot, probably the state—all of humanity was packed into that shameful apology the way she put it. The whole world had mistreated me. Hadn't it? But it was okay, because she understood. She accepted responsibility. She asked forgiveness.

I blinked hard in the sunrays that poured in through the big back door, savored the wholeness and powerful value of her wonderful phrase, then managed to rise on my elbows. Christopher appeared concerned. "It's not a problem," I said to the woman. I wanted her to feel better, not take all of it on herself. "No harm," I mumbled.

Her face was hidden, her back towards me. I had an impression of a fragrance, distinct from the animal musk that hung in the air, a vapor that came from her. She squatted beside the cage, her fingers intertwined in the mesh. I could make out the dark outline of the back of her head against the yellow morning sheen outside, her confident shoulders that remained still and unmoving when the creature continued to slam against the enclosure. On her upraised wrist, there was a bracelet. No: a ribbon or strip of pale red cloth. I could see the mud on the heels of her boots. I could also see that the apology had been meant for the coyote.

Then she rose, quick, stalked across the concrete, moved through the plastic slats of the wide door before I could get a good look at her. Although it seemed a man on his back on a hard floor might rate some attention, I wasn't at all sure she'd even noticed my presence. Maybe the coyote had been too interesting. She made the slats slap together loudly as she disappeared into the air-conditioned expanse of Lumpy's, and the rest of her clan followed, poured after her, their heads bowed. Walter departed last, but turned before leaving. He performed something like a backward hula dance: shook his hips and moved his arms back and forth in a way that, I suppose, was meant to convey his disgust with me, but only caused him to resemble Buddy Holly even more.

"Who was that?" I asked him.

"Yeah, right." He left, too.

"You okay, man?" Christopher asked. He got me sitting, then helped me stand.

"I'm fine. I think. What day is it?"

He frowned. "Yeah, right." Then, after making sure I wasn't going to topple, he too trailed the Sparrow Clan out the plastic slats of the door. He called after them. "You want the kielbasa to go or dine in?"

I stood a moment in the silence. Silence, that is, but for the sound of bone and fur against wire mesh. There were busted wooden pallets all over that place: some leaned against the corrugated aluminum walls, others had been stacked on top of something that looked like an unserviceable clothes dryer. There were two rows of wire racks like the ones that are in the back of nearly any service business that served as storage for miscellaneous cardboard boxes and plastic five-gallon tubs. It was all so tacky. To watch that wild animal back there with all that unnatural junk as it threw itself at the sides of the cage, again and again, was difficult. The coyote panted, looked exhausted, but never ceased in its attempts. It didn't register that I was even present. The coyote didn't care about me. It cared less about me than The Earth Our Mother did. There was no way I could get that cage into the back seat of the Elantra. There was no way I could get the thing out of there, either, without the cage.

I have to admit, I pondered the possibilities. I could see it. Dance in my face, Sparrow Clan? I'd get Mr. Coyote before they could come back, drive him away, stop somewhere along I-10, and let him go.

I knew if he could go, he would go and go and go.

I felt shaky. I watched the coyote and backed out of the room. The woman in the black leather jacket and her entourage were nowhere in sight. I clenched my Danish microbrews. At the checkout counter, I paid for them and the Lumpy's logoed hat. I went to the car, wedged a metal cap in the glove box and pulled down hard on the bottle to open it. I took a swig. Then I noticed I'd gotten a text from Chloe. I was thrilled, but I hesitated to read it. It was strange how I kept thinking of her that morning, kept conjuring her presence. I became a little reflective. What if she'd been there in the car with me? What if she'd been with me in Lumpy's? Would I have been capable of such a pathetic display with the Sparrow Clan if Chloe were also there, watching? I didn't think so. I knew if she was there, I'd have remained conscious. And that woman—I'd have kneeled beside her. I'd have joined her, and apologized to the coyote, too. Then I'd have gotten loud. This woman and I would have, together, insisted—like humans—that the right thing be done, while Chloe looked on and beamed pride and approval. Approval of me. If Chloe had been there, one way or another, that coyote would be free now.

She'd gotten the pic of the burning car, I guess. Her text read: "WTF? Is this about Leudecke?"

Leudecke? WTF was a Leudecke?

I didn't realize it then, but I'd just met one.

V.

I was back in Houston by nine, and went in to work, and at work I learned how in my absence I'd been put in charge of the Leudecke case. This was the case that would ruin my life, or save it, depending on how you look at these matters.

But it's more accurate to say I eventually I went in to work and found out about the case. It did turn out to be Tuesday, which meant I hadn't been to the firm in several days, since Friday, but it was one of those periods when to deal with work on top of everything else would have been just too much. I'd stayed away from the office quite a lot around that time, as a matter of fact. And after the weekend in Austin, and the drive in, the traffic, the long ride through the steadily ever more polluted ozone air, of course I needed to change from my four (or five) day old hotel weekend clothes, so I went home for a long shower and pulled dry-cleaned slacks and a shirt out of my closet.

Marisel and I did not share a closet. Maybe because we didn't share a bedroom. Nobody was home. Henry, I knew, would be seated at a table at that hour, across from some highly trained and impossibly patient young woman instructor, probably with straight, pulled-back, brown hair, at his mega-expensive school, where I thought, with luck, I could keep him enrolled at least through the holidays: but then what? With Henry out, my wife's little sister, Alexandria, was cut loose, too. God knows where my wife and her brother might have gotten to, but it was no doubt someplace that was at that moment costing me something. Everything Marisel did cost me something.

After getting cleaned up and dressed, I felt I must be hungry, so I drove to a deli I liked in a nearby shopping center where the parking lot was already full—had to drive around ten minutes to find any place to park—but I couldn't even eat anything once I got inside. I just had a beer, bought a newspaper and read it awhile. (Come to think of it, that's when I found out it was Tuesday.) It was the usual newspaper stuff. There'd been a propane truck explosion on the West Loop. Then, somebody had found a carpet roll on a mountain bike trail along a bayou, and inside the carpet there was a decomposed body. It didn't sound like the decomposed body of anyone I knew. So I finished reading most of the paper and it was on into the early afternoon when I finally got to the parking garage, took the elevator to the office, where Ruth, the hatchet-nosed receptionist with the skinny legs—the chain on her glasses so old-fashioned it had snapped back into vogue—glared at me as I came into the foyer. She gave me a not-so-neutral look that said "Look who's here," or "Where has he been?" or possibly "Say, there's that guy who ruined my life" (which I most certainly had not). But she alarmed me. It was like Ruth had aged so much since the week before. I'd never noticed there were folds of skin—flaps—under her jaw: skin that flapped on her neck. I stared at this skin awhile. On the high, narrow counter in front of her was an enormous envelope of the large, yellow, bubble-wrap-insulated kind. I was not in a position at Davison, Kohlhoeffer & Loeb, LLP to receive large, insulated envelopes, so I figured it had nothing to do with me.

I was wrong.

But the fact that Ruth was not quite asking me "Where have you been, Bent?" in her cold, foldy-necked, sinister way—like she somehow didn't ask me about my whereabouts since Friday in an ironic fashion—this didn't help me feel less sorry I'd spent four or five days at the Sheraton next to the Austin Convention Center, just because Alice had showed up one afternoon at my office with a bottle of wine.

I couldn't take it, Ruth and her attitude. I turned on my heel, spun, and moved back towards the elevators. I raised a palm to my forehead in the universal silent movie pose: Oh, I forgot . . . I'm supposed to be somewhere. . . .

"Bent!"

Stealthy, malevolent Ruth had croaked out my name. I turned and she tapped the thick package on the counter with two of her bony fingers.

"Yours."

I picked up the package. I figured I'd better stay. If I left now . . . went to a bar . . . went to Chinatown. . . .

If I did any of that, my therapist, Yvonne, was going to be just a little too pleased.

The package was heavy, like a book. It was labeled, but I ignored that for the present and walked past the cubicles, past the big conference room. I shook the package against my ear, checked for suspicious rattles or ticks. I went down the hall past the two small conference rooms, where, thankfully, I saw no one. Tentative, I raised my swipe card towards the door of my office. It was an exterior one—not a corner office, but near the end of a hallway, out of traffic—and featured an impressive view of the downtown skyline from the thirty-second floor. Impressive, yes, though in the hallway a fluorescent tube blinked the same spastic flash it had when I'd called maintenance about it two weeks before. I raised my card and felt a moment of suspense—or the usual moment of suspense—when it didn't seem like the lock mechanism would work. It was that instant of uncertainty when it appeared quite possible that there wasn't going to be a click and a whir today. This was it. Not the sort we like to keep at Davison, Kohlhoeffer & Loeb. You are out. Starting. Right. Now.

But then there was the click, and I pushed the door open, and had my other usual moment of uncertainty until I hit the lights and saw that the whole thing hadn't been cleared away. My books, binders, papers had not been packed in cardboard boxes and labeled for storage. There was the empty wine bottle on the credenza, the unwatered plant (looking bad). There, in the air, the whiff of something—gym locker?

I ignored the stack of folders on my desk, flipped on the computer, cranked up the blinds the whole way (fabulous view!), and started to open messages and e-mails without looking at them really. None of them made any sense, anyway. Some were from people who wanted to know things. Others came from people who wanted me to do things. Seven in a row came from Ngo Dinh Duc—that pain in the ass—which I deleted without reading. I did open one e-mail that seemed frantic (maybe it was the HELP ME! HELP ME! subject line) from a lady with an I-90 green card renewal issue but no understanding of subject-verb agreement. I got halfway through it before my eyes went fuzzy and I gave up and forwarded it to Loeb. Little Loeb, that is. The son of one of the founding partners.

I began to think that coming to the office had been a mistake. If I was to start my week on a Tuesday, maybe I should start somewhere else. With something easier than actual work. Maybe I should have taken the afternoon off to pick up Henry at Spectrum of Achievement (his hyper-expensive school), or signed up to take piano lessons. I'd always wanted to start piano lessons. At forty-eight? Why not? Or something simpler still.

Then Chloe and Loeb stuck their heads in my door, one from either side of the frame—stage left, stage right. Somewhere was the other Loeb, the partner with his name in brushed gold behind Ruth's wrinkly head in the foyer, a *Big Loeb*, but him, I'd never met. I'd seen him twice in maybe seventeen years. This was Little Loeb and his Little Chloe. And the two of them said, "Hey, Bent," and "Where you been, Bent?"

"Convention."

"Car-fire convention?" Chloe asked. "Looks to me like you went to a terrorist state."

"Just something I wanted you to see."

Chloe was young, twenty-five or twenty-six, and skinny, as young girls are—although, according to herself, she used to be a fat girl. It was possible. She packed some inertia behind those play punches she'd give me occasionally on the arm. Chloe did triathlons now, and wasn't fat anywhere. Maybe ankles. She grinned at me, like she was glad to see me, and her teeth were small—her mouth mostly pink gums with rows of small, sharp teeth on top and bottom. She tossed her hair, and in quick profile view Chloe's face was oddly flat, like a plate with a tiny nose on it. I swallowed hard.

"Glad you made it back," she said.

"We thought you were going to miss your four o'clock," said Little Loeb, who aimed a knowing look at Chloe.

Sure. Aim your knowing looks, Loeb.

"Yes, no way I'm missing my four o'clock." I stabbed at the keyboard and shuffled a folder on my desk to show I was busy, at work, deep in the middle of important acts pertinent to the Gulf Coast's large, lucrative immigrant population. I was not the smartest attorney in the world but knew how to handle . . . I-90 green card renewals, let's say. So I ignored them, playacted like I knew about the thing at four o'clock they were going on about.

"We don't have a lot of time to get over there." Chloe walked to my desk, tapped the large, overstuffed, bubble-wrap envelope I'd dropped on it. "Did you get a chance?" she asked. She looked excited.

I still hadn't opened it, hadn't even read the name on the label, so I continued to move folders and make keystrokes. "Not much time," I said. "And . . . just where are we on all that?" It probably involved some sort of meeting. Everything always involves some sort of meeting. I hit the "messages" button on my desk phone and began to pretend to go through those to have something to do. In general, on a normal day, during the course of a week, even, there were zero messages on there. But I could tell from the readout that there were . . . what the hell? Forty-six? So I bent close to make sure I wasn't mistaken about that. Mr. Duc seemed too busy for those kinds of shenanigans—unless he'd had his waiters do it—or had Alice gone batshit crazy with the voice mail again? I imagined her quasi-naked on the bed at the Sheraton, recording her venom for the past six hours, but then the messages started, and it wasn't Duc, and it wasn't Alice.

Pretty soon Chloe said "Oh my God, that's terrible!" Loeb leaned on my desk and said "That's terrible!" and "Is there anything I can do?" Because it was my mother's neighbor who'd called, a lady who lived next door to her in the chemical-plant suburb southeast of the city. The first message was from three seventeen in the morning, two days before. And Blanca, the neighbor, was tearful, and she went on about the ambulance, and the police, and the door kicked down, and "Harrison, you need to get over here," she said (no one calls me "Harrison"), and there seemed to be voices in the background, then *click*. The second message was calmer, but not much. Blanca was in her sixties, about ten years younger than my mother. She was the neighbor I always reminded Mom about when she fell into complaining how "Those Mexicans" had invaded her street, and "Everything is Spanish, now," and "The signs at Food Town are all in Spanish now, I can't understand the cashiers."

"What about Blanca?" I'd say to Mom. "Who helps you out? Comes over every day, and takes you to Food Town?"

"I'm not talking about Blanca. It's those *Mexicans*."

So the voice of Blanca now spoke to Chloe, Little Loeb, and myself from a couple of early mornings back, and she said the ambulance was there—I could actually hear a siren in the background of the message—and she said "Don't bother to come" if I got the message. "Don't come to the house. They are taking her to Saint Victoria's," then *click*.

Why hadn't they called my cell? I fished it out of my pocket and saw that the ringer had been silenced. Oh, yeah. I had done that on Saturday, I think. I hadn't wanted to be disturbed. It registered dozens of voice mail messages, too. Shame I hadn't noticed when I took the picture of the burning car.

Yes, a shame.

So after six or seven of these messages, it became clear that Mother hadn't been robbed—hadn't been attacked by angry Vietnamese gang members or anything like that—but had slipped and fallen in the kitchen. She'd been able to crawl to the phone and ring Blanca, but she couldn't make it to the front door to unlock it. So first responders had manfully kicked it out of its frame, bundled her up, and taken her to the nearest emergency room.

"Saint Victoria's," Chloe said. "Oh my God." But I could never be sure if her sentiments were sincere, especially when she spoke to me. It's just a doubt I always had. Her feelings seemed like text message feelings: "OMG" and such. Sometimes I sent her funny texts, little humorous e-mails, as I was trying to keep a connection with her. I was trying to keep that connection "fresh." And sometimes, she texted me back with some abbreviation, like: "LOL."

Really, Chloe? Out loud?

Chloe was in law school, a night-school ranger who worked her way through classes as a paralegal at the firm. (She told me I worked as a para-scapegoat at the firm. Hah. Hah.) Chloe and I had never done anything inappropriate together.

Maybe once.

So the next message was from the waiting room at St. Victoria's and Blanca said the doctors thought she had broken her hip—my mom, that is—that she would be moved to St. Vincent's and "Oh, that's bad," said Chloe, and "St. Vincent's is bad for anyone," said Loeb, "And at her age. . . ."—which I really needed: reports on hospital quality from Loeb. The oldest son of the founding partner, Loeb was reedy and trim, broad across the chest and fit like an athlete, but he played no sport, and that tan didn't come from the sun. He was a total gym and spa product. Any attorney who spent that much time at a gym and spa lacked sufficient billable hours. His was not the kind of athletic strength that would allow him to . . . save a drowning child, let's say. I glared at his flat belly and youth. He shot out his arms, repeated himself: "St. Vincent's is bad," and he turned his wrists, examined his square black cufflinks, first the left, then the right, each enameled with a milky pearl figure. An L? A bent over nude? I couldn't tell, but who the fuck wears cufflinks? On a Tuesday?

"Listen," Loeb said, "I can make your four o'clock."

"Yes," Chloe said. "Stuart and I can go. There's no need."

Stuart! That was his name. Like the name you'd give a gray cat or something. That the two of them were an item was an open scandalous fact of life in the firm. A picture of the pair at an office retreat, pinned to the break-room corkboard, did nothing to dispel such rumors. It was, as a matter of fact, a picture I'd been responsible for, more or less.

I waved them off. "There's no one making my four o'clock but me," I said.

Whatever it was.

"You've got to deal with your mom, Bent," said Chloe. "Besides. It's the Leudeckes."

"Right," said Loeb. "What about the Leudeckes?"

It was odd. On any normal day, I would have sent them in my place. But I knew Loeb had a "thing" for Chloe, and this in spite of his engagement to some rich River Oaks family's offspring. For that matter, Chloe had her thing for Loeb, too. It gnawed at me today, however, most likely because of what I realized in Austin as I watched that car seat bend submissively into the heat of the burning car.

Besides, if I didn't make my four o'clock, I might have to deal with mom.

"Well, what about these Leudeckes?" I asked. "Can I not deal with . . . those?"

"They did ask for—" said Chloe.

"Am I not an attorney? Attorney enough for any number of Leudeckes?"

Finally, the messages were into the next day, things like: "The doctor says she should walk again, but she'll need a cane," and "The insurance company won't call me back," and "Your mom thinks she is seeing spiders on the wall from all the drugs (which Blanca called *drogs*)."

"Spiders!" said Chloe, so horrified, so cute.

"That's from the anesthesia," said Loeb.

Thank you. Thank you, Doctor Stuart Little Loeb. But if he didn't work at Davison, Kohlhoeffer & Loeb, it's likely I wouldn't still be there either. To the extent I had my position, my view of the metropolis, my home and career, I owed it to Loeb, though not for the reason most people usually owe things like jobs to people like him.

Blanca said Mom was trying to shoo the spiders, and telling her to "Kill the spiders!" Then Blanca cried and said she was so worried, they wanted to replace the hip with a plastic hip, and they wanted to do it fast, and "Your mother's hair looks terrible," she said.

Then another voice, after a pause. "What would you do, Bent? I mean really. If I were to forgive you."

"Who's that?" asked Chloe.

I tried to shut off the messages, but I'd had so few of them in the past I couldn't quite remember how the thing worked.

"Would you approach me? Whisper in my ear: '*I can't stop*

thinking about what it would be like to fuck you. Fuck you from behind.'"

"Isn't that Alice Dowling at Bracewhite?" said Loeb.

". . . then wait for me to be coy, or would you flirt back?"

I finally forwarded the thing to the next message. Blanca resumed her rundown of hospital updates.

"Jesus, Bent," said Chloe. "Wasn't that your stalker?"

"I don't have a stalker."

She shrugged her bony shoulders. "You got that court order against her."

Chloe and I had fallen into a habit. We commonly exchanged deeply personal information about ourselves with each other. It was true: a year earlier, Alice had taken to dropping by my home at inappropriate hours, and calling maybe fifteen times a day: texting, e-mailing, asking things like "Why don't you want me? What's wrong with me? Alton never thought there was anything wrong with me." Fucking Alton. Until just the sound of Alice's voice would make me want to destroy things around the house, like the day I put my foot through my guitar. I asked Alice: "What in the hell am I supposed to say to my wife when you come by like this?"

But the court order was probably a bit much.

Loeb laughed. "Good thing about a stalker is: they're always there when you need them."

Asshole. There was a framed picture on my desk of Marisel, myself, and my son, Henry. Actually, there were a lot of pictures of Henry, since they took them at whatever school he ended up in, and sometimes he'd be in two or three a year, and I ordered, kept, and framed them all, whether they were any good or not. It was usually the first thing people commented on—as people will—when they came into my office: "What a killer!" and "Great-looking kid" and "Handsome boy." I agreed that he did indeed have that going for him, but this photo of my whole family was larger, and sat prominently at the front edge of my desk. Marisel and I had our usual posed photo faces. Henry—he was about seven at the time of the picture—looked worried. His eyes were suspicious, his mouth open. One new tooth in the front had grown in crooked and gave him a quizzical, attentive look he rarely otherwise sported unless someone opened a candy bar near him. The three of us were side by side on a bench in front of the crocodile cage at the zoo. Because it was bigger than the other photos, I considered picking it up and cracking it over Loeb's head.

Then: another voice, elderly, with a lilting accent.

"Where is my process? It has been six weeks. Do you know who I am, Mr. Bent? Do you have any idea who I am in this community?"

I fumbled some more, finally snapped the thing off, silencing Ngo Dinh Duc.

Chloe frowned. "What. . . ?"

I scanned my ten-years-service desk clock and pen stand: three thirty. "We better get started," I said. "If we're going to arrive on time." (Wherever it was.)

"It'll be impossible now," said Chloe.

"No, we can make it. We just need to get going. You come with me and review that." I pointed at the big, bulging envelope Chloe now cradled in her arms. I still had no idea where we were headed, or why, but I grabbed up my briefcase, told Chloe to get her coat and meet me at the elevator.

Loeb stood by my door, solemn. "Are you sure you don't want me to go?"

Oh, you'd like that. You'd like that a lot, wouldn't you? But I just said "Got it," and when Chloe came back I said: "Let's go see about these Leudeckes."

"Yes, well, one of them anyway."

"Exactly. That's what I meant," I said, and I had no idea just how screwed I was about to be.

vi.

It is hard to know how things happen—and very, very hard to know why—but sometimes I can pinpoint the when, like when I decided it was Chloe who I needed—that it was Chloe who could pull all of this together for me: Chloe who could put my life back in order overnight, if she'd only play along. That decision happened sometime during those few seconds, as I stood at the hotel window and watched the burning car.

It probably had its foundations in something my therapist Yvonne said to me one time. It came down to a question she'd asked me.

"I want to know what happens when you're excited, Bent," Yvonne said. "You are excited about things on occasion, correct?"

"Of course."

Yvonne continually asked me things. Then, she continually listened to whatever answers I came up with, and pondered those answers. Sometimes, as she pondered, she blinked in a way that made moist eye-blink noises. Occasionally, she'd reach for a palm-sized sponge ball covered in plastic prods or spines. She had a variety of these she used to massage her vertebrae to deal with some kind of chronic back problem. Typical of these sorts of people, she never told me what that problem actually was. Childhood spinal disease? Snowboarding last winter? I had no idea, but always, finally, she would talk. She would coach me in life. She would help me operate "in this world."

"So, when something good happens," she said, "a good thing in your life: who is it that you turn to first? Who would you want to be the first to know?"

On that particular day, I'd had no answer, but I knew as I watched the bizarre car burn, and watched the bizarre man who stood beside it, that I did not want to tell the authorities about it, or the hotel management, and I damn sure did not want to tell Alice. I wanted to tell Chloe. And, on that drive through North Houston, heading to a coffee shop to meet with someone called Marguerite "Maggie" Leudecke (the actual name of the person she and Loeb had been referencing), I knew for certain what I needed.

I was like those soldiers in movies, the young men who sign up to fight "The Great War," or whatever. In those stories, there is always an anchor, a focal point, a "girl back home," so the soldiers can get letters when they're off facing their perfect hell, so they can have someone to write letters back to. These soldiers write letters that are filled with lies because they don't want their best girl to worry. They don't write about the chaos or death they are experiencing but instead make up future scenarios filled with future hope and positive thoughts about how great the world could be someday when he, the soldier, and she, the girl, could be together. And the fact that, in these movies, this girl always ultimately writes a letter calling off the whole thing, one that describes some new love, or some change that had occurred when she realized that they had "drifted apart," maybe a realization that struck her in the midst of one of the mind-expanding college classes she took while he was off losing pieces of his soul, watching friends blown to vapor, learning to kill and die—this part about the "kiss-off letter" I always shoved aside in my mind, because that was the kind of life I was having. A hellish movie wartime life. It was an existence of chaos, uncertainty, unhappiness, and sadness, and I knew for certain that to survive it, I needed an anchor, a center, a girl-back-home. I needed Chloe.

Or someone like Chloe.

She ended up at the wheel of my car as I went through the bubble-wrap envelope and examined the papers she'd prepared concerning the Leudecke case. The text on the page did not come together for me. I was hungry, dizzy even, though I felt no more like eating anything than I had at the deli earlier. I did feel like I needed a drink. Maybe a

Xanax. Besides, the case was strange. I plowed through the paragraphs, and attempted to separate out the main point of the thing. It made me anxious. It concerned something about a freeway, or a highway, and eminent domain. Where was the immigration problem? It was difficult to concentrate because I kept thinking about the young girl with the skinny legs and the high forehead there behind the wheel of my car.

"What do you think?" she asked.

"I think we should turn around. An eminent domain case should go to Jefferson downstairs."

"The client asked for us . . . for you specifically."

Marguerite "Maggie" Leudecke had asked for me? I tried to place the name. It was vaguely familiar. On the other hand, what was the harm in talking to her, if it meant an afternoon out on the road with Chloe? I could turn it all over to Jefferson later, no harm, no foul.

That Chloe was beautiful wasn't a universal opinion among males at Davison, Kohlhoeffer & Loeb. But they're asswipes. Besides, I considered Chloe a friend of mine, a young friend who happened to be a woman and who, although she was attractive, I had this normal and healthy relationship with. We had gone out to lunch together from time to time, especially when she'd first started at the firm—that period when she'd labored under the misconception that I was an important part of the operation. Sometimes, we'd go to a matinee on Friday afternoons until, I think, she realized this was something none of the other attorneys ever did. She was a straight-haired, big-eared girl, and we got along well together, and could talk to one another. She'd listen to my troubles, and I'd listen to hers, and, of course, because she was so attractive—heart-freeze beautiful in a photograph, for example, if you ever saw one (Chloe photographed much better than she looked in three dimensions to tell the truth)—I did keep in the back of my mind this slim sliver of an almost hope that someday our relationship might turn a little less "appropriate." But the more she told me her troubles and confided in me, told me about her love life, the men who didn't treat her well, the One True Love of her life who didn't seem to be able to Make His Move, I realized that the chances of her and I getting together were becoming slimmer and slimmer. And as I tried to keep her attention with little stories of my own that I thought were entertaining, like about Alice, my "stalker," or the way Madame Chung would come into the room in the Chinatown massage parlor, come in with the two towels that had Elvis's picture on them, and the way she would say, "You want something special tonight? What you like? You like tall? You like petite?"

Anyway, as I told more and more of these stories to Chloe, the chances of ever having anything with her but an, in fact, healthy, honest, and platonic relationship were approaching nil and niller still, but that day, driving to North Houston, there was something about this girl that was making me think happiness wasn't impossible. For example, my wife would take my son, Henry, to camp in a couple of weeks. Also I hoped her sister would go. Maybe she would leave her brother—the fucking place was crawling with in-laws, but that was alright. I could send the brother out on a rigorous errand—like, to California or something. I'd have to get the exact dates, but I could have the house cleaned. I could turn my kicked-in guitar to the wall with its back showing, so Chloe couldn't see the damage. Basically, I'd set up my life, clear some space for Chloe, just as I'd told Alice I couldn't possibly do for her.

And it began to occur to me that I also could, with some effort, maybe get Chloe to think of me the way she had at first. It wouldn't be anything like that *skak* hotel where we'd gone that time (only that one time). That was the problem. That *skak* hotel. Like a *skank* hotel but not worth the extra consonant. A pinchy-faced brunette with skinny legs, big ears, and a big heart (she asked about my mother as she steered the Elantra, and suggested that, maybe after our meeting with Maggie Leudecke, we should go by St. Vincent's), such a person could find something in me that she needed, too. And she was a smart person, though inexperienced (her spelling was atrocious, I recalled), and a young person who probably had problems, because you can't go to law school at night and work as a paralegal during the day and not have problems. I could listen to these, and even help her out. None of this was beyond reach there for a few seconds, none of it seemed impossible, though I hadn't eaten much that day and was light-headed, and had passed out earlier on a concrete floor, but that didn't matter.

It was Chloe that could make me happy. And with that came a parallel observation: happy was what I wanted to be.

We were, by then, pretty far north of town, where there were signs like "Berries!" and "Pull in For Cigarettes" and "Catfish, Dressed or Undressed."

"Oh," I said. "Dressed by all means. But casually."

Chloe laughed and, though driving, reached across to hit me on the arm in that way she had that was friendly (I think), yet no joke. I really did have a perniciously, chronically sore shoulder: from all these "friendly" blows I took? From bursitis, arthritis, fibromyalgia? Excessive jerking off? I didn't know, and my "doctor" at the Jasmine Pain Treatment Center (a mobile home behind a quickie wedding chapel off the Gulf Freeway) didn't seem to know, either, or much care. Anyway, Chloe kickboxed in addition to her triathlon hobby, and packed more punch than she realized.

"What are you doing tonight?" I asked. "What's on? What's happening? What's the deal?" I considered again what day it was. Tuesday. It was still Tuesday, and I tried to count the days until Marisel took Henry to camp.

Chloe started to explain to me about how she really needed to get home after this meeting, as she was caught up at school and wanted to get in seven miles running this evening, then there was this guy she was "seeing," this man who was both a Certified Public Accountant and a jazz singer, who had made a date to pick her up and take her to a first-run play.

"Yeah, but we know who you'd rather see that play with."

"Mmmmph," she said, and hit me again on the arm in a way that was really starting to hurt. The deal was, Chloe and I went to dinner together sometimes, or those movies, and this was good because I needed to go and do these things in a "healthy" way now and then. And Chloe was so good-looking in that sort of "run herself thin" way, it was impossible not to forgive her when she left that dinner we'd been having to go meet some date; even when she'd spent the whole dinner texting Loeb, and I'd picked up the tab, it was all worth it.

"You know . . . " I started to say, but then we came to a stoplight. A guy stood there at the curb of the traffic island: a ratty-looking guy in a ratty jacket and stained trousers. He was a tall, very tall, dust-covered man with a creased face and a defeated expression. To top it off, he held a cardboard message. WILL WORK FOR FOOD, or HUNGRY AND NEED HELP—I don't know, something like that. He walked with his sign as he ate an orange, moved along the row of cars that had stopped at the light.

I told Chloe to wait. Hold on. "Roll down the window," I said, and I got my wallet out of my jacket, removed a dollar, passed it to her and she shook her head but didn't say anything. She'd seen it before. The first time she saw me give a street person a dollar, months back when we were on our way to a different meeting somewhere, she said, "That doesn't impress me."

"It's not for you."

The second time she said, "You're a twisted citizen," but now Chloe just took the bill, and rolled down the window. "Here," she said to the guy.

"What's that?" he asked. I couldn't see his face from my side of the car. His voice was rough, graveled, but it didn't give me the charge. It sounded different aimed at Chloe, not speaking to me directly.

It was a waste of a dollar, basically.

"It's yours," Chloe said, dismissing him.

"I didn't ask who it belongs to." He lowered his head to look into the car. I could see only one vacant eye. He spoke slowly. "I asked what it is."

"Hey," I said. He looked familiar. A client who'd hit hard times? Someone I'd gone to school with? "It's a dollar."

"A dollar!"

So help me he moved like a cat, the half-eaten orange suddenly crushed in his clenched fingers. His arm swung quickly, expertly, and I thought for sure he would smack—no *punch*—Chloe with the mangled fruit. He had the kind of reflexes I'd only seen at ringside in prize fights: that same "whoosh" as his arm moved through the air in front of her face. But his fist stopped: his grimy knuckles came to a halt maybe a quarter inch from her button nose, and Chloe drew back away from him and screeched.

"Hey, motherfucker," I hollered. "What are you doing?"

"Hey you motherfucker!" he said. And he began to grope towards me. His arm extended past Chloe, the juice from the orange dribbling over her, my gearshift, my upholstery. "Hey rich motherfucker with one dollar!"

The light changed and Chloe floored it. The filthy arm whipped past her face and out of the car as we sped away. I twisted around to look but he'd already turned his back. He walked up the traffic island.

I knew that guy, I was sure. But he was somehow totally out of context.

I wiped at some sticky juice on my jacket.

"You know . . . I've been thinking about us," I began.

"*Fucking Christ, Bent.* Will you stop giving those people money?"

"I didn't mean . . . I've given it a lot of thought is what I'm saying." But I hadn't, of course, and was feeling jittery, and empty-stomached besides. I still had some of the adrenaline charge from when that arm shot out towards me so unexpectedly. Chloe's skull had nearly been clobbered. I couldn't finish my thought before we pulled into a parking lot.

I began to wonder if this meeting was a good idea. Maybe Loeb should have come in my place after all. Maybe I should have had just a normal, sit-in-the-office-and-pretend-to-work sort of day. Possibly if I asked Chloe out to lunch tomorrow, that would be a good move. We hadn't done that in a while. I didn't think she'd turn me down for lunch.

"We're here," she said, checking her watch, flicking orange pulp off of her sleeve. "Against all odds. Here's your dollar back."

I nearly told her to keep it, but that was ridiculous. I folded the bill inside my wallet

The lot we'd pulled into was at an intersection off 488. We were parked in front of a Café Rico, which took up the prime corner spot of a single story strip center.

"They're building a freeway through a Café Rico?"

"She's meeting us at Café Rico. She doesn't want us in her home. It's her house that's having the freeway built through it, and her ranch property."

"She has a house and ranch property?"

"Well, she's a Leudecke."

I still didn't know what a Leudecke was, but was starting to get an idea.

"And she's a witch," Chloe said.

"Oh, no."

"Not like that. But you'll see. Her house is also a store, and meeting place. It's called the Cauldron of Magic. "

I had in my travels heard about the store for "All Things Wiccan" north of town. We got out of the car to go into the Café Rico. "So she doesn't want, then," I said, "to defile the witch place with. . . ."

"Lawyers," Chloe said. "And then there's the murder," and we went in. The bell on the heavy door went clang when we pushed it open.

vii.

People don't realize how immigration issues touch on so many other facets of life and law.

Practice in immigration requires strong familiarity with criminal statutes, for example, because something mundane like a DWI violation can throw a change of status into serious jeopardy: for *years*. I mean, why Mr. Duc should be so ghost-shit insane about a few weeks' or months' delay with his nephew's filing—the impatient old fuck—I had no idea. And I'd have told him so if I'd ever accidentally actually taken one of his calls. This stuff is tricky. And complicated.

Recently, I'd had to have someone look into pollution regulations when the son of a wealthy Mexican investor whose visa we were handling got a summer construction job and was told (as so many young Mexican construction workers are always told), "Dump this bucket in that creek." Water supply contamination was the charge, which could mean prison time, but even in hybrid misdemeanor form it put his green card in limbo and his bald hyper-wealthy father in a tizzy. When a kleptomaniacal daughter of an Indian information systems magnate was caught shoplifting via a dressing room camera at Marshall Field's (coal-black push-up bras) I found myself having to locate someone to delve into the Constitutional right to privacy in order to keep her in the country.

Really, very little of Davison, Kohlhoeffer & Loeb's work had to do with the path to citizenship. Employer-based, we focused on visas, hiring compliance, and helping our clients avoid encounters of any kind with Homeland Security, the Department of Labor, and most especially the dreaded ICE (Immigration and Customs Enforcement), those guys with the raids and—more common and more horrifying—the audits.

Probably 80 percent of our work was spent ensuring that those we represented did not know the immigration status of their workers and did not find out, as that would almost certainly make them complicit in unlawful hiring practices. When approached by any employee who, perhaps, mistook them for a helpful Latin-American-style *patron*, rather than the garden-variety labor exploiter they almost certainly were, we trained them in their responses: "Are you saying a *friend* has gotten a job with an unlawfully acquired work visa? Here," (handing over a D, K & L (LLP) business card). "Why don't you advise them to talk to an attorney?"

In reality, the bulk of our practice with actual foreigners mostly involved investors who sought residency for international trade: those folks from afar who wanted to sink substantial bucks into "Regional Centers"—entities that resembled corporations, but that were created out of thin air to construct shopping malls, hospitals, and recreational facilities using foreign funds. The EB-5 program could, by federal law, offer immigrant investors special resident status owing to their generous injections of capital into the national economy. In those cases even eminent domain could edge into play, albeit it in a marginal way, and always from clients hoping to invoke it to obtain frontage or easements. Hell, I understood (though not well) that our firm had its *own* Regional Center, managed by four junior partners in the Corporate and Project Finance Group on the 30th floor.

D, K & L, then, was about rich people. Still, a good immigration attorney, because the clientele could get dragged under by so many kinds of legal tentacles, could never stop thinking, could never stop learning or paying attention. That's why it was lucky there were so many good immigration attorneys around me who owed me so many favors, because otherwise I wasn't worth a shit.

So, you're thinking: we know what's up with him. Why he gives money to strangers, panhandlers on the street—can't pass one without pressing a dollar into his (or her) semi-psychotic hand. (That guy with the orange . . . where had I seen him before?) And why he attends especially to the creases, and the hardness in their voices. When he listens to those street people, he probably even believes he might be listening to himself a little bit. Right? His own future voice. Bent thinks he could be out there some day, under an overpass, holding a sign: WILL FILE I-864 FOR FOOD.

Or you're thinking I was trying to make myself feel better with the handouts, to make up for the laziness, the irresponsibility, the philandering. Or to make up for the poor job I'd done with my life; my career; my son, Henry.

I probably should have worried about all that, but you'd be wrong. Like with the philandering. My marriage was not a love match, but an arrangement. It was better to say a disarrangement the way it had worked out, but it was, at any rate, a deal I'd struck when I got into some hot water. I had just received an annual review and been handed the news: good old Bent, down in naturalization and immigration. Great guy, really. Has hit on some hard times, even, but he wasn't going to be joining the firm in any permanent way. Not on partner track (ha!). Not on equity track, even. He'd been around too long, accomplished too little, probably needed to start looking for employment elsewhere.

This was trouble. Besides, I had Henry to think of after my first wife did her business with the knife and left me . . . or I'd sent her away, depending on how you looked at it.

I was thinking about the boy.

I was just divorced, and toe to toe with uncertainty, when the word came down that a friend of one of the partners, a real estate mogul, was having trouble with his *au pair's* visa. The kids were grown, the girl was seeking another position but wanted permanent residency if possible, so I talked to her as a kind of favor, and listened to her. She was attractive, it was true, in a thick-bodied, mole on upper lip, *au pair* way. Her English was not so good, nor was my Spanish (and my Tagalog—right). So I had some trouble communicating with her, plus I didn't really want to deal with favors at that moment. I wondered how I could take care of Henry if he and I were out on the street, how we would survive. It would make for a very heartwarming scene of love and perseverance to watch in a movie of the week, maybe: father and son huddled in a cardboard box, facing the elements together. But to think

I would have to live such a life scared me like a screwdriver scraping bone.

Then, it kind of came to me. I asked this *au pair* what she knew about autism spectrum disorder, a question she didn't understand at all. I asked her what she knew about six-year-olds, and she smiled, so I closed my office door, sat on my desk, leaned in close.

I said: "You may not have considered a sure-fire path to citizenship."

So really, you can't fault me for my attempts at some other kind of life, a life outside my home, although the way I handled the Marisel issue must have registered deep in the inner chambers of the firm because when the full documentation with addendum to my annual report came down, it recommended "potential equity track" for me "in time," and I didn't leave after all. Then, Little Loeb showed up, fresh out of law school, more incompetent than me—vastly—and I was set. But my home life wasn't even personal (except the yelling), and wasn't sexual (maybe now and then). And Marisel wasn't doing that much with Henry, even, since her sister had moved in. And Marisel wasn't doing much of anything else, for that matter, since her brother had come to cook (and eat, and smoke Marlboros on the back porch). It got to where I spent as little time at home as possible. But I'm not so bad. Loeb's father—Big Loeb—his deal at home was, by all reports, much, much weirder than mine.

So, naturally, I thought a lot about Chloe as she and I took seats in the Café Rico. I thought about how Chloe was cute and smart, and not the possessive type. I thought about how she was nice. A breath of fresh air. I recalled how she was slutty enough to go to a *skak* hotel at least that once—might she agree to that again?

Chloe. My focus. My anchor.

Maggie Leudecke didn't seem to be there yet, and Chloe checked her watch again and again, like she was fearful she would miss out on her jazz-singing CPA if things didn't go according to schedule. "You're not a lawyer," I pointed out. "You could've gone to her house without me."

"I told her that. It didn't seem to help."

"So, are they building a stadium out here or what?"

"It's a loop. A road."

"For?" I asked. "Hospital? Shopping center?"

Chloe shrugged. "Road to nowhere," and she ordered a Honduran mocha from a skinny girl with a tattoo on her forearm, a tattoo I couldn't quite see. I ordered the "house grind" like I needed more coffee. I needed a hamburger, fries, a croissant, anything, but those Café Ricos don't serve food except sandwiches and wraps, and little containers of oddly colored potato salad and coleslaw, sealed in plastic and of questionable point of origin.

"And there's a murder," I said.

"Relax. A death. Probably an accident."

"Probably. Excellent."

"Cranked-up folks are just calling it a murder, raising a stink." She pulled out her phone. "A man from the construction company that surveyed the new freeway was found dead on her ranch."

"So, let's see: rancher, witch, and murderer? Should I remind you that I am just Good Old Bent?"

"Uh-huh."

"From down in naturalization and immigration? Not. . . ."

"I know! The Leudeckes asked for you, like I said."

"Are they trying to lose this case?"

"Right?" Chloe laughed and started texting.

I opened the envelope again, began to thumb through the documents, fearful to uncover the first inevitable misspelling since Chloe had a hand in their production. And now I'd ordered more coffee, even though I was shaky from all the caffeine I'd had that day, plus that six pack of the Danish Microbrew I'd sipped when I drove in that morning, and the beer while reading the newspaper. Then there were the pills—the "Houston Cocktail" combo that bubbled in my veins, sent in attack formation against that chronic pain that was so much a part of my day I wasn't even sure I still had it anymore (although that particular combination also delivered a little pharma-boost that helped make the climb out of bed in the morning an imaginable reality . . . though slightly less imaginable each morning). This replay of the day in my mind also caused me to remember the little coyote in the cage, and bile rose in my throat for my powerless role in that scene. Fucking mega-gas-station convenience store corporate shits . . . I wasn't really sure how to label them. Besides, those crazed *faux* First Nation motherfuckers who'd been as appalled as me were shits, too, with the possible exception of that woman. God, that woman. I recalled the sound of her words, and how they'd poured over me as she squatted on the concrete beside the cage: "I'm sorry."

I shook my head, flipped through the pages, and a folded sheet, a map, slipped onto the table: Maggie Leudecke's property. The map showed an irregular parcel of varying elevation with parallel lines, straight as Ginsu blades, that indicated the path of the concrete four-lane that would slice her property in half.

"Looks lucrative to me," I said.

"She doesn't want that road and she doesn't care about lucrative. She's a Leudecke."

Prominent in the package was a stiff photo, an 8 ½ by 11 glossy. I expected to see a picture of the threatened landscape, but it was a head shot, the kind a fashion model would have for PR, only, on closer examination, with the clothes, the expression, the sweaty brow, it was better to say mug shot. It was this young guy, vaguely Hispanic, his pupils floating up towards the top of his lids like the camera had been set above eye level. Shave-headed along the sides, the hair on the top of his head rose in spiky pompadour fashion, and his beard and mustache were both thin, carefully shaved, shaped lines. He didn't look happy.

"So she killed this guy to stop it?"

"An accident . . . probably. People are just saying she killed him."

"What people?"

Chloe shrugged. "Mexicans, mostly. I'm sorry, the Latino population. They want the road built. It's all in the file."

I rubbed my neck, felt that gel-brained pill-and-beer-lunch drop-down sensation weigh me to the chair. It was hard to concentrate on the paperwork. Plus, I hated these damn Café Ricos. I knew they were a franchised chain, but couldn't stop thinking I'd been in this particular one before, though it was the usual sort of place of its kind. So my Café Rico annoyance started to set in. The design was early wood-beams-across-ceiling, brick-showing-through-fallen-off-stucco Americana. It was one of those coffee shops with the god-awful, unframed, primary-colored cartoon art pieces on the walls. These, in particular, were paintings of what appeared to be dogs: four-legged creatures in each panel that resembled dogs more than they did anything else. The walls were covered with these puerile masterworks of cartoon doggery.

I started thinking: I didn't sign up for this. I shouldn't be faced with this kind of four o'clock meeting in this barge of a coffee shop north of town because the client was too important to come to the office and didn't want attorneys in her home rattling her *chi*. *Fenging* her *shui*. Chloe started back texting almost immediately so I looked around and saw they were all there: the "types" who usually hang out at places like Café Rico, with their long, black, fingerless gloves, clove cigarettes, and "journals." They were the kind who sipped java and wrote with fountain pens in fat, blank books, eyes wide as they gawked at the deepness of their fathomless selves. Or, there was one lady there like that, anyway, which was enough to make the whole place seem full of sensibilities. Others tipped back in overstuffed armchairs, read newspapers or paperbacks, and tapped on tablets. None of the furniture, dishware, or even the coffee mugs matched: a Café Rico trademark. Each piece was meant to seem artfully selected, as if from fabulous antique stores, uncovered by teams combing out-of-the-way secondhand shops in exotic lands.

And it was too warm in this place—though it was mid-October, approaching the downslope towards Halloween. A ceiling fan helicoptered overhead, but forget that. It was, of course, a horn-beast sort of hot in this city in summer, but on any given October day it could still hit 85 degrees, yet everyone in this coffee shop was layered: packed down with jackets, sweaters, vests. Meanwhile, piped in "world music" with airy drumming, Andean scales, and sad lyrics injected into peppy melodies undulated in the background: women vocalists wailing heartbreak, passion, and vengeance in that "alternative" way—except that every Café Rico played this soundtrack. Go into any of them and you would hear the same alternative.

It had been a mistake to come here. I'd have been better off anywhere else.

I didn't notice anybody who looked like a witch. A large opening that resembled the sprung doors of a carriage house connected to a garden with more tables, and out there I saw this guy I knew. He was someone I'd been helping out with an immigration issue. Then I remembered he had a Café Rico franchise, but I couldn't recall if he was from India or Pakistan, mainly because his wife couldn't remember either. It was one of "those kinds" of immigration deals. So, oh shit, that's why this place looked familiar. He talked to some women in the shade of the outside patio foliage, standing over them, being all Rico at the Café, friendly neighborhood Indian (or Pakistani) business owner style, but none of those women appeared witchy.

The waitress arrived with our coffee, and I could see now her tattoo was the outline of a wrench, as in the tool: the open-end sort with a 3/4 inch span on one end, 5/8 on the other. I touched her arm lightly after she'd put down the mugs. "What's with the wrench?"

"What?"

"I'm just wondering. Because I'm sort of into tattoos."

I could feel Chloe's eyes on me. Chloe has a tattoo, although not everyone has seen it.

I have.

"Because, you know," I said, "there's just a lot of tattoos here . . . in the caffeine district. Body art, piercing, but I've never seen anybody with a wrench."

This girl plucked my finger from her arm. "Lots of us have them."

"There are lots of you?"

"We are deconstructionists," she said and turned, went back to the coffee counter. She had another tattoo on the small of her back, visible in the space that showed skin and ample amounts of hip flab between shirt and pants. It wasn't a tool, though, but something winged and feathery.

"Tramp stamp," I whispered.

Chloe frowned at her phone.

"Same place you have one."

"Oh, boy," said Chloe.

I sat silent for a while, listened to her clicking at her screen. "A deconstructionist," I said. "Don't meet those so much these days. Think the witch is coming?"

"Look over the summaries." Chloe kept tapping. "Maggie . . . Ms. Leudecke is blocking the road with this suit, which is threatening other people along the easement who want it built. There's a *barrio* community near her ranch that really wants the revenue possibilities. They're all up in arms."

"Yup. Tramp stamp like yours."

Chloe stopped texting for a moment, looked around for the waitress. "What does it say?"

"What do they all say? *Hi! I have no gag reflex.*"

She kicked my ankle hard under the table and went back to texting.

"It's good," I said, and rubbed my ankle, "since I haven't seen you in a while, that we can visit."

"Uh-huh."

"And we've even got an excuse to do it."

She nodded, pressed something with finality on her phone, turned the device face down on her palm. "Excuse?"

"Oh, I don't know . . . just that . . . ." What did I mean? "I guess if anyone sees us here, there's a reason for us to be together." I spread my hands flat on the antique table. "No questions asked."

She grinned at me with her tiny, rice-like teeth. "Why the hell would there be?"

"Oh, just all that about tattoos."

"Alright." She glanced around, but still grinned.

"It makes me think of your tattoo. The last I saw of it."

"Okay, Bent."

"A dragonfly, as I recall."

"No, doofus. And I'm sure you see a lot of tattoos."

"Who are you texting anyway?" I leaned forward, rested comfortable on my forearms as if I really were close and comfortable with her. I asked about her texting even though

I already knew, because Chloe and Loeb were at it constantly. They communed electronically with each other all through the day (on company time!), and exchanged constant updates on the most unimportant shit. "Just bought cupcake," and like that.

"Loeb," she said. "I'm talking to Loeb."

"Ah." I thought it over. "I don't see that many tattoos." I sat for a moment and admired her sweet, razor smile, and her straight, stringy hair. It was probably best to just let things lie. Maybe raise the issue later. Don't push. Or at the very least, find some sneaky or clever way to work into the conversation. I could try something indirect.

And as I thought about being sneaky, it reminded me of LCS Industries, a garment distributor client of ours, which three weeks earlier had gotten popped by the Department of Labor for damages and back pay to the tune of several hundred thousand dollars. All of their employees were documented—Mexican nationals, in fact—but the company had thoughtfully arranged direct deposits to the workers' Sonoran bank accounts, paying in pesos. They were paying at the rate, it turned out, of about $1.97 per hour. "You're in compliance with immigration policy," Parker Harrell, head of naturalization and immigration at D, K & L (and *prick*) explained to them, "but you've played heck with the federal minimum wage requirement."

Parker Harrell didn't like to swear.

"It's like my feelings are pesos to you, aren't they?" I asked Chloe.

"What?"

"It's like they're in pesos and it takes a wheelbarrow of them to equal one of Loeb's Krugerrand sentiments."

"What the fuck is up with you today?"

"Nothing."

"What did I say," she asked, "to suddenly make you say a thing like that? Why would you?"

"Never mind. Not a big deal." I drank some of the coffee the deconstructionist brought in a squat, handmade mug that resembled a pencil holder. "Drink your coffee. It's got a shot of chocolate flavoring in it, I understand."

"Jesus, Bent." She leaned in closer. "You didn't set that car on fire, did you?"

"Hell no!"

"Was it your car?"

"A random, one. Burning. Beautifully burning." I thought about the guy standing next to it. Weird.

We sat silent for several minutes more. Waited for the witch. Be cool, Bent. Let it ride. Let it lie.

"I think it's right, though," I said. "I think that's pretty much how you consider me when you bother to think of me at all. As devalued."

She put down the phone. "I swore I wasn't going to feel guilty about any of that."

"There is no reason to. No reason to feel guilty about anything."

"We've been through this," she said. "What we did in the old days . . . it's one of the reasons I trust you now."

"It's true. More like the old *day*, but true."

"And why I feel like I can tell you things."

"More like the old *afternoon*."

"We're friends. Plus," she whispered, "I said at the time it was a bad idea—I told you it was."

"Yes. Yes you did."

She didn't though.

"So what suddenly prompts you?" she asked. "What suddenly makes you decide I don't value your feelings after all this time?"

That was unexpected. Whatever I was hoping for, it had nothing to do with hearing Chloe tell me that she actually valued my feelings. I had expected more snickers. Another arm punch. Though the fact is, at the time, back in *the day*, she was the one who thought it would be a good idea. Despite our age difference. She was the one who said, "Trust my judgment."

She looked upset. I felt something kindling in my stomach. It was that gut-burn I always got when I knew something was about to go away, float off, be it that balloon that slipped from my wrist at the circus when I was eight (my father tied it on; my father, though a pilot, was ironically enough not a man with practical skills), or . . . that ballet dancer I'd worked with on a defection case who'd gone into the Chinese Consulate and never come out. (I'd told him: *Do not go into the Chinese Consulate you will never come out*—but did he listen?)

Those kinds of things that are hard to get back.

"Nothing! No prompt. It's just a general feeling."

I thought that if maybe I left it right there, left it at that, the afternoon would be saved. I could take it up with her later at a better time, a better place. I could take her somewhere that didn't have deconstructionists or killer homeless street vagrants. I groped in my jacket pocket for my pills, knocked them together, heard the comforting sound of the plastic bottles snick against each other. I wondered if Yvonne would have some insight. How should I handle the case of Chloe?

I glanced out the window. It was October in North Houston through the window of a Café Rico. The short day seemed to have come to a close already: the arrival of darkness, a gloomy overcast. I decided to wait for the witch. Keep quiet. Chloe picked up her phone. Most likely she picked up where she had left off with Loeb.

I lifted the photo again. "Found dead where?"

"His name's Eladio Trejo. Drowned on the property."

"Shit. Poor guy."

"Well, yes."

"Guess nobody cares he's gone. Just like me. If I were gone."

"You *bastard*."

"Wouldn't be missed. You certainly wouldn't care."

"Alright, that's it." Chloe made as if to stand.

I groped towards her, unsteady, tried to hold her arm to the table, but she wriggled free. She took up her coffee. She took it up almost like she was about to rise and fling it at me, or find another table at least, but she stayed seated, sipped from it instead. She glowered into the cup's steam. It was true she hadn't hidden her affections for Loeb from me, and had done a poor job, probably, of hiding them from the rest of the firm as well. The two of them were "talked about" by busybodies of the kind all organizations harbor. She accepted this, too. "Better the company whore than the company bore," she'd told me one time.

"That is so unfair," Chloe said. "Just take me off your list of people that fuck you over and want to get rid of you."

"And . . . what is that? People who want to do what?"

"Never mind."

"There's a list? What list is that?"

"I said you had the list." But she put down her cup and went back to texting.

I sipped more coffee. Jesus. Somebody please just drag me out of here, now. Something please descend from the hills, take me away . . . cook me or even eat me raw in a cave . . . a damp cave. I didn't care. Anything would be better than this. Assault by an armed Vietnamese gang might be better than this.

Maybe not.

"What the hell is wrong with you anyway?" she asked.

I was a little dizzy, it was true, but something else was wrong, and I couldn't tell her because I didn't know. Then I saw her eyes looking beyond me and kind of upwards, following someone who approached our table, someone who had walked up behind me, so I turned in my chair. . . .

viii.

I had a strange experience, then, at the Café Rico.

It was her. No question. Yet, even from this better vantage, seated solidly at an oak table, it was hard to get a handle on her face. It was difficult, for example, to easily tell her age. She definitely had freckles, many of them across her cheeks, and as she approached, she smiled and gave a little wave of her hand. Her wrist was thin, the pale red ribbon fluttered as she moved her palm from left to right, a greeting. But it was as if something were wiped away, as if everything to the right of that hand was dissolved, then replaced by darkness that trailed it, like a movie transition that dropped the scene into black.

. . . a spackle of light, some kind of smudged brightness far away. I was flat on my back on the floor of the Café Rico. What the fuck. This time she had wiped me right off my chair with her little waving motion.

It occurred to me that if this person was to be following me in my life I'd have to examine the floor closely any time I walked into any place, as I'd likely be lying on it sooner or later. This one wasn't all that clean, for instance, and felt especially hard and very cold. A damp draft drifted from the direction of the door with its clanging bell clapper. I sensed something: a breath across my forehead. "That is kind of bizarre," Chloe said, as if she had been hired to do the voiceover narration of this scene, and "He's not feeling well today," she added. "Not himself." And then laughter and another voice joined in: dark and mysterious, smoky and low. It was that scorched-in-mansion-fire voice from earlier in the day: rough, but also deep and rich.

"I figured he doesn't do this often."

There was dampness in my ears—like after a shower—

and far away I heard plates, cups, and saucers being rinsed in a big sink in some distant chamber. The woman with the black hair and leather jacket floated above me. She had so many freckles under her jaw they formed constellations. She looked down at me. I was noticed, this time. Win! She smiled. Her eyes were dark, with gray circles of sleeplessness underneath and almost unnaturally large black irises. Fat wooden beams hung behind her as the blades of the worthless ceiling fan rose on one side of her face, fell on the other. Her hair draped towards me, fairly long, shot through with threads of gray I could see now, and it brushed against me when she leaned close. The sleeves of her shirt were big, covering thin arms. I examined her hand by clutching it when she offered it to shake—something different, shaking hands with a new client while flat on my back—but the hand she'd waved at me that wiped out the universe now seemed fish-boned and powerless. I knew better.

"Bent, this is Maggie Leudecke," Chloe said.

"We've met."

The woman narrowed her eyes but continued to smile. "Have we?"

I did a sort of inventory. I made sure I hadn't, as they say, released anything. Fluids. Semi-solids for that matter. It was so hot in there against the freezing floor. I wiped my brow with my palm, and then Maggie Leudecke—in a way that seemed both inappropriately familiar and completely natural—stroked the perspiration off my forehead, her fingers hard and almost leathery (had a ranch I reminded myself). She straightened my hair. She spread her fingers like a comb and brushed the tangled mess away from my eyes.

Then the Indian or Pakistani coffee shop franchise owner arrived, leaned over me, his palms on the back of one of the mismatched chairs. "What are you doing here?" he said. He looked worried. "Is any of the paperwork out of order? The pictures? Visa application?" It was obvious he was not there to see after my well-being, even though having people passed out on the floor couldn't be good for Café Rico business. Customers would think twice before eating that yellowish, day-old potato salad in the cooler tubs.

I told him everything was fine. My voice was a moisture-free croak. I was only there by chance, I told him. I started to get up. "I haven't eaten much today."

"Can we get a menu?" Chloe asked.

"I'm the owner, not the waiter."

I began to remember that I had no love for this guy, and had always felt sorry for his "wife," too.

"Is it the valentines?" he asked in a stage whisper. "Are they not believing about the valentines?"

I couldn't quite put it all together, but just then he turned to Maggie Leudecke, this Indian or Pakistani guy, and his face lengthened out. I don't know a better way to say it. Like a porous Play-Doh face, his nose and chin extended and he told Maggie Leudecke that she was the most beautiful woman in the coffee shop. He stood tall, raised a hand, made as if to lead her away. "Let me take care of this," he said, but Chloe took Maggie's arm, kept her near our table. The fake stucco swam a little behind them. The Indian or Pakistani owner, Mr. Pamalllanagaboomlon—I couldn't really remember his name—slapped his forehead. "Oh, hell. What am I saying? You're the most beautiful woman that has ever *been in* this coffee shop."

I sat up, gathered myself, and he bent over me, asked if I needed an ambulance, then told me not to claim later that he didn't offer to call one, and that this woman, this beautiful woman, would be his witness to that in court. Then he smiled, held out both hands, palms up, extended towards Maggie Leudecke again. I thought, My God, he's going to kiss her hand, and then he did.

Mr. Pamalangadangdong smacked around a while on the bumps of Maggie's delicate, though possibly chapped, knuckles, then gave me a low, dark look, and at some signal from him two girls dressed in the polo-shirt attire of the Café Rico franchise lifted me, their hands in my armpits. They brought me, unsteady, to my feet. Together, they stood me in a semblance of uprightness that I didn't feel I could really get behind.

"Are you alright?" one said.

"Ooof, heavy!" said the other.

My toes dragged as they duck-walked me towards the counter. Both Chloe and Maggie seemed to go in a direction other than mine, Chloe with the large envelope full of, I assumed, misspelled documentation, possibly even misspelled contractual arrangements.

It wasn't so much that I worried about the documents Chloe was about to put in front of Maggie Leudecke, but more that I couldn't quite bring them, their content, into focus. True, Chloe did not have sharp editing skills, but, more important: what exactly was Davison, Kohlhoeffer & Loeb advising Maggie Leudecke to do? And would I be able to remain conscious while we did it?

I noticed only then that one of the friendly female types who dragged me towards the counter was the tattoo woman—the waitress with the wrench on her forearm—and I considered requesting her not to hurt me. To undeconstruct me, if at all possible. They got me past the counter, through one of those behind-the-counter swinging waiter and busboy doors, then to the left into the strong-smelling "kitchen" area of the Café Rico. There was nothing Rico there. They lowered me onto a slashed vinyl couch that had been repaired with duct tape, the edges of the tape curly and brittle. I sat across from the open door of a fragrant employees' bathroom with a low, slanted ceiling over a yellow-colored john. This behind-the-Café-Rico workspace had the usual dry-erase panels, employee schedules on cork boards, dire hand-washing warnings, and wire racks along the walls—like the ones I'd seen at Lumpy's that morning. (Really? Just that morning?) But all these racks held boxes, each with plastic spigots, like boxes of that sickly sweet, diseased-tasting, undrinkable box party wine you find at really bad box wine parties. What the hell?

The girls propped me in the uncomfortable sofa-chair, patted my shoulder, and filed away one behind the other. I wanted out of there, out and away from this coffee shop. I wanted to be far from Maggie Leudecke, someplace where I could be alone. I wanted to be alone to think about Maggie Leudecke, quite possibly, and mull her over in my mind: her jacket, her freckles, her fatality. I needed to process the feel of her fingers on my forehead. The sound of her "I'm sorry" that had moved down my spine like a warm wave earlier that morning. And I was definitely not going to masturbate while I thought about her. That was out. She had cowboy boots. *Forget it.* I needed some kind of move, or exit. I'd find a back way, slip out, and wait for Chloe in the car.

"Do not say I didn't ask," said Mr. Proomalangabong, who had appeared again. He grew serious. "What is she telling you? What is she saying about me? Why can't I even visit? Does she think I am some kind of monster?" He pulled himself to his full height. "Maybe I should call the police," he said.

"Sure. You call the police on me." Because the little green card thing he had going with his "wife," to tell the truth, didn't strike me as being completely on the up and up. Little immigration things that are legal but not completely on the up and up were a kind of specialty of mine.

He dance-stepped backwards, pointed a finger, said: "You better think twice!" and "I offered to call the ambulance. Do not say I didn't," and then he moved away.

Then, in came Loeb.

There in the back of the Café Rico: him. Little Loeb, Little Stuart, breezing into this kitchen area with his sports coat, slacks, his jaunty bounce.

"What the hell?" I said.

Loeb didn't speak immediately. He stood. He stared into space. Loeb halted with his fake-muscled but actually weak spa and gym arms held in front of him, dangling like the arms of a *Tyrannosaurus rex.* Then he apologized. "Sorry, Bent," he said. "So sorry. I'm just looking at all these boxes with spigots on them." He was gape-mouthed, as if shocked. "What's the deal with those?"

"I don't know. Why are you here?"

"No, I shouldn't have ignored you," he said. "I'm sorry."

"It's alright. Those are pretty odd."

"I'm not good at paying attention."

"You're fine, don't worry about it. . . ."

. . . and damn it. This was something he did. Loeb drove me crazy with his shit sometimes. When someone was upset at Loeb, he had this way of apologizing, but apologizing for something else. So pretty soon you always found yourself telling him, "No, no, it's not your fault," and the thing he was actually responsible for was still hanging there. All the actual shit he caused he never took the blame for, although that was usually okay.

Taking blame was my job, after all. Still, it had been an open question to me over the past few years whether Loeb was a major boob or a master manipulator.

Just when I was about to ask him about this whole Leudecke ranch thing, he said, "She seems nice," and sank into the vinyl sofa beside me. He touched my shoulder. (That was another thing he always did. He touched.)

"She?"

"Doesn't look much like her pictures," he said. "A lot younger. Maggie Leudecke. My dad knows her dad pretty well." He took my wrist up in his hand, like checking my pulse. So now he was Dr. Loeb giving me an exam. "He really wanted you on this," he said.

"He did? Your father? Me?"

Loeb's lips were red like the lips of the cartoon dogs in the dreadful artwork in the coffee shop proper. He pointed to the racks along the walls. "Do you really think they get the coffee out of those? Don't brew it? Ever?"

"Something here is out of whack, Loeb. For example: what I know about eminent domain," I said, "is nothing."

"The partners think you can handle this one. Asked for you."

"They what? Listen. What I do know is that people are lining up to give away ranches, and everything else they own . . . hand it to the Department of Transportation in hopes of getting freeway-front property."

"Sorry, Bent. What's that you're saying?" He shook his head. "I can't get over these boxes back here."

"People want the state," I said, "to create some value for them, for their played out prairies . . . shoosh a freeway through them, and—now there's a drowning?"

"I'm sorry. The state will what? I'm not very focused today."

"No, no, you're fine," I said.

Fucking Loeb!

I tried again. "The other thing I know about eminent

domain . . . is that it is eminent. Hence the name. If for some reason the state wants to put a road through Maggie Leudecke's ranch, through her ranch is where it will go. No matter how many construction workers she kills with magical spells." I thought again of my two episodes of unconsciousness in one day. "And it will be a lucrative thing. The best we can do is make sure she gets . . . I don't know, a fair price. Market value."

"If that's the best you can do, Bent, it's the best you can do."

Asshole. Was he even listening? "Loeb, I'd like to get to the real issue here: what part of this has anything to do with my area of limited expertise?" I chewed over, momentarily, just what part of the law might even qualify as "expertise" when it came to me.

"Maggie doesn't think it's eminent. And she's no murderer. Probably."

"So what are we really doing here?"

"Or not the usual kind of murderer. But we'll see. I'm just here to give Chloe a ride to the courthouse." He had finally addressed the first question I'd put to him. "Depositions tonight."

Sure, I thought. No jazz-singing CPA date at all. I bet there were depositions. At the courthouse. Sure, Loeb. Lots of depositions taken at night.

"She really can't spell, though, that girl," and he shook his head in this way that was stern, like he didn't think Chloe's misspelling was cute. Which I didn't either, but the fact that he thought so made me want to defend her, like when he'd made the crack about my "stalker."

I mean . . . it was Chloe he insulted now. And, uhm, Alice. It was just spelling. And stalking.

I was about to say "I drove her here and can take her back," because I truly looked forward to the drive back to town with Chloe. It had been what I'd clung to as a way to salvage the day. But she came around the corner then.

"It's all settled," she said. "Maggie's signed a contract and is ready to proceed as soon as possible. I told her we'd save her ranch."

I was struck by a sudden stomach tremble. "You told

her what?"

"Oh, she likes you," said Chloe. "She's impressed with you. Wants you to handle everything."

I remained quiet. I listened to water drip from a faucet somewhere. Loeb didn't stir. He looked over his cufflinks again, maybe.

"No, no, really," she said. "Maggie claims she got a very good vibe off you, Bent."

I held my hands to either side. "And why not?" I tried to smooth my tie, found someone must have loosened it when I went to the floor. Also, my jacket was gone.

"Bent was just saying," said Loeb, "he didn't think it would be possible to save the ranch."

I cut him off. "Don't you have depositions?"

"Oh, right. We can't stay," said Loeb.

Stupid. My resume blows his out of the water completely, and my resume is thin. He wouldn't even be at Davison, Kohlhoeffer & Loeb without me. Or was it that I wouldn't be there without him?

He grinned.

"Yes," said Chloe, "I am feeling much better about the entire thing." Then she said that when she walked to the parking lot with Maggie Leudecke, she saw that Maggie drove a gigantic black truck, one with tires that lifted it so high off the ground it seemed about to topple. "And when she got in," Chloe said, "she crossed her legs. Like half-Lotus-style." Chloe bit her cute lower lip. "I think she drives like that, with her legs crossed."

"Well," I said. "We have to suffer a witch . . . to drive how she wants?"

"Especially a Leudecke," said Loeb. "Really, Bent, all the Leudeckes are impressed with you."

"They are? The Leudeckes?"

"And they know you'll help them out here." He shrugged. "Like the way you helped their maid."

He rose and Chloe handed me the thick envelope again. "Guard it with your life," she said. "We'll see you later."

"I almost brought you something," I said to Chloe. But she must not have heard, because she and Loeb were gone.

They weren't hand in hand or anything, but gone, swiftly, and a little too together.

"No big deal," I said to nobody. "Coyote."

I sat a moment, listened to the drip of the faucet, wondered about what might be in the boxes with the plastic spigots.

Something nagged at me. Maid? I helped the Leudecke's maid? It was a favor buried in all the citizenship cases I'd worked for the domestic staffs of wealthy people, I supposed, but then I got nervous. Friends of Big Loeb's. Maid with a problem. It started to sound familiar.

Only I realized, then, Loeb had it wrong: not a maid with an immigration problem, it was an *au pair*, and shit yes I helped her. I married the crazy Filipina bitch and had her whole family living with me.

ix.

I made myself rise from the sofa. I went back out into the coffee shop proper, located my jacket on a chair, and headed for the exit. Through the windows, it was October, for sure. Dusk had fallen early. The streetlights were on already and cast a sick, yellow glare. People banged in and out of the heavy coffee shop door. I headed for that exit in a kind of tunnel vision of flight.

Outside, I looped around the parking lot trying to find Loeb and Chloe, which was ridiculous. They were long gone. But I wanted to see if they might still be around, smooching it up, or doing other things, in Loeb's Hummer (yes, Hummer). Maybe they hadn't left yet; it had only been a few minutes. Maybe they needed help with that deposition (even though I knew better), or wanted to grab a drink by the courthouse. Only moments before, I'd been sick of Loeb and of his apologies. (I really don't ever apologize. I take the blame for things now and then, but that's not the same.) Now, a drink with him and Chloe didn't seem all that terrible, yet in the few minutes it had taken to leave the coffee shop, Loeb had managed to get who knew how far away with Chloe . . . Chloe . . . Chloe.

So I searched through the parking lot under the cones of sodium vapor light. And I looked around, behind the signs, behind the parked cars. I checked my Rolex. I had left Austin nearly fourteen hours before. I considered. Because while it's true she was an enormous pain in the ass, she was also somebody I could talk to, someone who seemed even to understand me. I had fallen into a mysterious place, and needed advice.

Alice.

I wondered if she had followed me. I wondered if she lurked nearby, had waited for me to come out. Because didn't she have to? Wasn't that her job? Her role?

What does it mean when your stalker abandons you?

So I wished Alice would come, and I got all nervous over the thought that she might not. I worried, suddenly, that if she ever clicked to just how badly I'd insulted her by leaving her at a hotel, a hotel in another city, I might not ever see her again. Truly, this didn't seem likely, but still. . . .

"Why do you want me at all?" I would ask her, because there didn't seem to be any obvious reason anyone would. "Chloe doesn't," I would say to her. "Chloe's gone with . . . that guy. Can't there be something about me that works?"

In fact, Alice had analyzed my qualities of attraction before—aside from my somewhat adequately if not impressively sized member and sickly demeanor—but her breakdown hadn't been particularly illuminating. I waited, and looked for her. I wouldn't mind hearing these, my attractive qualities, again. I tried to remember what she'd said.

"I like a man who has some mystery," she'd told me once.

"Do I have mystery?"

"Do you think you do?"

"No."

"You're right." She thought a while. "Men are attractive when they have that appropriate balance of intellectual curiosity and snark."

"Do you consider me intellectually curious?"

"But I do like men who are attractive," she went on, "and don't realize it. That's totally hot."

"It's true that I don't realize it."

"Yes. That part is true." She grew silent.

If she were there I would tell her it was important. It was important for me to know if anyone even wanted to be around me again in my life. I would explain how things were slipping away. Decisions were being made without my consent.

"When has that *not* been the case?" Alice would ask.

"But now, I'm fucking passed out on the floor when it's happening."

"I do know that I am not at all attracted to men who

were popular in high school," Alice once said. "I mean, high school and/or college." (I wondered, sometimes, if patent attorneys used that "and/or" construction a lot.) "There's just something wrong with them. Alton, for example, was never popular in high school."

"I was captain of the basketball team." I spoke this aloud to the parking lot of the Café Rico. I looked around for Alice, afraid someone had heard me.

I really wished, then, that she'd come up to me in her vinyl jacket and her thong. With that voice. That screech of a whine. I wished she'd ask me if I loved her. And why I couldn't be more like Alton. And why I couldn't love her.

I wished she would ask again: "Why are you just not capable of love?"

And I'd tell her: that's all I'm capable of, lady. That's all I ever do. I go around and love all day long and the thing is, it's just almost always in some inappropriate way.

But Alice wasn't out there.

Part II.

There is no tribe that forgets

i.

In the morning, Marisel complained about the cartoons her sister, Alexandria, had turned on for Henry in the living room, while Alexandria defended them. Henry ignored the crack and pow of the animated Japanese mega-transformer crusaders and fixated on the unlit Christmas tree in the corner. "*Lap leese,*" he said. "*Lap leese.*" Ours was the kind of household that kept an artificial Christmas tree up year round, by which I mean we forgot that we had one sitting there. We rarely bothered to light it, even at Christmas, unless Henry wanted to see the lights, which could be a notion he'd take up at any time.

Cheso "cooked" breakfast. At least, he stood at the microwave and popped small bowls into it, one after another. The bowls contained something dark-colored and liquefied that smelled of fish heads and Dr. Pepper. When I stepped into the kitchen, he lifted his aviator shades and gave me the thumbs up. Not everyone can get away with aviator shades indoors, especially when combined with hand gestures, but Cheso had both down pat. *That's right, bro*—I raised my own thumb—*another day in paradise.* Then I ducked back into the hall.

On my cell phone I tried to explain to Yvonne's featureless, android, automated female voice mail that it was "an emergency, kind of. Any openings you have." At 7 a.m. there'd be nobody there, but I sought any edge on an appointment. And it was an emergency, or a special circumstance at least. I needed to see Yvonne, although she wouldn't be pleased to have me back at an unscheduled time. Or—she'd be too pleased. She was hard to predict.

I'd spent the night sleepless. I checked my phone

constantly. I looked every few minutes to see if someone had e-mailed or texted. I looked to see if Chloe had called; I was just so down about her.

In the kitchen, Marisel sat on a stool pulled up to the white Formica island countertop and pecked at her laptop. It was a very white kitchen. Everything there—the breakfast bar, the cabinets, the tile-work—had been redone in pristine blankness, as white as snow blindness. This had been Marisel's attempt to lift what she called the "dank" she'd found when she moved in. She'd managed to uncover gaudiness in purity, however, as she filled all available space with white junk shop and eBay items, including—horrifyingly—knickknacks from the Home Shopping Network. These included a row of pale, carved, weathered duck decoys displayed across the cabinet tops, and under these another row of polished, bleached, driftwood slabs. One wood and wool item was meant to resemble, as far as I could tell, a scary, eyeless baby lamb.

"Number one:" she said, "do you realize your mother has broke her hip?"

"Nice." I glared. "You think I don't know about my own mother and her new hip—probably plastic—that she's getting?"

"Will you go see her? Do you intend to do something?"

"I'm actually not a geriatric orthopedic surgeon. But I'm on it." I got out my phone again.

Marisel seemed neither satisfied nor disposed to press the issue. "Number two: can you tell me what was wrong with the restaurants?"

I had no idea what she was talking about, but I could only shake my head because I had already redialed—there was something I'd forgotten to tell the automated voice message. I didn't want Yvonne to get the impression that an appointment on some morning other than that very morning would work. "Bent again," I said. "A special circumstance that I may not have mentioned. If it's possible to find an opening, because . . . the problem is, I'm not sure I can do what has to be done." I checked the rooster-themed, lacquered driftwood slab clock over the microwave where Cheso labored. (The rooster, at least, had a touch of color: a disturbing pinkish bloodstain touch.) "So I'd like to hear from you so I can work in your working me in is the thing, as I've got a busy day lined up . . . but. . . ."

"Do they have one?" asked Marisel. "A restaurant?"

". . . I'd like to try. So, whatever can be done, please do. And thanks."

Marisel turned the laptop towards me and indicated the screen with both hands. She had rings on nearly every finger, each a different eye-popping sparkler. "Did they *have* a restaurant, Bent?"

"What's the question?" The screen was lines, numbers, grids and made little sense. I stuffed my phone in my coat, picked up my briefcase from a captain's chair—another online Marisel acquisition. There was nothing in the case but an iPod and Chloe's Leudecke envelope. "What, what, *what?*"

"*Lap leese!*"

Marisel's fingers squirmed like a magician's above a hat. "Room service four times a day?"

The screen showed some kind of Sheraton Hotel and Spa invoice, itemized.

"I just got back! How did you even access that?"

"The firm don't care? You ever attend any panels at that conference?"

"Of course!" Although in reality it would be difficult to imagine anything more isolated than that room. It was all there. Bathroom facilities. Bed. Fucking. Cable. "Where did you get a word like 'panels?'"

She didn't dignify that with an answer, but turned to holler at her sister in the living room. "At least get him from the screen! He's so close! Those cartoons rot the brain."

"They don't!" from Alexandria. Henry sat beside her, his rump on his ankles. He bopped his curly head to some rhythm that had nothing to do with the sword-swinging aliens on the program.

My son was beautiful, in the way untouched things are often beautiful. His wavy hair shone, his skin was perfect, his brown eyes nearly bottomless black circles. For a long while, we were obsessively careful with his diet and kept him from sweets, processed foods, and glutens, but I don't think that gave him the healthy glow; besides, on the day he broke away from Marisel and myself in a Denny's on I-10 to ravenously scarf waffles from a neighboring table, we gave up on all that, yet the glow remained. I would like to say that he was pure, but if so, it was probably the purity of pure ego. He was a boy—a teenager now—who wanted: one who couldn't fathom the barriers between "want" and "have," let alone "wait," or "later." I suppose this was made up for by his wants being few and easily supplied.

"I don't think there was a conference."

"Don't pester the man, *hermana*." Cheso slapped one of the little bowls on the counter in front of me and handed me a spoon and a sheet off the paper towel roll. Cheso was not one for fancy, individual paper napkins. As usual, his taking up for me wasn't really taking up for me. We all knew who the man of the family was around here. Him. But occasionally, he'd toss me some support, just to let me know I had access to the tree house: the global brotherhood of guys. And guys worked together. Screwed off together. Ate exotic servings of brown liquid together, and without fear. I looked into the bowl. Oily blisters floated in red gravy over occasional flecks of dark . . . fish? In my opinion, it was some kind of marine animal at least. Truly, it was easier to swallow Cheso as an invading alpha male who'd taken over my house than to swallow his breakfasts. He was also given to baking breads of tooth cracking hardness, and often hovered over the stovetop all day, whistling as he stirred a greenish muck of some kind that simmered for hours until it was the consistency of hair gel, then was ladled out over questionable cuts of meat. Another of his specialties I'd labeled "sinew stew." The recipe involved some species of stringy, muscular animal flesh, and capers. All of Cheso's meals were barely edible, let alone digestible, and had brought me to thrashing sessions many times atop many commodes.

Damn fucking straight I got room service four times a day.

"He's working hard! Of course he was at a conference!" Cheso winked at me, as if we had a special understanding between us of just how versatile the word "conference" could be.

I put my briefcase on the floor, slid next to Marisel at the counter, prodded the bowl of red horror with the spoon. "*Sar'ap'*, man!" I raised a hand for a high five, which Cheso slapped. When he turned back to the microwave, I dumped the bowl's contents into the kitchen island's sink with its decorative bronze faucet that resembled pump handles encountered beside red barns in rural America. Or somebody's hallucinatory fantasy of rural America.

Marisel scowled. "You are not gracious."

"I need to go."

Compared to the whiteness of the kitchen the living room really was dank—or dark, anyway. Alexandria liked to watch TV—especially her favorite *anime*—with the lights low. She'd been recruited from Marisel's extended Manila family to look after Henry when Marisel discovered country club lunches, tennis lessons, and community events with her friend and doubles partner Sarah. Henry rocked, cross-legged, his fingers crooked in "The Wall"—a plastic grid set around the entertainment center meant to keep him from climbing and overturning it, and possibly killing himself. Of course, Henry was sixteen, and "The Wall," designed for toddlers, came only to his thighs, but it still served as deterrent. His pose reminded me of that mysterious figure—Maggie Leudecke as it had turned out—who had squatted so low and laced her fingers into the coyote's cage.

At the moment, all Henry's attention was on the dark and silent Christmas tree.

"Alexandria," I called into the living room. "He's saying 'light please.'"

"He likes it dark."

"*Lap leese.*" Henry nodded, smiled at one of his private jokes, but didn't look at me.

"The tree."

Thankfully, Alexandria hadn't followed her sister into brunches, visits to Visible Changes Hair Salon, or sports that required lessons and vitamin waters at expensive facilities, but had stuck close to Henry when he was at home, and when he went to school retired to her room to read thick fantasy novel series. So the fucking nerd girl was the only god of common sense in the household. She grinned now in recognition, got on her hands and knees, her little ass firm in her jeans under the glow of the *Shogun Time Warp Rangers* or whatever the hell it was, and she wormed her way under the tree. "Look, Henry! Look!" She withdrew a wire from the nest of plastic branches and plugged it into an extension cord. The tree flicked into action, all its tiny bulbs the same white color. The ornaments were all there, though many looked glazed, dusty, and random. I thought I even saw some cobwebs but didn't want to be caught having to clean the tree, or, God forbid— Marisel being in a mood this morning—asked to dismantle and store the entire thing.

Hell, it was just two months till Christmas.

Henry pulled his fingers from "The Wall" and went to stand by the festive lights. He smiled his smile. I had successfully translated his slurry hodgepodge.

Hey, I understood my son.

Sometimes.

Alexandria's ass had the same appeal as she backed out from the tree as it had when she had squirmed under. Some nights—those few I spent at home—I'd watch her: her high forehead, her gigantic glasses, her complete lack of the tasteless glamour Marisel had acquired almost immediately after our vows were exchanged with the justice of the peace . . . and on those nights I would want little Alexandria like crazy, but I'd also be depressed and wish I were dead.

"Your mother does keep calling," Cheso said. He drank that vile instant coffee he favored, leaned against the counter, finished, thankfully, with cooking. "Or her friend."

"Don't pick those up!" I said. "Everyone! Don't answer."

"Do something, please," said Marisel. "She's your mother."

"I'm on it."

"*Baboy ka,*" she said, which I had fair confidence was not a compliment. Though she had slanted the laptop away from me I could see Marisel was into the bank balances now. She poked a finger at the screen: probably she had located the cash withdrawals I'd made over the weekend, but it hadn't occurred to me she could get to hotel records so quickly. In the course of nine years, Marisel had morphed from a confused childcare worker cowering in my office to a matron with layer-cut hair, tailored multi-tone tennis dresses, and two-hundred-dollar Reeboks. She traced out my economic life trail in Excel at her redesigned kitchen island. She fed my numbers into her PowerBook and frowned.

Her attention to detail was something I couldn't have predicted, seeing her in my office on that first day. I didn't notice her obsessive behaviors, either, until it was too late. Marisel couldn't sleep before she checked the locks on all the doors—front, back, patio, and garage—multiple times. She turned at the levers to make sure they were locked, then pulled on the handles and knobs. Then she said "Okay, okay, okay" softly to herself before trying the lock again. She'd do this routine five or six times for every door.

"What did you learn at this conference?" Marisel asked. "Tell me one thing."

"When it's time to leave." I rose, grabbed my briefcase. "Big Loeb's actually given me something to do. Not sure when I'll be home."

"The Christmas cards," Marisel said.

"On it."

I poked my head into the living room, where Alexandria and Henry were blank silhouettes against the brightening lawn out the bay windows—exaggerated parody figures in outline like the cardboard shadows caricaturists make with scissors at fairgrounds. They were both templates of two beautiful children, really. And now, behind them, the Christmas tree lights winked. In the frame of the TV, laser beams, eye rays, and swishing sword blades sliced and swooshed. "Good-bye," I sang. "*Good-bye.*"

"*Good-bye, daddy.*" Alexandria cued Henry to the correct response.

"*Goory darry,*" sang Henry, though he never looked away from the tree and its small, white lights.

"No," said Alexandria. "*Good-bye, daddy.*"

"*Da dee dee die dinosaur.*"

Close enough.

"The Christmas cards," said Marisel. "I'll get the receipt."

"But that's two months away!"

She ignored me and headed for the second floor. She took two stairs at a time. Her powerful brown legs pumped in the short tennis dress. Marisel had her moments, but when she pulled out that laptop it made me sick as shit and cast a pall on the day.

I moved down the hall, past an inset "window" that held the landline telephone we never used any more. It had been that phone Chloe had called me on when she'd enticed me out to that *skaky* Pasadena hotel. Marisel had stood nearby, obviously wondering who I was talking to so intently. She rarely bothered eavesdropping any more.

But it had happened. It was one of those once-in-a-lifetime events. I was amazed I'd forgotten about it. Marisel had called me to the phone, cupped it in one hand, said "It's the office" and "Who's Chloe?" I took up the receiver and said "Intern," or something like that.

"Was that your wife?" Chloe had asked. "I told her it was about work."

"Yes. Uhm, yes."

"I told her I needed some help with something at the office, but what I really need is to meet you. Do you understand? The two of us?"

I was not misremembering this.

Now Cheso, however, had edged into the hall. He leaned on the doorframe in the foyer with his arms crossed, an unlit cigarette in his fingers. The smoker of my extended family, Cheso was thoughtful to do it only on the back patio, where a clay bowl spilled over with his Marlboro butts. Who the fuck smokes any more?

"A little advice, Harrison," he whispered.

"Do whatever they say, brother."

He smiled. "No, I have some. For you."

Helpful advice from Cheso had become more common as his fortunes rose and mine plummeted. Before his sister had brought him to Houston, he had worked in a giant tire store in Manila—one of the U.S. chains that had served to decimate all the tiny tire stores in the Philippines before it keeled over bankrupt itself. He'd been an assistant manager.

"They want to hear you're sorry."

"They?"

"All women, really. You think she doesn't give a shit what you do." He'd also gotten comfortable using expletives with me, as family members or bosses will. "Or how much you spend. She does. And she wants an apology."

Cheso once told me he'd nearly been married, but the girl's parents found out that the tire store had failed, and, besides, she had a cesarean scar he didn't like.

"That'll keep the lid on things for now, man. An apology."

"Keep a lid on things."

He shrugged. "She might be getting close to some limit is what I'm saying. Right now, an apology is all she wants."

"Of course." *All I want is some reason to call Homeland Security on your ass.* "Thanks, Cheso. Really." I heard determined footsteps descend the stairs and held out my hand. He grasped it firmly and winked.

Marisel appeared unsurprised to see her brother and myself together at the front door as we sealed with handclasp the mysterious manly pact we'd made in her absence. She placed two cardboard tabs of the kind photo stores use as receipts in my shirt pocket, along with a folded paper slip. "And some other things to buy when you get the cards."

The cards were items ready for pickup at the nearby Mega-Outlet mart, in the photo section, where a computer had placed a picture we had of Henry into a festive frame. I was to get the package of two hundred of these *Season's Greetings from the Bent Family* post-card-sized printouts suitable for mailing. The photo we ended up using—Henry smiling, his hand up under his chin—gave the impression of a common, everyday pose my boy struck all the time, like a neuro-typical kid might do if he mugged it up for the relations: a ham who played to the camera. Really, it was a one, one hundred and twenty-fifth of a second lucky slice out of a day of uncommunicative, hyperactive, unfocused muddle, with Cheso, Alexandria, myself, and Marisel exhausted after an afternoon of trying to get my boy to look into the camera lens. If there was one thing Marisel had, it was the ability to do a thing over and over, even hundreds of times, without becoming tired, especially a thing not particularly useful. Like practicing a second tennis serve. Or checking door latches. Or taking pictures of Henry.

"Did I mention I'm working today?"

"Anything else?" she asked. Cheso slunk back towards the kitchen. He still nodded and grinned at me behind her back.

"I did forget something." I leaned forward, one eye on Cheso. I lowered my voice. "There's something I want to say."

She looked skeptical. "What do you want to say?"

"I want to say—do you remember the Leudeckes?"

She flinched. "Of course I remember the Leudeckes."

"You worked for them."

"I worked for them fifteen years. You know that."

I nodded, although if I'd ever known that, I'd forgotten it. I got very close and lowered my voice even more. "Of course. And Marguerite? Or Maggie?" I whispered. An eavesdropper might well think we were having an intimate conversation of some kind. "Do you remember ever seeing her?"

"The crazy one? She gave Mr. Leudecke so much trouble."

"Ah."

"And then she killed her husband."

"What?"

"In Mexico. A few years ago."

This was more than I expected. "You're shitting me."

She turned away. "You're not gracious ever."

"Killed her husband? How? In Mexico?"

She shrugged. She pointed at her own head—possibly right at the very lobe that kicked off her bouts of obsessive compulsion. "She's crazy, like I said. Why are you asking?"

"Nothing." I leaned forward and kissed her cheek. Her skin was warm, nearly feverish—although I can never really tell about a person's temperature just by touch—and her hair smelled of powerful and expensive chemistry. I leaned back. Cheso, at the end of the hall, gave me the "thumbs-up" one last time.

"Yeah, nothing." Marisel tapped a Reebok once on the tile, shot her hip in the tennis dress as the door didn't quite but almost slammed behind me, and I crossed the lawn on the pebbly, decorative pavement stones she'd set from the porch to the garage. They were shaped like stars, armadillos, the state of Texas. Before I reached the car, I could hear the metallic clicks of the front door latches. Her voice barely registered through the thick panels.

"Okay, okay, okay."

Yvonne's secretary called as I backed out of the driveway. "Really?" she said. She was getting as bad as everyone else. "Shouldn't you take a break, Mr. Bent?"

ii.

"This is no country . . ." I said to Yvonne, who had worked me in before her first appointment—and this, by the way, was something I appreciated about her.

Yvonne was not the best therapist I'd ever had. Not the best "life coach" one could ask for. She would get snippy was the problem. But she was still better than most. She was much better than the last one, for example, who was ill tempered as shit. It's not that Yvonne didn't have a temper, but this one before her—I can't remember his name right now—he was bad. One day, he told me he couldn't see me any more. It was nothing personal, he said, just that he was about to relocate to another city. Out of state. Philadelphia. And he didn't really have any referrals, but was sure I'd find somebody, and was sure I'd be alright: "You always land on your feet," he said, and so on. So four months after I found Yvonne, I was in a liquor store and there he was: my ex-therapist. He was buying vermouth. He looked blank for a moment, then turned friendly, but held the vermouth bottle between us like he'd break it and use it to cut my jugular, if it came to that. He said he was back from Chicago, had come to visit friends, and I said, "I thought it was Philadelphia." At any rate, he squirmed away, but later I went up to where his office used to be and . . . it was still there. His name was still etched into the frosted glass door. When I looked inside, it seemed like the same magazines were stacked in the waiting room.

Yvonne stuck with me.

"This is no country," I said, "for an only child."

Yvonne closed her eyes, knocked herself on top of her own head with her closed fist. Knock, knock, knock. I supposed it to be a variation on the universal symbol for

"Hello? Anybody in there?"—or a bizarre version of *nugeee,
nugeee, nugeee* . . . which people don't usually do to themselves.

"Only child?" she said. "Have you ever considered you
are no child of any kind any more?"

"There are such limited opportunities for somebody
with my upbringing."

"Twenty-five years old?" she said. "Your intern?"

"She's twenty-six." (I didn't really know her age at all.)
"And a paralegal."

"Have you considered ceasing this . . . seeking a way of
stopping . . . ?"

"It's a bona fide profession. Paralegalism I believe it's
called. Plus she's in law school. Very mature."

"Stop," said Yvonne. "Just stop and consider . . . no
more. How about letting go of all these excuses?"

"Nobody can live without the possibility of love," I
said. "Big, big love."

"Everybody can, actually."

"And Alice. Being with her is not that weird."

"There's this idea that love is all." Yvonne leaned
forward. "That it's everything. An unquestionable true and
unadulterated good." She laced her fingers, prayer-like.
"Supposedly. I mean, we've all got to find it, got to have it.
But you're actually right, and even brave enough to say so.
Love is crap."

I stared at her. "I just said the opposite."

"With your life you say it, Bent. Every day. Your actions.
Like this Alice."

"A mistake," I said. "I admit it. A moment of weakness."

"Five days of weakness."

"Just four nights."

"Jay-zus. Don't you know when you skip work for . . .
however many days and go off with somebody like that, all
of society is telling you not to?" She raised a hand to her ear.
"Don't you hear it? No, really. Listen."

I didn't hear anything. I could, maybe, make out the
vague sound of people who milled around in the mall.
Yvonne's office was in the Galleria.

"That's society you hear, Bent. It's telling you to quit

before somebody gets hurt. If you want companionship," she said, "society is saying buy a fucking pet."

"That's funny, because I almost did, sort of."

"No. You won't. You never will."

Yvonne was hard to read sometimes. I think she was a person with problems, but I could never quite understand the best way to help her. Now, for example, I tried to figure out if I was being goaded by her or if she was actually disappointed in me. I was uncertain if such a thing were even possible. Was it? Was it possible that someone to whom you give one hundred and twenty-five dollars twice a week could ever truly be "disappointed" by anything you might do? I mean, she sort of banked on me having problems, right? But I thought maybe she'd just had it with me this time.

Yvonne glanced at her watch, her eyes wide. I had that old, primal fear: that our forty-five minutes had come to an end. In fact, by my Rolex, we'd gone three minutes over. That was weird. Was she actually worried about me this time? Because when it came to calling it quits, Yvonne was like those girls in Chinatown. Come to think of it, those girls operated in small rooms a lot like hers, and the rooms even sort of smelled like her office. There was, in both places, some unidentifiable unpleasantness masked behind cheap fragrance. And those Chinatown girls shut the door and told you to make yourself comfortable, but when the time was up they were *gone*; they nicked out from under you . . . *whizzzzz* . . . their little feet zipped past your right ear and you were left looking down at two towels with Elvis's picture on them and saying: "Well, let's go then."

But Yvonne took checks.

She squinted, waved her hands as if to wipe something clean. "Wait . . . this Chloe. Is this one of those girls . . . that hotel you take women to?"

"You make it sound like there are hundreds of girls. And this was a different hotel. She asked me to go. We did spend an afternoon. We're established, really." I laced my fingers behind my head, sank backwards into the couch, eyed the ceiling. "But then our affair was never really. . . ."

"That's not an affair."

"You are so negative these days. Do you realize that? All your advice is grim. Get a pet. Not an affair." I was pissed. "Chloe's good for me."

"Is she?"

"Only, she's kind of in love with someone else. So there's a drawback." I massaged my forehead, looking up into Yvonne's ceiling tiles. "One of the partner's sons."

"And you're afraid you might insult the partner? Or the son?"

"I'm not afraid of insulting anybody."

"That I believe."

"The partner, Loeb. Big Loeb. He's an odd one. I'm not sure he can be insulted. But hey . . . love triangle, right? Don't tell me you're not interested."

"I hope you don't pull all this crazy shit just to entertain me."

That possibility had never occurred to me. No. I had real problems. I needed real help. I removed the two folded cardboard stubs from my shirt pocket, then the folded paper. I shook the list from one corner to snap it open, held it out to Yvonne. She had to slip on her posh, frameless glasses to read it. She probably got them a few levels down at Eyemasters.

"Wife," I said. "Wants me to get groceries. She wants me to buy these items, on this paper, plus pick up Christmas cards while I'm at it. And so here I have it: a list. What are my chances, Yvonne?" I asked. "What do you think?"

"People have lists, Bent."

"You believe I could do that? I'm not really sure I can do that."

"Go to the store," Yvonne said. "He who takes a journey, any kind of journey, is already a hero." And she said that word, *hero*, the way many judges say the word *felon*. It was a platitude that she'd laid on me before. In fact, at times, she'd get on this journey binge, and yet she looked pretty much planted in the same place herself. I always visited her in the same office in the same mall. She always sat in the same chair. I didn't see her going anywhere. I don't think I'd ever seen her leave that sofa/recliner with ottoman. Yvonne had to keep her feet elevated because of the back trouble. An assortment of her devices sat on a glass-topped table by her chair, and these looked exciting enough in an adult-bookstore-toy-like way, but I knew they were for her vertebrae. She would halt her talk, her advice, her direction from time to time to grab up one of these and reach behind her neck with it. She would even occasionally drop the device down the back of the recliner and roll on it like a cat. Yvonne didn't go on journeys, I was pretty sure. It was difficult to imagine her scaling K9 with a bag of those back tinglers.

I was always having people give me advice they didn't think was good enough for themselves.

"Not an affair, a hookup," she said

"You weren't there."

"When did all this happen?"

I tried to think. "It was summertime."

"*Which* summertime?"

"A recent one."

She nodded. "Made an impression, then."

"A couple of years ago. I should know this, you're saying. I should know the date if it's that important to me?"

"Or wouldn't if it were some random encounter."

This was it. "I should remember the date, and what happened. Something went wrong, didn't it?"

"What do you mean?"

"At the hotel. On that afternoon. I did or said something . . . that made it all impossible. And you think if I remember what it is. . . ."

"Listen, sometimes people don't hit it off. Have you heard of that?"

"If I can remember, I can make it right."

"I didn't say anything of the kind."

I pondered a moment. "You're right, though. I really can't remember much about it. This morning, I thought about how she called to set it up. Called at my house." This seemed important. I searched my mind for a connection, an association, so I could keep talking. So Yvonne wouldn't tell me the time was up.

I said, "Listen. In the Philippines, Marisel claims there was an isolated tribe that scientists discovered. This tribe had no word in their language for 'loss.' If a man lost his hatchet, he forgot he had a hatchet. He didn't think about it."

Yvonne looked over her calendar book, ran her finger down a column. It was probably a list of people with actual appointments that she needed to get started on. "I heard about that tribe."

This was another thing Yvonne always did. She always claimed to know already the facts I tried to explain to her, but this time I kept going.

I said: "If a person died in this tribe—a mother or father—soon their children forgot there was such a person. They forgot the entire concept of Mother or Father. Life went on."

"That tribe was called the Gentle Tasaday."

"It must be a gift," I continued, "to be able to move forward like that without—"

"They were a hoax." She moved to the edge of her chair. "That tribe was a hoax set up to fool anthropologists. I saw it on PBS."

I didn't like to be wrong in front of Yvonne.

"There is no tribe that forgets," Yvonne said. "They just pretended to forget. Much more likely you'll forget something you still have than something you lost."

"I remember this affair."

"You remember this hook-up," Yvonne said. "People get laid. Don't blow it out of proportion. Go to the store for your wife," she said.

"It won't end well."

"And think about embracing your inner adult." She took up one of her spine toys and waved her hands towards the door.

iii.

The Christmas cards were a pain because I'd promised to pick them up but chores, I told myself, were getting in the way of my actual work, even though when I left the office to (ostensibly) get the cards it was after a (pretty short) morning of not being able to figure out anything to save the Leudecke ranch. Because what did I know about ways to save ranches anyway? Still, I spent some time that morning at research. I looked into how the state claimed property for public use. Or saw what Wikipedia had to say about it, anyway. I made a trip downstairs, too, to Real Property to find Rich Jefferson, who'd always been friendly with me and had written white papers on eminent domain. Why wasn't he taking care of this? His secretary told me he was at a conference in London, but still. "If it's eminent domain, Jefferson in London is going to be better than Bent in Houston," I told her. She only shrugged.

Googling recent news items easily brought up the demise of Eladio Trejo, an employee of the Dutch company DeVries Construction. Typical of state highway contracts, rather than investing local funds in local enterprises, the award for the "Road to Nowhere" was pending to a foreign company, one that would no doubt employ cheap illegal labor. Articles about his death included smaller versions of the mug-shot-like portrait I had in the manila envelope. They reported that Eladio, a surveyor, had started to map approaches for the freeway that would, someday, potentially, cut the Leudecke property almost exactly in half. The uproar over his death seemed out of line: he hadn't been shot or poisoned, after all—hadn't been found with the sharp end of a Leudecke family heirloom sword piercing his heart. He had been located one morning by the DeVries crew where he floated face down in one of the "tanks" on Maggie's ranch: one of the little man-made ponds cattle could drink from and wade in on hot days. An overturned canoe that belonged to Maggie—also in the tank—all pointed to accident, although why in the world he'd been surveying the pond at night nobody knew. And: "I don't know why he thought he could use my canoe, either," claimed a baffled Ms. L to a local news outlet.

There was no actionable offense, but this didn't alter the accusations of the Latino community, especially those who lived in the area of some place I'd never heard of, an unincorporated town called Bold Springs. "The Leudeckes will do anything to keep us from getting our road," said a Bold Springs spokesman. "We won't be scared off."

Holy shit. Why on earth would Davidson, Kohlhoeffer & Loeb, LLP let me even try to deal with all of this, especially if Big Loeb was in so tight with the Leudeckes? Obviously, as it appeared that "the other Loeb"—Big, Thomas Loeb— really was behind this, and had asked for me personally, the Leudeckes having reminded him of my "results" with the case of their *au pair*, then a sensible approach for myself might have been to go see him. The Man. Ask him, basically: what the fuck? But that was unlikely. For one, I had never spoken to him. I'd only seen him a handful of times. I'd been near him once as he lounged in a Speedo at a hotel swim-up bar—not a happy memory—but he had never called on me for any reason before Maggie Leudecke and her ranch had been threatened by this construction project. He had never poked his head in my office door, let's say, for friendly small talk, even though I worked for his department, technically, and had enacted wonders by keeping his son occupied and—at least these days—out of trouble.

It wasn't that he intimidated me. More that he intimidated the shit out of me.

Loeb *père* really was "big": a massive presence that loomed, especially his belly, which hung over his belt and moved before him in a way that defied gravity. Thomas Loeb's paunch was without visible support, like a flying balcony. Dark and swarthy, he bore a resemblance to a sumo version of Tony Orlando. His black hair was going white but—and this against all expectations of a founding partner of a major downtown firm—he kept that hair long, pulled back and away from his face in a steel-gray ponytail. This, along with his thick jowls and lips, gave him the appearance, as he walked our floor, of a Buddha in a Brooks Brothers suit, or possibly a tribal chief making the rounds of a massive reservation casino, though he had no Native American taciturnity. If Thomas Loeb had told me he'd just come from a sweat lodge, I'd have no problem picturing it, unlike the crazy convenience mart honkeys. I could imagine the hulk of his frame as he grinned into burning coals, his chest no doubt hung with breasts larger than many women's, his belly a sweaty globe. I could see it. Thinking of him sitting still in one place for long was another matter. A famous flirt, his reputation was simultaneously sullied and pristine. He never put the moves on anyone at the office, and had, in fact, kept the same executive assistant—an iron-willed and efficient administrative force named Ms. Speight (pronounced *spite*)—for several decades. All of his office advances were obviously offered in fun and accepted in that spirit, no matter that it was the twenty-first century, the era of sexual harassment grievances, and such advances were severely risky if not *passé*. It was also known that he roamed the city otherwise, had kept an apartment for a young socialite at one time—possibly more than one socialite if the truth be told—yet planned to remain in his massive home in the Memorial District until his two young daughters were grown. Although his wife was, according to those who'd met her, colorless and without personality, this didn't account for Little Stuart Loeb's own blankness, as he was sired of an earlier spouse. Thomas Loeb by all accounts was not fit to be married any more than he was fit to be a monk. He possessed all the privileges of personality—could easily have fit in as a late-night TV commercial lawyer—but had remained obscure among the city's most powerful attorneys and steered the region's eighth-largest labor and immigration department from behind the scenes, away from public eyes.

No, I wouldn't pierce the partnership veil to ask anything of Thomas Loeb, but I did have to wonder if my suspicions about being somehow forced, prodded, or tricked out of the firm were correct, with Marguerite Leudecke some tool to that end. Maybe Little Loeb himself was orchestrating it, although that was hard to imagine. It was, in fact, easier to imagine a lemur doing a tonsillectomy.

I rang Chloe on her cell, happy to hear her voice, happy to have a legitimate reason to contact her.

"I'm busy," she said.

"Just real quick: Maggie Leudecke's husband?"

A pause. "She doesn't have one."

"You mean any more."

"She's never been married. Oh, so now you think she's available."

"Not that. Just following up on some unreliable gossip."

"Or available enough for you."

"No, really."

"And I really have to go." She rang off.

The rest of my morning was spent in a different kind of research.

If my afternoon with Chloe had been so important, when had it taken place? As in: when exactly? I was firm in my belief it had happened two summers past, as the previous summer had been taken up with a masseuse, a real estate agent, and a high school AP English teacher. So I had the year and the season. Hotel receipts would be long gone, I was sure, as they weren't something I kept. I doubted the crappy Pasadena hotel had a record of our stay, either. I tried to recall: what else had occurred on that day? Or the day after? I'd been at the house just before I drove to the hotel, but time at my home was a painful austerity of boredom and discomfort, the sort of time that folded into itself: origami time. It was what made it so difficult to see the progress Alexandria had achieved with Henry. He was now toilet trained, for example (something I had considered, for many years, an impossible dream), and would these days, on request, kiss people on the cheek, even hug them in an awkward, stiff-armed way, all outlier activity for a child—or teen—with his condition. He would make those awkward, inwardly turned waves when saying hello or saying good-bye. All this I attributed to Alexandria, but I still couldn't bring myself to be cheerful about it. It had happened so slowly.

One time Yvonne attempted to convince me that my relation to my son was one of mourning.

"Dramatic," I said. "But he isn't dead."

"I see it sometimes," she went on. "In parents. Even good parents."

"Even those?"

"The child they envisioned, that they created in their mind, placed so many hopes in and projected so much of their futures onto . . . when that child doesn't show up, it can be a severe kind of loss. To mourn for that child is no reason for shame."

"I think I have better things to be ashamed of," I told her. "He's the son I have. I'm not moping over some . . . great, smart, friendly kid who doesn't exist." I really didn't like the way the conversation had turned. "Who might have turned out to be an asshole, by the way."

"I'm not saying you're blaming Henry."

"Blaming him for what?"

"Exactly. You accept him for what he is."

"I do. I do accept him."

"By spending so much quality time with him," said Yvonne, and she reached for one of her back tinglers. "As opposed to wasting it on masseurs, real estate agents, AP English teachers. . . ."

That Yvonne could be a pure bitch.

But such thoughts did not help me with my project for the day. I needed to know before I could move forward. I had to pin down that time with Chloe. When had it been?

It was a quandary.

I attempted to recall what day of the week our hotel adventure had happened, or if there had been anything notable in the news: any high-profile cases we might have had up and working at the firm that summer. I knew it had to be before a retreat Kohlhoeffer had us all attend in Galveston a couple years back, because I could recall how I was so down about Chloe there, after she'd told me that we couldn't do *that* any more. No offense. Nothing personal. But no more trips to *skak* hotels. And she wouldn't meet me at my room at the Hotel San Domingo after the panel sessions in Galveston, either.

"Not even to watch cable?"

"Nope."

Heartbreaking. In a foul mood (I admit it) at that Galveston retreat I'd stooped so low as to trick Loeb—Little Stuart, that is—into doing something pretty foolish: a stupid prank.

So, the afternoon I sought had been some time before that retreat. I sat in my office, looked out over the Houston skyline. A helicopter lifted from the Texas Commerce Bank tower. Steam-like clouds drifted towards the West. I couldn't do it. It was impossible to recall the date. Maybe Yvonne was right, and it hadn't mattered that much to me. I knitted my fingers, frowned over the megalopolis, and thought about a fried chicken bucket that had floated past me when I was sitting alongside a bayou when I was twelve. The bucket spun slowly in the murky current, showing, then hiding the goateed Colonel's likeness. "I wonder where that will end up?" I remembered asking myself at the time.

At this point, to find that chicken bucket seemed as likely as finding the day Chloe and I had gone to the Super 8 in Pasadena.

I could just ask her, but that sounded like a non-starter.

Then I remembered the swimming.

Chloe had been wearing a bathing suit under her jeans when we'd met at the hotel. In fact, on the phone that morning, it had been: "I'm still in my bikini, and all wet." Because she'd been at Yellburton's housewarming. Yellburton, that asshole in public law, who'd thrown a pool party because he was so proud to have a pool.

Like a pool is a huge fucking deal.

My computer was as much a mess as anything else in my life, because I never deleted anything on it—foolish, perhaps, but in this case, it allowed me to feed a few search terms into my e-mail system and soon I was looking at the invitation from two years before. "Join the Yellburton family for wild, wet fun! July 7, at 2210 Scarborough Lane. Be sure and bring the. . . ."

It had been absolutely not the sort of thing I had any intention of attending, but Chloe had gone. She had gone, gotten a little tipsy, maybe even smoked some grass with some summer interns behind the carriage house. Then she'd called me.

I had that much, then. I had the date. The all-important date.

It had been a good morning's work all around. What to do next?

What to do?

iv.

So: I spent most of the afternoon at Club Some, and by 10 p.m. I was still there. I enjoyed a few beverages. I listened to people talk. I asked myself the age-old question: does sitting alone in a suburban bar, drinking god-awful Cuba Tiránicas, while texting a guy's wife in San Antonio, an old girlfriend in California, and some fifty-six-year-old chick I commonly did S and M sexting with in Orlando qualify as rock bottom? Hypothetically, that is? Or should one, hypothetically, steel oneself for a further bottom to come?

And I hadn't gotten the Christmas cards at all, or anything else on the list. Too busy. Research. Brainstorming.

Oh, I'd had that issue earlier. I had stopped off before I settled into the club at a place on Tidwell Road, the place I'd been using recently for refills. I needed Vicodin. I needed Xanax. Possibly Soma. I parked in the ratty elevated garage, close to the ratty office park, and got some of "Doctor" Double-Wide's prescriptions out of the glove box. When I came down the metal stairs into the sun, I saw a long line of people and . . . oh, shit, not again.

They'd found my pharmacy.

Sure enough, when I walked to the front of this line I could tell they all obviously were waiting to get into the place I had wanted to run into quickly, then get out of fast: a first-floor tenant of this squatty building. The pharmacy had only been there for two weeks that I knew of. The masses work fast. People in the long row eyed me carefully, like I was some kind of authority, or—worse—somebody trying to cut in line. Some of these people were so gray, tired, and unwashed-looking I wondered if this was where I'd seen the guy who'd turned on us so viciously when Chloe had offered him a dollar the day before. I wondered if I'd stood next to him in line at some other Tidwell storefront on some other occasion—but that didn't seem right. A couple of leather-clad types stood stooped over, hugging themselves, wrapped up in spite of the rising heat. Others, absolute deadbeats, were there, too: unshaved in threadbare trousers. Then, there were, as always, the ubiquitous, better-dressed, but hyper-thin, pale, white suburban housewives. But so many!

I needed to keep moving, but thought it over and resigned myself. I took up my place at the end of the line next to a guy with a bright gray goatee, Bermuda shorts, bath slippers, and few teeth.

"Good morning, Mr. Bent."

I didn't know how they could have walked up to me so silently. It must be true what they say about those sneaky denizens of the East. Four Asian guys—oh, shit—skinny, young, with large, insincere grins, approached me as if from nowhere: like they'd been manufactured in a secret lab back in the gloom of the nearby parking garage. They smelled like chemicals, for one thing—or hair tonic—all of them, and each had sleeves fastened low at their wrists, hiding involved tattoo designs, no doubt. They wore identical white shirts and black vests. I didn't recognize them at all, but . . . fucking Ngo Dinh Duc. Surely he wasn't going to have me killed. Or maimed. Surely not in broad daylight on Tidwell Road. That would be truly crappy.

I needed to be careful.

"What the fuck?" I fingered the edge of the nearest one's vest. "You guys gang members, or waiters?"

Mr. No-Tooth in line ahead of me nearly turned, but decided mid-gawk he'd be better off if he ignored my existence. I felt I owed him some kind of explanation, but, on the other hand, why?

The four arranged themselves in a kind of diamond pattern, like a down-court zone defense, and one, the skinniest, whose vest I held, stood very close—the pointed tip of the diamond, the Vitalis leaking off of him. "We *are* waiters, Mr. Bent," he said: soft, polite. "I know you from La' Mai II."

That was one of Duc's restaurants. He had four. The

first stood at the edge of downtown on a lot that had held a gutted and burned Whataburger for nearly a decade, but was now home to his three-story flagship dining facility. It was open twenty-four hours and featured valet parking, catered deliveries, space for wedding receptions, and very questionable activities on its mysterious third floor. Madame Chung had turned me on to it a while back. Mr. Duc served awesome tamarind sweet crab, but hadn't risen to the top of the Houston food chain by his recipes. He knew ways around normal channels when it came to real estate, liquor licenses . . . his relatives' work visas.

"Small world," I said to this kid, who I absolutely did not recognize from La' Mai II. "Line forms at the rear."

"Mr. Duc said we would find you here."

"I do take office appointments."

"We have been here for three days."

"Guys!" I reached into my jacket pocket, but saw them stiffen. "Hey, hey. Business cards."

The man in front of me turned, shuffled away, disappeared into the gloom of the parking garage. Several others in line gave me sidelong glances.

I dealt out the four cards. "Next time, just call."

But the skinny kid moved my card aside in a way I did not like: something similar to Maggie Leudecke's wiping away of my consciousness with a wave of her hand. "Mr. Duc knew you'd be here. Sooner or later." The kid nearly smiled with his thin lips. "He knows everything about you."

"I need to talk to him. Is he here?" I looked around. "I just came from a therapist who hasn't got a clue about me."

"His nephew's visa has not appeared."

"It's hung up in processing."

He nodded. "Which is why he hired you. So there would be no 'hung up in processing.' Would you like to expand and clarify further?" What a smug little shit. His tone was annoyed, but soft, as if he'd asked if I needed more spring rolls. Then, however, he called out less softly, more generally to the parking lot and those who stood in it: "After all, he paid you in cash."

The line waved and whipped, Rockettes–style.

"This is not a long delay," I explained. "It's standard."

"An envelope with *five thousand dollars* in it." He didn't seem angry, just desirous that the amount be heard as far as possible. "An *on the table deal* I believe it's called."

"Under. The visa will be here as soon as I have a chance to file for it."

"And then you said. . . ." But this brought him up short. I noticed, behind him, a van had arrived at the ratty office building. Its brakes screeched, the front fender lowered as the top-heavy vehicle made a hard stop in a handicapped parking zone. On the roof was an alien-looking death ray device: a broadcast dish.

Channel 4.

"Wait," he said. "You haven't filed?"

"I can't without the five thousand."

This only brought more incomprehension. "He gave you five thousand."

"I spent it," I admitted. "On something else. But I'll have more soon, will file, and he'll get his nephew's visa."

He was stunned. Behind him, heavyset men in jeans and short-sleeve shirts poured out of the doors of the broadcast van. "This is not going to make . . . maybe you don't understand."

The line into the pharmacy began to break up. The nervous, older, undernourished white chicks backed away first. The guys in black vests probably thought it was because of them, but: Asian gangs bad, yes. Appearing on Channel 4 in bath robe clutching pain med prescription? Much worse.

One of the Channel 4 crew approached with a heavy video camera on his shoulder. His paunch shook as he broke into a trot. Another loped from the opposite side of the van with a microphone and wraps of black cord on a long boom. Then . . . well, shit. A third guy, his hand mike at the ready, turned out to be—fuck me—Isaac Mintor. Of *Isaac Mintor, Eyewitness Probe.* He was perhaps the Gulf Coast's fattest and most annoying local yellow media on-air personality—and that was saying something.

"I have to go," I said. "As I believe we all should." I forced the business card into the Vietnamese kid's fingers and headed for the parking garage. "But call with questions."

"You can't just spend the money."

"Isaac Mintor," Isaac Mintor said, appearing at the kid's shoulder, his handheld mic thrust forward. "*Eyewitness Probe*. We're wondering what you're waiting to purchase in this line, and where you got the prescription for it?"

The kid shoved Isaac away while his compadres wrestled with the boom operator and video guy. The news team was going to be pretty much stuck interviewing Vietnamese gangmember/waiters, as the line had rapidly dispersed. More people poured out of the front door of the office building as word spread.

"I'll have the money soon and he'll get his nephew's visa."

"Spent it on what?" the kid called out. He ignored the newsman easily, but couldn't seem to make himself comprehend what I'd told him. He asked, in other words, as if he really wanted to know.

"Henry," I called, then headed for the stairs and my car.

V.

So, like I said, after that debacle, Club Some was where I spent the afternoon. It was, in reality, the afternoon and on into the evening. It seemed wise to stay away from the office—home, too, for that matter. But, hey, Club Some was an informative place to hang out.

Some guy there was saying, "Riding mountain bikes, for instance. . . ." It could have been somebody who sat at the bar and whispered, or it might have been a person out on the patio who screamed in an effort to be heard over the music that pulsed from speakers out by the slime-and-algae-covered pond. I tried to find the voice, but couldn't among all the bar talk. I wanted to "tune in," as it were, and find that conversation. "Riding mountain bikes, for instance. . . ." For instance what? I don't find mountain bikes particularly interesting, but it's how I get sometimes. And Stuart Loeb was totally into mountain bikes. Maybe that's what I was hoping to hear in the conversation: *"Riding mountain bikes, for instance, indicates that a person is a goatfucking douche-bag. Science, in fact, has proven. . . ."*

But the actual conversation was absorbed into the backdrop of noise.

That was fine, because "Per Max Weber. . . ." said some other guy two barstools down. He was in a much-washed R.E.M. T-shirt with 1999 tour dates.

"Per whatzit?" asked the woman beside him. She was thin and dirty blond, in business attire, and had one of those ventriloquist dummy smiles—the kind with two hard lines down either side of her mouth. That smile looked familiar.

"Per Max Weber, charisma is a natural endowment . . . and only a natural endowment. . . ."

"So you're saying that you just really want it," said the

woman, her jaw sliding up and down, her voice low and lush.

". . . yet creates a form of domination."

"You want it because I'm so warm. You just want to get lost in me."

The guy in the R.E.M. T-shirt turned to someone, a friend, apparently, beside him: some guy in a knit cap with floppy Sherlock Holmes flaps. "If I get lost in her," he told this friend, "send a team after."

They high-fived.

Oh man. But the blond woman had a mouth just like my first wife. In more ways than one, I guess, but I meant those vertical lines. I was sure it wasn't Kelly. I squinted close to make double sure, however.

Kelly wasn't in a mental hospital (any more), but she wouldn't be at Club Some either. As far as I knew she was with her parents in North Carolina, and for a second I got that sadness, but then I remembered the knife, how she claimed later there was no knife, and I checked again to make sure the woman at the bar wasn't her, then got up from my stool. I walked, kept moving, circled as I'd done a half dozen times already that evening, orbited, passed the high stools, the legs, knees, overhanging asses . . . I moved through the lights. There were three massive trash-can-sized Hollywood Kliegs bolted to the ceiling at Club Some, each aimed at mirror balls that spun in spasms, but that wasn't the half of it when it came to illumination there. Against the darker walls, filtered bulbs behind colored shims gave much of the clientele an unhealthy zombie-like cast. I strolled into the courtyard, tired of making the bar circuit. I checked the perimeter. The pond—or better to say the-thing-that-resembled-a-pond, as it presented more as the swimming pool of a rich exile that had reverted to nature in his absence—I made quick work of. Nothing swam naked there (as on occasion). I leaned over and gave it a sniff anyway. And . . . that pond on the Leudecke ranch. The one that had caused the demise of . . . Eladio somebody. Could it prove to be a freeway construction barrier of a different kind? Snail darters? Rare toad habitat? I sniffed some more, researching, and made a note to check my big envelope of Leudecke ranch info that I had brought with me.

Uhm. Where was that?

I turned back towards the bar, vaguely panicked.

Inside, I loped through the lights and the *throm, throm* of recorded music, and—there. On the corner of the zinc bar, in front of my still empty stool, there was the envelope. I sat, held it tight in both hands. An out-of-season string of Christmas bulbs framed the rack over the bartenders' heads and made me recall the grimy tree in my living room, and that I really should have gotten the Christmas cards, and how a working man can't catch a break *goddammit*. But I held my envelope. I concentrated. I'd get the cards the next day. I promised.

I thought hard.

And that's when my idea arrived.

Well, not just then. I swung my legs pointlessly for another hour before the idea showed up. I sipped a Cuba Tiránica or two. Maybe it was more than an hour. I occasionally sent a text to one coast, then the other. First I attempted to make them appear intellectually curious. Then I attempted to make them appear snarky. I stopped trying to do either after a while, and looked in a desultory way at what the paperwork said about the two "tanks." The documents contained no mention of wildlife, but noted some Indian artifacts found in a midden on the banks of the biggest pond, left by a noble Native American tribe: the "Orcoquisacs." *Save the Orcoquisac Homeland* didn't have much of a ring to it, and the site had been surveyed by Southern Methodist University in the 1980s, then backfilled with gravel.

I felt the epileptic gerbil vibration of my cell phone. *Chloe!* "Hello, hello," I said. I had to scream into the thing over the background roar.

"Bent?"

"I have been working this problem," I said. "This case."

"*Bent?*"

"I got nothing."

"That's good."

"No, I said *I got nothing.*"

The call was breaking up. Frustrating. Something about "preliminary." Something about "easement." I started remembering why I'd kept out of property law. "I'm bringing you the cases," Chloe said. "Where are you?"

She was coming to me! But it seemed a sad thing for her to find me doing, sitting at a bar, drinking Cuba Tiránicas (like Cuba Libres but more oppressive), and having no clue. "I don't want to see you," I told her.

"I want to see you, too."

"No! To you . . . see me . . . like this."

"*What?*"

"Club Some. Downstairs."

She rang off.

We could share a rum specialty drink, maybe, as those were half price. Maybe we could come up with something together.

Because can there be anything better, especially when you're feeling low, than a solution to a problem? Like when nothing you want wants you, for example, and you've had a whole debacle of failure with Christmas cards on top of it. Hey . . . an idea would cure all that. One of those five, maybe eight bev-nap ideas: you just keep pulling them out of the black metal dispenser and you scribble and tear into them with the ballpoint. You draw back from the crowd, the scene, the family responsibilities. I could easily be engrossed in an idea in a place like Club Some.

If I had one.

Then I did.

It swam into my consciousness like a perch with a silk handkerchief in its pocket, paddled up from the muck of my past few hours, from exactly what I had been obsessing over. It was like in the Mafioso movie where the old guy says, "Louie," (or Rickie, or Lonzo), "*stay with what you know.*" What I knew was that I'd spent the previous night, plus some of that morning, pacing, checking my phone, seeing if anyone had called. I looked constantly to see if Chloe had left me a message, or maybe somebody from a hospital or police station had tried to contact me. I didn't want to miss any call that might come in to tell me there'd been a wreck . . . a terrible Hummer accident that killed . . . no, that *disfigured* Loeb, although she, Chloe, safely strapped in the passenger seat, had escaped unharmed. Perhaps, yes, she'd had parts of her memory mysteriously erased. Perhaps these had even been tawdry, cheap hotel parts. But there were no such calls, so after a few hours I'd sat up in bed, rubbed my eyebrows, and considered more proactive means.

At Club Some, I fell naturally into these same musings as I watched the lights and the people. How to get rid of him? How to do it in a way that would work and be final? And not point back to me? It wasn't like I hadn't already manipulated the poor schmuck for several years. I could murder him. *True.* Best, however, to keep such approaches on the down-low, so to speak, not mention them, but there they were: poison spy pellet . . . ceiling fan accident . . . voodoo spell. . . .

Voodoo spell.

It's amazing, really, that it wasn't until that moment that it occurred to me how some aspects of the Leudecke case and other factors from my own personal life interlocked in such a natural fashion. It was only at Club Some, that brain-jamming noise mill with the concrete floor that always seemed damp, the music so loud it was barely recognizable as music—a club that always reminded me of a soccer match, where everybody ran and bumped into each other, and nobody scored—it was only there that I hit on an idea good enough to get me to accept a ballpoint from behind a sweaty bartender's ear and pull seven bev-naps from the black metal dispenser.

I knew a guy who'd gotten a voodoo spell. He'd driven to New Orleans for it. It had to do with his ex-fiancé, or oil lease tax subsidies, I couldn't remember which. But *Voodoo Spell, Schmoodo Spell.* Why go to Louisiana and spend a wad when there was a witch right here? And a perfectly good one, with a house—no, a *ranch house*—full of who knew what? Cauldrons. Crawfish bladders. Spells (probably). It was, of course, my client—my newest, highest profile, community icon millionairess with the legal problem I had no idea how to solve and the personal aura that seemed to trigger personal brain seizure. I could ask Maggie Leudecke for a way to get Loeb out of my life. If I could stay conscious in her presence, I could buy a candle off of her. I could have her mix a packet of contagion, maybe, or prepare a velvet-lined clutch purse (with a gold clasp) filled with secret herbs and baby's blood. And the way my mind was running, it didn't occur to me at first, I admit, that it might be better, less unseemly, to just get a spell from Maggie Leudecke that would make Chloe love me. A potion.

No.

I wanted one that would harm him, or would make Chloe hate him, make him evil in her eyes . . . possibly dissipated. I wanted a spell that would do something to his cock, like turn it reddish with a pernicious, scaly rash. Surely Maggie Leudecke could handle that if she were worth her mojo.

I wondered if she took orders over the phone. Might be safer.

Hell, I'd be willing to do a ritual, if that's what it took. (I'd had several drinks by that time and the music was pounding.) I'd be willing to dance naked around a tree if I had to. I'd dance naked in both directions around the tree, I didn't care. . . .

. . . and. . . .

Chloe had said Maggie Leudecke was a "Wiccan." That was an actual religion last I'd heard, and I wondered, then, did she have any rituals, or any ceremonies, especially ones that she did on her ranch? Was the ranch in some way associated with the spiritual life beliefs, or practices, of this actual. . . .

I envisioned, momentarily, the Sparrow gang, or clan. Those kinds of people fried me, slipping into Indian spirituality like it was a shirt off the rack, but I remembered some cases, and in the state, too, that involved such groups and things like enchanted hills and power boulders. These were sacred spaces, associated specifically with geographic areas and spared from the developer's backhoes because yuppies had gone there to form drum circles.

Why the fuck not? It was something to pursue, anyway. It was something to go down into the library with Chloe to check out, and I was happy then for a while. I sipped more rum from the glass coated with diet cola syrup, tapped by the bartender straight from the pressurized cylinder under the soft-drink dispenser. I enjoyed a few more Cuba Tiránicas, sucked on limes, scribbled bev-naps with a flourish of pen. As always with this particular beverage, I was going through the requisite zone of dizziness required to achieve the level of drunkenness desired.

This just might work, I thought. It could easily work well enough for tonight, anyway. I could impress Chloe with the fact that I'd come up with something. Chloe, who would be arriving at Club Some, due any moment, and my take on her was that she was easily impressed, or used to be, and I wouldn't even need to have Loeb killed or reduced to fetid piles, because, just in time, I'd had an idea, and Chloe would love my idea and, hence, love me.

Maybe Maggie Leudecke would need some of my magic, too, after I saved her property: who knew? I gave good vibes when it came to Maggie Leudecke.

So I just had to sit there, quietly, and wait, but there was somebody making eyes at me. C'mon. Really? But yes. This was not the woman who resembled Kelly, but another one. She was a relatively short woman, tiny and dark-haired, in a large-winged, floppy hat. I felt there was something about her. Her face was cut into odd, shadowy planes, for one. Her small size, maybe, gave me a false sense of immensity. I sipped at my Cuba Tiránica and waited for Chloe to come with "the cases"—whatever those were—and my idea was ready to spring on her, but somehow I soon found that I'd risen to stand by this little woman's stool. Like a roulette ball, chance brought me to that spot, the one beside the floppy-hatted girl. It was so crowded, and there was no place to do anything like sit next to her, so I stood in front of her, wobbled a little. Diet cola syrup has a way of berserking the bloodstream.

I pointed my finger at the short girl, one eye closed, head cocked. The mixer behind the bar whined like Hell's iron shredder. When I say she was small, I don't want to give the impression she was malformed, or misshapen, like a dwarf, Pygmy, or midget. Everything was proportional. She was slender in her beige skirt and white top, with powerful-looking legs and that floppy hat.

"You don't recognize me," she said, before I could utter a word.

"What? How could I forget . . . the girl with the hat. . . ."

"No."

"Who I met in college?"

She shook her head. "I'm working on my GED. You're my lawyer, Mr. Bent."

That stopped me. I couldn't believe it. I said: "Oh, right."

"My counselor? My attorney?" She was one of those girls who turned statements into questions. "Or V.J.'s, anyway."

Now I was stooped over, my hands on my knees so I could lean close, be a little more eye to eye. She was just that small, even on a bar stool. I couldn't place her, or "V.J." for that matter, and then Chloe walked up. Chloe tapped me on the shoulder, and she had another manila envelope, only this was a smaller one than the big bubble-wrap mailer variety of the day before. And what had I done with that?

I panicked again. The envelope! I looked around, searched the floor, but "Hey, it's Chloe!" I said and tried to act nonchalant. "What are you having?" I looked for the bartender to get Chloe a drink, but mainly—what the fuck had happened to the envelope?

"Heya," she said.

Back at the corner of the zinc counter, a guy had taken my vacated barstool and rested his highball on the envelope, where it left damp rings.

Oh, guy.

"Look," I said. "It's Chloe, who is not short."

"What?" Chloe said.

"But who was fat once." I didn't want to get the envelope just then. I didn't want Chloe to know I was allowing her hard work to be used as a coaster at Club Some. "A fat, fat girl," I said. "At one time."

"Thanks for mentioning it." Chloe eyed the short girl: my client, apparently.

I was not communicating well, and the mixer seemed to be grinding a Mini Cooper to scrap.

"Bent?"

"But I wouldn't care if you, Chloe, were fat, is the thing," I said. "Which you don't care about either, or not any more."

That's the problem with Cuba Tiránicas. They hit you all at once or not at all, and never not at all.

The music cranked up loud, competing with the mixer.

"*Check this tonight.*" Chloe came very close to my ear because of the noise. I felt the warmth of her breath as she screamed. *"Stuart and I. Pick up Maggie. Take to the hearing. Tomorrow."* She'd been working all day on the Leudecke case, while I'd been dealing with Wikipedia, pharmaceuticals, not buying Christmas cards, and warming a stool at Club Some. She looked tired.

Oh, wait. I did something productive today. "July 7," I said.

"What?"

Right. She didn't care about July 7. "Listen," I said. "I can make the house not go through the freeway."

"You smell like a cruise ship," said Chloe. *"Having fun?"*

"I'm going to save. . . ." but then the mixer ground to a halt and Chloe flinched because I screamed into the sudden silence. *"SAVE THE RANCH!"* This idea got some applause from cheering, drunken bystanders, and I grinned and waved at them. Chloe rubbed her ear (her big, big ear) and I gathered myself. "To save the ranch." I glanced behind me. Envelope was still there.

Chloe patted my shoulder. "Yay!" But she didn't mean it. She said "Yay!" in this way that I knew meant the opposite: "Yay-not," or something.

But it was nice that she took the time to pretend to be supportive. Chloe was one of the few people I knew who never really attacked me, although she hurt me all the time with the way she treated my feelings like they didn't exist, like I wouldn't be hurt when she told me about Loeb: how Loeb was so great, and then she'd tell me about her boyfriend the CPA who she really, really didn't even much like. Couldn't talk to him was the way she put it: not the way she talked to me. But that didn't stop her from, on occasion, telling me about how she and the CPA went at it for eight hours one weekend. (And she would say the word "hours" like it had two syllables, possibly three.) And his chest was so this. And his arms were so that.

I have a chest. I have arms.

"So, you're saying you found the land grant?" she asked.

"What'sit?"

"This." She touched the new envelope. "Hasn't been challenged, even a big municipal case. In the tidelands."

"Ah. Municipal. Tidelands."

"Like Spanish land grant?" asked the short girl in the floppy hat.

"Don't listen to her." I raised my hand to whisper behind it. "GED."

"That, yes. Exactly. Given to the old Texas pioneers by the Viceroy. But then they became Mexican land grants in 1821."

"Now look here," I said. "A Mexican is *dead*."

"And were kind of in limbo until the Treaty of Guadalupe Hidalgo in 1846. Which was when the smart and rich people—like the Leudeckes"—she directed that part at me—"got surveys and proper recognition of their titles. This is from an international treaty, Bent."

"I prefer to think of it as *trans*national . . . but. . . ?"

"Article XIII of the Treaty states these old grants are *inviolably respected* by the United States." Chloe stopped there, leaned forward, extended a hand to the girl. "We haven't met."

"Look," I said, taking her hand away from the short woman's vicinity. "I have to make two things very, very clear between us, right now."

"Yes?"

"The first is that I have never seen this person before in my life." I stuck my thumb towards the small girl with the hat.

"He doesn't remember," she said.

But then I had it. I snapped my fingers simultaneously, both hands, and pointed at her, quick-draw style. "Mrs. Panglomadangadong!"

"Nine o'clock at the annex," Chloe said, then turned to the small girl, offered her hand again, stated her own name. "Nice to meet you Ms. . . ."

"Amy." The girl grasped Chloe's fingers daintily. She shrugged. "I can't pronounce it either."

"Have you called your mother, Bent?"

"Getting on that." But this gave me an idea. "I need to get by the hospital. Just don't want to go alone."

Chloe looked over my shoulder towards the big, circular bar where the lights flashed and spun with the loud music.

"Maybe you and I could run over there and—"

"Gotta go." Chloe backed into the chaos of the crowd. "Read it. Nine o'clock. Annex. Nine o'clock."

And then she was gone.

I stood awhile. The music started in again, deafening. I turned to Amy, shouted in her ear. "She left!"

"Yes, she's gone."

"There was one other thing. That I had to get clear between us."

"Do you remember what it was?"

"No. No." I leaned on the bar, snaked my arm behind Amy, close.

She put down the glass she'd been holding, took up her small clutch purse. "Do you have twenty dollars?"

"Yes."

"Cash?"

"Yes."

"Do you want to come with me to the ladies' restroom?"

"Yes," I said. "Yes I do."

vi.

The saddest thing I remember out of all the sad things I remember about my ex-wife is the night she spent strapped to the emergency room gurney, where sedatives and anti-psychotics dripped into her through IV tubes. Slowly, the drugs lowered her below and away from whatever irrational nightmare episode it was she thrashed through. She wrestled against the restraints as she went down, down . . . into what the doctor on duty promised would be unconscious oblivion.

C'mon unconscious oblivion.

I don't like to draw attention to myself. Standing next to a screaming woman in a crowded emergency room with five people holding her pressed against a gurney was not my scene. But then, when the pharmaceuticals got some traction, finally, but before the stupor, she edged into a transitional zone, somewhere between insane and blacked out. Her incoherent screech wound low, then trailed away. I suppose she must have found herself momentarily afloat in an eddy of clarity.

"Good God," she said to the four or five medical personnel who held her limbs and forced her onto the mattress. Her voice was hoarse. She scanned her surroundings, looked everyone in the eye. "I'm being such an asshole."

"Oh, no," the security guard said. I'm pretty sure he meant it ironically. They'd put this giant guard at the foot of her bed the hour before, and he'd twice stopped her from pulling out her tubes, twice again stopped her from choking herself with her own hands, or trying to. That was when they'd brought out the restraints. She had already, that afternoon, attempted to kill herself with a knife, wrestled with me, and deeply bruised my forearm as I struggled to get help on the phone, then assaulted the sheriff who arrived before the ambulance, kicking at him ridiculously with her high-heel boots.

She turned to me. Her wrists were fastened in straps and bands attached to the bedframe in a way that made her arms look broken or frozen at unnatural angles, like the wings of flying dinosaur fossils. "I want to go home," she said. "Bent, can we go home?"

That was the sad thing.

"What did you tell her?" Yvonne had really wanted to know that part when I'd explained about Kelly. It was one of our first meetings, back when I'd first started seeing Yvonne. "What did you say?" She waited. "I mean, it would be one of those make or break moments in a marriage, don't you think?"

"I don't remember," I told her, though I did—and Yvonne knew it, too. It's terrible to get so down on yourself you start lying to people you're paying hundreds of dollars to just so you can have somebody you don't have to lie to. I remembered. When Kelly asked if she could go home, I looked at all those people around her, dripping drugs into her, restraining her, all of them anxious and exhausted.

I said: "What the fuck do you think?"

At Club Some, I glanced a last time at the woman with the R.E.M. T-shirt dude, making sure it wasn't Kelly, then slipped over to retrieve my envelope from under the guy's sweaty highball glass. "Sorry, left something, no harm," and the like.

"No problem, Mr. Bent."

I had my *two* envelopes, then, firmly in hand, and Amy tugged me by an elbow across the damp concrete towards the doors to the restrooms. I thought about Chloe. It was like her touch remained on the manila envelopes. I wished she was still there, yelling over this shit music, her breath warm in my ear. I missed her already. I missed her high-pitched little-girl voice; the smell of her body wash; the baseball cap she'd worn to that *skak* hotel, turned backwards. I thought about Chloe, who had backed away into the crowd at Club Some: a sort of terrible, aching, iconic version of *leaving*, and I had a craving, then, for her legs, her arms . . . for her wrists . . . those thick ankles and overwide hips. I believed, then, this must have been some image that I kept stored in a cabinet in my brain: a glass case in one of the back hallways of the cerebellum, labeled with a printed card in a little frame: "Front of Woman (Backing Away): Ideal." It was a specimen that had been there decades before I ever knew Chloe (years before she was *born?*), but that looked just like her.

And . . . hey, what the fuck?

I spun around, but the barstool was empty, the guy who'd rested his beverage on my envelope gone. I retained some residual memory of broad shoulders, a sports coat. Tall. He'd had very bushy eyebrows that met over his nose.

He'd called me by my name.

"Did you see that guy? Who gave me my envelope?" I twisted the brad holding it closed, and looked inside. I didn't completely know what had been in there in the first place, though. How to tell if something was missing?

"Guy?" Amy, the woman with the quasi-legal marriage to the Indian or Pakistani who had the Café Rico franchise, had brought us nearly to the wide-swung LADIES door. Inside, the facility appeared filled to maximum occupation already by both sexes, who milled. The restrooms at Some were more an annex of the bar than private, gender-specific havens of genital evacuation, although divisions and the doorless stalls allowed for at least semi-private fluid (and other) transactions of various kinds. Around us moved several waves of talk, including an earnest, chesty blond who said "Let's get real. No, really. It's time we get real." She kept repeating this, although she didn't appear to be speaking to anyone in particular. Then "Actual obliteration of the mind" from a guy in soccer shorts, knee socks, no shirt. Jagged, triangular tattoos decorated each forearm. "The mind and the spiritual consciousness as well, plunging both into a suffocating—"

Thanks, moving on. Where was that man with the eyebrows and the envelope? I had a bad feeling about him.

Then a dialogue:

HE: I mean, it's not like, rub this. Suck that.

SHE: I do not want to know.

HE: There's an alarm system anyway. Or if anyone's left out.

SHE: Alarm system?

HE: Or feeling left out. A code.

SHE: Fuck! With levels? Are there levels of alarm, Carter?

HE: Calm it!

SHE: Does it go from concern to. . . .

HE: Just say Code Nine, Melissa.

SHE: . . . to soul-shattering existential crisis?

HE: Say Code Nine and—

SHE: What?

HE: We reconfigure.

Amy repeated herself several times. "I'm going to the restroom. I'm going to the restroom." I didn't mind girls who repeated themselves when drunk. It filled time that otherwise might be taken up with awkward silence or—worse—attempts to *get real*. "If you lose me," she said, "just call back," and I noticed then she was speaking into a cell phone, the device mostly hidden by her hair.

I was about to follow Amy into the restroom when there he was, this guy I knew, coming out of the LADIES. He was this attorney who I hadn't seen in a while, but I knew him. I went to law school with him, and he was doing well. This guy owned outright one of those low-rent immigration and traffic violation storefront operations in the East End: ABOGADOS Y MÁS. He was on TV, advertising his services in heavy rotation. The Latino Guy. Which sounds bad, my calling him that, but that's how he marketed himself, too: "Latino and having troubles with the courts? Call The Latino Guy!" And: "Latino and involved in an accident that's not your fault? The Latino Guy can help." Even: "Have a DWI violation and you're not Latino—just Latino-curious? Call!" He had a huge operation running down on Navigation Street, but shit, true to fucking white-male stereotype, I couldn't recall his name, even though it was a common one, the name mentioned in all his ads, the same name he'd had when we went to school together, when we'd run around and gotten drunk together. He was even dressed like he did on the ads, right down to the beige jacket and white straw fedora with the black band.

Alberto Martinez. No. Fernando Hernandez? Something

like that, but . . . Eladio Trejo! Shit no, that was the dead guy in the pond.

I was afraid to pick a name, so just said "Hey . . . man," and went to shake his hand, but he had just come out of the restroom and it was the restroom of Club Some, so we both simultaneously thought better of the hands and the shaking.

"Bent!" (Oh, great.) His face was shiny. It kind of shocked me to see him there. When I saw people I knew in the sort of places I hung out, I always lost a little respect for them. Maybe he felt the same because: "I am surprised to see you, Bent," said the Latino Guy.

"I'm still in town."

"I'm surprised to see you alive, motherfucker." He frisked my arms and shoulders, reassured himself of my reality. He indicated the manila envelopes. "And on the case. You really working?" He pulled a bev-nap out of my pocket, dabbed his forehead, then held it before him. Sweat-splotched, it contained only one word:

"OMPHALOS? What the fuck, Bent?"

"Sacred navel . . . thing," I said. "Foundation stone. The Earth. Uhm. Our Mother."

He withdrew another from my pocket. "*Spirituality*," he read, concentrating hard. "*Look into it*. Yes! Dude, I haven't seen notes like this outside a dorm room in years."

"Anyway." I gathered my bev-naps, stuffed them into my coat.

Amy, still on her cell phone, became emphatic: "*I said I am go-ing to the rest-room.*"

"Listen," The Latino Guy said. He reached into his own pocket. "Man, I haven't got any business cards on me. But you can find me, right?"

I thought about the heavy rotation TV commercials.

"I might have something for you," he said. "Laters."

"Wait! Do you know someone . . . with big eyebrows?"

The Latino Guy laughed. "I'll bite. No. I mean yes."

"You do?"

"Everyone knows someone with big eyebrows, Bent."

"This one . . . I think he might burn cars."

"Shit, man. You never change." He saluted with two

fingers along the rim of his hat, winked—as he always did in his ads, come to think of it—and wandered away.

Amy tugged at my sleeve, covered her phone with her palm. "He's crazy, Mr. Bent."

"He's eccentric, but successful as shit."

"I mean V.J. Is there anything I can do?"

"Your husband?"

She stopped. Said "No!" At first I thought she was still on the phone, or had loudly denied my statement of her espousal, but it was actually terror. Her statement quickly turned into "No, no, no!" then she grabbed my neck, brought her lips up close to mine. I thought I was about to get some action right there in the doorway of the LADIES, but "Up!" she said and I saw then what was snaking out of the restroom: a menacing stream, a flow of water, more river than puddle, that spilled out onto the dance floor. Something in that restroom had begun to gush. In my mind, as The Latino Guy had just left from there, I connected the problem with him: like he'd dropped a cherry bomb in a commode before strolling casually away. The liquid spread, looked half an inch deep in places, and no telling what was floating in it. I didn't much want to step into it myself, but Amy had open-toed shoes, and . . . what kind of gentleman takes a lady into a club restroom and then lets a toilet juice her feet?

I looped my forearm under her little bottom and lifted, cupped her ass with my manila envelopes. She was surprisingly heavy, as women are when you actually pick them up.

"C'mon, we still need to go in," she said.

"Of course." Why exactly was that?

I carried her in my arms as I waded into the LADIES. Amy was so small (though not necessarily light) that I could hold her up pretty much the way I used to hold Henry when he was seven or eight, right up until ten or twelve, when he needed to be calmed after coming home from some direction other than the direction Marisel or I usually brought him, or when he moved a chair into the kitchen and opened the freezer and found there were no frozen popsicles, or when he saw a cat. Cats terrified Henry. Then, sometimes, when the air conditioner turned itself off, he couldn't stand it, and he would begin to howl. "*On! On! On!*" He wanted to sit by the big intake vent by the hall telephone—put his face next to the vent and smile, and keep smiling—but he couldn't do that if the thing continued to cycle off, so he would scream like shit until we'd lower the temperature to get the fan to move again, or until he got picked up. It was something like that, holding my client as the liquid sloshed over my shoes.

Once anointed, there was no point being worried about it, so I carried her deeper into the restroom, and was surprised once inside to find that a complicated work of conceptual art had been displayed in there, bolted against one tiled wall. "That's a damn odd place to put a work of conceptual art," I said to Amy, right over the stainless steel sinks (though, to call them *stain*-less would be kind), and though Amy was heavy and still chatting away or at least listening to somebody on her cell phone, I couldn't help but examine this thing . . . imagine it, in fact, over the desk in my office. It was the sort of piece that gave an impression, and looked to be a representation—in gelatin—of a pummeled and bruised two-headed sea mammal, possibly one found piled on a beach by tides after a rough passage over coral reefs. Hair streamed from behind the ears of this creature like bad wiring, and its exposed heart was a bright orange rectangle. Then the heart fluttered and moved, and I heard the electronic throb from the "dance floor" outside and it was like coming out of anesthesia. The beast became a horrifying two-headed anthro-morph humanoid with four arms and two befuddled expressions, and the glowing, Virgin-of-Guadalupe-like fringed halo around the two-headed creature's two heads was no longer a halo but a floppy hat. I was looking into a filmy mirror and it was myself and Amy Praomongijanklang reflected back: her lifted in my arms so she wouldn't get goopy toes. Her feet, wrapped around my torso, seemed unnaturally large in the reflection. The orange rectangle: Chloe's Leudecke file.

"God," I said. I meant it. I called God.

Amy watched me in the mirror. She looked right at me, as two people who look in mirrors will sometimes do. There was something both odd and familiar about the way she felt in my arms. She unwound one elbow from my neck to push at a string of hair plastered flat to my sweaty forehead, then daubed the moisture with what I took to be a towelette of some kind. She pushed at it, but the hair wisp wouldn't budge, just kept springing back into my eyes. I was reminded of Maggie Leudecke's leathery fingers. When I looked again, I realized Amy had wiped my brow with my twenty-dollar bill.

"I'm losing you," she said into the phone. "Yes, yes, I promise. Bye-eeeee." She folded the phone, dropped it into her little purse, all of which seemed odd for her to be doing while I carried her around.

"The Indian or Pakistani guy?"

"Which is it anyway?" she asked. "C'mon. You've got to know the right people in this world."

She directed me farther into the restroom by pointing the damp twenty and steering me with her knees. I still couldn't tell where the flood was coming from, but it was being generally ignored, the room damp but full of men and women, the music in there more *thump* than roar.

"Amy!" said a guy with a beard and a nasty neck rash who walked out and waved. She waved back, guided me towards the last stall at the rear of the restroom where a group of people gathered and sweated beside a blond woman with a thick chin.

"X!" Amy said, and she held out the cash, moist with bits of me.

The blond woman slit the seal on a sandwich lunch bag with her thumb. "Amy!" She dipped a broken glass pipette into some off-white powder, then held the unbroken end towards Amy, who leaned forward in my arms. I leaned back to counterbalance, the effort reminding me of hooking tuna offshore on a deep-sea boat rental with some exploration petroleum guys one autumn. Something in my shoulder made a sudden *scritch*, and I stood, expecting trouble, a wave of pain. Instead, it seemed to feel better. I was ready for anything.

"Is that X?" I asked Amy. "I've never had it."

The lady with the chin said, "I'm X. X is my name."

"What's this, then?"

Amy snurfed the mystery crystal into her nostril from the glass, and X unhinged her big mouth, but no words came. Then she shrugged, her lips parted like she was about to blow out birthday candles. Lots of them. I looked into the water of the john, where flecks of billowy cotton-like wisps of white twisted in currents. Some guy in a long black coat leaned over it and spat—which explained the cotton-like wisps, but didn't help the effect.

"Him," Amy said, and when X placed the glass in my nostril Amy held the other closed with a forefinger.

Could be heaven. Could be Drano. I sucked it in.

"Ah," I said.

"Ah," said Amy.

So we ended up at another place after that, one that was right next door, called Emo's Club, owned by the same people who own Club Some and, so, spelled it backwards, but the crowd was younger . . . terribly, terribly younger, which wasn't so bad for Amy Prangalingatam, who looked to be in her twenties, but as I examined the crowd in there I remembered the wrinkled sea mammal in the mirror, the burning car, my recent slip into unconsciousness at both a convenience mega-mart and a Café Rico, those Christmas cards I hadn't gotten, and I felt my years. This was more a dance place than a drinking place. It had the same looped, palpitating white noise, but a lot more flailing, and I felt breakable and self-conscious wading into the youthful, thrashing crowd. Amy got us some drinks and I sipped mine, but put it down after a while, then lost it (it tasted vaguely of cranberry juice and hotel room disinfectant), and Amy danced while I hovered over and around her, imitated the motions of the human figures nearby as best I could. Young, T-shirted, sweating: some had no hair, some had long braids that slashed the air. A thin, brunette girl with very red lips and green eye shadow whipped and ducked so violently I was prepared to catch her head when it snapped off her neck. In a smoky corner, piled-up cushions smelled of dust and cum when Amy and I dropped onto them, and we dripped with sweat. She stroked my face and simultaneously rubbed her own ribs, legs, and head. We both ignored the clamor of her cell phone when it rang every five minutes. Amy whispered in my ear, but I couldn't really understand what she was saying as she rimmed the outside of it with her tongue at the same time, and her tongue was rougher, more sandpapery than I expected.

"We need to go to my place," Amy said. "While you are sober enough to drive." She grinned, draped a leg over my hip. Her phone rang.

"He calls a lot."

"He actually tries to visit me."

Lovely: a near admission of what I had nearly suspected all along but did not want to hear: that the "marriage" between these two was an immigration scheme. I hadn't taken the case of a couple of cohabitants after all, an acceptable legal category where gaining citizenship was concerned. Amy, probably, had been paid by "Vijay" (his name—not initials—I finally recalled) in goods, services, money, or whatever. Maybe she got an apartment and a computer. He got a green card and the ability to remain in the U.S. and run his coffee franchise. I remembered now how they'd shown up at my office with letters and a month or so's worth of e-mails . . . so I asked about the valentines. With a spring wedding, there'd need to be some cards to show Homeland Security these were "people in love."

"We left those at home," said Mr. Promalongabong.

An hour later, they brought some totally sappy cards with totally sappy messages scrawled inside, especially Mr. P's to Amy. The guy had a tendency to go overboard in his written messages, but in a staccato, English-as-second-language way that gave them the tone of Love Telegrams. "I will wrench out my heart. Without you I will. Also soul," and the like, but it's not my job to investigate, it's my job to guide the clientele past the I-130, through to the I-485, to arrive safely at an adjustment of status. I did not, now, want to know they had left my office after our initial consult only to find a Hallmark store and buy a stack of sentiments they could back-date in the parking lot before returning, and I told Amy this very thing, but she didn't grow silent, just more animated.

"He wants me to visit his parents! In Karachi! Are you fucking kidding me? That would be the last anyone ever saw of me. Do you know, to keep up this sham marriage. . . ."

"See?" I said. "This is exactly what I'm talking about." I was driving by then and couldn't stick my fingers in my ears, jump on one foot, pretend the music drowned out the content like back at the bar. I couldn't do all that and still keep the Elantra on the road. We had left after what seemed several grueling hours of dance, noise, and sweat at Club Emo's—but by my watch it had only been forty-five minutes. "Do not tell me about sham marriages."

"To keep up this sham marriage he continually comes over to put stuff in my apartment. Or our apartment, but it's mine, not his."

"Oh, shit." She told me things that could easily get me disbarred. Of course, it's not like I was a stranger to hearing things that could get me disbarred.

"That was the deal. He'd pay for . . . this project I'm working on. But it's *my* project, only now it's all his clothes, coats, underwear, socks in the chest of drawers. He's got a golf bag. One of those things full of golf clubs? On wheels?"

"So if anyone checks . . . but wait, who's paying for this apartment?" And where was it? Her directions had taken me in what seemed a spiral pattern through the Montrose district, and she'd given no indication that we were drawing any closer to her home.

"He doesn't play golf!" Then her phone rang.

"Can't you turn that off?"

Instead, she conversed with her "husband," told him she would be out a while longer. She began to sound testy. "No, because I do not want to be bothered tonight. No, because I do not want my friends bothered either."

We passed an unfamiliar-looking Pancake House under some spreading oaks that was enough to give me a feeling. It was a *déjà-vu*-like feeling, or better, its opposite. That feeling of *I've never been here before*, and I got it from the Pancake House, the empty laundromat beside it (it was 2 a.m. by this time), the tiny woman in the car beside me who chattered. All of it seemed new, unfamiliar, and wrong.

Thank God it was only a preliminary hearing in the morning.

I considered a call to Marisel to tell her I'd be late. But all the people . . . all my people were probably in bed asleep, and didn't expect me home anyway.

"I wonder if this is going to be a problem," Amy said

when Mr. Pinglamagloom finally rang off. "I wonder if I'll ever have a normal family life?"

She asked this six or seven times, and her head lolled on the headrest while I propped my eyes open with my fingers to help me concentrate on the road. I needed some level of alertness, so began to think about the damn Christmas cards that were such a pain in the ass, the damn Christmas cards that made me want to slam my palm down on the steering wheel. Amy began to slip lower in the seat. Her feet shoved aside the hamburger wrappers and the empty cigarette boxes from months back. I didn't even smoke any more. Nobody smokes. Her short legs nestled among the briefs and wadded up Department of Homeland Security forms.

Finally, we took a left on Hawthorne and I found the number Amy had mentioned—but by the time I'd parked, pinning in some other car (hey, how long could this take?), she was snoring not so softly in the seat beside me, her legs parted in the short skirt. Her apartment building was a square, red-brick, two-story horseshoe around a swimming pool that seemed to have resisted the urban press of condo construction, office parks, and high-rise executive suites: all the old house and apartment building demolishers that had eaten away at this older section of the city. After a few shakes, a few groans, she reached her little arms around my neck and kissed me. It was nice. Not great, but nice.

That sandpaper tongue.

"Are you just a lonely boy?" she asked.

"Finally, somebody understands."

We went into the courtyard through a combination-pad gate. Amy led me past a wrought-iron fence to the edge of a pool that almost filled the cramped square. There were twenty or thirty units around the pool, a laundry room in one corner, not much else.

"Is it better to go to your place, or mine?" she asked.

"We already decided on, have driven to, and now arrived at yours, unless I'm mistaken."

"But my place is a mess!"

"Mine is not nearby and includes a wife, child, in-laws, and possibly a car full of armed Asians parked at the curb."

"Scary!" She giggled and slapped at my chest. "Oh, lonely boy." She placed her head against me and paused, childlike, as if waiting to count my heartbeats, but soon she slid down onto her knees, then onto her hands and knees, then lurched over to the edge of the pool and threw up in it.

"Maybe tonight's not so good," I said.

vii.

I did what I always do in such situations: moved upwind, first, to avoid the stench and get some distance on the splatter. Then, I held her hat and lifted her hair out of the water. I considered putting her onto one of the poolside loungers so that she could stretch out comfortably. It was, after all, a relatively warm October evening. If I snuck away, it probably wouldn't rain on her. Yes, I ought to at least see her inside her door, but my knees ached from the "dancing," and I had no idea which of these twenty to thirty doors was hers. Hey, I'd gotten her pretty close to home. I rubbed her back.

"Oh," she said after a while, and then her phone rang in her purse, so she stopped retching a moment, dug it out, started to retch again, and loops and whorls and chunks the size of eyes poured out of her, plopped into the pool where they swirled cloud-like in the underwater lights. "Hello? Oh, hi. No." She paused a moment. "No," she said, then snapped the phone closed and tossed it into the pool. Then she retched more.

I watched the phone drop. It turned like a leaf, deeper into the water. "You could," I said, "have shut it off."

Her vomit-spackled, emotionless face regarded me a moment. "He'll get me another one. My place is a mess."

I kind of half carried, half dragged her to number eleven, which was where it turned out she lived—thankfully on the ground floor—and she dug around in her little purse, and removed an enormous ring of keys, but found the right one even in the unlit murk of the courtyard. In one corner of the square apartment arrangement stood a leafless tree and, somewhere in it, a confused bird—disoriented, maybe, by the pool lights—sang away like it was 7 a.m. When her door opened, I worried immediately: the apartment was completely lit, and noisy, too. The TV blared. It was a rerun episode of *Columbo*. Peter Falk said, "You know, there's just one thing I don't understand. . . ." It concerned me that "Vijay" could be in there, that he might be lurking behind the door, 6-iron in hand, maybe about to swing it for the first time. Surprise. Or did she have a roommate? What kind of person would leave all these lights and appliances on, then go out for an evening of drinks and dancing? I thought of her apparently hostile relations with Pamapamayangalon and decided it would be the kind of person who wasn't paying the electric bill and didn't much like the guy who did. But Amy kept going in and I sidestepped behind her, still fearing lurkers, and *Columbo* was loud. "It's just that this one thing has been on my mind a while," Peter Falk said, blasting his suspicions through the whole apartment and into the courtyard. She closed the door behind us, and hugged me as she applied the lock.

Amy was right. Her place was a mess. It looked like a shop where bicycles went to be butchered. There were parts, chains, frames, sprockets, pedals, and dirty piles of those tight-fitting bike pants. Three helmets were stacked one inside the other on the kitchen counter. Did three crazed cyclists live here? Two apparently complete bicycles hung from ceiling mounts over the breakfast nook. "This looks serious," I said.

"I have a dream."

I wondered if the project, the one the Indian or Pakistani fuck had agreed to bankroll in exchange for marriage—and citizenship—had something to do with designing a . . . what? New bicycle? Great bicycle? Mega-bicycle? I yawned.

She went to the sofa and moved some loose papers, a sneaker, and a phone book before she dropped onto the cushion. A bit of vomitous spittle still drizzled from her lips. There were also piled up ashtrays on the coffee table (a smoking cyclist?) and one of those European-style squeeze-lid coffee makers on the floor beside the sofa, half-filled with amber liquid. I sat, removed another sneaker from my spine, and began to consider a gallant exit. It's not like I'd never done it with a woman who's thrown up before—thrown up on herself, even—but that was back in the day.

"Are you my lawyer?" she asked, then pulled the white blouse over her head and sat beside me, her nipples small and brown, a very flat-chested girl. Amy looked at me like I was a strange idea she'd just had.

Maybe if she brushed her teeth it would be feasible.

I got her around a corner door, through her bedroom (also full of parts of bicycles, rumors of bicycles), to a bathroom draped not in bicycle parts but in clothes: skirts, blouses, slacks, dainty undergarments, linens, and towels. All of this was clipped to an overhead clothesline and draped over odd racks. The racks seemed to be rich cousins of clothes hangers, but with pins, snaps, and Velcro attachments no everyday clothes hanger could afford. Everything smelled of the powdery, fragranced, interior mystery chamber of girl.

Amy went limp on me, however, somewhere between living room and bathroom sink, such that to urge her along wasn't enough—she had to be lugged the last few steps. I got my hands into her warm underarms and lifted, which made her sound out something more than a whine, but less than a scream. "Wah," she said. "Wah, wah."

"Let's do some face wash." I leaned her against me. "Can you step this way?"

"Nooooo."

I tried to get her in a bear hug and lift her towards the sink, but she wouldn't budge. She just let out little screeches, until finally she pointed at the floor.

"Oh." I'd been standing on her foot.

I cured that issue, found a cup with a toothbrush in it, dug around in a white plastic basket of mirrors, toenail clippers, combs, the odd bottle of petroleum jelly, and found a toothpaste tube, squeezed nearly flat. Amy mumbled while I gave her teeth a bit of a clean then looked for some mouthwash or neutralizing agent to swish in her mouth. Amy truly had no tits, but was damn cute as she jabbered and spat in this bright room hung with colorful clothes. When I turned, a fabric of some kind draped my face—damp and towelly—so I pulled that down, wet a corner, wiped her face with some soap, then tried for some rinse action. The apartment didn't seem to have hot water, even when I tried the tub behind a bizarre, fish-covered shower curtain. It sported a grinning dolphin surrounded by bubbles, tiny sea horses, big-clawed crawfish, and the occasional peeping clam. Then, finally, as she whimpered and limped on the foot I'd crushed, I got her to the bedroom and into bed.

I got her shoes off. I removed my pants and shirt. The TV in the bright living room still blared, as I hadn't had a chance to turn it off, and I smiled, leaned over, took one of her tiny nipples in my lips, and was about to say something, but she sat up.

"You know what?"

"What?"

She threw up again, on my lap this time. Her vomit was warm, like spilled vegetable soup.

I must have said something, maybe made a deleterious remark or a loud profane comment there in the heat of somewhat nearly inflamed (but not quite) enpassionment . . . anyway, I must have made a disappointed murmur after being thrown up on, because she seemed hurt. Then a phone rang somewhere out in the living room, and Amy started to cry, then shake and gag a little. She hugged me tight and a bracky liquid spilled out of her onto my collarbone.

"Why won't it stop? Why won't it stop?"

"It will." I regained my cool. "Not to worry."

"Is the room spinning? I thought that was a . . . figure of speech."

"It might be spinning."

"Don't say that!" The phone stopped eventually and it was back to the bathroom, though the evening was beginning to seem like the end of a rope ladder dropped into a well. I'd reached the last rung, had one leg stuck out as I groped for solid foothold, but could find nothing below me, save snapping noises. I began to think it might not be "all that" to hang out with Amy tonight. I should be home, even, rather than with this girl with no tits and a GED. I could come back tomorrow. But it would be rude to leave, too, and she seemed responsive and even passionate with the way she swished the toothpaste and looked into my eyes on our second trip to the bathroom. Her eyes . . . they definitely did give the impression that there was somebody in there.

So I got her back into bed and saw then the set of golf clubs leaned against an open closet: inside, two suits, several polo shirts on hangers, all of it new, none of it liable to fool anybody. I shrugged. Amy was still in her skirt but I was naked when I climbed in beside her—my boxer briefs being vomit-soaked—and she reached under the skirt, pulled off a pair of black panties, and then she was on top of me. She kissed me, and began stroking with her short little fingers. Okay. It had been a long time, after all.

Wait, it had been a couple of days, that's right, Alice in Austin, but this was good. An actual flesh and blood and skin and muscle and woman-smelling woman (though she smelled sweaty by now, too), and Alice was a lot older than Amy, and more upholstered: not so muscular, not so tight along her back and shoulder blades. The girl rocked on top of me, the inside of one thigh rubbing my leg through the skirt, and she moved fast, almost violently. I had a hard time keeping up, getting the rhythm of it, and she kept saying "Mr. Bent. Mr. Bent."

"Just Bent," I said, and I held onto her bare feet, although—now that I could hold them in my hands, my impression from the mirror at the club seemed correct. Those were some big feet.

I kissed and licked the crusty corners of her lips. Peter Falk said: "There's just one thing I'm trying to understand here," and sounded befuddled. I attempted to coax her higher onto the bed, where I could get to her throat, shoulders, underarms, chest, but I had no traction. The bed was small: my feet dangled off the edge. Amy had gray-green eyes, but her lids were drooping. *I am about to lose her*, I thought, and I saw some zits under her jaw, acne pimples. Not like Maggie Leudecke's freckles at all. One of these pimples was large and pulsed an angry red color. *Won't you drive my sleigh tonight?* Then I realized what was wrong and I bolted up quickly.

"Excuse me," I said.

She moved her chin away from me. Her eyelids slid down like stage curtains.

"Did I bring that brief in here? A couple of manila envelopes?"

"I dunno." She began licking my chest.

"I kind of need it."

"You can't always get what you want."

"I said need. I need to see something. Or read something." I got out of bed, and rummaged on the floor for my trousers, my keys. When I bent down I must have moved awkwardly, because one of those pains I get in my shoulder shot through me. I stood, rotating the arm.

Seemed okay.

"I really do need to get those."

"Now?"

"You're coming, too. Wear this."

I dug up something like a shirt for her from the pile by her dresser, slipped into my own pants, put on my shoes sans socks, then, by steering her shoulders, got her out the front door, into the courtyard, though she was smelling not so fresh with this T-shirt pulled off her pile. Amy was barefoot, but decent on the whole, because I had thought ahead. I knew she would have to hold the security gate while I went to the car. We passed the pool, where wispy chunks still writhed in the shallow end, and I half-propped her in the open wrought-iron door to make sure it didn't close while I went to the Elantra and retrieved the envelopes from the floorboard where they'd fallen.

As my luck had been running, Amy should have wandered away from the gate, left, passed out behind a bush, and I'd have been locked out, away from her apartment and the oh so important room I needed to get back to oh so quickly. This is the other aspect of the Cuba Tiránica, or maybe a normal side effect when one drinks straight diet cola syrup from a pressurized fountain tank—with or without rum—but Amy was there when I got back. She pushed against the gate and shook her head as if to clear it. She looked cute and sweaty and tired in the T-shirt and skirt, under which I knew there were absolutely no black panties.

I held up the envelopes. "I like to multitask."

"You're kidding."

It was damp outside, getting to be early morning, and the confused bird continued his performance, his song echoing off the units. "I have to do something," I said. "Then we'll get back . . . where we were."

In the apartment, in the bathroom, I closed the door, ducked through the towels, pants, bras, harnesses of various kinds. I split open—with some difficulty—a shrink-wrapped box of candles propped inexplicably beside the tub, and pried out one of the only slightly warped, waxy cylinders. I stuck it in the glass with the pastes and ointments, looked for matches in a drawer by the sink. There are always matches in a drawer by the sink and, sure enough, I found those, struck one, lit the candle. Little Amy would thank me for this later, I knew. I settled onto her toilet, which turned out to be more difficult than I thought. Did they make small toilets for small people? This one seemed three-quarter size, a learner's john, and it didn't help that she'd installed a shaggy bun-warming seat cushion that made the available hole space smaller than any found in nature. I folded myself into this toilet, and after some adjustment settled in as best I could. Amy, in her bedroom, sighed deeply, the mattress compressing under her weight.

"We could be in for a bit of a haul," I called, but got no reply.

The crankcase gunk-like nature of my intestinal goo had become a life issue in recent years, but I had anticipated an immediate effect and knew that the syrupy black liquid I'd imbibed at Club Some would be exiting soon. I was fooled. The feeling passed, and a few minutes trying to get it back didn't help, nor did a few minutes of trying to force it back. Outrageously loud snores came out of the bedroom, nearly cartoonish in volume, which wasn't promising, but did promise me uninterrupted time.

I was surprised by what I found in the new envelope. Chloe had the argument organized by case law, laid out in a continuous, logical, even readable narrative, back through nearly one hundred and eighty years of precedent, since the time of Spanish settlement, Mexican colonization, and the fight for Texan Independence. That was the point: the descendants of old claimants, original settlers on their original properties, back from the time that the place had been its own Republic, held impressive privileges in the state courts. No one had ever challenged the Leudeckes on these holdings, but families *like* the Leudeckes had faced generation after generation of courtroom challenges to their land rights, down to 1999 and an abandoned three-acre lot in a small gulf-side coastal village. Private zoned downtown commercial property now abutted this parcel, and the village lusted to acquire it to—presto!—change three acres of johnsongrass into tax-producing revenue: shops, restaurants, even covered parking (five stories) for the beach tourist trade.

The family that had inherited it claimed "vested rights" recognized under the Treaty of Guadalupe Hidalgo. The commercialization had all been blocked by the courts.

Really?

Despite other claims, which included eminent domain arguments of community benefit and several recent cases where these "vested rights" were trumped by necessities of national defense (these mainly involving angry families along the border who didn't want "the fence" on their property—I suppose these folks unpatriotically imagined that terrorists would enter the country with plane tickets or some shit), the boundaries and assigns given the old Texas Heroes stood firm in the eyes of law and society.

What a fucked-up state.

Chloe really did seem to have found the thing. Exactly why it would work wasn't at all clear to me, more just that it had, time after time in the courts, and that would be good enough for Maggie Leudecke's ranch, no doubt. To set it aside as a sacred space, put up a historical marker, find a rare species of minnow—none of that would be necessary, and the only wonder was that nobody in the grand, sweeping, mega-rich Leudecke clan hadn't already clicked to this before consulting the services of Davison, Kohlhoeffer & Loeb.

What kind of moguls were these people?

To trace Maggie Leudecke's claim back to the time of the Anglo revolution that separated Texas from Mexico might not sit well with the vociferous—and largely Hispanic—complainants in Bold Springs: or the family of poor, drowned Eladio what's-his-name. Still, sitting there on Amy's john, I started to feel a bit lawyerly, in spite of being nude, hunched, and in pain. I pushed and pressed. As I thrashed, I returned to the other envelope, read through the summaries, thrashed a bit more, tried to get something to work loose in the crusty, dried mud-like substance that lined my colon. I worried, as it was often a bloody mess coming out, too: ripping and tearing. But Chloe had turned out to be a competent, even talented, object for my affections. She was on her way to really being something. I simultaneously had a jealous thought: that the polish of the documents had come from Loeb. It could be that Loeb had helped her with all this and made the subtle connection with the historical land grants, or that his father had even done it. It could be that Chloe didn't figure this out at all.

But Loeb? It didn't seem possible.

I spent nearly another twenty minutes producing little more than strained black noodles. I took the paperwork, finally, and returned it to Chloe's envelope, although something about the whole thing nagged at me as I opened a shag-covered (to match the bun-warmer) toilet paper dispenser. Finally I left the bathroom, marched past the snoring girl into the living room, where *Magnum, P.I.* was now blaring. Tom Selleck wiggled his eyebrows at the camera. I had forgotten how bad that show sucked. I stepped over wheels and spokes, frames and sprockets, to look for the remote, but no go.

Alright, let it blare. Let's do this thing. Make it happen. Nail Amy. Go home.

I considered that I should just do the second part. I could find all my clothes among the piles and bike parts, get dressed, locate some paper or a plastic bag for my underwear, get in the Elantra, locate Amy's number somewhere in the Pamalamabog file and call her the next day to make sure she was okay. I'd tell her how I'd let her sleep, beauty rest and all that.

On the other hand, though it was true she was asleep (and just not coming awake, either, no matter how much I jiggled, prodded, or elbowed)—and might well have been more passed out than, let's say, snoozing—it was also true that less than a half-hour before, right in that bed, she had called my name with desire. Or said "Mr. Bent, Mr. Bent," anyway. Perhaps she was not exactly conscious, or aware of being conscious, at the moment, but before I'd been attacked from within, Amy had had her arm around my neck, her leg thrown over me, her thin, half-naked torso hugged up tight against me. It seemed, if not proper, at least allowable to get things back to that position and see what happened. She'd pulled her panties from under that skirt, after all, and taken me in hand.

If, in other words, she'd had no objections to performing any of these acts or services while wide awake, did it not make sense to assume she would have little opposition to them while semi-conscious as well?

So I slipped off the T-shirt to get her back to that point and took her arm to crook around my neck (though it kept sliding off), kissed her, licked her here and there, said "Amy, oh, Amy," and so forth. In fact, she responded. A little bit. The snores ceased, for example. She uttered a series of guttural snorts. Then her breathing came regularly. When I transferred my thoughts to the actual woman, her heart-shaped mouth, her scent of garlic and gin, the old urges started to work on me, and I began to develop a level of near excitement that bordered, practically, on the lower reaches of a nearly high-pitched frenzy . . . that edgy almost-vibration and itch.

I pretended a little bit. I imagined that we were together, Amy and I, but not in this ratty Montrose apartment with eighties TV drama blaring, but in a nice hotel. Or on a beach. Or: I was on a beach with Chloe, not Amy. Chloe and I were naked under a bright yellow beach umbrella, where the wind came in off the Gulf and caressed our skin.

Amy started to snore again. This was off-putting, especially as I had made so much effort to give her what she so unconsciously desired, but I had one more thing I could try. As she snorted and rocked in her sleep, I tugged at the little beige skirt, her last item of clothing. I drew it down the length of her legs, over her big feet, leaving her completely open, naked, beautiful, and asleep before me, and she turned, and when she did her penis turned as well, flipped against the inside of her right thigh because she had a penis, is the thing, Amy had a penis.

I had two weird thoughts. Or weird thoughts to be having at a time like that. I did begin to gather my clothes. I located socks and vomit-soaked underwear here. Found my shoes over there. It's not that I don't enjoy trying new things, but it had been a long day. If it had been a new kind of fabric softener, or shampoo and conditioner in one, or crack, I might have gone for it, but no. In the kitchen I found a plastic bag for my boxer briefs so I could just carry those out. I attempted to get my belt through the loops of my trousers without much luck, and so grabbed my coat. I did not forget my two envelopes. I made sure to snuff out the candle in the bathroom, which I'd forgotten about (yikes!). In the living room—son of a bitch—there on a low glass table, finally, I spied the TV remote, so I turned off the noise, and the silence rocked my head. I ground my teeth. And the first odd thought I'd had seeing Amy's not terribly tumescent though respectably sized (especially for such a brief frame) surprise was that it wasn't a surprise. "I knew that," I thought, and recalled her tongue, her feet, how she . . . or he had felt when lifted in my arms. Sometimes, I only notice what I want to notice: a bad habit. The second odd thought had nothing to do with her, penises, or really anything in the immediate vicinity. It was the thought that maybe Loeb hadn't been doing Chloe's work for her, but that it was the other way around. Maybe the reason his output had changed so drastically in the last year was that she'd done his work for him. And then . . . what had been nagging at me? What was wrong?

In the living room, I opened the bulging envelope with the maps and summaries, shuffled through the papers, pulled them out, shook the contents onto Amy's carpet, checked the other envelope, too. Down on my hands and knees, I fanned through the whole contents of both, several times.

The photograph of Eladio Trejo was gone.

Then the front door opened, and in came Mr. Pramalongabang.

He was all *shocked*. *Flabbergasted* and such. "What are you doing here?" he said.

"Just leaving." I scooped up all the paperwork.

"What are you doing *everywhere*! It is four in the morning!"

I rose. "Oh, shit. I have to get up early." I started to push past him.

"Hey! You!" Spittle sprayed from his large lips. "I am *angry*!"

"I'm frustrated," I said. "Raw and sore besides."

"You . . . you . . . What do you have there?" He eyed my envelopes.

"And on edge. Like the way people say they will leap out of their own skin? You know that phrase?"

"What?"

"That's me!" It did seem possible that whatever "X" had inserted in my nostril had made me jumpy, and made me grind my teeth, too, but it seemed to have done little else of consequence. The thought of my having inhaled illegal substances—and that photograph now gone that had so resembled a criminal incarceration picture—reminded me. "Hey, this marriage is bullshit."

"What?"

"I've got proof." I coughed. I walked past him, my chest out. I made an exit, out into the courtyard. I spat something unpleasant onto the sidewalk while the poor bird squawked and squawked in its tree. "I'll use it. So get in there and . . . prepare to. . . . "

It didn't work. He followed close behind. "Are those the papers?" he said. "Is it the e-mails, or the valentines?"

"On further review," I said, "I can't represent you any more. I'm calling the feds." I shook the envelopes in his face and felt a little like Nikita Khrushchev waving blank pages of "evidence" in front of the UN Assembly. "Deportation. Or something. Jail."

He took my elbow. "I'll sue you!"

At that moment, I pulled the belt out of my trousers: not to thrash him, I had just given up on getting the damn thing through the loops. But he backed up in alarm.

"If you must know," I said, "your marriage will not fly."

"I married her already. I have my green card." His eyes narrowed, though he watched the belt. "It is done."

"Fraud!" I said. "You can't marry one of those." I wasn't totally sure what out of a number of possibilities Amy was, but had fair certainty that she . . . or he . . . didn't fit a category the state would recognize for nuptials. "Even if you want to," I said.

"You're wrong. I checked it online."

"Oh, well . . . that settles that." I remembered again what she'd said about her "project." Guess it wasn't bicycle-related after all.

"None of this explains what you are doing here. I don't care if she's Jewish."

"I'm just an attorney, after all," I said. "You . . . what?"

Echoes came off the corners of the courtyard, the surface of the pool. The bird seemed to be singing the name of a month: June, June, June. Or maybe it had picked up on Vijay's words. Jew, Jew, Jew.

Against all of my expectations, he stood still, dropped his head, and brought his palms against his eyes. "Why does she hate me so much?"

"Uhhh."

"Why won't she even let me try?"

It occurred to me that the revelation flipped against "Amy's" inside left thigh in her apartment bedroom (circumcised, incidentally) might be news to Vijay Pramalangagang.

"Look," I said. "You cannot convince me that this is about . . . the real thing."

"For convenience, sure," he said. He looked up from his hands. They were damp with tears. "Somebody brokered it."

"Don't tell me that."

"I thought you knew!"

"I do now. You can get me into a lot of. . . ."

"Afterwards, that's when . . . I can prove myself to her, but she won't even let me." He grew quiet. "I didn't know she'd be so hot."

I shuffled my feet a few moments. "It's possible she's not that hot."

"You fucker!" He pointed his finger again, damp, like it had been in his mouth. "I don't like it, Mr. Bent. And won't have it. Your being here at this hour." He thrust his damp, slobbery hands into his pants pockets. His breath steamed in the night, but his voice sank back, flowed downwards, like his eyebrows. "If I hadn't gotten that call, I wouldn't have known. I might not have caught you at all! Tell me. What are you doing here, really?"

I swallowed. "Consulting? But what call? Someone called you?"

"Of course someone called me. That's why I'm here." He stared at me. Vijay Pramgalonamang looked like his father was no better at tying balloons onto wrists than mine.

"Called you about what?"

"About my goddamn lawyer being in my goddamn apartment!"

"Not really your apartment," I said. "Did you recognize the voice?"

"What is going on?"

I had to be careful. "Look, your wife is . . . pretty drunk. Somewhat ill. And very asleep." I pointed at the still open door of her apartment, the lights from the living room warm and yellow as the sun started to smudge away the stars. I didn't mention that she was stoned, naked, and some form of ladyman.

"You get out," he said.

I felt I should put a supportive hand on his shoulder. "If you want to keep things the way they are, if you're smart, we'll go over and lock her door, and you'll leave with me right now."

"I have to see her."

"No."

"Make sure she's alright."

"I assure you she is. By most contemporary standards."

"What?"

"You can see her later."

"Am I supposed to believe nothing happened between you?"

I was tired. "I don't give a shit what you believe. Listen, did you recognize the voice of the person who called you, or not? Was it a man? A woman?"

"What difference does it make? Some man. Someone looking out for me."

"I'm looking out for you." But I was freaked. I glanced around. Had someone shadowed my every move? Was it someone with a large frame and bushy unibrow? Had Mr. Duc hired somebody? Or Alice? The Leudeckes?

The law firm?

"Take my advice," I said. "Leave now or be stupid."

"No one listens to me. No one believes in my love."

Poor Indian or Pakistani fuck. He truly didn't realize there was another scam wrapped inside his scam marriage.

"I will prove it," he said. "It doesn't matter what I have to do, and I don't care about you. Or anyone."

"She's someone you want in your life, is that it?"

"She is in my life."

"Then, you want her?"

"Yes."

"Have you been drinking?"

"Yes."

I did walk up to him, then, took him by his shoulders. "Even if she's gone? And it's against all odds? Even if there is no getting her back, you don't care?"

"What are you saying?"

"You're going to get her anyway? Is that the thing?"

"I just said so!"

"You know what? I believe you. Let's go lock that door."

We went, flipped the lock on Amy's front doorknob, closed it, and I led him to the parking lot. I got him into his vehicle—a Nissan sedan, the back seat filled with more of those boxes with spigots. I leaned on the door after he got behind the wheel. "I believe in you," I said, and he started the engine and drove slowly away. On the street, a pickup truck approached, and a man inside tossed newspapers into the lawns of the houses along Hawthorne. I eyed him with suspicion, but it was just some guy. He continued driving and tossing papers.

I sighed. The things we do for love, etc. Now I had, maybe, four hours to get ready for Maggie Leudecke's preliminary hearing with the Board of Transportation, but it wouldn't matter if I got ready or not, because, unfortunately, I was going to sleep through it.

Part III

Quagmire

i.

I must have fallen asleep with my phone on my chest, because that's where I grabbed at it, frantic, the next morning— well, the next afternoon—unsure if it had rung in reality or in my dream, which was the circus dream, where the tent falls, and keeps falling, and the performance is ruined. "Put your back into it!" the man with the stovepipe hat orders, but you can't get the canvas back up, the salty-tasting fabric keeps coming down . . . and Amy was there. Little Amy, naked—but vaguely naked, no real detail—and she . . . or he . . . tugged and tugged on my sleeve: "Will I ever have a normal family life?"

"I dunno. I dunno."

So I thought my phone rang, but I was also unsure it wasn't in the dream, or wasn't just my heart clanging in my rib cage, as it would from time to time, in imitation of the cell's vibrator mode. "Hello?" I tried. I shook the thing. "Hello?"

"You fuck," said Chloe.

I sat up, rubbed my eyes. I rubbed my hair. A quick glance at the digital alarm (1:17 p.m.) caused me to rise. I did not lounge, not for a second. I didn't get out of bed, either, but did grab my pants slung over the bedpost and bring them up over my pajama bottoms. I favor pajama bottoms only, even in chillier months. It's something I enjoy, having as much of the bedclothes against my skin as possible without allowing it to touch the lower part of my body. By getting dressed, I reasoned, dressed even just a little, I could say what I was about to say without lying.

"I'm on my way!"

Chloe brought her face to within inches of mine. "I said: you fuck!"

I jerked back from those sharp, grim teeth. "You . . . give a guy. . . ."

"She's not on the phone, man." Cheso leaned against my bedroom door. He sounded sorry for me.

"Moron." I tossed the phone on the carpet, shot up from bed. Chloe was in my bedroom. I was half dressed. I was more than half dressed if you counted trousers brought partway over pajama bottoms. Shirtless, I wondered if she could tell I'd been working out (though not recently).

"I'm not a moron," said Cheso. "She wanted in."

"It's fine."

"*No it's not,*" said Chloe.

"I set an alarm! I don't know. . . ." I moved my shoulder, worked out the morning stiffness. Except I guess it was more an early afternoon stiffness. "It's like you're dressed for court."

"You really had a nine o'clock?" said Cheso.

"Beat it." I was on my feet by then, and I moved across the room to slam the door on him. Then I opened it. "And get us some coffee."

"There's only instant."

"Get it instantly."

Chloe was in tears.

I was highly aware of my state of undress. It was something like Pasadena on that hot, July 7 afternoon, only she hadn't been dressed then either, and certainly not in blue pinstripes. Then she'd had on a sweatshirt, tight jeans, and bikini bottoms underneath. Oh, and she wore that baseball cap that she'd turned backwards. Now I looked down on her dish-like face, came closer, smelled her hair. She'd never looked better. Maybe once.

"So . . . how did it go?"

She hit me with a force similar to that she used on those surprisingly powerful shoulder slugs, but flat-handed across my face. It was a real slap. I lost my balance, rocked against the dresser.

"I didn't deserve that," I managed to say.

"That sounds right." Chloe dropped onto my bed, her arms folded. "You deserve lots worse." Threads of tears pointed into the corners of her mouth, dribbled off her chin. My own face stung from right eye to jawline. Had the world gone crazy?

"You do not slap over preliminary hearings."

"This is your case. Why am I the one who has to look like a fool?"

"You don't. Won't. What are you talking about?"

She trapped her hands between her knees, squeezed them tightly, shook her head at the floor. "We thought we were in the wrong place. We went to the assigned room and . . . it was an auditorium."

Gingerly, I sat next to her. I rubbed my jaw. "You should have called me."

"Fucker. We called and called. Stuart was about to ask for you at the office, but I stopped him."

Because somebody might have put it together that I wasn't where I was supposed to be. Somebody important.

"Always looking out for me, nice, but no slapping."

She shook her head. "Never again. No looking out."

She opened her knees, released her fingers, and took another swing, but I caught most of it across my forearms, then clamped down on her wrists.

"I apologize," I said. This wasn't like the universal species apology Maggie Leudecke had given the coyote. This one was all on me.

"There were two hundred people there, Bent!" Her cheeks scrunched into unattractive wrinkles, and I made a mental note to explain to her . . . later, later . . . that scrunching her cheeks like that did nothing for her looks. She rearranged herself on the bed roughly, scooted away from me, and recrossed her legs. In fact, there was a kind of finality to the force with which she recrossed her legs. "What, were you out all night with Mrs. Pantydragger?"

"It shouldn't have been in an auditorium," I said. "Preliminary hearing. Two hundred people?" I began to get a bad feeling.

"And the press."

"Impossible."

"It was about her." Chloe brushed hair from her eyes. "Maggie and her ranch and Eladio Trejo and . . . fucking social justice."

"What two hundred people would attend anything

as arcane as a Transportation Department preliminary hearing?"

"Pissed people." She started crying again. She dug her clanging cell phone from a small purse, brought it to her ear. "Oh, that's primo," she said after a few moments, then thumbed it off without another word. She wrinkled her face more.

"Stuart says Channel Four's posted the video."

"Video of a meeting of the Transportation Board?"

The house had gone quiet. I had a feeling Cheso had run away, or was out back smoking rather than helping me with something as difficult as instant coffee in my time of need. I recalled, from a kitchen counter note I'd found when I'd dragged in earlier in the morning, that Marisel was with Sarah and her cronies at . . . well, ironically enough, it was at a local Café Rico, to plan some kind of benefit or doubles tournament or who knows what. Alexandria and Henry were at camp, a swim lesson, a pre-Halloween Party . . . there was something planned for him every day, hard to keep up with it all. So I went down the hall to Marisel's room, grabbed her laptop, found one of the local news homepages online, and returned. I sat next to Chloe again on the bed. She really did smell good.

"Maybe we should get some lunch."

"Fuck you."

"I guarantee you do not want to eat here."

"I don't want to be here. I've got a class, then I'm going to go look for a job."

"Now, now."

Near the top of Channel Four's page was a banner with a picture of double-chinned Isaac Minter alongside a clickable link: *Feeling no Pain at Houston Pill Mills*. Pass. But then another link: *Citizens Weigh In at Transportation Hearing*. In a tiny thumbnail image, Maggie Leudecke held her hand aloft as if taking an oath. Her red ribbon dangled from her thin wrist.

"You don't have to be sworn in to talk to the goddamn Department of Transportation."

"I'm going to kill you," Chloe said, but without force. Her damp eyes seemed dead.

PRETTY ENOUGH FOR YOU—143

"Well, if you're clueless, doesn't Loeb know anything?"

I put my arm around her to give her the benefit of my calming influence, which resulted in her shoving that arm away with distaste and asking me to put on a shirt, which I didn't. But I clicked through the pages to an even less favorable headline: *HER PROBLEM WITH PROGRESS: Millionaire Heiress Halts Community Revitalization.* From the copy, and Chloe's angry explanation, I began to put it together.

It hadn't helped that Maggie Leudecke had decided, at the last moment, not to be picked up by Chloe and Loeb, then had arrived late and couldn't be briefed by them before proceedings started; irresponsible, really, but it probably wouldn't have mattered. There was no intention of revealing the "Texas hero" exemption at this hearing. No suits had even been filed. Still, it turned out Chloe, Loeb, and Maggie had walked into not a preliminary anything but an orchestrated ambush. In the auditorium were parties or representatives of parties of landowners whose properties would abut the new road along its entire length. There were land developers among them, but also business owners, some farmers and ranchers, citizens, citizen action groups, local and city government board members, and officials from a number of small towns along the proposed route of the loop, all of whom were in a sulk, all of whom frowned down at Maggie, Stuart, and Chloe, as did the entire Board of Transportation from its raised dais: the chair and all four of his commissioners present.

"Hell," I said. "I didn't know they really met at all."

"A witch hunt, Bent."

"Literally."

Also prominent among the crowd were poster-sized images of the deceased Trejo, obvious even on the small screen by the uptilting outline of his pyramidical pompadour. Oh, shit.

The narrative, from a certain perspective, was pretty newsworthy.

The page included a written synopsis and another link to a video of the testimony. According to Channel Four, Maggie stood in the way—was the only thing standing in the way—of a project that would raise property values for everyone north and west of FM 1960 over the space of three counties, affecting 25,000 suburbanites and especially altering the fortunes of the low-income incorporated community of Tidemont, an enclave of black families settled outside the city after emancipation. Maggie Leudecke, daughter of privilege and witch, had set about destroying the lives of the descendants of freedmen. Though not specifically mentioned, I didn't doubt that there were a few EB-5 "target areas" among the groups represented: economically disadvantaged zones (or places that had successfully argued economic disadvantage) that the Federal Government would set aside for foreign investment, and the visas to go along with it. Then, that non-incorporated pocket of largely Hispanic homeowners—labeled *Bold Springs* on the displayed topographic map that demonstrated the extent of the havoc Maggie was personally wreaking—also stood to benefit at the planned route's westernmost arc, so two Latino community organizers were present who looked after those interests.

In a photo of the assembled crowd, I noticed a straw hat and beige sports coat. "My man," I said to the little screen. "What's-his-name."

Architectural firms had been retained to work up schematics for a hospital and two shopping centers set for groundbreaking on this "major artery into the northernmost regions of the tri-counties, planned as a response to population growth over the next two decades." The project had all been approved, save for one thing: Maggie and her intractability. This had now been complicated by the unfortunate drowning of an employee of the Dutch company pegged to build the road—a victim, according to the Hispanic community of Bold Springs, of a veritable lynching by the elite Leudecke family: a warning of the kind the Klan might have orchestrated in our fair region sixty years earlier.

"That's a bit much," I said.

I clicked the play button to see a streaming image of Maggie, seated behind a microphone, her back very straight. The lighting wasn't good, and accentuated the roughness of her skin and the dark eye rings. She didn't blink, which made the image seem like a still photo but for the way the crowd in the seats behind her writhed, as did the several otherwise immobile faces of Eladio Trejo that were waved aloft on placards. I noticed how the threads of gray in Maggie's hair were completely invisible on television. The medium seemed to make her look simultaneously younger and more haggard. Maggie listened to a question from off-camera: a droning, East Texas drawl that made little attempt to be civil.

"Ma'am, do you have some rationale for your opposition?"

Maggie Leudecke lowered her head to place her mouth closer to the microphone and spoke.

The carpet in my bedroom needed cleaning. The pile strands tickled my cheek, my nose . . . the fibers redolent of church bazaars, used-car lots, misspent youth . . . although I guess it was mainly residue from shoes and bare feet. I was down, my recently slapped, stung cheek flat against the bedroom floor. Probably there was also dead skin, dust, and the leavings of desultory vacuuming done by a woman we hired to clean, since the woman I married to do the cleaning had better things to do, as did her brother and sister.

"Bent? Where are you now?"

"Haven't gone anywhere."

"Why are you so fucking worthless?"

I attempted to reach out to Chloe and her angry, distant, high-pitched voice, but without success. It was like trying, from deep sleep, to grope for a snooze button attached to a restless goat.

Were even low-res internet streams of Maggie Leudecke going to do this to me?

I propped myself against the dresser, tipped forward in a wave of dizziness, but also leaned into a cushion of clarity. It came suddenly. Those posters of Eladio must have triggered it.

That guy. At Club Some. Who'd called me "Mr. Bent." I needed to warn my team.

"Someone is following us, Chloe," I said. "Don't be alarmed, but he got our dead Mexican picture."

I got to my knees, shaky, managed to click off the video stream before the next whining, nasal question came from the commissioner. Carefully, I began to scan the transcript— Maggie's words minus her voice. Hopefully, those wouldn't knock me on my ass. Her answer to the question about her rationale, however, had been straightforward, and clearly set forth her reason for blocking access to the land:

"It's mine."

"It's not that bad," I said to Chloe from where I kneeled beside the bed, evening-prayer style. (It was. It was very bad.) "Everything will be fine," (doubtful), "and you, Chloe, have done a good job and shouldn't worry." (Oh, please). "And . . . you ask . . . where was I when you needed me? Because I should have been there, it's true. I have fallen down on the job." I knew the art of taking blame. I might not know much, but that much I understood. "Man, that 'truth and whole truth' pose really makes a person look *guilty* of something, doesn't it?" I got to my feet. I wanted a slight elevation on Chloe while I navigated my excuses. "There's no time to go into why I might, or might not, be in one place or another," I said.

"Where's the girl?" Cheso stood in the doorway with two mugs.

Downstairs, the front door slammed.

"Look, Harrison," he said. (Nobody I actually know ever calls me by my first name, but since I didn't want to know Cheso, I never pointed that out to him.) "I don't mind bringing you coffee, but it's not really my job." He gave me a cup, leaned against the dresser, began to sip from the other. "Somebody named Stuart something called and wants you at the office right away."

"Did he say that? Right away?"

"I think so. Who does he think he is, huh?" Cheso sipped his coffee and laughed. "Girl's kinda hot, though." He shrugged. "Kinda."

ii.

Immigration law. Is it exciting? Is it gratifying?

It is arcane and requires that many forms be filed, many deadlines kept, lots of I-9 compliance record-keeping, background checks, and evidence of residence maintained. Consistency is surprisingly important. To say that an applicant for an H1-B visa was forty-three years old on one document but mistakenly claim on another he was forty-four would be enough to ban that person from legal entry to the country. For *years*. Add in that "the rules" concerning waivers, bars, and deadlines all shift underfoot constantly, the fault lines tending to appear out of nowhere as courts, legislatures, and agencies without much in the way of notice alter opinions, rulings, and obsessions—including each other's—and you can see there's room for error. Immigration law does not require genius or even talent. At least, I've never claimed to bring any of these to the table. But competence . . . oh, competence.

It's specialized, esoteric even—in the way you could consider a quagmire to be esoteric if you looked at it long enough—and not terribly concerned with issues of justice. Giving myself, Loeb, and Chloe the Leudecke case was not a complete invitation to disaster. Like on a transatlantic flight, having a heart surgeon handle an emergency childbirth: that might make sense if there were nobody else, if he'd paid attention to his schooling, if his competence was up there.

But there were plenty of people better able to handle the Leudecke case at the firm, and I had not really paid attention to my schooling, or anything since my schooling, and whatever Loeb's fine qualities, competence wasn't one of them.

He had demonstrated his aptitude for carelessness when he first arrived to start work for his dad. Big Loeb had encouraged him to clerk at other firms, where, I suppose, he left a path of ruinous error before somehow passing the bar and arriving at D, K & L, where, in just his first month on the job, Stuart Loeb mistakenly ruined the life of one Emmanuel Adeyemi—a Nigerian anesthesiologist who was seeking residency after a ten-year marriage to a U.S. citizen (a noted podiatrist). Loeb suggested that this man's waiver of unlawful presence would have to be taken care of at an embassy in his home country, which was true—or would have been true prior to January 1. Thus young Loeb sent Dr. Adeyemi packing to Lagos, unaware that this policy had changed in the current calendar year. The anesthesiologist could have handled it at the federal office on Northpoint Drive, which he no doubt drove past on his way to the airport to catch his expensive and unnecessary international flight. Once in Nigeria, complications ensued. Then more complications. Apparently, tempers flared in the scalding Nigerian sun. In short, Loeb's advice caused a man to separate himself from his wife and daughter (both U.S. citizens), not for a few days, or even weeks as he'd thought, but—well—now it had been three fucking years. Though he had lost his job at St. Luke's Hospital, Dr. Adeyemi (we understood) was able to find another sweeping a medical supply warehouse in Abuja while he awaited action from the consulate.

It was the kind of mistake that might have been common at a general practitioner's office that, let's say, did immigration on the side. It could also easily happen at an operation like ABOGADOS Y MÁS, as operated by my friend from law school, a firm that existed on high volume and was staffed by dozens of mainly young, mainly just-starting-out attorneys who handled actual at-risk deportation hearings—and even trials, like in court—and did so at rock-bottom prices. Though making money hand over fist, my bud probably also had difficulty tracking all the policy changes. It was exactly the sort of problem people like Emmanuel Adeyemi and his foot specialist spouse paid the enormous hourly rates of Davidson, Kohlhoeffer & Loeb to avoid.

Shrug. Loeb screwed up, so it sucks to be Emmanuel. But his case, bizarrely, like my marriage to Marisel, marked a turn in my career.

To this day I don't know if my actions were sentimental, strategic, or just a product of a hangover that had left me very desirous to avoid a long afternoon meeting in the stifling and gloomily oak-paneled big conference room on the thirty-second floor. I wanted to cover for the neophyte, true. My first impression of Loeb wasn't necessarily negative. After all, as a partner's son, there were all kinds of people around who wanted him to fail, even if they kept this desire to themselves. You have to pull for a guy in a situation like that. At the hastily called emergency summit (after we'd heard from Adeyemi's new attorneys), Parker Harrell (called, behind his back, "the young master" because of his youthful demeanor and New England prep school attitudes), who acted as head of naturalization and immigration in all matters the senior partners didn't want to lay a finger on, dropped the Adeyemi file heavily on the big conference room's oval table like he'd dropped a cleaver and glared around the room. "Shut the fucking door," he ordered. Harrell couldn't really pull off swearing—the syllables always sounded phony coming from him, like when children start to repeat cuss words before they know what they mean, or when white people try to use the N-word in an off-hand way, as black comedians can do on stage (but white people cannot convincingly do anywhere—something I discovered the hard way, incidentally). When it closed, the conference room door sounded deep and metallic like those big jailhouse panels that *schwump* behind you when you visit a client. It was the kind of sound that always made you feel trapped, even if you were just passing through to get some paperwork signed. "This cannot happen," Harrell said. "These are lives at stake, ladies and gentlemen. Our reputation. What do you have to say for yourselves?"

All knew who was to blame, but that person was the young and extremely well-groomed son of a founding partner, so Harrell did the smart thing: began to spread that blame as quickly, thickly, and widely as possible. Everyone in the room knew this would make things easier for him, and ultimately for us, too.

It was going to be a long meeting, an uncomfortable one, perhaps even epically so. It might have been talked about in the firm right down until today except that I stumbled onto my secret then, one that I've utilized ever since. My window office, my ability to take long weekend junkets at will, the fact that I hadn't seen an actual case through to change of status for the past five years . . . even Chloe's presence as my paralegal: much was owed to my actions concerning the Emmanuel Adeyemi debacle. Maybe I understood there could be no downside to helping Loeb. Or maybe I did it altruistically, without thinking through the consequences at all. Or it could have been that throbbing headache I mentioned.

I don't know why I did it. Many of my actions are just that way.

At any rate, it came down to what I said into the silence that filled the room after Harrell's tirade, which was, ironically, the same thing Maggie had told the coyote, only with an entirely different intent.

"I'm sorry."

"What's that?" Harrell blinked hard.

"I said: I'm sorry." I shook my head. I looked down at my legal pad. There was nothing on it but a doodle of a Volkswagen being chased by a giant seagull. I covered this with my forearm. "I can't believe it got past me. It won't happen again."

You could feel the heat drain out of Harrell, out of the entire room, really.

"Well, what the hell," Harrell said (unconvincingly). "Why didn't you say something when you realized?"

Crap! Loeb had kept quiet about it, too? "I . . . I didn't realize it. Until. . . ."

"Until we were sued by Bracewright & Connell?" asked Kebba Jobe. He was always willing to jump in and help me get deeper into trouble. Nearly an ideal form of the human specimen, Kebba was Gambian: tall, black, shave-pated, and distantly related, by rumor, to African tribal royalty. He'd studied in England and done his law school at the University of Texas. He loved to get under my skin.

By this point, I was accepting more blame than I'd planned. To screw up is bad. To tell nobody about it: oh, boy. But I was in for an inch, so: "I'm an idiot," I said, which, arguably, was a true statement.

PRETTY ENOUGH FOR YOU—151

Harrell and the others laughed. The door that had locked us in with a *clump* a few moments before now seemed an easy escape route. There were more statements about an *ad hoc* committee for spreading the word on governmental policy changes in the future, a handful of other matters, and we left in fifteen minutes. Everybody knew it was complete bullshit. Nobody cared. I hadn't been anywhere near Emmanuel Adeyemi's appeal, and shit yes, I'd kept quiet about the problem, because I hadn't known there was one. Everybody knew who I was covering for.

Kebba Jobe gave me a sidewise grin from on high as he left the room. He understood. It didn't matter. The blame had been secured. A long meeting had been avoided. Happy hour awaited across the street at Warren's. So many times it's easy to cut off trouble if you step in and do one simple thing:

Sacrifice yourself.

Loeb, incidentally, never raised his head during the meeting or acknowledged that I had snatched him out of a bad place. Basically, he never thanked me. Although that was not totally true, as someone at the firm I really got along with—good old Alan—left for his native New Hampshire a few weeks later, and his window office became available. I'd spent quite a bit of time in that office in the past, shooting the shit with him, having a beverage or two after a hard day's work. Or a day's work, anyway. So I was sad about Alan leaving, but to my surprise, I received a card under my door the next Friday afternoon telling me that facilities would move me to his space over the weekend. At least two others probably had priorities on that window.

On that day, I leaned back in my chair and flicked at the facilities card a few times with my thumb. I imagined a trajectory for myself: a new orbit that the presence of Young Loeb had made attainable. The fact was, if the firm had been smaller, there would be no place for a person like me to hide, especially given my proven inability either to attract new clients or grind away at billable hours in service to existing ones. On the other hand, at a larger firm, no particular partner out of the galaxy of those that commonly existed in big organizations would be able to wield sufficient power to keep me safe, keep me employed, keep me nepotistically in place, merely as protection for a family member.

D, K & L, however, was just right.

"Thank you," I said. "And you're welcome."

The ways in which I used this sin-eating to my advantage when it came to Loeb were as arcane as the labyrinthine policies, statutes, and affidavits that governed the rat's maze that is American immigration. I had to count on Loeb to carry some of the weight with his fat, colorful, ponytailed old man when I pulled his nuts out of the fire—something I never asked for, and something he never failed to provide. Ultimately, he turned out to be not quite incompetent enough. I discovered a way around this without having to leave anyone stranded outside of our nation's borders. This happened at the same time I discovered I despised Loeb with all my heart.

I'd started to hear the rumors not long after Chloe had pointed out to me that our affair had been a mistake . . . or, fine, whatever Yvonne and society decided to call our hotel afternoon had been a mistake, at least as Chloe saw it, although I can distinctly remember not feeling that way. Even back then—it must have been only a few months after our July encounter—I'd felt I could get her back. All it would take would be patience (which is the one thing that seems to never work, actually), but by then that guy from real estate law with the queer-as-a-three-dollar-bill mannerisms, Dalton Harpe, started in on me in the break room.

"It must be nice," Dalton said. He liked to lean in close and confidential when he spoke to anyone. He did have this engaging voice, melodious, which was always a comfort to listen to. I'm not into guys, and if I were, it wouldn't be guys like Dalton, but he did make me tend to move closer, loosen the muscles in my shoulders. Probably that's why he was such an effective gossip, come to think of it.

"What must be nice?"

"Fucking twenty-four-year-olds. That Chloe of yours."

I was actually prepared for this. I had been for a while: ready to deny any liaison between Chloe and myself, since, after all, she'd asked me to do so—and wouldn't that impress her if I actually did? How gallant. Maybe this would make her realize that having a liaison wouldn't be such a bad idea. (No surprise: this kind of gallantry in my experience also never works.) But I'd been waiting for someone to accuse me, in fact, just for the excuse to pull out the reaction I'd prepared, which I thought a good one, too. Nearly foolproof.

"I'm forty-six, Dalton. Do you really think Chloe would go for me?"

"*You!*" He laughed. Sort of guffawed. I wasn't sure I'd ever actually seen anyone guffaw before. "What?"

"Not me!" I agreed.

"That would be a good one."

"Right?"

Asshole! What the hell kind of a gossip was this guy, anyway? If not me, who?

"Loeb the Lesser," Dalton said.

Great. I was not only unable to deny what I had been completely prepared to disavow, but also suddenly introduced to something I could hardly accept. "Impossible."

"The IT department thinks so."

Oh, man. How they should know anything is beyond me, but it's true. They always do.

"There's something up between those two, anyway," said Dalton, and he departed with his coffee from the machine. That coffee made Cheso's instant taste like Blue Mountain roast. I thought it might have heroin in it, because it was almost impossible for me to start the day without one of those paper cups of liquid gunk to wash down my morning medicinals.

It didn't seem to me like there was anything between Chloe and Loeb, but maybe that was an act. Wouldn't it be better, by all rights, in all possible ways, to just have me?

Chloe and I held no secrets from each other, but I put off asking her about Loeb, as this was the same week we were set for Kohlhoeffer's retreat in Galveston.

Kohlhoeffer—the oldest in years of the original partners, and in times past the all-powerful overseer of anything labor-related (hence, by extension, naturalization and immigration)—was a fan of the group activities I despised most in life: planned programs where colleagues saw each other outside of the normal, day-to-day office setting and worked the problem, whatever the problem might be. I'm all about leaving the day-to-day, but not for mystery nights, trust sessions, teambuilding, or the other kinds of organized fun where people trip over themselves as they force-fit enjoyment and business into a lump-filled botch. That year, an organizer from Phoenix, Arizona, ran the retreat, and she turned everything into an adventure. Or labeled it one. Casino games were "an adventure of chance." Teambuilding exercises were "occupational community adventures." There was a comedian. There was always a comedian, but this one was "adventurous," and obviously had been fed information about us, because we were part of his act. He brought the house down when he captured one of the common catchphrases of the Big Partner, Thomas Loeb, who actually appeared at the dinner where this funnyman presided. This retreat was one of the few times I'd seen him in person. The comic delivered up what was considered to be Big Loeb's catch phrase, albeit in a high-pitched and mincing rather than booming voice:

"Why do you have to do it *that way*?" the comedian asked, and he swished an imaginary ponytail.

The crowd—including Thomas Loeb—ate it up. The comedian was more adventurous, still, by his liberal sprinklings of innuendo, mainly the tired joke he used many times that combined unlikely names as romantic pairs, all with a healthy dose of inferences, nods, and winks. A little of that is fine, but some aspects of his shtick approached the cruel. Heidi Cross, the—to put it politely—Rubenesque labor law litigator who was approaching her seventieth year but still appeared in the office each week day even though she couldn't walk—the hum of her Hoveround a familiar background motif to the office noise on the thirty-second floor—was linked to several young men in the firm with much feigned shock. Heidi loved it, but the whole thing made me queasy, especially since Chloe and I had been in a ratty Pasadena hotel only a few months before, and even more especially because she had made it so clear we would never visit such a hotel again

When my own mention came, it was merely an imitation of Kohlhoeffer himself asking "Where's Bent? Has anyone seen Bent?"

Big laughs.

The comedian did not, as a joke or otherwise, pair Chloe and Loeb.

I myself spent most of the meetings, buffet suppers, midnight buffets, and continental breakfasts in search of evidence of heat between the two of them. I felt that my mind was in chains—like the ones the third night's magician slipped out of in less than sixty seconds (though sewn into a linen bag and locked in a trunk).

On Saturday, I'd gone to bed early. Really, I'd been in bed since about 11:30 that morning, fed up by the fourth day with the seminar adventures, training adventures, and especially the "adventuretainment." I had myself made a presentation on dealing with new per-country numerical limitations that morning, which was just as exciting as it sounds. I walked out of that panel alone, but heard Heidi's enhanced mobility device as it bore down on me in the hallway.

"Bent, you are the only one unlinked to me." She spread her arms, slab-like in her sleeveless sundress. "Romantically, that is. Guess we fooled them."

"Yes. Avoided the breath of scandal once again."

Although I should have expected it, she surprised me. Heidi grabbed my crotch.

"Advantage of operating at this level." She winked at me.

"Shit!"

"I just need some company. These people. . . ." She let go of me long enough to hold her nose. "Boring."

I laughed, backed away.

"Come to my room," she pleaded. I couldn't tell if she meant it or not.

"Stuff to do, counselor. You know."

"We'll just watch cable!"

I got out of there. I'd brought a novel with me, one of those things a person always brings on business trips but never has time to read.

I read the novel.

Somewhere around 1 a.m., I picked up the room phone. I had it in mind to ask to be connected with Chloe, who'd come as part of the staff and had been mainly out of sight, working to make sure everything ran smoothly. For some reason, I asked for Loeb instead. He sounded groggy and possibly a little buzzed. I knew there'd been an open bar after an ERISA executive compensation panel that evening. I figured Chloe had attended. Mainly, I needed some kind of reassurance she wasn't with him. I think, in fact, I'd called with something fairly straightforward in mind. "Say, Loeb, I'm looking for Chloe. You haven't seen her?" But before my mouth could open, I realized—no, I should have called her after all. That would have made sense. What did I expect him to say? Or: did I expect to hear her, somehow, in the background of the phone call?

Was she with him at that very moment?

I should have hung up. I don't know why what happened next did happen. I did not think it through (I promise). Somehow, I discovered that I had lowered my voice an octave below what I considered my normal speaking tone and added a trace of an accent: something vaguely Eastern European.

"I am calling patrons, sir . . . there has been emergency."

Loeb coughed a few times. "Alright."

"Emergency with leak, and you are under advisement."

"What?"

"Gas. Gas leaked in hallway, sir." I tried myself to pin down the region from which my accent originated, but without much certainty. There was a vague Russian lilt to it, I noticed, as all my articles had disappeared.

"Is it toxic? Or flammable?"

"I'll say. Do not go in hallway. There has been emergency. Hurry please."

"Wait. Hurry and do what? Who is this?"

I didn't know if Chloe was with him, but I suddenly clicked to a way of finding out.

"This is Vasily. Vasily. . . ." I blanked for a moment, and attempted to settle on a believable name. Ultimately, I decided to go with the unexpected. "Cobb. Vasily Cobb of Hotel San Domingo advisory staff, calling patrons to tell of hallway gas leak and advising hurry."

"I should leave?" There was a sound of rustling in the background. Rustling for two?

"I call, advising air circulation," I said. "And ask patrons please, and quickly, open their windows. Please, sir. At this time open window."

More rustling. Some knocking. "It . . . there isn't a way to open this window."

Of course. "Breaking the window, please, sir. Break window to circulate air."

"It's sealed. Damn hotel." I heard more rustling, but no voice of high-pitched feminine concern in the background. "I think I can break it with the nightstand. The drawer from the nightstand?"

Jesus. Such ingenuity.

"Careful, sir. But to hurry."

I snapped off my own lights, stretched the phone's cord to the window, opened the room curtains, and peered into the courtyard. The San Domingo was a hollow stucco cube, built around a pool and swim-up bar. Below, a handful still congregated, sitting in deck chairs around umbrellas in the early morning hours—possibly some of the D, K & L crowd, gabbing it up in the heavy air. A massive, dark, muscular shape lounged in one of the poolside chairs. Kebba? He'd come to the retreat alone, although recently married, according to himself, to a beautiful blond woman, a picture of whom he constantly pulled from his wallet when encountering colleagues for any reason.

"My fifth wife," he said. The picture was black and white, and obviously the product of a professional studio. The new spouse wore a long evening gown and pearls: a classic skinny blond with overlarge teeth.

The moment I saw that picture I thought, *She looks like a fifth wife.* "Do you mean fifth consecutive?" I asked Kebba. "Or concurrent?"

"*Haw, haw, haw.* Oh, Bent."

From my hotel room window, I heard what sounded like rocks hammered by a chain gang, but then the distinctive tinkle-of-glass-on-concrete confirmation that Loeb had, indeed, used some part of the nightstand to do a very stupid thing.

I covered the receiver with my palm. "No fucking way," I said to the empty room.

The three figures seated poolside simultaneously turned their heads towards the lighted second-floor window, where a shadowy figure wrestled a large, boxlike blackness. Loeb's silhouette against the curtains seemed that of a cowled monk who had lifted a Gutenberg Bible to begin a scripture reading but then decided instead to shove it out into the congregation. The remaining panes broke, the nightstand drawer clattered into some bushes below his window.

"Okay," Loeb said. "Is there anything else I can do?" His voice was like a tiny insect trapped in the handset. "Should I help evacuate others?"

"Please to . . . I authorize, sir. You are on second floor. You must leave."

"I'm getting out of here."

"Not hallway! Gas! Gas!"

"Oh, man."

"I authorize you. Put mattress through window."

"The mattress? The entire mattress?"

Several of those gathered around the pool now stood and pointed towards Loeb's room.

"This will clear glass," I said. "And soften fall."

"I . . . should jump?"

I clamped my teeth momentarily. "Recommend escape. Avoid asphyxiation. Must go."

When I left the room, the mattress was just beginning to protrude from the window like a slowly extended, folded tongue. I arrived on the sidewalk of the hotel's pool court to find—beyond believability—Stuart Loeb on the ground, on that hotel mattress, the queen-sized item still in its fitted sheet. He was dressed only in white briefs, his legs spread before him. In fact, I believe he is the only man I've ever known—let me say the only full-grown man I've ever known—who wore skivvies rather than boxers. He had his hands on his hips. He yelled something to me about hallways and asphyxiation.

"Loeb?"

"Gas leak, Bent. We need to get out of here."

"Oh no."

And it was then that I got my idea. Is there anything better than getting an idea?

"Loeb, Loeb, Loeb," I said. "Don't tell me. Get up."

He seemed comfortable enough on his mattress for someone so openly exposed. Of course, he did have that barrel chest, those powerful-looking arms. Dare I say: his body made an impression on me in the moonlight?

"Loeb. Not the gas-leak-in-the-hallway, break-the-window, jump-out-on-the mattress prank. You didn't."

"I . . . ?"

I handed him my room key quickly, started to remove my shirt. "Fast. Up the back stairs. Wait for me in my room."

He glanced towards his window. "Who do you think did this? Shit, I'm going to have to pay, aren't I?"

I pulled off my shoes and pants. The group from the pool came towards the mattress from some distance, apparently unwilling to approach until they'd secured refills at the swim-up bar. Kebba Jobe was easily discernible in the crowd, a head taller than the rest and dressed only in a Speedo. Room lights blinked on in the courtyard windows.

"Hurry, Loeb."

"You're sure there's not a gas leak? I don't want to. . . ."

I handed him my clothes, placing them mainly over those tighty whities. "Move," I said. "You want your father to see you?"

That did it. And so the poolside people came to find me on the mattress. I spoke to them of the phone call I'd received, while in the light of an open doorway entrance I watched him enter, then back out, caught short as he made room for someone.

Chloe exited, wrapped in a bathrobe. She wore flip-flops, her hair pulled back straight, no makeup. She looked a little pockmarked under the hard doorway light, but pretty enough.

Chloe glanced at Loeb's still exposed chest and legs—otherwise, thankfully, he was covered by the bundle of my pants and shirt—then she stepped around him and came out into the courtyard. They didn't speak or even nod to one another. No eye contact.

Kebba, though he'd started over first, was one of the last from the firm to arrive. "Don't tell me you fell for the gas leak call, Bent." His tones, as ever, were powerful as they echoed across the courtyard walls. Truly, I wondered if he hadn't seen my exchange with Loeb and hung back so he wouldn't have to acknowledge he knew what I'd done.

Chloe held closed her bathrobe at the throat as she came over—so cute—and surveyed the windows above us. "Is that even your room?"

"I feel like an idiot," I said, repeating my favorite label for myself at the firm. That's what the comedian should have been saying. "Where's Bent? Where's that idiot?" By that time custodial help arrived, fully dressed and ready for action with pails and brooms at one in the morning. They needled angrily at each other in rapid-fire Spanish as they manhandled the mattress out of the courtyard. While the gathering crowd appeared to see the situation—as I explained it—as ever more humorous, the workers were none too pleased.

I stood in my boxers (at least I had boxers) next to the powerful African giant with the perfect, triangular upper torso. There was some word that Kebba had been an Olympian and played basketball for his small country's national team. That was my game, but I had no interest in going one on one with him. As I stood next to him, I felt soft and possibly genetically deficient.

"Awesome," said Kebba. He glanced between myself and Chloe.

This was, incidentally, the closest I ever came to actually meeting Thomas Loeb. He had been among the crowd at the swim-up bar and, like Kebba, wore a Speedo only—to completely different effect. I could see his laugh on his belly when he heard what happened to me, although he never approached, didn't say a word to me personally. He never asked my name that I know of. He began to herd the others, reached around his own bare, massive stomach to steer with his flabby arms. "Drinks on me!" he said. Kebba, Chloe, and the others followed him, uncertainly I thought. They left me in my boxers, but I was relatively happy.

I knew she wasn't in Loeb's room now. I knew that Dalton Harpe, and even the infallible IT department, had made a mistake concerning Chloe and Loeb.

"To the beach!" bellowed the elder Loeb, which was the

last I heard from that group as they disappeared, dissolved into darkness in the direction of the seawall. Chloe went with them, headed—although I didn't know it—for disaster.

The next day the news of what Kebba called my "awesome punking" spread quickly, but it wasn't like such things hadn't happened to me before. Only: who was responsible? Most likely, they wanted to congratulate such a person. There were plenty of theories, but my own approach had been solidified. From then on, I determined just what it was that Loeb made a mess of. I became proactive in regards to his incompetence and could better choose those things for which I took the blame.

I guess I got cocky.

The "retreat" continued through its final day with nothing accomplished and work, no doubt, piled high back at the offices of Davidson, Kohlhoeffer & Loeb. Loeb and I negotiated his window repair bill with the management, who regretfully agreed someone had been victimized. The rest of the gathering offered Chloe absolutely no more reason to interact with the favored son, his broad chest, or his healthy head of hair. It's the picture, the photograph pinned to the cork board in the break room on the thirtieth floor, that tells the rest.

In the photo, all the retreat participants are seated, positioned around a long wooden table under canvas umbrellas in the great out of doors, tall tropical drinks in hand, and with empty and half-empty plates of Mexican food piled precariously at each elbow. Kohlhoeffer was at one end of the banquet with his red, red sunburned wife seated on his lap. Kohlhoeffer beamed. The wife—a well-upholstered woman— was a bit subdued, and leaned thoughtfully on the table so as not to crush her partner, the partner. Her cheeks were crossed with a fire-engine glow. Semi-retired, he took little part in the day-to-day operations of the firm any more. As Dalton loved to whisper in a tone of delight, Kohlhoeffer was "forgotten, but not gone." Dalton beams in the photo as well: the joker in the deck always smiles such a smile. Kebba looked natural and at ease in shorts, polo shirt, and smirk—at home anywhere on the globe: the absolute opposite of the "Young Master,"

Harrell, who seemed to have just been kidnapped from a boardroom, his hands rising often to arrange some phantom tie he didn't wear. The organizer—Miss Adventure Phoenix—snapped a photograph, but was none-too-pleased with the arrangement. "It looks so professional," she complained.

"Oh, no," said Kohlhoeffer, dryly, to which we all dutifully laughed.

In the final picture, I stick out like the cockroach in the rice bowl because everyone else is seated in someone's lap, or has an arm draped around a colleague's shoulder, or a hand on a support personnel operative's knee. Ruth the receptionist leans her head on the EEOC counsel's arm. Dalton, with a show of sweaty delight, is plopped onto Kebba's lap, the big man retaining the exact same air of nonchalance. This gave me my cue. I steered Chloe to Loeb, pushed her on top of him, propped her across both of his firm knees. His hand rested lightly on her tummy to steady her as she started to slip off, and it was a very large, very flat and delicate hand.

If there was any heat there, I'd know it now for sure.

Then:

"We need big hugs," said the photographer. "Hug on three."

"*Ah haaaah*," said Kebba.

And that's why that picture is the way it is, and why it became such an opportunity for fun and games, rumor, innuendo . . . gibes, jabs, insults, and who knows what all over the next year and a half. "Look at them," Dalton said a few weeks later, again in the break room, indicating Loeb and Chloe. "I told you. And breaking the first rule, too."

"Rule?"

"Of office romance. No pictures."

"Bullshit," I said. "You were there—it's all posed."

He turned away, but pointed his chin over his shoulder as he left. "It ain't posed according to IT."

Once I understood how important Chloe was to me, I returned to that photograph in dark times. I came to believe Dalton and the IT department had indeed been wrong before the Galveston retreat—there had been nothing between Chloe and Loeb after all—but as she began to confide in me about her attraction to Loeb, I realized that must have been it. That picture. That moment. A record of the beginning of whatever it was that had occurred between them.

And I'd started it.

iii.

So. That Stuart Loeb, who would have been bulging out of his undies in front of the senior counsel at a posh Gulf-side resort hotel if not for me, was now calling me in. Right away.

Fuck him. It was Thursday afternoon—Friday afternoon was, after all, only a day away. I stopped at a donut shop. I had some crullers, Vicodin, and coffee, and read the afternoon paper. Not a word about the Leudecke scandal until the business section, but, sure as shit, there Maggie and her guilt-projecting hand were prominently displayed. I rolled the paper under my arm, made it to the firm about an hour before closing time.

I hated Loeb's office. It was one of those spaces where the framed pictures and certificates were perfectly aligned on the wall, placed like props rather than actual personal accent pieces. I saw only one book on his shelf—Loeb being one of the new digital casework generation—and that was a *Black's Dictionary,* which, I'm sorry, I don't even own a copy of any more. I think it was part of the box of items I'd pawned after my divorce. My law school casebooks, plus my gold wedding band, got me enough for a carton of cigarettes and a sixteen-ounce Diet Coke.

Well, I was out of cigarettes and Diet Coke.

"Loeb," I said. "Despite my sketchy . . . let's say non-existent expertise in matters having to do with state-funded highway construction, I think I might have taken one look at that situation and. . . ."

"What? What, Bent? Enlighten me." He was testy in a way I had not seen.

I, however, was calm. Almost properly medicated, I moved to navigate carefully and tack into the pushback of his anger at just the right angle. "Look," I said. "Just because you screwed this up doesn't mean we're in trouble, because Chloe. . . ."

"There wasn't anything I could have done!"

"You couldn't have asked for an extension? I mean, let's boil this down. Were there any documents dumped on you?"

He thought about it. "Maps."

"Is that one of them?" A large multicolored paper roll sat across his otherwise pristine desk. I took it to be the bad news on ranch dissection.

"I'll get to that," said Loeb.

"Did we have a chance to examine these maps? We have a right to look over anything new," I said, not totally certain that was the case. "Nor did we receive any notice of this being a public hearing."

"Dad is adamant that you handle this, although I myself no longer think it's a good idea."

"Oh, you yourself don't." I sat in one of the chairs in front of his desk. It was stiff-cushioned and seemed brand new. I wondered if anyone else had ever even been in this movie set of an office. The décor told as little about Loeb as the wall accessories might about a hotel room occupant. "You know, I can't figure out why your dad is adamant about anything having to do with me."

"You are going to explain to Maggie how this happened."

"I'm happy to!" Now we were getting somewhere. "Chloe and I will tell her about the land grants. I mean, she's actually got a good case."

"The historical thing?"

I shrugged. "Don't you know? Ask Chloe about it. Ms. Leudecke will have no problem impoverishing these pesky property developers and minority groups."

"You don't take anything seriously. This is an important client! She and her family asked for you specifically. You're in trouble. Unless you stop all this shit and listen to me."

I'm sorry, but I believed him. I didn't consider him much of an authority on my troubles, but in this case . . . I remembered him, momentarily, sitting with his arms in his lap on that hotel mattress, dressed in his skivvies, and put my hand over my eyes. Great. This was the person who was going to help me. The walls closed in; the fluorescent light over his desk flickered, like a lantern viewed through an airplane propeller.

I rubbed my forehead. "So, fill me in," I whispered.

"I have a job for you."

I got a job for you, too, pal.

As Loeb told it, at the hearing that morning, aside from the hisses and sounds of discontent from the assembled crowd, many of the proceedings had consisted of the board pulling forth map after map of highly detailed topographic elevations, demonstrating to Maggie Leudecke how the highway could—by the state's invocation of its right of easement—be constructed in such a manner that it separated her home from a low pasture area on the south side of her properties: acreage, however, presently being used for nothing beyond a party-place for prairie grasses. "Or," said Loeb, "if she didn't play along. . . ."

"Are we talking about the Board of Transportation or the Mafia here? They gave her ultimatums?"

"They had a route they much preferred that would separate her living room from her kitchen."

It was nearly funny. Still, Chloe's researched discoveries about the sanctity of the Leudecke properties did seem ironclad. The state would have to go against a shelf of honored precedent: the legal kind, sure, but also the Leudecke ancestors were bona-fide heroes of . . . Goliad, the Alamo, or San Jacinto? I figured that the last guy to try to bully the Leudecke family out of property had been Santa Anna.

I made a note to look up exactly what the ancient Leudeckes had done to get their grant.

"I'll see Maggie today," I said.

"No!" He became suddenly even more energized. "No, but you'll leave today. Ruth has your ticket."

"What do you mean? What ticket?"

"You do know Maggie splits her time between here and Mexico."

"Of course." I had no idea. "She's gone to Mexico? Now?"

"I got the impression she was in a hurry to leave," Loeb

said, an attempt to be arch. He removed a pen from his pocket and placed it on his desk. Perhaps he'd seen someone remove a pen from a pocket for effect in a movie about lawyers, I don't know, but it was perfectly aligned with his calendar blotter. I forgot to mention that there were several prints on Loeb's office wall: pictures of giraffes. I have never known any male to so prominently feature that particular species in his personal space. There was a carved specimen on his filing cabinet, too. Yet, as with everything, even these decorations didn't seem to be about him.

"I hate to say it this way, Bent, but Dad really wants me to take this over after the mess you've made."

"You just said he wanted the opposite."

"He wants you to deal with Maggie while I straighten this out."

"Hah! If you're taking over, then you go to Mexico, and I'm going downstairs and throwing myself on the mercy of Rich Jefferson. Or I'll fly to London and drag his ass back here. In fact," and here I stood, rested one knee on his pristine desk, and leaned in close. "I've got a wild notion, Loeb. This might be an excellent opportunity, really, to move this whole thing . . . not to somebody like you or me at all, but an attorney who deals with the state. I don't know. A real estate, or property, or eminent domain expert. The kind of person who should have been doing this all along."

"Or a person who shows up at hearings."

"Low, Loeb. Very."

"Besides, that department can't handle this one."

"What?"

"There's a conflict of interest."

I couldn't follow it. "What the hell? We have a conflict of interest with ourselves?"

"Think about it and you'll understand. Shit, Bent, you've really done it this time."

"What does that mean? You . . . Chloe was saying something like that the other day. You better. . . ."

"She likes you. That's what's important now."

"What?" I fingered the large rolled map on his desk. "Chloe said that?"

"*Maggie* likes you. Go to Mexico and calm her down."

I got quiet. "What's really going on here, Loeb?" I whispered. "Just tell me. Who's been following me around? Who killed Eladio what's-his-name?"

"A canoe accident killed him."

"A canoe accident never kills anyone."

"And you only have to have one word with her. Go to San Judas and tell her everything will be alright."

"Sam what-the-fuck?"

"San Judas Tadeo. It's a town."

"How close to Cancún is this town?"

"I told Dad you'd leave today."

"I'm not even the best person to explain this to her. I'm taking Chloe with me, then, and. . . ."

Holy fuck.

At that moment it struck me how I had been looking at this the wrong way entirely. A few days—or weeks—with Chloe? In Mexico? Oh, man. Especially now. Now that she was so pissed at me.

Sometimes you think the world is chaos, and that there's no way to move against the forces that dog you, no way to get over these barriers that rise, and rise again, or to touch, let alone grab, what you want. It's like: *shit,* that last barrier, man. Too big! Right when I thought I was onto something! But then my head cleared. Chloe and I, together in Bumfuck Judas, Mexico?

Would she even be able to text from there?

I could have a chance . . . not to influence her, no, but to explain. Explain how we really hadn't even tried that time before. When was it? July 7. Two summers past. How, given everything, the situation, the context, she'd be so much better off with me than with Loeb. Oh sure, yes. He was wealthy. Well connected. Certain to be a partner someday, and single, at least for now. Nice-looking, yes, yes, and she loved him. *Lurved* him. But seriously, that wasn't ever going to work out for her.

I, on the other hand, would try to give her what she wanted, keep out of her way otherwise, stay out of her business. Hell, if Loeb ever got . . . what was the Spanish term? (I dug into my imperfect vocabulary, considered how I'd have to polish my language skills for the trip.) If he ever grew *cojones*, I'd step back. No problem, Chloe. I know how you feel about the guy. Maybe he'll even leave that millionairess fiancé for you. (Right.) Until that happens, is there really anything better for you with which to fill your lonesome hours? Anything better than your beloved Bent?

Who you know you've got a connection with already, and. . . .

I could dedicate the entire plane ride just to explaining how I was really, really sorry that I hadn't shown up for the preliminary hearing.

"In twenty minutes, Chloe is meeting with my father to explain this grant landing angle," said Loeb.

"Land grant."

"And will be with the partners through tomorrow and the next day. You go by yourself. Find Maggie Leudecke now."

"So . . . that's a terrible idea. I should wait till Chloe's finished."

Loeb reached for and unrolled his map, which turned out to be several maps, but not of the Leudecke ranch.

"Fly into Mexico City tonight, then get a cab to the northern bus station for the trip to San Judas."

"Tonight!"

". . . where Maggie has a hacienda, although I guess it's more like a townhouse or something." Loeb handed over the addresses and an itinerary typed on the firm's stationary. I snatched it from his hand.

"I have to ride a bus?"

"Although she might not be there, or might have come and gone."

"Will there be chickens on the bus? I hear there are chickens on buses in Mexico." I examined the listings. "The Bar El Infierno? Where are you sending me, Loeb?"

"A hangout of hers in San Judas, but mainly, there you want to connect with a man named Yucatán Bob."

"Get out of here."

"You need to listen to this carefully!" said Loeb. I'd never seen him so angry. Or was it fear?

"None of this is going to happen, Loeb. And what's

the rush? *Yucatán Bob?* What exactly have you gotten yourself into?"

"Shut up and pay attention."

"Am I supposed to take him a plain wrapped package?" Because the itinerary began to make more and more sense . . . for a contraband transfer of some kind. I was to know Yucatán Bob by his false leg. (Naturally.) He'd be the one to take me out into the mountainous countryside, where Maggie had a much larger hacienda, and where she was most likely headed. "He's some kind of sculptor and Maggie's part-time caretaker in Mexico," said Loeb.

"He's expecting me?"

"The Leudeckes are getting hold of him. He'll be there." Loeb explained how the trip to this second ranch would take seven hours in Bob's van. "Probably you'll see snakeskins and hawks for sale in front of palm-roofed lean-to's," said Loeb. "The usual tree-trunk electric poles become concrete with trees being in such short supply."

"Do you *know* this place?"

Loeb shrugged. "I've been to San Judas. It's a destination." The town, he explained, was approachable only through a long tunnel drilled through the Tadeo range during the silver mine era. "It's a one-way tunnel, but the drivers call ahead to the other side to make sure no vehicles are coming."

"And she's in this town?"

"Like I said, probably at her hacienda, several miles outside it." Loeb unrolled another map—this one hand-drawn, albeit it in some detail—and traced his finger along a dotted line. "You get there on a dangerous shelf road."

"You're actually calling it that?"

"Yucatán Bob will probably get you to walk out in front of the van to watch the wheels."

"Not going."

"Because he's only got that one leg. Well, one is prosthetic. After a few hours, you'll get to the canyon floor; then it's about thirty kilometers across some dunes, and you'll find her house." He stopped. "We're trusting you with this, Bent."

We, indeed.

"Alright," I said. "When I've flown to the capital, taken the bus through the impenetrable mountain stronghold to the colonial village, passed along the *dangerous shelf road*, and crossed thirty clicks of desert . . . basically gone to Mexico's asshole and then fifty miles up it with a one-legged sculptor . . . what exactly have I been sent there to do?"

His eyes momentarily lost their I-fucking-hate-you stare.

"Calm her down. See Ruth about the ticket."

"Not going."

"She said you gave her a vibe, Bent." He waved his arms at me. He was like Yvonne, telling me my time was up. "Go to Mexico," he said.

"And Chloe?"

He smiled in a way I did not like. "Stays here with me."

iv.

Ruth handed me a printout for an Aeroméxico flight that evening—which left me about three hours to pack if I gave myself buffer time to get through the international terminal and its double security checks. I stood in the parking garage beside my car and tried to decide. Three hours. Things could go one way or the other.

Yucatán Bob?

On my phone, I pulled up Google and searched for San Judas Tadeo, trying to get some idea of just how far off the map Loeb was trying to get me while he trained his vaunted incompetence upon the Leudecke ranch. I didn't see how I could leave the country at this important juncture. This was shaping up to become an ultimate defeat. It was my case, after all, and it was going badly. When I returned, Maggie's entire properties were liable to be covered by the concrete they so richly deserved to be buried under. But I couldn't even find the town online, just its namesake saint who was, as it turned out, the patron of lost causes. I tried to decide if that was off-putting or appropriate.

And what did it mean that the proper department at the firm couldn't take up the eminent domain question?

Hell, maybe I should just go. The case was starting to become a sticky problem. It wouldn't be the first difficulty I'd solved through flight. It wouldn't even be the first that week. But Chloe certainly seemed down on me. This kind of running and hiding wouldn't help me much to shine in her eyes. By this point, finding some way to shine in Chloe's eyes was my whole purpose for even pursuing Maggie Leudecke's plans to block construction of that road across her property.

Wikipedia included a ritualistic prayer to San Judas,

which turned out to involve a candle (of course) and an incantation. *Come to my aid in this time of great need* and such. *I am alone and without help.* I murmured the words under my breath. It all applied, basically. Help me out a little, saint.

In answer, a taxicab went past. Its tires squealed as it entered the nearby down-ramp and began to corkscrew towards street level. The last I saw of it was the ad panel on the trunk: a phone number, a straw hat, a face, and a wink.

Necesitas un Abogado? Llame Tony Ruiz, the Latino Guy!

I slapped my fist into my palm. Fuck yes. Tony Ruiz. That was the motherfucker's name. He was in this Road to Nowhere crap up to his hat band, and he represented that little town . . . what's its name: Bold Springs.

Bold Springs, I thought. Time for me to make one, and I got into my car.

ABOGADOS Y MÁS was blimp-hangar huge, an aluminum-sided monstrosity situated among other just normally oversized warehouse shells on Navigation Street. The main workspace encompassed an area the size of two dancehalls. I arrived well after 6 p.m., but it was open for business, filled with attorneys still hard at work, seated at desk after wooden desk, the whole arranged in no particular pattern across the gigantic floor, all of the lawyers operating without benefit of cubicles. Tony Ruiz—my friend, my good friend from law school—had made it much bigger than I'd thought. His personal office space was obvious, though similarly without walls. At the back of this cavernous room on a raised platform, the hat and sports jacket from the commercials hung conspicuously on a rack behind a desk four times the size of the others: the clothes seeming more "on display" than conveniently stored. It was like the way you occasionally see Elvis's duds in traveling expositions. Tony was not obviously present, but every lawyer at every desk was occupied, deep in conversation with the largely Hispanic clientele. The waiting area, nearly the same size as the consultation room, was filled to capacity, mostly with families by the looks of them, all waiting to see one of these tyro-attorneys. If Davidson, Kohlhoeffer & Loeb's reception area resembled the lobby of a luxury high-rise, this one looked more like the foyer of the Department of Motor Vehicles. It was easy to see that unlike the well-heeled clientele of my firm—who would occasionally have to arrange a work visa to, let's say, fly their horse trainer in from Portugal—Ruiz's bread and butter was the "transpedestrian" immigrants of America. They had arrived in the country on foot.

One of the three receptionists made several phone calls before she handed the youngest among them the duty of walking me back to see Tony Ruiz. Nice. No waiting. I walked down an aisle flanked by attorneys, floated through a familiar chatter of I-180s, waivers, birth certificates, and proof of residency.

We went out the back of the cavernous room, made a hard left, and were outside the building. We crossed Navigation at a traffic light.

"So." I indicated the hulking warehouses. "Tony's leasing more than one of these?"

"He owns them." She smiled, looked north up the street, her eyes and hair raven-dark in the diminishing fall light. "I'm not even sure how much of this is his."

We passed through the glass door of a metal building across the street. After a small foyer, a hallway opened into another cavernous, flood-lit area, but here metal bleachers against one side gave it the appearance of an arena. I looked carefully. Far away, a scoreboard, its bulbs unlit, showed the characteristic square "eighty-eight" pattern both for VISITORS and for HOME.

"This is a baseball diamond," I said.

"Mr. Ruiz sometimes has ex-Astros in to coach. He knows lots of ball players."

I had that feeling I get sometimes. Tony and I had left Bates College simultaneously. His work wasn't glamorous. (I'd heard him described once as running a *maquiladora*—a cheap labor sweatshop—of immigration.) Hell, his work might not even be responsible in all cases, but if he could bring Astros in to teach baseball to kids in the East End?

And yeah, I also had to admit that while it wasn't hard to take cheap shots at Tony, on the other hand, that room full of actual attorneys back there represented a resource in a city full of rip-off *notarios* and scam artists who pecked at the flesh of the hyper-vulnerable undocumented. It was high-volume, yes, but by all reports an honest service, and rendered at affordable prices, no matter how cheesy the hat, beige sports coat, and commercials.

I felt myself deflate in stature. What would it be like to be able to give this much to a community, and make this much profit, too? And, yes, I thought about Ngo Dinh Duc's nephew and the cash-filled envelope I'd used to keep my Henry enrolled in applied behavioral occupational training for one more bank-account-emptying month. I couldn't cover it. It was all slipping away. I wiped sweat off my brow with my sleeve.

We walked along the first-base line to another door, then a hallway, and into a somewhat smaller warehouse where two extremely fit-looking guys worked with two spud-shaped women on weight machines in a fully outfitted gym that appeared twice its size because of the mirrored walls. The women probably appeared twice their size, too, working out alongside those two hard bodies.

"Those are his professional trainers," said the young woman.

I noticed that I had neglected to get her name, as I'd had the impression she'd only walk me a short distance. Now I didn't know a good way to ask for it. "So, those women . . . is it a company fitness program?"

"Those are Tony's aunts. They're trying to lose weight," she smirked.

"It's great they can use all this stuff."

"It's for them," she said. "This is all pretty much just for his family."

"Wait," I said, but she didn't wait. We left this building, quickly went to the curb to cross Navigation again. At least, I thought it was still Navigation. "This is all for his family?"

"And some friends."

"The ball field?"

"For his sons. One wants to be a professional." She smirked once more. "I don't think he's going to make it in MLB, though."

The woman struck me as someone who didn't suffer

fools. Such people always intimidated me, especially since I spent so much time trying to decide if I was, myself, a fool. It was not an easy call, but she seemed perfectly capable of settling the question.

She opened another door across the street. "This is for his horse."

Sure enough, inside was a covered, air-conditioned stable. In the middle of the large circular paddock stood one brown-colored horse.

"He told you to take me around and impress the shit out of me."

She laughed. "No. I'm just not sure where he is."

The next building was outfitted with more books on shelves than my middle school had in its library when I was a kid, plus whiteboards, maps, globes, and several computers. "For the sons," I guessed.

"They're home schooled."

"I'll say."

"Señorita Valdez is their tutor. I haven't seen her today." She searched down the aisles of books. "She has a master's degree."

We went past a lunchroom pretty much the size of D, K & L's, but full of people—young attorneys, apparently, who grabbed a bite between shifts. ABOGADOS Y MÁS obviously did not close at 5 p.m. I knew it was a common training ground for those who'd just passed the bar but for whatever reason hadn't been spending their time interning for judges, in government offices, or in larger firms downtown. The worked-themselves-through-law-school-at-night crowd. Then a hard left, through a metal door and. . . .

. . . we were back in the original giant hall of attorneys, beside Tony Ruiz's massive desk on its raised platform. Only now, he was there with seven or eight men gathered around him in heated conversation.

"Oh, he was here the whole time." The young woman grinned and walked off, back towards the reception desk, her bell-shaped ass, walking away—so nice.

Good-bye, good-bye. . . .

"Bent!" said The Latino Guy himself. "I thought I'd find you here sooner or later."

"It's the place to be."

"We could have just met at Club Some if you wanted to party." He grinned. "Look, I have to handle a couple of things, then I'm right with you." He turned to the group. "So, how many cars do we have?"

"We got forty cars, Mr. Ruiz," said a sharp-looking twenty-something with a bushy mustache and creased, ironed jeans. All these men who surrounded Tony were young, with polished boots and stiff-collared Western-wear shirts.

Ruiz appeared deep in calculation. "New cars?"

"*Por supuesto que sí.*"

"Make it forty-five. That'll work."

All seven or eight of them agreed that forty-five was a better number, and, with not a lot of other ritual, the group dispersed, stepped off the platform, into the sea of lawyers, citizenship applicants, and deportation defendants, headed for the exits. They were off to buy, I guessed, five more new cars.

For?

"One more thing I have to deal with. I have to watch this video." Ruiz put a disc into the sliding drawer of his desk computer. "Then we can gab."

Only one of the men from the convocation remained, and he and Tony Ruiz began to watch the video on the desktop monitor. I looked over the back of a woman attorney in a desk below me—young, a little heavyset, earnest in the way she spoke to an old lady and a middle-aged man who sat before her. Despite the video and the general cacophony of the warehouse, I could still easily hear the exchange between the lawyer and her clients.

"It'll be fine. We'll tell the judge he has a company, señora. He employs twelve people in the community."

The older woman put in: "He supports veterans."

"Oh, such a good son you've got."

To tell the truth, the man didn't look like a "good son" to me. I may be predisposed to mistrust angry-looking people with tattoo sleeves that feature writhing snake designs, especially when they slither among skulls that grin with sharp, pointed teeth.

"His daughter who chose him over her mother," the attorney continued, heartfelt. "His poor little boy who passed.

It's so sad: a powerful exceptional circumstance. I'm sure any judge will see him as an asset."

"Everyone after Miguel in the family was born here," said the mother.

"And your whole family is citizens, that's good. It's all good. Your own testimony will help the judge understand who Miguel really is."

"It will be fine," said the mother.

Miguel looked away. There were more tattoos in bands around his ankles and calves. He wore basketball shorts, so I could see his skinny legs. Who wears basketball shorts to meet their lawyer? With their mom?

"But you need to know everything before we get to the hearing," the attorney said, and she lowered her tone. "Which is why I have to tell you. This is something your son doesn't want you to know about, and has been keeping from you."

The mother turned from the attorney to stare down her "boy," who appeared to be pushing forty, by my eye, and also seemed no community asset. But who knows? He supported veterans . . . somehow. Sounded like he'd lost a kid. Maybe all the tattoos were pictures of this lost child (doubtful). Meanwhile, the DVD in Ruiz's computer spit out a smooth, salesman-like pitch:

"With sixty-three years of experience, your unipolar or bipolar knee prosthesis is guaranteed perfect quality and perfect sterility."

"Señora Perez, Miguel has a conviction from the 1980s for drug possession."

It is difficult to describe the scream that issued from the Señora Perez. She directed it towards her own lap as she looked down and winced in what appeared to be excruciating physical pain. It was more like the way a mother might sound upon learning her son was dead, not upon learning he had a thirty-year-old drug conviction.

Mothers.

Heads turned across the ballroom-sized hall, including Tony's and the guy he was watching the video with. The giant room grew silent enough for the video to broadcast loud to all corners:

"We are licensed by FDA India for production of orthopedic implants on license form twenty-eight!"

"We will see him through this," said the woman attorney. She sounded not at all businesslike. Although I was looking mainly at the back of her head, I could tell she was nearly crying. I was totally falling in love with her. "Señora Perez, your boy is not to blame. He was with some friends, and it was *their* drugs, but you know how it is. Tell her, Miguel."

"C'mon, Ma." Miguel shrugged and thrust his bare legs and his Air Jordans out in front of him, like the whole process was beneath his dignity. I wondered what "business" he ran that employed twelve people.

"Thank God his father is not alive to *see*," wailed Señora Perez. "That's the knee you want?" Tony asked his client.

"That's a good knee."

"Okay, I'll get you that knee. Now let me talk to this palooka."

When we left, the counselor at the desk below me was wrapping up arrangements for court. "It's like he has two mothers helping him, Señora Perez: you and me. He will be like a son to me."

"Hey," said my college friend, who stopped to look down from his platform. "Miguel's got an extra father on his side, too." While he'd juggled the car deal (whatever it was) and the knee implant, the whole time he'd also been listening to the immigration saga of Señora Perez's good, good son. He jabbed a thumb into his own chest. "He's got Tony Ruiz."

V.

"I would suppose this to be some kind of parallel universe," I said to Tony. "Except maybe more like perpendicular."

Once again, we'd gone through the metal back door, past an area filled with document boxes stored in what didn't appear to be particularly well-ordered sequences, then out the back of the building. It turned out to have started raining. "It's not far," Tony said, and he started to jog past some barrels to a gate in a wooden fence. We both pushed on it to swing it wide on its badly rusted hinges as the rain started to pepper down, and beyond the gate were picnic tables and a covered patio, like a beer garden. Then, we went up some wooden steps, through a door, and, like that, we were in a bar. There was a jukebox, darts, twenty beers on tap: an actual bar.

"Sweet," I said.

"The Cantina Henderson," said Tony. "There's a real entrance on Bering, but I love this. I live over the office, so it makes me feel like there's a cool watering hole in my backyard."

We took stools at the bar and Tony ordered us drafts. Something made me think he might well own the Cantina Henderson, too.

"Yet I have to assume you didn't come here to hang with your bud," he said, and glanced around the cantina as if seeking someone he knew, though the place was thoroughly empty. Did Tony Ruiz keep this completely stocked bar just for himself? Was it like the ballpark for his boys, the trainer for his aunts, or the paddock for his one brown horse? "You're working for her, right?"

"Her?"

He gave me the low eye. "She who cannot be moved!

So, what's Davison, Kohlhoeffer, and those fucks into? Construction? Commercial interests?"

"Okay, well. I saw—on TV actually—that you were at her preliminary hearing."

"Nasty, right?" He seemed delighted.

"So, of course, we at Davison and those fucks are trying to protect an innocent millionairess from the police state."

"You what! No!" But his fake shock disappeared quickly. "Like I don't know that."

"Why do you ask if you already know?"

"That is a proven lawyerly technique . . . of lawyerness. You should start doing that, Bent. You ask too many questions looking for answers."

He had me there.

"Because really, you're not even down here working for her, are you? It's Koelpepper and Davidson and them who got you by the balls."

"Fine."

"You ever want to cut out on them, let me know. Listen. . . ." He sighed, then laughed. Then he laughed some more. "Oh, heh. Sorry. I was going to say I would hire you, motherfucker."

"Couldn't hold it, could you?"

The Latino Guy shook his head. "That's why I can't tell jokes! But you're playing a dangerous game with those people. That woman. Rich witch. She's a menace." He leaned forward over the bar, though there was no one to overhear us. "I know."

"That to all appearances was a simple canoe accident."

"You're not listening. I said, *I know*."

"You know her?" This intrigued me. "Look, I have to ask. She affects you?"

"It's like she put a spell on me."

"So it's not just me."

"No, we're all susceptible."

I moved closer. "What happens?" I asked. "When you're near her? Do you lose your head?"

"Oh, yeah."

"No, I mean really. Like, keel over unconscious?"

"I'm conscious," said Tony. "*Uber*-conscious. I don't keel over; I keel up."

"Fine."

"I lost my wife and family because of her."

"You what?"

"Unfortunately," said Tony, "they found me."

The barmaid, it turned out, was eavesdropping on our conversation. She wiped the tray under the taps, snickered, and shook her head. She'd heard that one before. Was she there only to serve Tony Ruiz on his occasional visits?

"So, Tony: why are you attending preliminary hearings of the Transportation Board?"

With a moment's thought, I should have been able to put it together from what I'd just seen, and from what I knew about supporters of the new loop. For one, according to The Latino Guy, "that bad news trouble bitch" it turned out was, by her actions, running completely counter to nature. "Look at the world, crazy *puta*. That world is a *barrio*. Why stand in the way of the world?"

"Philosophical, but I accept it. Only there's more."

"Only, so, mainly she's also running counter to the interests of Bold Springs." He described the Hispanic enclave (unincorporated) that stood to gain enormous economic advantage given the present projected arc of the Road to Nowhere, not only in increased land value, but also in tax revenue from business income. "Maybe even a lot of business, if it can be swung. And it is being swung alright—right out from under us."

"Maybe it's only because I just took a grand tour of your holdings on Navigation Street," I said, "but I still have to ask. You don't own any properties in Bold Springs, do you?"

"You're one to talk. You and your Regional Center parked right in the middle of that road."

"Me?" I blinked. "You mean the firm? That's impossible."

He shrugged. "It's what I hear."

"Those are for foreign investors. I think if D, K & L had a Regional Center, the immigration department would have heard about it."

"Maybe you should go ask."

I considered it. "I mean, we have such things, but there can't be one connected to this road, or we wouldn't be handling . . . she who cannot be moved." I sipped my beer while he sat silent. "Would we?"

"Look, Bent, serious now. We need to talk."

"We are talking."

"Lives hang in the balance. Real people."

He sounded like Harrell concerning Emmanuel Adeyemi. I wondered if the anesthesiologist was still sweeping Nigerian warehouses. "Maggie Leudecke is a real person," I tried.

He gave me one of the clearest *you-don't-even-believe-what-the-fuck-you-just-said* looks I'd ever received. And I've received a few.

"Put it this way," Tony said. "I won't mention names, but this is a story about myself and a woman I loved. In fact, I was crazy about her. Totally fucking crazy! It was Maggie! Maggie Leudecke."

"I thought no names."

Tony showed his big eyes, stubbled chin, and his red gums. "This isn't the story I want to tell you. I'll tell you that in a second. But I started studying the occult because of her. Tarot. Candles. All that shit. Mainly just because she was so into it. It's garbage, Bent."

"Alright."

"But the thing was, she had this boyfriend. Or, as I always thought of him," he grew quiet, "she had this obstacle. This guy. Whose name was Roy. And Maggie Leudecke was always telling me how much better Roy was than me."

"He was so totally better than you in every category," said the barmaid, who put a stack of envelopes into a clip on top of the cash register—I guessed that's where the mailman would pick them up. "Did you even have a job, then?"

"I had prospects." He spread his arms wide for the barmaid. "I mean, she could have had all this."

"Roy," I said. Another character. "Never heard of him. So it was . . . when you were in college?"

"After." Tony leaned forward again, but made no effort

to lower his voice. "I would follow her, even, down to these properties she has in Mexico."

"I've heard about them."

"But this Roy was always blocking my cock. According to her, this guy, Roy, he had this great singing voice. He was a 'singer.'" Tony raised his crooked fingers as quotation marks. "Hey, I sing, I told her. You know what she said? She said not really."

"You suck," said the barmaid. "That's true."

"Not really, Maggie said! And Roy was a musician, and could play all these instruments. So I said, Hey, I can play a lot of instruments."

"This is all truly fascinating," I said. I thought about my rapidly approaching Aeroméxico departure time.

"She told me I just owned a lot of instruments. So it was totally hopeless. But—and this is key, Bent—the word comes down. I'm sitting right over there at ABOGADOS Y MÁS, working, right? And someone who knows Maggie in Mexico comes in and tells me. Roy is dead. That's right. Roy dies," said Tony. "Turned out he died of a heroin overdose, down there in Mexico. Oh, that Maggie, she owns all this shit in Mexico."

"So I hear. But wait, my wife, Marisel. . . ."

"Oh yeah. How's she doing?"

"Fine, fine."

"Send her my love, will you, Bent? She needs to get some from somewhere."

"Alright. Marisel says the word is Maggie killed her husband in Mexico. Is that this Roy?"

Tony shook his head. "She never married. Could be this guy, but she didn't kill him. Some people came through and gave him heroin."

"He was some kind of druggy?"

"He was clean for years, I guess, but he slipped up. Yeah, man." He sighed. "Even his addictions were more interesting than my addictions. But, look, here's the point: it got me to thinking. Singing. Playing instruments. Whatever. Doesn't matter how good he is at any of that now. I have to be better than a dead boyfriend." Tony stood up. "Let's go outside."

We took our beers, walked out the rear door, stepped

to the edge of an awning overlooking the patio tables, and stood where he could hold his flat palm into the steady rain. I had the impression he didn't often stand still, if ever. He was a Latino Thomas Loeb, maybe minus a hundred pounds.

"So . . . Roy is dead," I reminded him.

"I will tell you something I know. It is something you can have. Keep it forever. I know this for a certainty, will know it for eternity, and know it for an absolute. I know other things, too, but I'll tell you those later, after I tell you this." He looked at me. "Do you have any idea what this knowledge is?"

"There's no way to compete with a dead boyfriend."

Tony Ruiz seemed disappointed. "Figures you'd know that already."

We sat on sticky-wet wooden stools.

"I told Maggie and told her," Tony said, "it's not going to matter."

"What's not?"

"There will be no road."

We really were out of earshot now, especially with the rain on the tin awning as noisy background cover. It occurred to me he'd separated us from the barmaid for some actual privacy.

"I'm pretty sure," I said, "although my client doesn't want to hear this, there will be a road."

"Nope." The Latino Guy grinned, pulled up his pant legs, revealed expensive-looking—possibly silk—socks, and scratched an ankle.

"I've seen the plat," I said. "There could be a road through Maggie's living room this time next year."

I didn't want to let on that my personal choice would now be for her to compromise: admit that although her status as a "founding family" pioneer descendent gave her some clout, she'd be willing to give over property she didn't use. She'd be better off in every possible way; plus she would keep the highway apart from the house and the important sections of the ranching enterprise. For that matter, were there actually cattle on the Leudecke property? I couldn't remember them mentioned in any of the summaries.

"It won't happen. Listen, what is it you're thinking to tell the Board, Bent, when the lawsuits start to fly?"

"Of Transportation? If you represent the fine citizens of Bold Springs, Texas, I'm pretty sure I'm not going to reveal that."

He shrugged. "Those transportation motherfuckers are way too powerful. And take things personal, too. But what? Historical exemption?"

I wanted to run it past him, but checked myself. I also wanted to get home and pack, if I was actually going to go where I was supposed to go. I squeezed water out of my eyelashes. "I have no response at this time."

"You people. You're all like Roy. Better than everyone at everything. Have to put up a plaque every place one of those cracker land thieves took a shit." He moved his hand, as if taking an eraser to one of those chalkboards in his private school/warehouse. "Or, let's say, biological. A rare nematode in one of those ponds."

"They're called tanks." He was up to something. "But okay, let's go with that."

Tony Ruiz gave me "the look"—the one that's on the billboards and cab trunks, the one winking eye—then faced the empty gazebo-like rails and tables. "You think the Road to Nowhere is a highway. A loop. Or something else. You're thinking this is about subdivisions, right? Utility connections."

"Construction," I added. "Houses, mortgages, driveways . . . tricycles sitting on driveways."

"An enormous new tax base, targeted Regional Centers . . . and the ranch has to go to make all this possible."

"But what if Maggie doesn't want her ranch replaced with dwellings, mortgages, and tricycles?"

"It never will be!" He was loud, grinning wide. "Look. It's nothing personal. The ranch is a quirk."

"My client—uhm, the love of your life—disagrees."

"It's a story, Bent. She'll be sitting on her ranch when she's an old crone. When you *bolillos* drag her off to be burned at the stake, that ranch still won't have been touched." He sighed. "At least she'll have her memories of our time together."

I wasn't following him. "Give it to me with the nematode example."

"Perfect! So there's a pond on her property, with this endangered species. *Nematodas Bent-a-phonus.*"

"Lovely."

"Which translates to *anus worm.* So there it is, the pond, complete with rare endangered wiggler." He held his hands out, shaped space, pointed at the picnic tables, the irregular surfaces of which were indeed now ponding in the rain. "And over here?" He gestured towards the X-shaped wooden rail frames, stools shoved against them, some upside down, flipped atop other stools. "Your construction crews. Your grading machines, dozers, earth movers . . . guys with lunch boxes made of metal . . . visible butt cracks."

There was a trick in this somewhere. "You're going to ask me what's going to keep the lowly pond worm from being wiped out by the force of man and machine."

"I'm going to ask you: what's at risk, Bent? In this picture? What's in trouble? 'Cause it ain't the nematode."

"It ain't?"

"Or the pond. Or the land. Or Marguerite Leudecke's cosmic aura and great-smelling neck. It's those guys with the butt cracks that are gonna get it, man. It's that bulldozer. Because what's looming over them are the packages. The deals. Options, including tradable ones. Possibilities for making some real money *now*, while the business of building something so mundane as a fucking road gets traded . . . down the road, so to speak. Bought and sold by people who don't give a shit about roads in the first place, if they go nowhere or not."

Options trading. Put this together with real estate easements and I now had represented, in one case, two of the many areas of the law about which I knew the least.

"Maybe," I said.

"Damn sure certain! They want some dough for the land, right? For the option to build."

"And the real road?"

"Never built at all! Or maybe decades from now, but who needs a fucking four-lane loop out there? Who lives there except crazy millionaire witches, and the good people of Bold Springs?" He closed an eye again, like he was aiming something at me. "They, my clients, want some of that pass-along money. That's all. They want some clean profit, then sell, cash in, and get the fuck out. Can you blame them?"

I hadn't thought of it that way. Still, the Board of Transportation with its bullying tactics seemed so intent on the road, and once they had rights over the property . . . hell, they were liable to go ahead and build it whether it was worthless or not, just from inertia. It was how things worked in this state, as Tony well knew. And, anyway: "If that's true, I'm pretty insulted," I said. "Why am I even wasting my time on this?"

"Hell, don't ask me; it's your case. But you get to hang out with Maggie Leudecke, right? What do you think all this law shit is for?"

I recalled some of our late-night law school conversations. "Meeting chicks?"

"Thank you!"

Still, I had a feeling the "It's not really a real road" argument wouldn't fly with Maggie and her ironclad possessiveness when it came to her ranch.

"Even now, there's one bank in Bold Springs," Tony said. "And that joker is out there, trying to screw the people out of the profit, foreclose on them, and buy them out for next to nothing."

"I'm supposed to go and see her," I said. "Maggie, I mean. I fly out tonight."

"Flying?"

"Well . . . uhm. That's one thing I was wondering. You want another free beer from your bar?"

"I shouldn't."

"Then . . . you want to go to Mexico?"

"Mexico!"

"Or maybe there's someone in one of your warehouses who could go with me? Somebody bilingual." I thought about the raven-haired receptionist, whose name I'd missed. "It might be in all our interests. Including Bold Springs."

I retrieved the now somewhat damp itinerary from the pocket of my coat and gave him the rundown of the mountain towns, the tunnels, the "shelf roads." "She's gone back to her hacienda, where you so artfully courted her."

"Interesting."

"It'd be a lot better if you were there, and we could, you know . . . reason with her, maybe. Lay out the whole thing together."

"I don't think she's there."

"She's there, or will be soon."

"I saw her an hour ago out at her store on the ranch. And I don't think she looked like she was fleeing the country."

"Not in Mexico?"

"She had a brisket going for one thing."

Fucking Loeb.

I looked over my itinerary. I was right about the whole thing: an attempt to get me out of the way.

Maybe.

"And I'll tell you what I told her," Tony said. "She's done. There's not even anybody in her own family that wants her to stonewall that road."

"It's her family who sent her to us. One of the partners is their big pal."

"Think about it, Bent. I'm telling you, your partners have property interests out there. They've already spent some of the money that's come in on their Regional Center, and there's not even a road yet."

"They can't do that."

Tonto! There are so many ways to hide that shit. Shells inside of shells inside of boxes. Oh, yeah, believe it: they're taking investor dollars and screwing those poor defenseless foreign millionaires."

I thought again of Mr. Duc.

"She'll cost them a fortune," Tony said. "Hanging onto her precious ranch that's not going to be taken away from her anyway. Hell, the Leudeckes themselves don't even give a damn about her or Texas any more. Right now they're out in Colorado, buying the whole state acre by acre."

Colorado! I felt dizzy and a bit hungry.

The Latino Guy put his hand on my shoulder. "You need to get out of that place," he said. "That Kohlhoeffer deal. They do not appreciate you there, man. They are not telling you everything. And that Loeb. Jesus. Crazy, horny motherfucker."

"I assume we speak of our founder. Devoted to his wife and children."

"He's left them in the lurch. Already divorced the lady."

"No," I said. "He plays around on them, on her. But he's not leaving while those kids are still at home." Here I was, defending a man I didn't trust and hadn't really met. Out of what? Firm loyalty?

"That's not what I heard, but oh well. Those aren't my people." He pointed a finger—pistol fashion—at his own head, let the thumb trigger go. "Crazy fucks. You need to look out."

I nodded, but then began to wonder if he'd heard something. It seemed lately that everyone knew D, K & L's plans for me, except myself. "I'm trying real hard for them to just put up with me."

"That won't happen. Among quartzes, the diamond is outlawed, motherfucker."

I thought of the heartfelt counselor and her spiel about the "two mothers." It had an appeal. "So I will come here and work for you."

"Who asked you?"

Oh.

Right.

vi.

On that day, July 7, two summers back, I stood in my hallway after Marisel gave me the phone, and it was Chloe who pressed, Chloe who pushed. "I told your wife that I need some help with something at the office. But what I really need is to meet you. Do you understand? The two of us?"

"Yes."

"We need to meet."

"I think that's fine," I said. "Are you sure?"

What I really wanted to ask was "Are you sober?" But that was difficult with Marisel standing at the edge of the kitchen. I could feel the suspicion rise from her, a thermal lift.

"I've been at a pool party. And I smoked something." She must have read my mind. "But it's just synthetic."

"Ah, synthetic," I said, wondering what that meant. I listened to myself, tried to gauge and consider how the conversation presented to Marisel standing right there, but also I wondered what I sounded like to myself. If she was as high as all that, should she be driving? Could I be taking advantage of her?

"I'm still in my bikini, and so wet."

Fuck yes I could be taking advantage of her. And soon. "I better see about that, then."

"I'm sorry to call at home, but I really need to meet you. You can tell her there's something at the office."

"Yes, that's right."

"That really has to be done."

"So you think it's a worthwhile proceeding at this time"

"Trust my judgment," she said. "Unless you're just another man with no follow-through."

"Well," I said, and Marisel glared from the kitchen. "I

understand." I looked right at my wife. "It needs to be taken care of immediately."

That's how we set it up, and I listened to her tell me the location—on the La Porte Freeway, nearly in Pasadena. That was a city away, which was something Chloe would think of. I have follow-through. I have guts. I do things. Sometimes, they're wrong.

I'd done the wrong thing, somehow, that afternoon in July, and I'd find out what I'd done wrong, and make it right. But how?

After walking out of Tony's compound, I sat in my car in the rain and put in a call to the firm.

"Oh," Ruth said. "You."

"Any developments?"

"Pretty funny coming from you, isn't it?"

"Okay, I really don't get that. Can you connect me with Chloe?"

Silence. For some reason, though the rain drummed its background beat, I felt I could still hear Ruth shaking her headset: no.

"Ruth," I said. "If there's no change, can I ask that?"

"Even funnier."

"Let me talk to Loeb or Chloe or let me get on about my business."

"You don't sound like you're at the airport," she said.

Occasionally, passing cars swished along the damp pavement of Navigation Street, which I guessed she could hear even over my crappy cell phone. It was not an airport sound. I glanced down the long rows of warehouses—how many of them owned by Ruiz?

"And yet, I am here, very much so, at the airport with that lovely ticket you gave me."

There was more silence, then some kind of faraway switching or clicking.

"Bent."

It was her.

"I've been thinking about you a lot," I said to Chloe. "There's so much going on here that . . . I think you'd find. . . ."

"I can't really talk. Look, Bent." Her voice was lowered, which was odd for her. She wasn't the lowered voice type. "Something here is not right."

"Well . . . I need to discuss it with you, because the fact is, I'm not even sure Maggie has made it to Mexico."

"It's the Leudeckes," she said. "I'm getting an odd impression about them."

"Shit, sweetie. Nobody wants Maggie to keep her ranch, let alone the Leudeckes."

"I'm not your sweetie, and you're going to have to get help for Maggie."

"A term of endearment." I felt I wouldn't have long to talk with her.

"It's like they don't want her to know about the land grant." I could hear papers shuffled in the background. There was the sound of briefcase latches being flipped open or snapped closed.

"These are Loeb's, Big Loeb's, friends," I said. "They probably want Maggie to just agree to let the freeway run through that pasture, and everything will be fine, so we end up holding her hand while she loses her appeal. But we'll get her fair market value. And look. . . ." I was not at all sure Tony was right about this, but it seemed an idea worth floating. "There's a good chance the road won't be built even if the land is sold."

I felt in command. I was the experienced mentor, impressing my disciple with my grasp of the situation.

There were a few beats of silence. "That's awful. Tom wouldn't do that."

"Tom. Who's Tom?" I didn't know any Toms.

"Mr. Loeb, I mean. You've got to find Maggie. Are you in Mexico yet?"

"I just don't think she's there. I mean here." I took a deep breath. I suddenly felt more powerless than usual. "Look," I said to Chloe. "I think I might not bother looking for her. . . ."

"How can you say that? You've got to! Find her, Bent, show her the grant precedent. It's ironclad. We . . . you can actually win this. This case." She paused. "For a change."

Oh, man. "Well, we should be looking for her at her ranch, I think."

"Listen," she said. "I'm glad you called. I might . . . I might have screwed something up."

"No. The worst that can happen isn't all that bad. I mean, really . . . if Maggie succeeds, that's when people are going to get hurt."

"I'm sorry. I said something to Loeb. Told him something. I thought it wouldn't matter at the time."

"You said something to Mr. Loeb?"

"No, moron. Stuart."

I shook my head, feeling a radical shortness of clarity. Still, this seemed hopeful. A problem with Little Loeb? Had she said something that pissed him off? Mentioned something that he reacted to in a way that revealed to her just how shallow, insipid . . . how worthless and incompetent the guy really was, despite his clothes, his haircuts, his shoes and high-powered connections? Had she made some kind of ultimatum in regards to that rich fiancé?

"And I think he's really pissed," she said. "At you."

"Don't worry about it. He can't get to me." A bit of bluster seemed appropriate. Definitely, it was time for a little of the old *Hey, look at me. Now look at him. Which one is it really, babe?* "It's not like I have anything to lose," I said, still pushing it. "Besides, who takes him seriously?"

A woman in a poncho with a backpack came down Navigation, talking on a cell phone.

"When I heard he'd sent you down there, it occurred to me how he might be getting back at you," she said. "Bent, I told him about . . . you know."

"No," I said. I didn't. I was clueless.

"That little thing. The hotel secret."

"Oh."

I sat still. Wind rattled some waxy leaves that overhung the gravel in the ABOGADOS Y MÁS parking lot, and it lifted the edges of the woman's yellow poncho.

Man.

I had never known Chloe to even admit to me that she remembered there being "that little thing . . . the hotel secret."

Now: it was on her mind. And Loeb, for some reason, had dropped in her estimation.

"That's none of his business. And if I'm asked, I'll just say I've never even been to a Super 8 Motel in Pasadena."

"What?"

I couldn't believe she was actually talking to me about this. "Certainly not two years ago on July 7."

"I mean Galveston. You're such an asshole. When you made him jump out of the window."

"Ah." I had, at some point, in some late-entry effort to impress her, fessed up to the gas-leak gaslighting.

"Shit. I've got to go," she said. "We'll talk tomorrow."

"Wait! You don't have to ever. . . ."

The line was dead.

My mouth open, I stared at the phone, glanced up in the rain to see the dark-hooded face of the woman in the poncho. Only, there was something wrong there. Then I noticed the highness of the cheekbones, the dark-tanned complexion. She had a blue-stained chin, like a five-o'clock shadow, and a long, long eyebrow across her entire forehead. That cell phone she'd talked into before she now held and looked at in that way people do when they are taking pictures. Which she was.

She was taking a picture of me.

I got out, stepped into the rain. "Hey!" But the guy took off, because it obviously was a guy. His long, muscular, hairy legs jutted out of the dress he had on under the rain suit. His flip-flop shoes smacked down into the puddles, the pink backpack slipped from side to side, most likely empty. I went after him as his powerful thighs came down and he turned, splashed across Navigation.

I had to wait for two cars to pass, then crossed, ran behind him through the rain along an uneven sidewalk for twenty yards, when—cat-like—he dodged towards the right, into some kind of recession between metal buildings. I got to that space in time to watch his arm disappear over an impossibly tall corrugated wall, then heard him land on the other side. The sound of his shoes flapped into the distance.

I came up to the wall, put my hands along its smooth, curved metal. It was at least twelve or fifteen feet high: straight up. I looked at its sharp top edge as the rain came at my eyes in lines from the darkened sky.

"*Give me my head shot of Eladio Trejo!*" But my voice was mostly drowned out by rain on metal and the tires of passing cars.

vii.

"I saw her an hour ago," Tony had said. "At her store on the ranch."

Getting to Maggie's ranch, or house, or witch emporium—depending on what you wanted to call it—wasn't particularly easy. The sun had nearly set by the time I made the 105 exit and had driven past the little town of Montgomery with its square of micro-businesses that, to all appearances, were completely boarded up. One had been a beauty supply store. Another sold consumer electronics. There was even, oddly enough, a closed-down Persian Rug Emporium. But there were no economic woes here that a massive freeway project—or even the promise of a massive freeway project—couldn't fix. Then, following the directions in Chloe's big yellow envelope, I made a right turn on a two-lane farm-to-market road that eventually became a much narrower two-lane with very little right of way, and I was nearly there. A wild turkey strolled along the verge in the gathering dusk. After a mile, a concrete bridge spanned a clear creek: indicated on the map of Maggie's property by a squiggle line, though nameless. I knew I must be approaching her haven—or coven? I was about to invade, unannounced, that place where she made peace with the years, the songbirds, the deer . . . the forces of darkness. I pulled off the road when I saw her ground-mounted business sign that glistened in the rain under its own electric lamp:

CAULDRON OF MAGIK
Conjurings. Tarot. Past Life Regression.
Future Life *Prog*ression.
Special Massage.
Major Credit Cards Accepted.

Two actual cauldrons hung from either end of the sign.

I ran the engine, kept the wipers going, and sat in the rainy gloom. I had Maggie's contact info—including her home number—somewhere in my summary packet, so I could call the ranch house. This would tell me whether she was there, plus warn her that I was coming besides. It would also serve as a useful test: it would allow me to hear her voice, put my weight on the beam, as it were, while it was still only a few feet off the ground. I could see if I could deal with the sound of her, if only over the phone. Then, maybe, I could ease into her actual presence without slipping into unconsciousness. But what was I going to tell her? And what about her strong desire to keep creatures so detestable as lawyers off of her sacred grounds? I glanced again at the list of services on her promotional billboard.

Chloe had wanted me to tell her about her Spanish-era exemption, but with all the balls presently juggled in the air concerning this case, I wasn't sure that was a good idea. Something on her sign made me think I might take a different approach and still learn something. I could come at her on the slant, and possibly even settle some things for myself.

It might work. Nothing else made any sense anyway.

I nibbled a Xanax and steered onto the winding gravel path that led through the trees to the witch's house.

Her ranch home/witch store resembled nothing so much as a rundown steakhouse, mainly because of its unfortunate log-cabin design. An ungated, contoured rock wall surrounded the house itself—a wall that would stop a tank. The whole compound—there was no better word for it—sat on a low rise near the ruins of an unboarded barn frame where chickens roosted. Also, and completely out of context, a wrecker truck was parked on her scrubby lawn. The MILLIONAIR-ESS FIGHTING PROGRESS seemed to have won that battle when it came to the wrecker: deflated tires that had sunk into the sod indicated several years of immobility. Once past the opening in the wall, the house itself was ratty as shit: paint flaked off the eaves and the broken balustrade on the rough-hewn country porch. What I assumed to be the big black truck she'd arrived in at the coffee shop was in the muddy, grassless yard, and behind it was a gooseneck trailer, its bed loaded with piles of random, half-dismantled large appliances—prepped for copper stripping, I assumed.

I was glad we weren't pursuing the nematode approach, as it would have taken a lot of convincing the Board of Transportation (or the press) that Maggie Leudecke had any interest at all in ecology. I worried at what might be floating in the narrow ditch that trickled down the hill from the debris-filled yard. Large, blue, trash-filled forty-gallon barrels stood upright against the side of the house, but most of the trash hadn't made it into them: there was plastic sheeting in rolls held together by weathered duct tape, odd lengths of narrow PVC, flattened cardboard boxes and tubes (from shipments of witch supplies?), a desk, and a case of little drawers—like mail slots—constructed from pale plywood, all warped from exposure to the damp. A few busted pallets, a couch, a broken workbench, and what looked to be the guts of a water heater didn't begin to complete the inventory.

Now her stated rationale—"It's mine"—seemed not the words of a greedy, privileged aristocrat so much as of an unhinged hoarder: one of those narrow minded, narrow-eyed, Gulf Coast swampland crackpots so common to the region. I definitely did not feel I was standing before the home of the enticing Siren-like force of nature I'd seen at Lumpy's and met at the coffee shop. I began to feel simultaneously more confident and more disgusted.

Or: was I in the wrong place? Had I accidentally stumbled upon some, as Tony Ruiz would say, "inbred cracker's" property adjoining Maggie's? Some guy with more dogs than teeth who had homesteaded in a confusing turnoff along her road? Was I about to be shot dead?

But when I got out of the car, I noticed two more cauldrons on the porch and between these a cottage door with HOURS OF OPERATION displayed on a hanging signboard. The place's business availability was shown prominently and at some length:

10 A.M.-5:00 P.M.
Sometimes OPEN as early as **8:00 or 9:00 A.M.** and
occasionally we CLOSE as late as **7 P.M.,**

> but not that often.
> This does not include **vacations, holidays**
> and **random times of "playing hokie"** in Mexico.
> Bringing your coven from a great distance?
> **Call** so we can accommodate.

This was followed by colorful rectangles that indicated, as had the sign on the road, that The Cauldron accepted all major credit cards. I noticed "hooky" had been misspelled, and above the door was a notice: ENCHANT CONJURINGS . . . which seemed a bit off, like a typo. Enchanted? Enchanting?

On the doorknob, there hung a simpler card on a string: CLOSED.

The doorbell was one of those mechanical twisting kinds. It was chancy. For one, definitely this was after business hours. When the door creaked open, Maggie stood before me in a jeans jacket, jeans, and her muddy boots. She seemed shorter than I remembered, but it was the first time I'd actually been around her while standing. I grinned.

"How many more lawyers do I have to deal with today?"

I reached out, very tentatively, and laughed. I shook her hand, and noticed again the toughness of her fingers.

"Well," I said, "Still standing."

She didn't seem to realize I was talking about myself, and looked around her porch and eaves. "I'm expecting it to fall over any day. But I don't care, Mr. Bent."

"Because it's yours." I nodded. I felt okay. A little hungry, maybe.

"Can I help you?"

"I know Tony—counselor Ruiz—was here. I don't think you have to pay any attention to him." I shrugged. "I mean about the ranch. He could be right, but . . . we can make sure there's no highways run through here—real or imaginary."

"Wonderful," she said, without emotion. She remained standing in the doorway, her back very straight, as I'd noticed on the news video. I also felt my instincts had been correct. From her coldness, I could tell there would be no opening for a discussion of the Treaty of Guadalupe Hidalgo.

"I'm here for another reason."

She moved her eyes along the side of the house. Was there someone else around? A boyfriend? A bodyguard? A protective demon?

"I'm here," I said, "about a woman."

She nodded. "You *are* having a problem. It's that skinny one with the high voice."

"You're good." I didn't bother to defend Chloe's voice or frame at the moment. Maggie probably held some ill feelings towards my paralegal because of the hearing. She probably had some left over for me as well. I went for broke. "No one can help me."

All of this seemed to satisfy her, and she turned to go inside, then indicated that I should follow, which I did, though I feared at any moment I would keel over in a blackout. She seemed distant: not the same Maggie Leudecke I'd met before . . . although, really, I hadn't met her, and didn't know her. I'd only had one view of her back as she comforted a wild animal, another nearly unconscious coffee shop encounter, then seen some news footage and collected a few-third person accounts.

Was meeting her in her inner lair the secret to dealing with her awesome powers?

Inside the house, I felt immediately creeped out. Perhaps it was that Maggie Leudecke would have to be a woman of substantial resources to allow strangers into her home in the middle of nowhere, in the middle of the night, and so I assumed a sniper hidden in a corner: someone who watched me through crosshairs at some remove.

Or, it might have just been the darkness of the interior: the flooring and paneling were stained a brown so deep it edged into blue. It took my eyes a moment to adjust to the gloom and make out that the space after the entryway—where most homes would have a living room—was instead decked out for retail, although in a jumbled, disorganized fashion. It was as if a bookstore had taken a jewelry store to a candle shop to assault it. In addition to the book-filled walls, glass cases held cups and saucers that displayed powdery substances: dried-looking lumps and roots. These were spiritual herbs, I supposed, as were probably the bundles of desiccated sticks tied together with colored string. Behind the counter, a display of hundreds of odd trinkets hung on chains, items I could only assume were sacred stones, or protective amulets. A ceramic owl glowered at me from a high shelf. It looked like a cookie jar, but—who could know its mysteries?

We didn't linger in this storefront, but settled on padded aluminum chairs at a dinette in her kitchen. It was complete with checkered oilcloth tablecloth, salt and pepper shakers in a silver basket, and even one of those vertical paper towel dispensers, the kind that made the handing around of napkins unnecessary. Cheso would have loved it. The light from a single bulb spilled yellow and warm into her iron sink. So far, the Leudecke ranch had presented as junkyard, gift shop, and austere rural home of the kind I'd often visited as a kid going to see the aunts and grandmas. From the kitchen, it was just another comfortable country house gone to seed, complete with the odor of mold.

I'd been in several homes of millionaires. This one was not like those.

"Your life is bad, isn't it?" she asked, when we'd settled.

"I wouldn't say that."

"Empty. You keep putting store in things that don't pay off."

"No pleasantries, then," I said. "You are about to sound like my therapist, I'm pretty sure. You think Chloe is another one of those losing enterprises."

"I don't know, but I know she wasn't all that into you at the coffee shop."

"You picked up on some . . . pervading influence?"

"No, I'm a chick," she said. She smirked, then considered a moment. "I remember her not keeping her cool very well at that hearing, but I found her to be very opened."

There it was again, like ENCHANT CONJURINGS above the door. *Opened?* How about *very open?*

"Is she nice to you?" Maggie asked. "Does she listen to you?"

"Well, you know," I said, and I crossed my legs and got comfortable. "That part's great." And at that moment, I felt it was. I wished Chloe were with me right then rather than this woman I couldn't pin down. "She really gets me. We talk about everything with each other."

"Oh."

"What? What's wrong with that?"

"Nothing, it's just that . . . you fool around a bit, don't you?"

"Define 'a bit.'"

"And you tell Chloe about these exploits?"

"Well . . . I hear about her dates, too, and. . . ."

"Do you have a cell phone?"

I looked around. Couldn't we get some Tarot cards, a crystal ball, a steamy pot boiling over a big fire? "This sounds more like interrogation than conjuring," I said.

"If this Chloe called you, called you right now, at this moment, while you were here talking to me, after driving all this way . . . and probably having lots of doubts over whether or not you even should talk to me. . . ."

"Reasonable doubts," I mumbled.

"If she called and told you she needed . . . I don't know. A cheeseburger. Or help changing a tire. Or a copy of *Anna Karenina*. What would you do?"

"You're saying, no matter what crazy shit she called and asked me to do, no matter how busy I was . . . would I drop everything and. . . . ?"

"That's the question."

I smiled.

"As I thought, Mr. Bent."

"Just Bent."

She frowned. "That's weird. But, see, it's hopeless. You'll never have her."

"We had an affair before."

"I bet."

"Why doesn't anybody buy that part?"

"Either way, you can't have an affair with her now . . . or ever."

I scanned the kitchen for evidence of New Age witchery, but found nothing beyond a box of pancake mix and a container of Pringles. "This is your professional prediction?"

"This is me telling you. You're in the friend zone."

"Come again?"

"You're her friend. You might be her friend for life,

even her highly valued friend, but she's never going to see you as . . . well. . . ."

"A man?"

"Thank you. Not going to happen. Or not again."

"But this is your business, right?" I leaned close, tried to act confidential. I considered all the twigs and powders in the display case we'd passed. "There must be some way."

"Mr. Bent, people think the craziest things about witches. There's nothing I can do to make Chloe love you."

"Love." I chewed on the word.

"Or make anyone else love you. Nor can I remove a rival. Like this Loeb."

I hadn't mentioned Loeb. "You're really good," I said, "or I'm really transparent."

"You're a jellyfish. At least you can't get rid of him with anything any sane person would want to try. Believe me. It'll turn back on you, and it won't be pretty. Love's got to be there in the first place for love to work."

"Profound."

She leaned back, stretched her arms as if tired from lifting heavy appliances in her yard. "Sorry."

"I'm not easily discouraged."

"And I like that about you, but trust me. If Chloe were dead, I might be able to put you in touch with her in the spirit realm." She snorted through her nose in a not-attractive manner. "But brother, there's no way I can get you in touch with her bootie from the friend zone."

I waved this off. It seemed odd that she hadn't offered me any coffee. Since when did anyone sit at one of these dinettes in a country house without coffee? "My request is simpler anyway."

"How's that?"

"July 7. Two summers ago. Your sign says 'past-life regression.'"

She looked at me as if she had caught me stealing from her garbage cans: more pitying than appalled. "You don't get it. Because of the intertwining, spiral nature of time, it would be easier . . . far easier to reconstruct a week from your childhood than any single day from last July."

"Two Julys back."

"It would be easier to let you look in on a past life you lived in the Middle Ages." She reached out and touched my hand with her right hand. The length of red ribbon was still tied to her wrist. "Go home to your wife, Mr. Bent. Or . . . just find somebody else. I mean, she's not all that."

I nodded, but wondered what she had in mind. Her hand was warm, yet nearly weightless. Again I had the sensation of fish bones. Or the whiskery legs of insects. I shuddered a little. "It may come to that, but . . . okay, the sign says 'hypnotism' then. I just want to be 'taken back.' Can that happen? I just want to go to that day, that afternoon. I want to revisit a certain hotel room. Where I did something wrong."

"Afternoon hotel room." She shook her head, but then smiled. A smiling Maggie Leudecke looked ten years younger than the dour, serious version, and her hand grew warmer on top of mine. She didn't remove it. "That sounds about right for your 'affair.' I doubt you did anything wrong. And if you did, it's not something you could fix then or now."

"If you can't do it, you can't do it." I made to rise. "I guess I'll see you . . . well, not really in court. There'll be other hearings." I slid my hand from under hers.

"You'll attend them?"

"Sorry about that. By the way, I was told I had to look for you in Mexico."

"Who told you that?"

"Doesn't matter. Good night, then." I wasn't certain, however, that I knew how to get out of the place.

"Mr. Bent." She rose with me, took my hand again, led me to a hallway. "You said July 7? Two years ago?" She thought a moment. "A Thursday, I believe. I'm almost certain I went waterskiing that day."

"How can you remember that? I had to reconstruct. . . ."

"She put her finger to her mouth. "I got ticketed for parking my truck off the road by Lake Somerville. I remember the date on the court summons."

"Waterskiing. Is that helpful for my case?"

She bit her lip. I noticed there was a mole on it,

either a flesh-colored rise or something she'd covered with makeup.

"We'll try a light trance."

"Really?"

"It'll be $40. A heavy trance is more like $90."

"Sure."

She stopped. "In advance, counselor."

viii.

I came down from her log cabin under a gridded trestle that crossed the porch gables. The rain had stopped, and some birds that had settled in to sleep in the dark treetops past the stone wall peeped like voice-mail alerts. Every step I took down the porch stairs seemed to drop the temperature of the air five degrees until I stood and shivered in the muddy, cluttered yard. I found my car in the darkness and got turned around in the walled enclosure, hummed to myself, and pretended to be cheerful. "She's not all that," Maggie had said.

But then, driving home, something happened. It made me huddle over the steering wheel as I turned onto 105. I nearly crouched down in the car seat, because it was big. It was dark and black, and definitely passed nearby. It was almost like I'd seen something wolfish in the rear-view mirror, red in the taillights. Or sensed that it followed the car, loped along behind me—its eyes bright, hunting. Only it was huge. I thought I was about to be covered by it, but then . . . it was gone. I pulled over, sat alongside the dark road a moment. A dirty white van went by, but nothing else. I threw the Elantra into gear.

I thought I'd better not let it get ahead of me.

Crazy. People shouldn't operate machinery after hypnotic trances.

The feeling was strong that I had to catch up to this thing. I rushed ahead, speeding. The suspension complained as the car hit the rising angles of the two-lane. I couldn't seem to slow down, pause, or take note of my surroundings: the closed-down venders and shops in the town (and speed trap) of Montgomery went past in a blur. For some reason, no sheriff stopped me. I wondered if Maggie Leudecke had cloaked me in invisibility.

If I'd been without a car, it would have been like running. I moved in the Elantra with everything I had . . . not to escape, but to catch up with that thing that had passed me by.

What was it?

At I-45, the looming parkway overpass, covered on its underside with black vines, graffiti, and thick air, swept by on my left below the moon—a giant single parenthesis of glowing crescent. I looked at the ribbed reinforcements of the road under each overpass, and at the thick, iron rods of the safety rails along the on-ramps—corrugated metal with nuts cinched tightly down on them that held the barriers to their squat wooden breakaway posts. Driving forward on the cracked on-ramp while looking around at rails, reinforcements, moons . . . it was precarious. I was just asking for some kind of wreck on the still-wet pavement. To drive home safely or to accordion the Elantra against a concrete column—the difference between these was a question of only the slightest positioning of the steering wheel.

The chasm between love and friendship was the difference, maybe, of a single gesture.

Whatever it was I chased, I didn't catch up to it.

At home, as on many nights, I sat in the empty living room of my house. My "people" were asleep by the time I pulled into the garage. I almost looked in on Henry. It was something I liked to do. I liked to check which pajamas he had on. The blue dolphins? The T-rex's? I especially liked to see him asleep on his back, the covers kicked away, his hands turned towards his own chest, the same way he waved, his mouth heart-shaped as he lightly snored. I would lean low just to make sure he breathed in, then wait to see that he breathed out, too. But I was too depressed to get off the sofa, so I didn't go upstairs, just breathed out myself—tried to exhale the day's tensions. I started in on my regular routine of watching TV programs in pajama bottoms while I drank heavily. Scotch. J&B. Why not have a few? I watched TV, tinkled the ice in my glass, sometimes touched my own arms or legs, thought about how those appendages, by all rights, should at that moment be somewhere in Mexico, maybe on a bus with chickens. I felt guilty and a little cheated to be missing out on the bus, really. On television, a flying saucer wobbled against a starred background, obviously suspended by thin filament thread. This bored me, so I went to the front window to stare at the long driveway that arched towards the tree line that hid the street from my house and vice versa. The pines were familiar now, but when Kelly and I had first moved in, they loomed overhead like fate.

Kelly.

Maybe an hour and who knows how many icy glasses of Scotch later, down on my hands and knees in my bedroom, I shuffled a stack of papers by the bed. Yes. Here. I found a letter from my friend who'd moved: the guy whose office I now occupied at D, K & L. Alan had written this letter to send me his new address, and new phone number, too. I found it! He wasn't a good friend—a rather surly type—but one of the few people at the firm I would actually speak to on a regular basis. He'd gone back to his home state seeking greener pastures.

"This," I said, holding the letter to the lamp, "allows me to pinpoint his position with total accuracy."

When I dialed, the number went on forever.

"Alan," I said. "I am the victim of a cheap trance."

"Shit." The voice sounded thick and distant. "It's three in the morning."

I remembered then that my not-so-good friend had moved to New Hampshire—that's why he'd sent me his new address, new phone number, too—and there was a one-hour time difference.

"Also, something passed me in the dark."

"I see."

"Something bad. And I was wondering what you were doing on July 7. Two years ago."

"Bent?"

"I just want to collect everyone's experiences. How they perceived the day. I want to form around myself a sort of aura."

"Bent, is that you?"

I was impressed that my good, good friend could tell it was me, and from such a great distance, too. Gosh, I loved that guy. Old Alan. Perhaps all was not lost. "So far,"

I said, "all I know is that it was a Thursday, and a witch went waterskiing."

He laughed for no discernible reason. Frivolous asshole.

Good Lord. Was I the only person concerned about the hotel, the affair, and the youthful paralegal? It seemed everyone else should trouble themselves with these matters as well.

So I tried carefully to explain to him how it had been no good. How everything had been just no good at all. I hadn't ever gone into anything you might call a trance. Oh, yeah, my arms felt light and tingly, but that was it. When I closed my eyes, I had the feeling I was leaned forward, though I knew for sure I sat perfectly upright. This couldn't constitute a trance.

"For one thing, I was preoccupied with the hypnotist," I said. "Her voice was so low, so sexy. It kept disturbing me. Like the way a fly might disturb you if you were trying to do a handstand. You know."

"No."

"Plus my shoulder has been killing me again. And she had a red ribbon on her wrist. What am I supposed to do with that? Then there was her candor: the thoughtful way she tried to save me money, like she knew money was a problem for me. Which it is."

It was true. Maggie had been thoughtful and reasonable, and promised nothing, but I'd also been painfully aware I would receive only the forty-dollar version—the two twenty-dollar bills I handed over to her perhaps from among those that had rested in Ngo Dinh Duc's beige envelope: my loan. I could expect a trance adequate enough maybe for quitting smoking or the reconstruction of a past life, but I wanted an entire afternoon. I wanted my afternoon with Chloe, and in detail—her tight jeans, her baseball cap turned backwards, the air conditioning in the room that didn't work—so I could watch events, pay attention, keep an eye on her, keep an eye on how and if she was pleased and by what. I would not remove my gaze from her until I was sure I knew what happened. And, of course, maybe I'd done everything right. Maybe there was something wrong with her.

This, also, would be good to know.

As I went back into the almost trance, I'd seen—or had

the feeling of seeing—that there was a crescent moon on July 7. Also, I recalled that this was the day when hundreds were killed in a Japanese air disaster.

Terrific. For this I'd paid forty dollars and dropped into a state of arm-tingling forward-tippiness? I could have gone to a library and looked up those things. I could have found this info about July 7 in an old newspaper. But what had Chloe said on the telephone? What had she smelled like? What socks had I worn?

"What about the socks, Alan? What about the girl?"

"What socks?"

"And it's not like I won't get the fucking dink his nephew's visa. And then I started to remember things that have nothing to do with July 7, at all. I started remembering what I had forgotten . . . about Kelly, and what happened to me back when I . . . had some trouble. And these eyebrows are following me. Plus . . . a canoe drowned. Alan . . . Alan, I must find my way into the past."

"Bent?"

"In fact, I'm just now thinking . . . that here it is only two. Two in the morning. And there, you say it's already three. . . ."

"Bent, my advice to you is the same as all of my advice to you has always been, and always will be. You say there's a girl?"

"An hour difference," I insisted. "So it's sort of like I'm talking to you from the past already. Isn't that right?"

"Stay away from the girl. Stay away from that hypnotist and the other one, too."

"But, if it is two here, and three there, aren't I, then, already a voice from the past?"

"Women are nasty, brutish, and short. And don't go back to that therapist of yours, either. Seriously? Taking advice from the enemy?"

"I feel so lost."

"Women are unpredictable, unreliable, and a breeding ground for harmful bacteria."

"Never mind, then."

He yawned. "I'm pretty sure that you are not literally a voice from the past."

Wrong again. I slapped at my pajama bottoms. "Again, again, again."

"Bent? Excuse my asking, but have you lost your fucking mind?"

"She was thoughtful enough to just charge me fifty more for the full treatment. I mean, she's thoughtful, Alan. And has that ribbon."

With the ninety-dollar trance, we'd gotten a little further. The familiar arm tingling began. Maggie's voice guided me as if from a distance, like a radio program that drifted in and out from a background of static. She told me to concentrate on the seventh. I remembered that there was actually a mild earthquake on that day, in Los Angeles. Maggie told me that the earthquake could have important consequences for our goal, given the intertwining, spiral nature of time—though I didn't really understand the connection. Yes, and the plane crash in Japan, which happened on that day. Then—like a breakthrough—I saw it. I saw my breakfast, the breakfast I ate at The Kettle on Taft Street on the morning of the seventh.

"Where is Chloe?" Maggie's voice was soft, as if spoken through gauze.

"I don't know."

"Keep looking."

"I see two eggs. Two turkey sausage patties, coffee. . . ."

"Look for the girl!"

"Don't yell at me while I'm in deep trance!"

"You're right, you're right." Her disembodied voice continued. "You are dropping away. You are dropping away. . . ."

I knew where I was dropping—right into that memory that I both did and did not want to deal with. "Where's the puppy?" I asked Kelly one night. I'd come home late, as usual. "Henry's puppy? Where is it?"

She hadn't slept in several days. Her answer was a little too long in coming. "A good home."

This was . . . what . . . seven or eight years before the earthquake, the Japanese plane crash, and the Pasadena hotel. How the hell did you dial in the time on this trance thing, anyway? I saw Kelly, then: an image of her a few days later, going for the knife drawer. When I slammed that shut, she found the other knife on the counter. I heard myself ask her what the fuck she was doing. I watched myself wrestle with her, try to call 911 at the same time. I had to with one hand attempt to reach some help on the cell phone, but also to grab her around the waist, keep her out of the kitchen, away from cutlery, while Henry stood nearby and howled.

I believe I shouted at this point: "No!" When I looked around, Maggie was rubbing my cheeks.

"Go in there," she said. "Take off your clothes."

"I don't feel like. . . ."

"Do it."

In an adjacent room, I wrapped myself in a sheet and lay face down on a table, which had a hole provided for my head. The room smelled of lemon. Under the table, Maggie's carpet was gold-colored. When she came in, she switched on a boom box that sat on a crate in the corner. Some kind of strumming guitar instrumental played, and she rubbed lemony oil into her palms to warm it to begin what I supposed to be the "special massage." Was this included in the ninety dollars? I watched the gold carpet and decided not to worry about it.

Although I was naked under the sheet and her hands were firm, knowledgeable, and seemed much less leathery with the oil, I wasn't the least bit aroused by this treatment, not even when she rubbed my "footsies." (That was what she called them. A professional, offhand demeanor, I supposed, developed for massage purposes.) When Maggie rubbed my feet, I thought for a moment she'd break through the skin and actually start to caress the bones inside. There was a certain amount of arousal, yes, when she stroked my forehead. Only then.

Odd.

She moved me like a doll, tugged me upright to walk in my sheet to another room in this labyrinth of the steakhouse-style mansion, where she propped me on a sofa with cushions under my arms and waved a chain before me. A sliver of stone—like flint—swung at its end without turning, as if the flat face of the stone were trained to align itself with my own face. "For the rhythm," she said. "That's all. Nothing spooky about it."

It was the least spooky thing I'd seen in the whole place.

Still, I couldn't say any of this actually put me in a trance. Yes, no question, we had a conversation. We had a very deep conversation. We discussed the old days. The good old days. Back when I'd been somebody and gotten things done. Back when Chloe had loved me.

"She never loved you, Mr. Bent," said Maggie.

"Just Bent. Will the trance be still deeper than this?"

"Good Lord."

"I thought about trying another witch, but that didn't seem right."

"Fucker," she said. "Listen." Her low voice pushed me forward for a while, then trailed behind like toppled trees. There was music in the background—a guitar instrumental, I thought it was. Wait: I'd already had that thought. A flint sliver at the end of its very pale chain swept forwards and backwards. . . .

. . . I might have fallen asleep.

What was the use? Nobody knew. Nobody understood, or cared. If there had been a plane crash, they would have noticed. Or an earthquake. My problems amounted to nothing for these people, and this seemed incredibly short-sighted of them. What were they spending their time worrying about if it were not Chloe and how I could force her to love me? Instead, maddeningly, I got Kelly, waiting for me in the lobby of Cypress Pines.

Fucking Cypress Pines.

I'd been so elated to drive over there. I was set to meet with Kelly, give her some paperwork, and wait with her until a cab came to take her to the bus station. It was exhilarating. I was uncertain, still, about how I could get Henry looked after, but the dark, dark future also seemed a world of possibilities. It was a time of new beginnings. I'd put together an exciting package in a transparent plastic bag with all I needed for the trip to the hospital: divorce papers, a ballpoint for signing them (she could keep that for her journey), the bus ticket, a cashier's check for when she got to North Carolina, cab fare, plus even a little more cash. It was a freedom bag, and I looked at its contents fondly on the passenger seat of the car as I drove to Cypress Pines.

I may not be an ideal husband. Possibly. I may not really

be marriage material at all. And I'd spent too much time away from home, sought out excuses to stay away. I'm sure Kelly had been stressed, but I'd tried to make my time with her and Henry quality time, or, at least, when I couldn't be with them, I worried about it. That is, I did my best to keep her happy.

The wife of my youth.

I suppose if a person takes a knife to themselves in front of their husband and son, they're not all that happy.

I found her in the lobby, already released by her doctors and a court order. She was in jeans, straw hat, and T-shirt—traveling clothes—and had a sheaf of papers on her lap, her little suitcase at her feet. I think she'd taken that suitcase on our honeymoon to San Antonio.

At Cypress Pines, she'd asked more than once why she was in jail, and until the medication leveled her out, I kept having to try to convince her she wasn't. From the windows overlooking the courtyard, true, the place looked grim, and the uniformed guard posted at the metal detector by the reception desk didn't do much to alter this impression. The lobby itself, however, was Early American: magazines stacked on end tables, standing lamps, and a throw rug.

"Looky, I'm free," she said, and held up her court order. "And here—a whole report on me. I can read about how fucked up I am on the bus."

"It's just an eighteen-hour ride."

She laughed. She put a hand behind her head, held her own neck as she tossed her hair in that way she had. "Bent," she said. "I want to come home." It was the same request she'd made in the emergency room, only calm now. There was the promise of reason, hard work, compromise in the statement, rather than just pain and urgency.

"See your folks awhile. It's home, too."

I handed over the transparent sandwich bag and she examined its contents. "This isn't for a temporary trip."

"It's Ziploc, not Samsonite. We've discussed this." I took back the bag, pulled it open, and removed the cash so she could put it safely in her purse. "More of this coming. Texas is a community property state, so you'll have more checks, but I'll need to provide for Henry, so. . . ."

"They all said, 'Never marry a lawyer.' Did I listen?" She handed back the divorce pages, unsigned.

"Nope." I returned them, placed them on her lap.

"Seriously. I'm sick, Bent. A disease. Right? If I had cancer or leukemia, would you send me away?"

"I'm not sending you away." I had my own personal understanding of this, somehow, but had difficulty putting this understanding into convincing terms. "You're just going away. For a while. We agreed."

"If it was cancer, would you make me something like this?" She held up the bag again.

Being what I am, I had to think about it. Jeez. Would I abandon a cancerous wife? In the past I never had much use for such husbands, either in the abstract or those I had actually met. (There are more of them in the legal profession than you might think.)

On the other hand, cancer sucks. Best to cut it out. Right? I went back and forth on the question while the security guard flipped the pages of a *Newsweek* that had a picture of a turbaned terrorist on the cover.

"Not fair," I told her.

Her mistake was to zero in on the package. *Would you make me something like this?* Her attack on the travel kit I'd gone to all that trouble to put together only made me recall how I'd felt driving to the hospital, seeing it there in the passenger seat, knowing I'd soon be free. It had reminded me of how I could sleep in my bed, or in Henry's bed with him—he'd taken a fancy to having me there since she'd been gone, or I imagined he had such a fancy—and how I could feel safe in my house and not have to worry about a blade in the night. I wouldn't have to worry about coming home to chaos. Or . . . just where the fuck was the puppy, anyway?

I wasn't ready to give up that happy feeling of seeing the bag in the passenger seat, so I took it from her, unzipped its ziplock again, and dug out the ballpoint pen so she could sign.

"Probably just some electron jumped a shell in the brain," she said. "Right? A chemical misfire."

"Probably, but we decided."

"Yeah." She took up the pen, steadied the documents

on her leg, and signed without reading. She handed them back. "I love you."

"I love you, too," I said, but I could hear how the words were practiced, worn. They were said the way I might say to a waiter: "I'll have the fish."

"I always will," she said.

"I'll send you copies."

We stood, hugged. It was a bad, friend-like hug. The cab arrived and waited at the curb. She looked around and out into the severe, bricked courtyard.

"You should check in here sometime, Bent."

"Probably."

She held up the papers she'd been reading when I came in. "You might find your report interesting," she said, and she picked up her little suitcase. "And a deep disappointment."

"I still don't remember anything about the afternoon," I said to Maggie Leudecke.

"No." She seemed distant. She held her leathery fingers to her lips, pulled her mouth down at the corners.

"An interesting experience," I said.

"Alan," I said into the phone. "Cypress Pines. Ninety dollars and that's all I have."

"Let me get this straight," he said. "Cheap trance. Stolen photo. Bad marriage. Marisel on your case. This . . . paralegal thinks you're a piece of shit, obviously."

"Oh yeah."

"Left stalker in Austin. Eminent domain case snatched out of your hands."

"Out of my hands!" I said with indignation. "My case!" I must have, in some semi-conscious way, blabbed to him about everything going on in my life. "Why are people making all my decisions for me?"

He yawned again. "Yes, snatched out of your completely incompetent hands . . . let's see. You're being followed by a superhuman wall jumper, and a one-legged guy in Mexico is waiting to get a package from you. Am I missing anything?"

I tried to tick it all off in my mind. I felt he was

overlooking some important aspect of the situation. Oh. Right.

"*Burning car.* Oh, and trying to make my way back in time."

"Go to Mexico," Alan said. "You have a ticket. Go."

"They'd like that. They'd love it."

I could almost hear him shrug over the line. "Yes. They always do. Nancy's wondering what I'm up to. I need to get back to bed. Go to San Judas."

"Shit. You heard of it, too?"

"With the one-way tunnel? And the heroin? Christ, Bent. Everybody knows San Judas Tadeo. It's not even real Mexico. Place for tourists, artists, and other substance abusers."

"I hate those losing losers who go to places like that," I said. I shook my head violently. For some reason, I wished those people who'd gone to the "sweat lodge" were around, so I could fight them. Maggie included. Back before I even knew she was Maggie. "Damn losers."

"And you have a ticket there. Just do what they want. Who cares what it is?"

"That's just admitting . . . and Maggie's not there!"

"Yes, finally!" he said with some exaggeration. "Good. Admit it. Going where she isn't is the best possible answer! This is a woman, Bent."

"But. . . ."

"And this is you. Is there anything good that can come if you keep interacting with her? Go and lay low, where they can't get to you. Because, Bent. . . ."

"Yes?"

"You always let them get to you. Goddammit, protect yourself for once and let some of this happen without you, or you're just going to get sucked in."

I frowned. This sounded a lot like what I'd been hearing from many sources. "Maybe."

"Absolutely, and this time . . . you really could be ruined, man. You, and your kid. How you going to raise Little H if they start crapping on you at D, K & L? The Leudeckes are big players, so just leave. Stay out of the way if they want you out of the way so bad. Come back when it's blown over. Escape."

PRETTY ENOUGH FOR YOU—219

"And warn the others."

"What? I gotta go, man."

He rang off.

Jerk.

I thought about it awhile. I made some late-night Aeroméxico reservation calls. I arranged for the transfer fee since I'd missed the scheduled flight, and scribbled out a note for the "family" that I planned to leave on the breakfast bar:

GONE TO MEXICO

That seemed a bit terse, so I augmented it some:

GONE TO MEXICO.
DO NOT OPEN DOOR TO ASIANS

I went into the kitchen to tape it to the "Americana" well-pump faucet, but there was something already there: a sheet of paper with writing on it hanging from the fixture. Shit—had I left a message without remembering? And what was all this other stuff? Rectangular images covered the white countertop of the white kitchen island: photographs. They were 8 ½ by 11 glossies, by the look of them, and they were some terrible pictures, too, of extremely low quality, obviously taken by someone with few skills at framing or composition. Each was grainy and high-contrast with very little detail in either the light or dark areas. I had to get up pretty close to them to make them out at all, and only after a few moments realized they were of me. There was one, for instance, of me bending over a stool in a crowded bar of some kind, standing very close to a figure in a giant hat. There was another of me from behind, carrying something rather large and cumbersome into a lighted doorway—above it square block letters: LADIES.

Me.

I grabbed them up. The major points of the evening at Club Some, Club Emo's, and the Montrose apartment were all there. Which had been . . . what . . . just the night before for Christ's sake. Amy Pramalamabam and I on the cushion, her . . . or his . . . leg thrown over mine at Emo's. Amy and I getting into the Elantra. A rather romantic pose in a poorly lighted setting, with Amy's face against my chest—which would have been more romantic had I not known it was taken milliseconds before an episode of vomit.

Me and Amy going into apartment 11.

I snatched the paper from the Americana well-pump faucet and scanned it quickly as I went up the stairs, moved from room to room. Marisel's room: empty. Henry's as well. I stood in the hallway reading, not bothering to check on Cheso and Alexandria because I knew they'd be gone, too.

Bent:

These are from someone. I do not know. He looks after me. You are a worthless and ungracious. I would tell you to your face if you were ever home how much worthless, but this is it. My lawyer—you have to have a lawyer to fight a lawyer is what I always think—says this is enough but there is more also, so it is over, and he says Texas is a community poverty state, but I will have Henry with me, so. . . .

I crumpled the paper. He looks after you? The motherfucker with the single eyebrow had been sent by Marisel? I saw that I still had the GONE TO MEXICO note as well, so crumpled it, too, and stood awhile and looked at the wads of paper in my hands. Marisel's note had gone on to tell me to expect a visit from this lawyer, and that something or other would be for the best. I tried to swallow but couldn't work up the saliva.

What to do?

I stomped around the house. Marisel did not respond on her cell number. Did she have anywhere to go? Her tennis partner's house? Sarah? Where the fuck was that bitch's number? First in Marisel's room, then back in the minimalist kitchen, I searched obvious places for where my wife might have kept phone numbers, but found nothing.

Really? Now? Now, when I was so busy? When I had to get away from all the work I was supposed to do at the firm?

There was absolutely no fucking way, especially the

part about Henry, and I would make it stop . . . wouldn't I? Or could I?

How to deal with this on top of everything else?

I could hear Alan's words as if he were still on the phone. "Go and lay low, where they can't get to you."

Soon, I was locking up the Elantra at the Park 'N Fly and climbing on a shuttle van with my duffle bag. The driver, a big black girl just a little too cheerful for the predawn hours, played hip-hop—loud—all the way to the international terminal, while I dialed Marisel over and over. Visit from her lawyer, my ass. If he wanted to serve me papers in San Judas Tadeo he was free to try. I could at least buy some time.

When I rode up the escalator to the departure gates, my cell phone made its annoying vibrating clang and I snatched it to my mouth.

"You cunt."

"And good morning to you," said a male voice. "Want to know a good way to die?"

I imagined hard-planed cheekbones, powerful legs under a skirt, and a unibrow. "*Who are you? What do you want? She's not getting away with this.*" I must have yelled these things pretty loud, because a man in a hunting vest going down on the opposite escalator glanced over, concerned.

"Bent? Bent, it's me. You going to Mexico?"

Ruiz. "What the hell, Tony. It's 6 a.m."

"Listen, I found out something. About this Trejo character. The dead one."

"Oh." I couldn't imagine anyone or anything I wanted less to hear about at that moment than the drowned surveyor.

"She knows him. Or knew him. It's like he was her boyfriend or something."

"She?" In my mind, I connected Marisel and Eladio Trejo in a secret liaison. I should have had that bitch followed by a detective.

"Maggie, man," he said. "Who the hell else is a 'she' in this thing? In San Judas. That's where he's from, Bent."

"What? It's not a good time, Tony."

"A good way to die is to get all up alongside our girl, man. She's fatal. I don't have the details, but if you still want to help the fine people of Bold Springs, you might go down there on the Kohlhoeffer dime and look into it, eh? Can you do that for me, Bent?"

I frowned, deeply. I watched my reflection in some Plexiglas panels that I levitated past on the long escalator. When I rose to the next floor, beyond the magazine stands and coffee wagons, I could see the noses of parked airliners that loomed through large glass windows overlooking the tarmac. I felt old, transparent, and dematerialized into odd angles.

"Seriously," he begged. "Is there any way?"

I was about to lose my son. I had to wonder whether he might not truly be better off without me. But that was impossible: he couldn't be. But maybe he could. And this, after a day where I'd allowed myself to be punted aside by Loeb, someone I considered barely competent, even compared to me. Plus, I couldn't be too certain that when I got back from Mexico, I'd still be on my equity track "in time," or that I'd have an office, or insurance, or ways to pay to keep Henry in his special school, while I also paid child support to that immigrant bitch. Community *poverty* state: she'd accidentally gotten that part of her note correct. But no. I was his dad. His biological progenitor. No court would go for that. Would it? I needed family law help, and fast, because none of this could be allowed to happen; yet I couldn't see a way forward, either. Except. . . .

If I could climb out of it . . . if I could somehow turn things around, even starting, as I was, from the bottom of such a deep trench, that would be something, wouldn't it?

I stepped off the escalator. "What you're saying is: if I can find out why Trejo is dead, that would be kind of impressive."

"Well, sure, okay. Yes."

"People would notice it, is what you're saying."

"I'm not sure where you're going with this. Oh, but yeah. Chicks dig that kind of thing, Bent, no question."

I stood for a moment and looked out the windows at the noses of the giant planes. I had so many chicks who needed to start digging me, and soon.

"You know what?" I said as I moved towards my gate. "You talked me into it."

Ninety minutes later, the sun pissed out an unhealthy pink-yellow wash across a landscape stretched far below: territory that was either Texas or already Mexico, I had no idea. It was, to all appearances, just some broken, unwanted terrain, wrinkled like an electron microscope photograph of a rice grain. In the lurching 727, I brought the first bourbon of the morning to my lips. "Prepare to have your death avenged, motherfucker," I said, and saluted Eladio Trejo. I sipped, took only a little, nodded.

Down, down, as straight down as I could look out of the plastic window, cloudy bodies of water, like sightless eyes, gaped up at me, and they did not blink.

Part IV.

The Patron of Lost Causes

i.

For the three days I spent in San Judas, life took on a pattern. For three days, I did the same good, pointless things, in a kind of consistent rotation.

Every afternoon, I walked, for example, to the plaza to use the payphone in front of the bank. My many attempts to raise Marisel on her phone came to nothing. When I could connect, the line would ring and ring and never go to voice mail. Bitch! I thought of Amy's cell as it rocked back and forth, sinking deeper into the apartment swimming pool. That evening was going to cost me, alright, and what had it gotten me? I needed to change my ways, no question, and vowed to do so. And where was Henry? I didn't seriously think he'd be in any danger with my extended Manila family, but not knowing made me feel empty and sad.

Giving up, I would eventually call work to see if Ruth would let me talk to Chloe, or let me talk to Loeb. I even tried to get her to say something to me other than "Await contact from the one-legged guy."

"Ruth, I have asked about the one-legged guy, and he has not been heard from in a while. I can also tell you: he is not well thought of."

"Sooner or later he'll show up and take you to Ms. Leudecke. That's all I've got."

I knew Maggie probably would not surface. "May I talk to Chloe?"

"She's in a meeting and asked not to be disturbed."

"Ruth, she's a paralegal. Go disturb her and put her on the line."

"I misspoke. She's with Mr. Loeb. *He* asked not to be disturbed."

"So? It's Loeb."

"Sorry."

Then I would call Tony Ruiz.

"I have asked about Eladio Trejo. He is also not well thought of."

"Also?"

"Sorry. I'm looking for somebody else down here, too. One-legged guy. You know, the usual." I shook my head.

"He'd been romancing her, right? Trejo, I mean, and Maggie."

"Well, no. As far as I can tell, he'd been going out with some friend of hers. Or is." I tried to explain to him what I'd noticed. Many people I spoke to in town, the expatriate community especially, knew Eladio, and many also said to stay away from him. "But that's the thing. They talk about him in the present tense. Like he's alive."

Tony pondered it. "It's possible they don't know. That's a pretty isolated chicken coop of a town down there. Or are you saying there's somebody walking around San Judas? Some other Eladio?"

"Or was the drowned corpse in Texas even him?"

"Oh, shit. This is not helpful." He whistled. "So who was up here working for the Dutch? And what was he doing on her property? And why was he murdered?"

"I'm sure you mean to ask why he became the victim of an unfortunate canoe accident, but I'll see what I can find in my continuing investigation. I promise."

My "investigation"—the actions I'd actually done—consisted of, in good faith, walking for three straight mornings to Maggie's "house" on Calle Aparecido, where I rattled the structure's stucco walls as I knocked on the thin planks of the front door. It was not really, as Loeb had called it, a hacienda: more a shanty/slum version of a condo, attached to other "houses" on each side, one of which somebody had either turned into a barn or was allowing his donkey the living room to hang out in. Of course, she did not answer. A hundred feet down the hill was the saloon door entrance to the Bar El Infierno, an expatriate watering hole, which was where I repaired after checking Maggie's house to await contact by the mysterious Yucatán Bob. This person was also, day after day, a no-show.

"Oh," said Javier, the El Infierno's bartender and basically my main source of information when it came to *Messieurs* Bob and Trejo: "You don't want to meet Yucatán B. That's a bad man."

Others agreed. At the El Infierno, Maggie—and her "caretaker"—were known quantities, if divisive figures. Every North American I spoke to, and there were dozens, either knew and loved, or knew and hated, Maggie Leudecke. None, however, had seen her for months. Oddly, they also seemed genuinely sorry she wasn't around, and this included the ones—nearly all men, nearly all crippled in some way (walking sticks, crutches, not-terribly-hygienic-looking eye patches)—who despised her. They also seemed generally broke, and constantly begged drinks off of me, which I, in general, supplied. Oh, expense accounts. None loosened their tongues enough to tell me anything valuable about Maggie, however, or Bob for that matter.

I stopped myself from asking if they dropped into a coma every time she opened her mouth. But what did it matter? I knew where she was, or figured I did: seated at her kitchen dinette north of Houston. She was probably grinding eye of newt into a fine powder in a ceramic bowl with a pestle made of unicorn horn. My being in San Judas Tadeo was useless, which was the thing I had to admit, of course. It was what Alan had been talking about.

I was useless. I was safely stashed out of the way.

But there was my mission for Tony Ruiz, so I had also asked about Eladio Trejo.

"Him you definitely want to stay away from," said Javier. "A bad man."

"*Exacto.* A very bad man," said Javier. It was from him, and some of the expatriates, that I learned he'd been "dating" a friend of Maggie's. In fact, as soon as I began to ask about the expired (if he *was* expired) land surveyor, interested patrons of the El Infierno began to call me aside. Then, after a series of frustrating exchanges that made absolutely no sense whatsoever but added to my bar tab, I would learn nothing. I began to suspect I was being scammed. My experience with a guy named Paul (dirty eye bandage) can stand in for most of my interactions with all of them.

I met Paul on my first day in town. After I bought him the drink he asked me to buy him, he said, "I hear you're looking for Eladio Trejo."

This wasn't exactly true, but seemed a good start. "What do you know about him?"

"Never heard of him."

"Okay. Then why do you. . . ."

"But I can get you what you want from him, without him knowing."

"That's really confusing."

"If you want to know more, I'll need something from you. Obviously."

"Obviously." I looked to Javier for help, but he studiously ignored me. "Want me to buy you another drink?"

"Yes."

I bought him another drink. "Is there something else?"

Paul leaned back and hooked his thumbs in his black vest. He was a painter, so naturally he wore a black vest. "Oh, yes. There's something else."

I thought about the possibilities. "Money?"

"Of course, money."

What were expense accounts for? "How much would you like?"

"Exactly. How much?"

"Look, help me out a little here." Since Paul was one of those who spoke of Trejo as if he were still alive, I tried a different approach. "How much to take me to him?"

"First the word."

"I'm sorry?"

"The word for what you want. Tell me the word, and I'll take you to Eladio."

"Who you don't know."

"Never heard of him."

I had conversations similar to this with someone named Stephen (crutches and foot injury), and someone else named Mohammed (walking stick). I would always make it as far as "the word," then hit a wall. It was as if information about Trejo were somehow password-protected.

"How about you, Javier? Can you tell me about Eladio Trejo?"

"I also never heard of him."

"You just told me he's dating a friend of Maggie's."

"Yes."

"And I should stay away from him."

"A *bad* man."

Finally, upon entering the El Infierno on Tuesday, I found Paul alone, leaning on his elbows at a table under a drooping potted fern. He was pretty much wasted, impressively so for 11 a.m.

"Alright," I said. "What are you having?"

"Alcohol."

"Can't be a little more specific?"

He wasn't meeting my eye that morning, not even with his one good one. "I dispute that I am having anything specific."

"Paul's celebrating," said Javier behind the bar. "He finished a painting today."

"Congratulations."

"He never finishes shit," said the bartender. "So it's quite an achievement."

"Want to buy it?" Paul asked.

I considered it. "I'll buy it if you'll tell me the word."

"Oh, man."

"Because I'm really getting nowhere without the word."

He groaned and put his head on the table. "Shit, man. Can't you just buy it for some other reason? I'm broke."

I told Javier to get the guy some alcohol . . . of some non-specific kind. Javier laughed. "Nobody ever buys his paintings."

"Okay, how about you just tell me about Trejo, and you've got a sale." I wondered what manner of creepy picture I'd purchased that nobody else wanted anything to do with. I also wondered how big it was, and where I might discard it before heading back to Houston.

"Shhhh." Paul seemed nearly as paranoid as he did plastered. "Don't say the name if you won't say the word."

Javier brought the guy a clear liquid in a small glass.

"I've thought it over," I tried, "and have decided it's time. I'll give you the word."

"Really?"

"Oh, yeah."

"Me? Not Stephen? Not Mohammed?" He eyed the room with suspicion. "You're not playing me?"

"I don't play."

He sipped some of the clear liquid, shook away some cobwebs, and smiled. "Nice."

I still had no clue what he was talking about, but . . . what the hell? "Here we go, then." I thought about it. "Canoe."

Paul stared blankly with his one eye. His cheek began to quiver. He looked like his feelings were really hurt.

"Okay. How about 'canoe accident'?"

He began to register panic.

"Fine, never mind canoes. How about: 'DeVries?' Or 'DeVries Construction.' That's two words."

He rose with a start, pointed his finger at me. "You need to watch your shit and not start any more trouble."

"I just. . . ."

"We're both in danger here, as you know."

I looked around the El Infierno. "I'm not in any danger, and. . . ."

He was gone.

I moved to the bar. "Maybe I should just go to the police and ask them about Bob and Trejo."

"Are you crazy? You don't want to do that."

"Listen, is there something going on here, Javier, that you're not telling me?"

"Not telling you about what?"

But I had a feeling he was probably right about the police, although as far as I could tell, local law enforcement consisted of two fat guys who drove pointlessly through the streets in a patrol car and another skinnier type, who sat by the open door of the *policía* office on the square, situated most of the day in an open doorframe where everyone could see his epaulettes. Given my luck with police in general, it could easily prove counterproductive to approach them. I could only

hope that with my questions to Javier, Paul, and the others—
with nearly the entire expatriate community that frequented
El Infierno eavesdropping on me—maybe the word of my
"investigation" might get out.

Sure enough, it did.

After I spent the warm, middle portion of each day at
the bar, I would stroll to the main square by the parochial
church, away from that part of San Judas people called the
Aparecido, which (according to the guidebook I bought to
replace the guidebook that was stolen when my clothes were
stolen) was the hangout of painters, gallery owners, sculptors,
and other losers: it was the neighborhood where artists, writers,
and those Javier labeled "vampires" all lived. ("The ones
who only come at night," he explained.) I would trek to the
plaza a little buzzed, walk down the hillside along the more
commercial Calle Reforma, a narrow street with a pebbly spine
raised in its middle. At first, I would get all the way to the plaza
and wait under the awning of the Hotel Emperador for the
rain to quit—it always rained by the time I got there, and I
would always forget to bring the umbrella (which I'd bought
to replace the umbrella that had been stolen) before making
my pointless payphone calls ("One legged-guy. Await contact"
from Ruth, and: "Good work, Bent. Keep on it" from Ruiz,
and no answer at all—not a peep—from Marisel), then I would
lift a bottle of beer from the ice barrel cart on the *jardín*, pay the
señora, and head to the gazebo to listen to the awful orchestra
awhile. But as the three days wore on, the afternoon rains came
earlier and earlier, until finally, on the Tuesday I made Paul so
inexplicably upset, I walked out of the bar into a downpour.

I ran out of El Infierno and past a steamy, boiling hot
dog stand that smelled like the death of the galaxy. Its metal
sides sizzled under the big drops. The word *EXQUISITOS*
had been stenciled on its side in thick letters. The hot dog
vendor that day lay under it—the way someone would who
was changing crankcase oil, but obviously he sought protection
from the elements, his hat pulled low over his face. He was
not somebody I would have ever noticed, except now I was
jumpy and felt "in danger." I searched for tall unibrowed men
at every corner, and considered as well the possibility that I

would run into some second, phantom Eladio Trejo who still walked the earth in this bizarre parallel universe. Some kids, two boys with scraped legs, came towards me down a side alley, like myself running in the rain. They threw a tennis ball at each other. I suspected a small, handheld bomb, or that one of the boys would pull a knife and slit my throat as he jogged past. When the ball bounced off the cobblestones, it spun out Saturn rings. They splashed by me onto the Calle Reforma without incident.

The road turned muddy. Fallen raindrops bubbled into impossibly round, brown spheres when they hit the dirt, like perfect bearings made of turd. I turned down the Calle Mesones, *slippity slidey* in my definitely-not-made-for-running-on-muddy-cobblestone Florsheims, and lowered my head into my jacket. On apartment balconies overhead, nobody bothered to bring clothes off the lines. It rained every afternoon at some point or another: all part of the San Judas rinse cycle. A concrete pipe crooked overhead, like a finger with swollen joints, and shot a water jet into the street where I passed under it, getting splattered, since I judged it wrong and it was late afternoon so I was a little drunk and unsteady. I was also running low on my prescriptions, though I understood I could walk into any *farmacia* and just ask for them by name.

That hardly seemed sporting.

So, anyway, on that Tuesday, I got soaked, and the cold water dribbled down inside my shirt as I ran, miserable, yet I still couldn't help think about being there with Chloe. Misery loves company, after all, and in my experience, continually asking *What the fuck are we doing here?* is so much better than asking *What the fuck am I doing here?*—especially when asking someone you love. Besides which, Chloe, I'm sure, would see the good in it. She would enjoy the stores (VENDO QUESO, LA FIEBRE CAFÉ, LA CLINICA FACIAL), the little bakery, the tortilla factory from which a rhythmic mechanical *clack* rang out all day long. There was, at the bottom of the hill, of all things, a shoemaker. Today he stood inside his front door, out of the weather, and talked with a neighbor while he swished his homemade flyswatter: a leather heel spliced to the end of a thick, twisted wire.

It was just the kind of flyswatter Chloe would absolutely *love*. At least, that cheery Chloe that I created and kept in my mind: she'd possibly love the flyswatter for sure. The shoemaker, now that I noticed it, resembled the panhandler who had nearly belted her one through the car window when she'd passed over my dollar to him. He followed me with his dark eyes.

Everybody was starting to look suspicious.

Near the cathedral, I got to an open space where the rain was damn coming down, and there was no point trying to stay dry. The wind through the hills sounded like a jet airplane, total black overhead, but on the horizon, a green-blue strip of light appeared. The wind was cold, and there, lower down the hill, the barking dogs started nipping at me, but I knew they were bluffing after the second day. Dogs are so easy to understand, especially compared to millionaire witches, drunk expatriate painters, and dead Mexican land surveyors. I thought, not for the first time, about a dog for Henry. I'd remained wary of replacing the one Kelly had "disappeared," but maybe it was time. It would be something for him to take care of, and interact with. I knew Marisel's common objections would only come up again. "You're never here. I'll have to take care of it," and so on. Like taking care of a dog is such a big deal, and. . . .

Oh. Maybe she wouldn't be around to take care of it. Maybe Henry wouldn't be there to enjoy it either.

Unless.

I would get something on Eladio Trejo. I would return home, reconstruct my family, reconstruct my relationship with my paralegal. I would get my son a dog.

Under the eaves of the Plaza Emperador, I finally found cover, stood, and dripped for a few moments over barrels planted with prickly pear, mesquite, and some kind of miniature banzai saguaro. The *calle* was a river of mud.

I went into the lobby to wait out the rain, sat on one of the most uncomfortable hotel lobby sofas I'd encountered in my life—it seemed to be made of knobbed branches upholstered with worn towels—but I didn't want to ruin one of the better cowhide-variety lounges under the portrait of vaqueros at sunset between the two big-racked deer heads. I sat and listened to a child pick out a beginner's version of "Some Day My Prince Will Come" on the Emperador's baby grand.

I must have dropped off for a while into a beer, pill, and frustration haze. I fell into a jerkily choreographed dream— more like a musing—of my father, and his secretary, and her coming to me at his funeral. "I loved him, Harrison. I loved him so much." Except she had never done that, or said that. She'd already left for Florida by the time he keeled over from a heart attack. (I was, at the time he died—yes, believe it—at a violin lesson. Old days, old days.)

Occasionally, I cracked open an eye, rustled the newspaper I'd picked up and placed on my lap, and pretended to read. I didn't think anyone would bother a gringo at the Hotel Emperador, soaked through and wearing an orange-striped guayabera shirt under his jacket or no.

"Some Day My Prince Will Come" lurched and echoed in the tiled room. I remembered being surprised at finding expatriate bars, CLINICA FACIALS, and baby grand pianos in San Judas, which had just seemed so remote on arrival. Already my troubles getting there were beginning to draw back into a distant, nearly mythological time: some pre-San-Judas eon that included the chaos of the Distrito Federal airport; my belief that fifty dollars was too much to pay for a cab ride to a bus station in the northern part of the city; my paying it anyway; and my now very firm belief that a bus station in the northern part of Mexico City was no place to turn one's back on a duffle bag, even for an instant.

"*Dónde está mi* . . . uhm, duffle bag?" I asked those standing around me. I also asked a ticket vendor, as well as a couple of customers at a nearby newsstand, but without result or response. I might have asked about *el lápiz de mi padre* while I was at it.

But I'd transferred my pain killers and muscle relaxants to my jacket pocket, and so felt kind of lucky and self-contained. Fuck clothes (and guidebooks, and umbrellas): I kept going.

Rusted pedestrian bridges, smog-stained concrete panels, damp markets where stooped women clung to net bags and packages—all of these shuttled in quick succession past the windows of the bus as we reeled out of the capital. No chickens came for the ride. It took most of an afternoon to navigate away from the city, and at dusk, uplifted debris and treacherous stones replaced shanties and business districts in the bus's headlights. From outside came the smell of something organic mixed with diesel, and then all the other aromas I remembered from the portion of my youth I'd misspent in this country, before I began misspending my adulthood in Europe. There was the aromatic hybrid smell of raw sewage and machine oil mixed with (I thought) bug spray. I tasted the air like a connoisseur of the atmosphere (but was still pissed about the duffle bag, the clothes, guidebook, and umbrella). I picked up on kerosene, the rich manure of horses, and cattle, rotted fruit . . . the Chanel of a lady who sat two rows ahead of me with a cardboard box on her lap labeled *Limones*, although there was no smell of limes. The box turned out to be full of compact discs, one of which she gave the driver in exchange for the ride when she got off the bus. And I smelled sweat. Stale sweat.

Oh, that was me.

At a refuel place where we stopped at midnight, I had a beer and walked out back where this shirtless kid jumped on top of an angry-looking horse under the hard light of a single bulb hanging from a tree. He looped a long rope in his hand as the thing spun under him, more or less out of control. We left before I found out whether he was killed or not. Feeling gamey, I bought a guayabera shirt off a lady with a rack of them in front of another bus station, the orange horizontal stripes probably not a good choice. I doused my armpits in the station restroom. The face in the metal mirror had black rings under its eyes, an anvil jaw, and scary gray teeth. Farther north the next morning, a ghost-white burro came to my bus window and stared me down with Chinese eyes—*nice to see ya*—while behind him, a covered gazebo blinked pale lights like the unrepaired fluorescent outside my office door. At some point I opened my eyes long enough to see a tractor cutting across dry soil alongside a faraway hill, pulling a long, red dust twist. Some of the trucks and taxis going past had the personalized look of backyard experiments.

Every mile of the way I thought: the key is Eladio. Eladio is the key.

I wanted it to end, but it didn't. In Matehuala, I burned several empty hours on the square, then transferred to another vehicle—more like a school bus than a Greyhound—that took its passengers climbing up into the passes of the Sierra Tadeo. The engine choked and gargled in the thin air on the steeper grades. Cliffsides rose around us. Now and then clusters of ruins appeared to either side, and a grandmother across the aisle kept asking "*La Luz?*" but a little boy beside her told her "*No, no todavía.*" At switchbacks I could see into deep chasms where darkness had settled, but at the far horizon, the desert glowed like a white subpoena.

Without my guidebook, I had no idea where we were.

We had the headlights on by the time of the tunnel entrance—two days total in transit since Houston. I could make out an inverted black grimace under an arch in the side of a mountain. Before it and to the right hulked the nearly deserted town of La Luz, where the boy and the granny disembarked. The only illumination came from above the tunnel's opening—a streetlamp—and a man appeared from this cavernous hole. He carried a radio handset to the window of our bus for a momentary conversation with the driver. Then we were off.

It was a very narrow tunnel. Through the open window I could smell rock dampness a few inches away. The space in the mountain seemed just about bus-sized, not a dust-speck more. A line of flickering overhead fluorescents leaked a green glow onto the passage, and I'm not sure how we squeezed under some of the dangling fixtures. I noticed that my hands clenched deep impressions into the seat cushion, probably because the path through the mountain, for some reason, had not been excavated in a straight line. Kinks and elbow-curves brought boulders looming, and several times it looked like we'd reached the end. Something obviously had shifted in the mountain and sealed away the entrance to San Judas Tadeo forever. The narrow roadway always swerved at the last moment, however, into more blind open tunnel ahead. I could see the driver's nostrils flare in dashboard lights reflected off the big windshield, and hear the tires on the pavement *shooshing* like seashell waves.

When it seemed the walls were only centimeters from removing layers of bus paint, the overhead lamps vanished and we emerged in blackness, like another tunnel only darker, longer. Our headlights chewed over rough mud with no sign of road or track, until finally the bus shuddered to a halt at a low tin building under another streetlamp on an iron frame.

I got out and stretched my legs, back, and fingers. It wasn't at all obvious where I should go from there—although one of San Judas's dozen or so taxis would soon arrive to take me up the hill to my hotel in the Aparecido district. But for a few moments, I felt the strange breeze, looked into the clouded, obscured sky so oppressive it seemed to sag just overhead, like the lobby ceiling of an abandoned theater. The lamp over the shed buzzed, and there was a bumping bass-line from a faraway radio. My cell phone showed zero bars.

It was very much like traveling a long, exhausting way to arrive nowhere.

I awoke on the uncomfortable lobby sofa, shot up with a start, but hopefully not with a snort. When I walked out of the Emperador, the rain had slacked, but it was starting to come on dusk. On the square I got my bottle of beer, then claimed a space on one of the empty, short sandstone benches with hearts carved on them across from the cathedral. I watched people cleaning up with mops and brooms, pushing the water off the cobblestones around the gazebo and setting up folding chairs for the terrible orchestra. They looked young, well dressed.

A police car—that is, the police car—pulled up on the curb before me. It was a green Nissan, indistinguishable from the green taxis that crawled up and down the hill save for the bank of lights on top and a loudspeaker set square in the center of the hood. I'd already heard them making the rounds in the mornings, broadcasting "*Atención, atención*" about something I couldn't catch with my poor Spanish. Sure enough, the fat officers I'd noticed before—I thought of one as "The Chin" and the other as "No Neck" for reasons too obvious to go into—both unfolded themselves from the car. No Neck advanced first. He looked me over in a way I didn't like. Both fingered their night sticks. The Chin, as if he had clicked to an afterthought, stopped, walked backwards heavily without taking his eyes off of me, leaned into the patrol car, and reached to activate the flashing lights. Then, at my side appeared a spindly kid, also in uniform, including those epaulettes so visible through the *policía* doorway—with shiny boots, besides. Oh, man. He'd probably walked over from the station, which was also on the square beside the cathedral.

"Good evening, Señor Bent," said this uniformed kid.

Trouble. I made a determination to myself to be civil and accommodating. After all, I was a guest in a foreign country. No taunting, Bent. No taunting.

"You didn't bring enough men to take me alive," I said.

"It's the whole force!" said the kid. His English sounded North American—maybe a hint of the San Fernando Valley. "And who said we need you alive?"

"I know my rights. I'm an attorney."

He pushed his hat higher on his forehead. "Marguerite Leudecke's attorney, from Houston. Which means you probably know, really, you don't have any rights. Right?"

"Eh." He had me there.

The kid was either in charge—the much spiffier uniform seemed to indicate yes, his extreme youth no—or else he was the only one who spoke English. He definitely sounded like a Californian: maybe a USC grad. "So, we hear you're looking to buy heroin."

I was thrown a bit. I wiped at the condensation on my beer bottle with a finger. Looking to buy heroin was one of the few things I wasn't doing in Mexico. It was obviously a trick, but I decided to play it safe and cooperate to the extent of my abilities.

"Prove it, asshole."

The kid laughed. "It's not a joke, Señor Bent."

"Still, if you have no evidence. . . ."

"If we have no evidence we'll arrest you anyway, but see, it's like this: you're looking for drug dealers, so you must be looking for drugs."

"I'm looking for drug dealers?"

"Right."

"Name seven."

He chuckled again. "I have to tell you: you're just what we expected."

Fuck, were they talking about me behind my back everywhere?

"I'll just name two. They're two of the biggies, though. I mean, you know, for our modest region: Roberto and Eladio Trejo."

"Roberto who? And Eladio . . . he's dead."

I hadn't really meant to say that, but it obviously brought the kid up short. He said something to the larger officers so quickly in Spanish I couldn't catch it at all, and No Neck and The Chin stopped slapping their palms with their wooden sticks, shot glances at each other.

The three were silent for a moment. "Dead how?" asked the kid.

"Drowned," I should have said. Simple as that. Instead I went with: "I don't see how that's any of your business."

He nodded. "You better come with us."

"I'm staying right here, and I don't know any Roberto Trejo."

He took me up under an arm, gently. I didn't much want to leave: the terrible orchestra was about to start, after all. But I was thinking jail. I was thinking prison. Latin American prison. My whole scheme of self-redemption seemed suddenly ridiculous, even childish. I had no idea what was going on, and now the police would put me at hard labor in a desert fortress far away, where I would be fed seven beans a day until I starved.

"The one with no leg," said the kid as he tugged at me. "Maybe you know him as Yucatán Bob? And you might want to get off the street before the people who killed him take a crack at you."

I rose, then. "Yucatán Bob's dead?"

"Well, gee, I don't see how that's any of your business. Oh, and leave the beer here." He pointed at the bottle while he waved at the wagon across the square. "The señora will want the deposit."

ii.

When I left the *policía* several hours later, against the wall of the cathedral somebody was projecting, of all things, a PowerPoint presentation. A towering image of a child darkened suddenly, then changed into a snapshot of one of the green taxicabs, beneath it a phone number to call for service. I remembered I had my own call to make—I was half an hour late—so went and found the payphone (unoccupied, luckily) and sat on the rickety stool. I dropped in enough coins to reach the international operator. The firm had neglected to provide me with a telephone card. Oversight or sabotage, it had made it difficult to communicate with the office, and to successfully connect with work via an international collect call depended much on ancient Aztec phone gods and their capricious moods. This evening, they smiled.

"Oh," Ruth said after she accepted my charges. "You."

"If you're going to tell me to wait for the one-legged guy, don't bother."

"Bent?" It was a man's voice.

My God, she'd actually put me through to somebody.

"I'm not happy about all this," the voice said. "At all."

"Kebba?"

It was, indeed, the African prince. "They are doing this woman wrong, Bent, and it is your fault."

"What's happened?"

"This will not be an effective path to the top for her."

"Chloe? What are you talking about?"

"Listen. Are you listening to me?"

It was difficult to hear him, and I leaned forward on the stool in a near panic. I strained, as if attempting to get my ear closer to Houston. The terrible orchestra on the square had been playing awhile, and presently unwound a tumbling, atonal, arhythmic version of the "Love Theme" from *Dr. Zhivago* (I think).

"I can't really talk. Look, Bent." His voice lowered. "As you know, something here is not right."

"Well, hell yes, I know that, nothing is right anywhere. But, tell me what's going on, because the fact is I'm not even sure . . . that our client is here. And I completely need to leave."

"The Leudeckes," he said. "That is a crazy case for you, man."

"Shit, yes! I fear for my life."

"Oh, well," he sounded preoccupied.

"No, I mean it! Look, I'm coming back."

"She wants you to call her, Bent, but tonight."

Really? Chloe wanted me to call her? "What? Why?"

"I think she's in trouble with Loeb, and needs your help."

"Well, tell her . . . she can't really screw anything up. I think the Leudeckes are liquidating all their real estate assets anyway, and. . . ."

"No. Not that. It's got nothing to do with the stupid Leudeckes, man!"

I was clueless. Nothing to do with the Leudeckes, or heroin, or murder? In that case, under the circumstances, I had difficulty imagining Chloe's problems reaching the threshold of "trouble." She was in trouble with Loeb? She'd said something that caused him, finally, to blow his stack? So? Dump the asshole.

"Call back here at nine. And Bent."

"Yes."

"If she marries Loeb, I will blame you."

"*What!*"

"Nine o'clock," Kebba said, and then he was gone.

I rubbed the stubble along my chin and jaw, shook my head a few times.

The M-word.

I was torn between leaving immediately for Texas and waiting the two hours or so to make the call. But buses traveled out of San Judas, through the long, long tunnel, only in the mornings—much as they traveled into the town only late in the afternoon and evening. Still, I could go and pack. I could be ready to move. Plus, I might very well be safer off the street, if what the police chief had told me was true. As I wandered back onto the square, I noticed that the crowd had grown, and I began to catch on that there were dancers near the bank and under the lights of the cathedral who moved to the music. They weren't just colorfully dressed, but elaborately costumed. Or else my mind was playing tricks. I was still stunned, first by the possibility that Chloe might actually marry that fucking Loeb, but maybe even more by the possibility that she wanted to talk to me after everything that had happened. Oh, and that about Yucatán Bob and my life being in grave danger—that, too.

The officers had taken me to the *policía* station, sat me in front of the one desk in the one chair positioned squarely before it. Beneath the chair was a large stain roughly resembling the state of Georgia. As far as I could tell, the station consisted of that desk, that chair, a cell to one side big enough, possibly, for two people—its window a deep socket set into the thick wall, barred with grid-like wire—and, beside the cell door, a poster advertising a chamber music festival from several years past. The kid—who did turn out to be in charge, a Lieutenant Montez—sat behind the desk and folded his arms while I explained as best I could what I was doing in San Judas, how it had nothing whatsoever to do with contraband of any kind, and how Eladio Trejo had been found in Maggie Leudecke's stock tank.

"It's weird, is the thing," he said. "See, Yucatán Bob was also drowned. Kinda."

"How do you get drowned 'kinda'?" I really hadn't meant to take these local yokels seriously. On the other hand, I realized how many days it had been since I'd had a real conversation with anyone, the language barrier being such a hindrance, and the expatriate drunks at El Infierno being so incomprehensible. "I mean, I don't actually know, uhm . . . Bob."

"Mr. Bent, you've satisfactorily explained, *kinda*, why you've been asking about Eladio—although how it will impress a woman I'm still fuzzy about." In fact, Montez had clarified a few things for me, such as how by making an obvious nuisance of myself in the town and asking after Eladio Trejo but never uttering the magic "H-word," I had, no doubt, unwittingly performed a convincing impersonation of a narc: specifically an American DEA agent. "Who notoriously avoid charges of entrapment by making the other guy mention drugs first while they do their secret recordings. No wonder you're driving those losers up there as crazy as rats in a coffee can. But why have you been asking about Roberto?"

"I've never met him, but I'm supposed to be waiting for him. He's the caretaker. I was told he was the caretaker to the Leudecke properties."

Montez shook his head. "You can stop waiting. Thing is, we found him only this morning, in his bathtub. In fact, he's still there."

"You left him?"

"Pretty much."

"Wow, you guys are really on top of shit down here, aren't you?"

Montez grinned. The guy loved me. "See, he's been missing for like a month, and nobody knew where he was. I can tell you, the heroin-imbibing community has been in kind of a tizzy."

"Oh, no."

"So this morning we checked out his studio in the Aparecido."

"And found him in the tub."

"Covered in plaster."

"What?"

Montez raised his hand, flattened, to eye level. "Up to the brim. We had to chisel down into it for a couple hours, then, sure enough. There's Bob."

"Holy shit."

"Right? The stuff he used in his sculpture work, you know?" Montez pulled down his cap: he seemed continually unsatisfied with the way it rode on his head. "So, unfortunately, we haven't quite got him out yet. His fake leg was sitting up on top of the plaster, or we might not have even thought to bust into it. Or not thought about it for a while."

"Like I said, I thought he was a caretaker, not a drug dealer."

Montez shrugged. "He was a multitasker, true. He actually made sculptures, even. Art. Which is somewhat rare for artists around here, especially you gringos, of course."

"Of course."

"I think that's the only reason Señorita Leudecke had anything to do with him. Only, I'm not sure he was doing much caretaking, because the Leudeckes are selling out."

"What? Maggie's leaving the hacienda?"

Montez shrugged. "There are agents showing it to rich foreigners right now. I think San Judas Tadeo is about to be rid of that whole clan, and I won't miss them."

How could I have not been told all of this? "And you say Eladio is . . . was Roberto's brother?"

He nodded. "Eladio has lived in the States a long time, but comes occasionally with Señorita Leudecke's old friend. Janet? Jane?" He looked at the two hulking officers who were leaning against the stone wall. No Neck with his hands thrust unprofessionally deep into his pockets shrugged first, then The Chin followed suit.

"Some plain name like that," said Montez. "They'd visit Señorita Leudecke. You know, and sell heroin on the side."

"Look." I leaned closer to the desk but they'd placed me too far away to rest my elbows, and I for some reason feared moving the chair from the center of the ugly, Georgia-shaped stain. "At home, there's some talk that Eladio . . . well, that his demise wasn't an accident. People think he was killed to discourage some road construction."

"Some *what?*" Montez laughed again. "How much crazy shit were these guys into?"

"I'm not even sure any more."

"Who wants to discourage road construction?"

"It's a long story." I tried to explain the media hullaballoo over the Road to Nowhere and eminent domain. "But why do you think his brother was . . . is in the tub?"

"If I knew, Señor Bent," he shook his head, "I probably couldn't say. I mean, with all of this excitement, my first instinct should be to confiscate your passport and tell you not to leave town." He raised his hands before I could start my protest. "But the Leudeckes are important around here. So my second instinct is to tell you to get the hell out, and fast, and this really is for your own good. I mean, it could be whoever did this has no interest in you at all."

"But it could be. . . ."

"Totally. Besides, if you're waiting for Roberto Trejo to show up and take you someplace. . . ."

I definitely did not want to have anything to do with people who took plaster baths.

So I needed to get all my new information back to the firm, and felt it was a good idea to fill in Tony Ruiz, too. On the other hand, I wasn't totally sure about Tony, who was technically working against my client's interests. How did Trejo's drug connections with the now plaster-cast Bob figure into his working for DeVries Construction and being in Maggie's tank? My head ached. And my conversation with Kebba had definitely thrown me off. I decided not to call Tony yet—maybe when I got back to Mexico City—and just headed for my hotel to, at least, get ready to leave.

Something like the theme to *Star Wars* began to accelerate in tempo from the bandstand. It must have been movie night on the plaza. The dance had definitely attained a crescendo of crazy I didn't need, as, like I said, many of the citizens had crowded the square in costume for some reason, and the disguises started to make me nervous. I already didn't know who the fuck anybody was, or who among all these unknown persons might want me deader than shit, and now they were wearing masks?

As I got to the street, I saw that the dance participants were also mostly drunk: many had to hold their rubber gorilla and donkey heads onto their heads as they spun around, unbalanced. A bunch of these animal faces—with damn spooky eyes, nearly all of them (the sort of eyes those moms have who put their kids in trunks and drive into lakes)—a whole latex zoo of these faces was out there, tottering above the shoulders of women in evening gowns and the tuxedo jackets of men. A few of the blowsy Renaissance ladies turned out to be, on closer inspection, men also—their pitted faces rouged around mustaches and beards. I thought of the "woman" with the poncho on Navigation Street who could leap twelve foot walls.

Oh, great.

I turned towards the Reforma to go back up the hill to pack, because that was definitely what I'd tell Chloe tonight on the phone when I called in at nine. *I'll be there, babe.* Except she wouldn't want me calling her "babe." I tried some other phrases in my mind, but after I paralleled the dancers a half block or so, I got a little more sleepy and chilled—still wet from that earlier downpour. I kept expecting to see Maggie Leudecke, for one thing, or—drowsy as I was, this might not seem so loopy as it sounds—someone in a Maggie Leudecke mask, because she seemed to have acquired some local fame, after all. Or local infamy. The Leudeckes wouldn't be missed, according to Montez. Hell. How many of them were down here, besides Maggie?

How many of them were there, period?

I'd come a long way to do God knows what, totally unprepared.

In front of the gazebo, the crowd really milled now. Maybe I should have that beer I didn't finish before? The screeches of groups of kids were starting to disrupt the grating rhythms of the orchestra. On a grassy rise alongside the bench where I'd originally been sitting, a half-dozen boys, all in gaudy wrestler masks, played at some kind of kung-fu battle. They jerked like robots, oblivious to the music (which was pretty easy to be oblivious to) and the dancing revelers, too (much harder to ignore, but I guessed the kids were used to such displays). I sat back down on my same carved limestone bench next to the rowdy boys playing at violence and tried to gather my thoughts.

Marry Loeb?

Drowned in plaster?

Marry Loeb?

On the grassy knoll, one larger kid—misplaced, really, among the much younger ones—never seemed to be out of the action. His wrestler mask was gold lamé, brighter than the others, and he glared through its oriental eye-slits. This boy, simply and impressively, rejected the possibility of being the victim of attack. He refused to fall in slow motion to the grass with a grimace of fatality.

On the square a child—or possibly a midget?—dressed in white shirt and tie and wearing a mask I recognized as that sour-faced new ultra-conservative *Presidente de la Republica* . . . this little figure rubbed the chest of a pantomime horse. No, it was a pantomime bull. Nearby, a nearly seven-foot-tall dragon swung its tail made from rolled newspapers and helped to arrange three dancing "ladies" into a human pyramid: all of them showing their bloomers to the crowd. When they'd accomplished this, their strong arms never trembling, the dragon pushed them over into a hairy, petticoated, shouting heap, and ran for it. Another dancer had come as a tourist: he raised a camera the size of a crate to his eye constantly. His shirt, unfortunately, was one of the guayabera variety, with horizontal orange stripes.

Ha, ha.

In front of me, the battling kung-fu boys mouthed sounds of heavy impact, then sank into grass, careened towards a low concrete wall, and sometimes approached my own stone bench. I held out a palm to cushion one young, bony shoulder. It was odd to be touching one of the humans in this place, even a kid. I couldn't tell if all this craziness was refreshing or just bringing on an imbalance in my thinking, but I leaned towards the latter. Beyond the children, the pantomime bull kicked and bellowed with the tiny *Presidente*. A cowboy drew plastic guns—they were plastic, right?—and aimed at the hem of a ghost. Long rows of dancers joined, formed columns, rolled across the bricks to the music, spread out like limbs, and a short fireworks tower erupted into light and spark, but not much noise.

Beside me, the larger crime fighter got brought down finally by two smaller boys who snuck up behind him and dragged him to the ground. The big kid was kind of a bully, but I was pulling for him. The two round-faced youngsters could have been twins. The big kid howled and got up quick, brushed off some grass. He yanked the gold mask from his face so it deflated like gaping skin. "*No juego*," he said, disgusted. He sulked, but the twins tackled him again around the knees, slapped at his large legs with fake karate blows. Then the big kid turned on them, kicked one in the groin with the tip of his shoe.

The tiny boy stood—stunned for seconds before he thought to grab himself—and so the bully, like a scientist who'd made a remarkable discovery, kicked the other one in the same way. Both of them doubled over, their mouths round like car stereo speakers in their wrestler's masks. They called out:

"*MAAAA-MAAAAA.*"

You think it didn't surprise me to realize I was holding that big kid's white collar, staring into his sweaty face? You think I wasn't stunned when I said: "What do you think you're doing?" and tightened my grip on the little guy? I said: "They were just playing."

A man in a gray sports coat with his hands crossed behind him turned away and walked through the crowd in a manner I understood. He was trying to get away from me and the embarrassment I had created for myself. Other heads bobbed at the outskirts of the square, craned to get a better look: rows of black eyes turned towards me, along with their wrinkled brows, the sweat across their cheeks yellow under the scooplights of the cathedral. All of them watched me.

The twins, sobbing, plunged into the crowd. They looked scared. Possibly, I figured, scared of me. I was kind of glad their *maamaa* hadn't shown up after all, but I was left holding this stunned kid by his damp shirt, and I pushed through the folds of my Spanish, then tried to think how to tell him not to kick harmless children in the nuts. I actually thought I did have the vocabulary for that, but couldn't thread it together. There was a whole row of young men, teenagers, now looking at me, and they all smiled shit-eating grins.

I shook the kid, but just a little. I kind of rattled his shirt. "They were just playing," I said. And: "Where are your parents, anyway?" The kid held his mask and tried to look away, his eyes swollen. I knew that look. I could feel it coming over my own face. My own cheeks grew warm and capillary. I knew I was doing something damn wrong. Why else would everybody be staring?

When I let go of his shirt I smoothed it some. I flicked

some grass and lint off his shoulder. There. No harm. And "No" I said in a way that might have sounded directed at him, but probably it was something I was telling myself. As in: no more getting into shit, go home and help Chloe and stay away from drug dealers, and so on, but sure enough that pantomime bull gave me the eye. I think it kind of frowned, too. The music had stopped. The orchestra ground to a halt right in the middle of "There's A Place for Us" from *Romeo and Juliet*. A tall and mindless-looking Queen Isabella type with bushy eyebrows fluttered his or her fan. The costumed dancers pressed against one of the cathedral buttresses, the whole crowd coming to see me, spilling into the dance area of the courtyard. On the cathedral wall, the PowerPoint show was still going: a campfire . . . then a water tower . . . then the dark shadow of a man in a hat, who crossed in front of the projector, blocking the picture, and I moved, shouldered past a couple of guys seated on a low concrete wall, jumped a terrace to the plaza's second level. I don't think I used the steps. I wasn't running away, exactly, but it was a bit like not wanting to be bothered by anyone at the office, so: grab up something—a file, a package, some law books. Pretend you're on your way somewhere. I had, by hanging around, now done exactly what Lieutenant Montez had advised against: drawn attention to myself. And what kind of attention?

Who knew?

I went under some general's statue—passed pretty close to the tail of the upreared horse he was pointing his sword from—and looked around to locate the corner that would lead me up the hill to where all the annoying gringos, like myself, stayed in safe hotels.

"Señor!"

It was a woman's wail from behind me but I didn't want to deal with it. I passed a hand over my hair. The fabric of my shirt was sharp and cool in the place where the rain had gone down my back.

She can't marry Loeb! Emergency. Stand aside!

"Señor!" And then this woman trotted up, blocked my way to the sidewalk. She turned out to be an aged señora, followed by a widening triangle of children and others—

onlookers. A tall, snake-eyed teenager with tight black pants tromped up close behind her to whisper in her ear.

I told them I *busco*ed the Calle Aparecido, *por favor*.

But they didn't give me directions as far as I could tell. The old woman poked me in the chest. I couldn't follow any of what she said . . . I mean, nothing, which happens when I get flustered. My Spanish, which is poor, just goes sometimes, and the harder I tried to understand, the less chance I had. I looked around to see if anybody could clarify.

"Mi hijo," she started saying then. *"Mi hijo."* But surely this old woman had to be a grandmother, not a mother. Her gray hair swept back like wings and the deep creases of her cheeks shot arrows into her twist of mouth, and for a second there, I didn't know if I was looking at an old woman or a mask of an old woman, or a mask of my first wife, Kelly, as she would look were she a cadaver buried several years but come back to life: Kelly as she'd look if she clawed her way out of the grave a century from now to ask one last time if she could come home with me.

A knot of people then caught up with me under the tail of the bronze horse. The orchestra looked out over its raised platform, and masked characters arrived at the statue to point and berate. Dracula waved a pale hand, his rubber vampire mouth immobile, but garbled words flying. The cardboard and newspaper dragon skipped, clapped its hands. The dragon reminded me of someone I couldn't place. There was no way I could keep up with the chatter. I couldn't think of how to say "kick," or even "fight," and "fight" was an easy one I knew from watching boxing on cable. Maybe I should make a break towards the Emperador across the street. But then the tall, snake-eyed teen in the black pants dropped a familiar arm around the little shit-bully whose shirt I'd grabbed. *"Mi hijo,"* the woman kept saying. Her eyes were shockingly pale in the dark plaza. The cave hole of her mouth showed rows of black teeth—like oily rail ties sunk back in a mineshaft.

A yellow mini-bus stopped at the corner and then all the people in the damn bus started looking over at me, too.

So . . . fuck this, I said to myself, and stepped through them all, made the sidewalk, started up the hill, but Snake Boy, this teen with the tight pants, with the faint mustache, with the arm that had been draped over the bully-kid, he plucked at my jacket from behind. I was a foot taller than this guy and swept at him with an arm, but mainly wanted him to leave me alone. Then footfalls of all these people crossed the street, their shoes slapping the stonework like applause.

I got past an intersection, but that was it. It was full-on dark then, away from the plaza, the lamps, fireworks, all gone, and, oh, shit, there was a whole load of them, suddenly, young teens: some who'd stood behind me at the dance, others who seemed to have energized out of the bricks of the street. They were all young men in boots and jeans. They had lean jaws. Their heads tilted back, they came like they were cautious, but not cautious enough to stop coming, and in some dark pocket off the street, they fell on me like the ocean, and I flailed with my arms.

And, true, they weren't really hurting me so much. At first. I could pass it off as a kind of joke, albeit one I didn't understand. I said: "Stop it!" and laughed. I said, "*No juego.*"

Then a boot heel in the tangle speared my shin, a glancing blow but *ouch*. And so maybe this was really something and I was fucked, and. . . . and then I thought about, oh shit, the poor heroin-selling, one-legged sculptor, Yucatán Bob, encased in plaster, and a scary claustrophobic wave washed over me as my assailants pressed closer.

I screamed: *"Policía!"*

Where were they? Where was bullet headed No Neck, with his scratched nightstick and evil eye? Where was The Chin, and that Montez kid?

I had this feeling they were all nearby and ignoring me.

Another boot point hooked behind my knee and I fell under the leaning weight of them. My head cracked on the cobbles in the gutter, and I breathed in a street smell as damp as a cellar. The Calle Mesones was upside down, lit from below like a Frankenstein movie. Faces appeared in the bright doors of a liquor store and some place called the Tienda Dolores, and faces appeared above the swinging saloon slats of El Gato Negro. The guy in the dragon costume came by. Was the whole town coming to beat me up because I yelled at a youngster, or were they, more specifically, some enemies of the Trejo brothers? Or, hell, some friends of the Trejo brothers? Either way, it could only mean shit for me, and I couldn't explain why I was there.

These boys, they pulled at my left arm, separated it with purpose from the rest of my body, and a heel settled onto my left palm, too, until I felt like I was holding a friend's foot, about to give him a boost. There were too many legs in my face to see. A knee in my chest held me down; someone else pinned my other arm. Down there with my head in the street, I heard the insect click of boot-leather on rock and dirt, then the stroke of a wet palm across my cheek.

Then the boot point levered down, twisted, forced my fingers into the cobblestones, and I felt something give, loosen . . . and depart. . . .

I yelled.

My watch, motherfuckers!

That was when I heard the scorching sound. There was a snapping, like a whip, and soon somebody else screamed with me. This weird aria of pain started to echo in the narrow street.

"Get off," a woman said in English. Very calm. I heard footsteps.

One of the guys—I couldn't tell which in the commotion—danced face down on the street. His mouth was in the road, his teeth *click, click, clicking* either against the cobbles or each other, his knees knocking as he convulsed and screamed. "*Hombreeee!*" he bellowed, in a tone of deep disappointment, possibly betrayal. Somebody pulled the others off of me, shoved them down the street. Phrases and idioms came rapid-fire from this woman. "*Dejalo. Vaya. Get the fuck off.*"

The dragon, who had followed all the action, clapped his hands one last time, as if gleeful, then scampered away.

When I looked, I saw the lights of the *calle* reflected off her brown vinyl jacket as she wound the cables of her Taser between elbow and palm and grimly manhandled and kicked at the boys, her recharging battery emitting an upwardly pitched whine.

"Why, hello, Bent," said Alice.

iii.

People pretty much do want to be loved. On the other hand, it's not always that great.

The town of San Judas Tadeo is named for that saint I mentioned, the patron of lost causes, a carved wooden statue of whom stands inside the entrance of the parochial chapel, where I'd gone a day after arriving in town. There was a little framed card by the carving, and the way I deciphered the Spanish it explained how this particular saint had always had troubles—mainly because of his unfortunate name—and that an invocation or offering to him (there was a small donation box) would help in anyone's endeavors of any kind. He was an especially good saint to invoke for those who needed assistance. "Help me find a friend in these efforts, for I am alone and without help." So I dropped some coins in the box. And I have little other reason to believe Alice had come upon me on the street at just the right moment other than—no question—some kind of saintly intervention.

Thanks a lot, Mr. *Judas.*

Of course, whether she had saved my life, my wallet, or even just my pride, I knew that her coming along in such a timely, spiritually induced manner was not to say she came along by accident.

If The Latino Guy, Tony Ruiz, had suddenly appeared, that would be one thing, and I even had a feeling Tony, were he to materialize, might have a theory or explanation. He'd theorize that these hoodlums would prove to be henchmen under the control of the nefarious Maggie Leudecke: or a gang charged with the protection of Leudecke interests in Mexico, there to make sure that there would be no distribution of capital to the hard-working *campesinos* of downtrodden Bold

Springs, Texas. The police—were they not in hiding—might well consider the group a gang well versed in the mixing of large amounts of sculpture-grade plaster.

My own theory could be reduced to a single word: Rolex.

Alice didn't need an explanation. That hoodlums would descend on Bent in a foreign country and beat the shit out of him . . . "And why not?" she said, and shrugged.

"You followed me? Here?"

"Like I'd follow anyone all the way to this dump."

"Anyone else, you mean."

"I happened to be in the neighborhood."

"Uh-huh."

"Bent, please! Why on earth would I hurt you?"

"I have no . . . hurt me? Who said anything about hurting me?"

"These aren't easy to get into the country by the way," she said, and raised the business end of the Taser before she dropped the mechanism into her shoulder purse.

"Or legal," I added.

"Can we go to your hotel room to discuss this?"

"How long, Alice? When did you get here? Have you been waiting till you could separate me from the herd to bag me?"

She continued to rummage through the purse. "It's true; since we both happen to be here, there are some things we should go over. So we can clear the air." We walked up the hillside, towards my hotel, but she stopped suddenly, peered into a doorway of a dark restaurant. "Let's go in here, Bent, if you won't take me to your hotel and/or take me out to eat."

I shrugged. "Look, I appreciate . . . what you did back there."

"Oh, Bent, really." She gave me one of her classic big smiles. "We are so close to putting our past behind us and embarking on an incredible life together."

I swallowed hard. "Can't you just tase me instead?"

"Silly."

The place was called the Restaurante La Fuagua, and we went to a booth where she came quickly to my side and—while I attempted to fend her off—hiked up the right leg of my pants to see if my shin was broken. It and my left hand were the only parts even scraped. I was sound enough, so we did have a couple of drinks inside this beery and damp place. Two cones of light showed side bars to the right and left, and a row of busboys carried chairs out into the *restaurante* hand to hand, like sandbags in a disaster. We'd arrived a few minutes before official opening.

I did not want to be there.

"To the future," Alice said, and raised her beer glass.

"Speaking of which, at nine o'clock, I have to be somewhere."

"And the past is gone," she said. She flicked moisture off her fingers, as if these droplets were, indeed, the past, and to get rid of it required no more effort. "There's nothing between us now, nothing to keep us from the fun we're about to have."

"Oh, fun."

"Because deep down, we truly need each other."

I ordered tequila after my second beer. When the waiter placed it before me, I stared into the little glass. "I left you. Abandoned you in a hotel one hundred and fifty miles from home."

"I believe it's pretty obvious just how much time and space I've been giving you to think over that mistake. But, Bent." Here, she reached across and took my hand before I could get the glass to my mouth. I sloshed. "You aren't the only one with needs."

"I don't think I'll need anyone else neutralized."

"When a relationship is unbalanced, it won't work. Am I wrong? We can uncover the good out of this experience, trim the bad, and go from there."

I simply couldn't see it. "What has been good," I asked, "about your experience with me?"

"For instance, now we both know that honesty is the best policy." She narrowed her eyes. "The only policy, really."

"I honestly would like you to leave me alone. I want to go back to my hotel room. Also alone."

She sighed. "She's hurt you more than I thought. It makes me feel so sorry for you, Bent. Really."

Lord. Marisel again. Marisel never hurt me. Well, not

until this deeply injurious business about divorce and custody of my son. I couldn't seem to make Alice understand how it had been more like a business arrangement, anyway. And, true, maybe it was time for the arrangement to end. I sighed deep. I bit my tongue, gestured towards the nearest side bar, and indicated my need for another tequila. Then I called for another after that, which I used to wash down two each of my pills—I was hurting—while Alice continued with her monologue about how badly I'd been damaged by this terrible woman. She went on to point out that I had become dependent upon her—had latched onto her—and was frightened, even, that I might lose this woman, when really, hadn't she already proven that she didn't care about me? Certainly she didn't care about me as much as she, herself, Alice, did. Didn't our past together prove all of that?

Whatevah.

And it took me quite a while—possibly because at first I didn't listen all that carefully—to realize who she was talking about.

"Who does the little bitch think she is, anyway? What's one afternoon in a bad hotel room going to prove?"

"I . . . what?"

"Alton always said: the first time doesn't tell you anything. You can only truly learn about each other over the course of several encounters, Bent. Besides: night school?"

"Stop."

"I went to Columbia Law."

I pointed a finger. I noticed that my nails were dirty from the . . . what? The street fighting I'd been doing.

Street fighting?

I felt a sneeze coming on, and had to close my eyes down to blink in a way that didn't improve Alice's features in the hard light from the side bar of the La Fuagua. "You are shitting me."

"She's wrong for you, Bent. And has hurt you badly. She's about to hurt you so much more."

I absolutely did not remember ever having any conversation with Alice about Chloe. Nothing was lining up. "Have you . . . did you kidnap my therapist?"

Alice giggled.

"You are officially messing with things that are not your business."

"What does she offer you? Hell, you'd be better off at home with that other one."

"I am at home with that other one." Except that I wasn't. But I needed to get back to the payphone, or some payphone, to contact Chloe. "I have to go." What time was it? Shit. My Rolex was gone. I couldn't tell. I motioned to pay the waiter.

Outside, the tops of the roofs glowed in sharp outline. The moon that sharked over the parochial chapel was tinted blue, looked mottled and grained, like the surface of Alice's nose. Cheek of Tranquility. Ocean of Pores. Was this really the same crescent I'd seen over I-45 a few days back? Its horns seemed pointed in the wrong direction. Did Mexico have its own moon?

Alice chattered happily, walked a few paces behind me, and I had no misconception that we'd now separate of our own devices, or that she'd disappear into the night much as she'd appeared. No. Life's patterns began to open before me. It was pretty good tequila after all—and pretty good Vicodin . . . Xanax . . . and I could see the warp meeting the woof. Oh, yes. The line of people in my life stretched back, a long queue that waited to enter the *farmacia* at the end of the universe . . . who knew how far into the past? I concentrated, couldn't follow the details, yet could make out the broad pattern. All of the people I wanted didn't want me, and wouldn't come near me any more, ever again. Meanwhile, all the others I could barely stand, who absolutely would not disappear or go away, would reenter my life, cut in line ahead of me, time after time, most often when least expected or desired. And yet, it was true, I'd been disoriented in a foreign land for a few days now. Everything had been so confusing. I'd been lonely. And Alice knew me. And now, she knew about Chloe, too, somehow. I almost began to fear that she might walk off without me.

"Your hotel?" she asked.

On paper, she seemed alright, even accomplished and talented. But in person, even her jacket gave me pause. My understanding was she argued in the Supreme Court in 1996 wearing that brown vinyl jacket. I never should have been nice to her in the first place was the problem, but who understands the unintended consequences of being nice?

"What time is it?" I asked. "Do you know?"

"Seven forty-five."

"Fine, we can go to my hotel for a while, but then I have to go back into town. Alone, Alice." I looked for familiar landmarks, located the spire of the parochial church. "I think I can find it from here."

"Don't worry, we can find the La Huerta."

"How do you know where I'm staying?"

"And when we do, I'm sure we'll find room 304 without difficulty." She put her arm in mine, smiled, and led me up the hill.

iv.

We moved generally uphill along a street that was new to me, and soon the lights became fewer and farther between. The architecture morphed from colonial to medieval in the space of a few blocks. A dirty white truck with a throaty tailpipe came by, passed us, and I saw the *calle* change under its headlights, go from rough cobblestones and cracked pavement to slatted ruts of grunge just like that. We were walking along some kind of burro lane. The truck stopped, shifted into a three-point reverse, and coughed back the way it came, but we walked on.

"It's true San Judas isn't Mexico," one of the expatriates had said to me once in El Infierno, "but it's a pretty short walk to Mexico from here," and I grew worried as we made a hairpin intersection. A circle of lights and a clearing of some kind atop the hill made me think we were taking some new route to the hotel, so I kept us steered basically towards that. As long as she would stop talking about our "issues" I figured we could do this and I could still make it back to the bank for my call, but I did have to wonder how long I'd been followed. "Say," I said. "You didn't steal my duffle out of a bus station in Mexico City, did you?"

Alice laughed. "Bent, why would you even ask such a thing?"

Uh-oh.

"I don't think," she went on, "that we should let our life preservers float away as we cling to a sinking dingy."

"Metaphors!" I said.

"Although the thought has crossed my mind to let you go, Bent. Oh yes. As I'm sure it has also occurred to you." She aimed her chin into the sky that loomed ever more darkly as the light fixtures fell behind us. "But if I feel forgiveness in my heart, why can't I express it?"

"Because I don't want it?"

"Why does it have to be bad? No matter what, we both need to stop seeing each other as fragile. We can take the truth from each other. Own up to our mistakes and feelings. Who knows, maybe it needed to play out this way for us to learn about ourselves, how. . . ."

And so on: her continuing to tell me I should communicate my feelings; me telling her that my feelings were mainly centered around disgust; and her ignoring these feelings to further request more communication of feelings. After a while, we passed a building with a single illumination above a screen door, and beside it a stocky man with no shirt, his back turned to us, swayed gently while the sound of his urine made a broth-like, oddly comforting splash on the ground. I guess it was comforting because there are otherwise few explanations for stocky shirtless men to turn their backs on you.

"Water cycle!" said Alice.

"Shush."

"Public micturition! Misdemeanor."

"If you haven't noticed, this isn't exactly public."

She went into a mode that resembled an address to a learned assembly. "Why, Bent and I had the *loveliest* time in Mexico. And we met the most delightful man!" She laughed that laugh of hers.

Then something arch-backed and scurrying passed in front of us in the faint light from the screen door, and I was about to shoo away this cat when I saw it was a . . . fucking giant Mexican rat of some kind with a bad attitude (no doubt), and, uhm . . . *skin lice* (probably), so I jumped, but Alice kicked at it. She wore heels and didn't connect, but the thing understood: scared shitless, no doubt, by the ascending presence that was Alice and the perfume that preceded her up the hill. I trembled, but continued to climb, and the evening grew chilly. Light flashed above us. Headlights or lightning? Where was the La Huerta?

"I know she's hurt you, Bent."

"You don't, she hasn't, and it's none of your business."

"It might be therapeutic if you stopped to think about why this particular little girl has damaged you so badly. It's probably not even about her."

"No probably about it."

"Your pride has taken a hit. Or your masculinity." This made her chuckle grimly in a way I did not find seemly. "What is it, Bent, that makes real love impossible for you? Can you trace this back to some prime cause? Toilet training? Mommy issues?"

"Oh, boy."

"Did you live, as a child, fearful of monsters in your closet? If you can get to the root of this, you might move out into the adult world, and. . . . "

I felt my ears beginning to vibrate, like they were plugged into an electric current, and when I shoved my hands into my pockets against a slight chill, my shoulder gave its familiar creaking pang. It was time to medicate. Oh, I already had. Then, unexpectedly, the smudge of light on the hilltop showed itself to be not the Hotel La Huerta at all. Our trail led under a delicate, well-lit, arched entrance way, *PARQUE JUAREZ* written in gold leaf across its span, and past it, beyond some rusty swings, was a buckled cement basketball court, still lighted at that hour, though empty of players. The basket was made of thick chainlink. Beyond this, past empty, sag-wheeled carts where venders sold drinks and cigarettes during the day, a garden trail started: a walkway to stroll among the variety of labeled botanical specimens. Probably it was a lovely path in the daytime, but it was a spooky and humid foliage tunnel at night, and no place I desired to enter. Alice, naturally, took my hand and drew us towards it. Soon she found us an aromatic space under drooping flowers. The romantic, secluded spot smelled of jasmine and sewer, and I moved closer to her as I recalled the giant rat. I spread my jacket onto the loam so we'd have a place to sit, and resigned myself to some kind of encounter with filth.

"I'm glad we're doing this," she said.

Like Harrell I began to fiddle with my tie without really loosening it. "What are we doing?"

"No one will see us here."

"What? Here?"

"You know, you think people mistreat you—like this Chloe—but your neurotic self-hatred comes from things you do to yourself, not external rejection."

Amazing the insights a person can gather. "I don't do anything to myself. Ever." I still thought "rodent." I scooted as close to her on the jacket as I could get without seeming to initiate anything intense. "Hardly."

"You need to find a way to forgive yourself for all the bad things you've done. And the damage you've caused. The catastrophic damage."

"Alright!"

"The hurt you've created. You need to move on."

Alice sat partly on her vinyl jacket, hugged herself around the knees with one arm, and rested her other hand in the mulch of this garden. She had it in her head that Chloe had somehow harmed me—however she'd found out about Chloe in the first place. "The past is gone, Bent. Holding onto it is pathetic. Especially if it's just one afternoon."

"Oh for Christ's sake."

"In July. The seventh, to be exact."

I would sue Yvonne. I could imagine no other place Alice could have gotten this information aside from a shattering of the therapist/client privilege.

Of course, this also made Alice someone I could talk to.

And someone I absolutely could not trust.

"Austin was a dark time for me, Bent. I had to call in a lot of debts at the capital. A federal agent I know helped me out. Well, it was Alton, actually."

"I thought he was in Dallas."

"He has studied sex, Bent."

"Yes, yes."

"Researched it. He's watched videos. He sits and strategizes in advance how he will blow a woman's mind." She began to unbutton her top. "Or a man's, you know. Oh, Bent. Alton makes me feel, sometimes, like I have three clits."

Alice was not considering at all how the tropics are the petri-dish girdle of bacteria the planet wears, the place where advanced viruses are born, then—aided by various modes of aerial and ground-based transportation—spread throughout the globe. She was about to get naked in Germ Central, but didn't care.

"I don't think we should be here," I said.

"Anyway, I was furious at you. But when I finally got home, there was a big box at my front door. My new underwear from The Secret Boudoir catalogue!" She pulled off her blouse, revealed a wave of her heavy perfume—something sharp that, as I recalled, she'd gotten in the Middle East. She also revealed a lacy black bra. It was hard to see many fashion details in the gloom. "It turned my whole attitude around."

She went on in her way, and told me about all the items that had arrived in the mail, some of which she was wearing right then. She told how her life was suddenly no longer about seeking revenge against me. "New panties give new hope, Bent! You wonder: who will be the first to see this thong? Who will put his hand up my skirt? Touch my wet pussy?" She took my hand in hers, began to move it across her scaly thigh, her chilly knee. "Who will unsnap this bra and hold my breasts in his palms?"

She reached behind her back expertly. The bra dropped away.

"Don't you just believe in consuming passion, Bent? I mean, we do follow the same religion there, right? I'm not talking about vicious revenge sex, either."

"Oh, man."

"Or pity sex. I mean just being totally into another person's body, with climax after climax. . . ."

It's not that I disagreed with anything she was saying. It was more the manner, or tone. Or maybe it was just the source. Or, possibly, none of it sounded real. It didn't sound like the way sex actually worked, what with gravity, getting winded, cheap carpeting on kneecaps, all that. Plus, I couldn't help being nagged by all the things people knew about me—including things I didn't even know myself. Yes, Alice apparently had laid pipe to my secret soul, but it wasn't only her. Chloe seemed to think there was some kind of word out about me at the office, and Tony Ruiz hadn't quelled any of my fears concerning my reputation in the city. I'd often had that thought recently: that when the end came—my end—people would know it before me. They would start to act strangely, would pick up, perhaps, on a smell. Like putridity. I wouldn't notice, as I lived with it in my nostrils, but others would realize. Like, maybe they would go to a hotel room with me one afternoon, but pick up a whiff of that oncoming onslaught of limitation, and so make sure never to repeat that awful experience.

I thought maybe I should just bury my face in Alice's tits after all, while I still could. Who would find out? Shouldn't I grab it while I had breath? I knew I had to, as Montez put it, "Get out of town." Did I really have to phone the office at all?

I met her halfway, and put my cheek on her shoulder.

"Oh, Bent. I do hate spending the holidays alone."

"Okay." I checked my watch but . . . shit. "Do you know what time it is now?"

She held the plane of her own tiny wristwatch to the basketball lights and squinted. "Eight forty-eight."

Oh, man.

"Actually, Alton gave me this watch."

"Look," I said, and I took up my coat from the sludge. "We've got to get going. I need to be at the bank."

"Do that later." She held her arms towards me.

And I did want Alice just then, sort of, there under the flowers in the mulchy-smelling Parque Juarez, with the light from the bare bulb that raked her nipples, both of which rose in the night chill. But I also wanted to get away from bugs, night soil, and rats.

"Let me run back down the hill," I said. "I'll make my call, then we'll take up where we left off."

"Bent." She looked very serious. Somber. She returned to hugging her knees in the dark. She was vulnerable-looking in that position. That was the problem with Alice. That was always the problem.

"Meet me at the hotel, then."

"No. Come back to me. Here." Alice liked the out of doors. "If you don't," she said, "this time we're through."

"Oh, no," I said.

V.

I felt, as I hurried down the hill, that I really did need to get back to the Parque, that I needed to get back to Alice, and wanted to, even wanted to badly. What might she do if I didn't? "We both need to stop seeing each other as fragile," she'd said. Like hell. One wrong move and I knew she'd explode into a million dangerous shards. But it was also back there in the corner of my mind that should I not for some reason—should I receive word from this phone call that was life-altering, that required an immediate return to Houston, a return in a hurry. . . .

Tonight, I'd either make love to Alice under the moonlight on a hill of dung, or never see her again. Both possibilities had their appeal.

I shook it off and hurried down the goat tromp with my jacket rolled like a bundle over my arm. The town resolved itself upwards towards me through fog. Approaching streetlights acted like blowtorches that illuminated circular peepholes of wall, window, and refuse. It was like finding both prizes and flies as you ate down into a bowl of black bean soup. The odd topography caused the square at the raised center of town to appear first; the dome of the chapel nudged against the fountain like an areola, the terrain wrinkled around that central rise. Soon I could see rings of stone apartments, occasionally abandoned warehouses, then a furious circle of crumbled, roofless structures. There were cacti growing in the windows of the houses I passed, which were ruins of cheap adobe. The whole while Alice's oversweet fragrance followed me, I supposed from her contact with my jacket.

Finally, I arrived back on the square. The musicians had gone, and I saw none of the youths who'd taken my Rolex, thankfully. Should I report the theft to my good pals, the police? I was definitely sour on seeing them again, ever. I skirted the light of their big, open door. I felt like an unreal ghost as I stepped onto the raised walkway that surrounded the bank. I stayed in the shadows, edged towards the stool beside the payphone. I got an operator. Again! I made it known, in my broken way, my intentions with the collect call. Couples, families, and children were still out in the *jardín*, but it was a much different, much calmer crowd than before: the costumed freaks and their dance had, no doubt, moved into nearby clubs or restaurants. The phone line ticked and squawked, and I wondered at how I came to be there, on a stool in front of this square in the darkness. I again half expected to see Maggie Leudecke come strolling by, but there was no one I recognized. And I wondered: if I went back up the hill, saw Alice up there, dealt with Alice on the hilltop, would that mean I'd be stuck with her? Would she want to travel back to the States with me? Would it mean I'd have to make kind and meaningless movements around this woman for at least . . . what? . . . two more days of travel? I tried to recall what had been so appealing about her, ever. (Was it possible that everything had appeal—at first—under basketball-court light?) Nothing impressive about her especially came to mind, just an ill-defined aura of panic and desperation with a stillness at its center.

Would she hound me about Christmas all the way back to Texas?

When the connection was made, the phone picked up after one ring, but it wasn't Ruth.

"Bent," Chloe said. "I think I've made a mistake. With Loeb. I need your help."

"Yes, of course."

"Bent, I think I need *you*."

I couldn't believe it.

"Come back. Please."

I folded my jacket a few times over my arm. My mouth was so dry. First a flimsy blouse, then a black brassiere slipped onto the pavement. Both were redolent of Middle Eastern musk. Uh-oh. I bent, scrambled to scoop them back into the folds of the jacket, while a family of four strolled past.

"What the fuck?" I said to Chloe.

"Can you come back now?"

I could see through the window of a bar across the street, Hildi and Martin's. Against its far back wall was a kerosene lamp with a bulb screwed into it—some adaptation to electricity—that illuminated a nook featuring a picture of the Virgin. Also on the walls were stars trimmed from aluminum foil, a hanging trumpet, and soft-drink cans on the shelves. The place was full of people who laughed and smiled. Families strolled around the *jardín*, and a tourist girl was being chatted up by a couple of local boys. None of them was worried about making equity partner.

I wanted to shout *Hell yes I can come back now* into the payphone, but felt that the populace of San Judas Tadeo was like Marisel, standing at the end of the hall, overhearing my conversation.

"You're saying something needs to be taken care of?"

"What?

"You need me there?"

"Yes, Bent. Please."

"I'll make it happen." I was calm. Cool. "Don't worry."

The connection broke. Either she hung up, or some disruption occurred along the line, but it didn't matter. I returned the handset, and shook, I think, with happiness. Then I went to find the trail up to the Parque, but I couldn't seem to locate it in my muddled state. I recalled then that there were many taxicabs, and that I didn't have to wait for the morning buses. A cab could take me through the mountain pass and into La Luz that night. Then I thought I did find the right street, and hurried, clutched my jacket and Alice's clothes, breathed hard. It was so much more difficult to climb at those altitudes than scoot downhill. But soon I stood in front of the long stairway that led to the Hotel La Huerta. Somehow, in the dark, I'd missed the road to the hilltop basketball court and ended up where Alice and I had intended to go in the first place.

Give us your blessing to touch upon this problem, I said into the stars. She knew where I was staying. I went up to room 304 and started to pack. I expected Alice at any moment, but maybe she got lost as well. Should I wait for her? Should I go out and search for that mysterious hillside *parque*?

"*Pray for me, saint,*" I said as I folded myself into a green cab that waited with its lights on and engine running on the upper portal of the Aparecido. *"For I am without help."*

Part V.

Procession

i.

I drove the Elantra directly from the Park 'N Fly to the office, but Kebba Jobe stopped me in the garage before I could get into the building. "My heart is broken," he said.

"You, too?"

"Oh, you've done well, asshole." The roundness of his mouth and his emphasis accented the "hole." "I almost left my wife for her, you know. Betrayer!"

"Your fifth wife? But who are we talking about?"

"Chloe is so beautiful. We had an affair, you know."

Oh, boy. I just nodded.

"And an understanding."

"Are you sure it wasn't just a hookup?"

Kebba surveyed me length and breadth with his eyes only, not moving his head. It was as if he had actually noticed me for the first time in his life. He squinted and walked away. I probably was a bit gamey after my trip back. I stood with my duty-free paper bag. Both my cheap sandals and the guayabera shirt were beginning to come apart.

"Wait," I called after him. "Where is Chloe?"

He placed a long, powerful finger alongside his ear, pointed directly upwards, towards the upper floors of our building, and continued to walk down the row of parked cars in the ugly fluorescent light. The garage seemed a low-contrast Xerox copy of itself printed on gray paper. "Bent, quit screwing around. I'm trying to tell you something actually important."

I ground my teeth. "Kebba, come on. It'll be okay."

I watched him disappear around a corner. Was he kidding? Or crazy? How many afternoons had Chloe spent, in how many *skak* hotels? Better the company whore than . . . etc.

I didn't care.

She'd said "Come back." She'd said "I need you."

I got off the elevator with the paper bag wrapped tightly around my duty-free rum and my sunglasses riding low so I could see over them. A few people I didn't recognize headed towards the elevator, pulling on coats. Yellburton stopped me as I noticed Ruth, who glanced up from behind the front counter. Her expression, as far as I could tell, approximated terror. She turned to her receptionist bank and began to push buttons.

"Great job," Yellburton said. He was the public law prick, so proud to have his house and his pool. "Any encores, Bent?"

"It's going to be alright," I said—again, as with Kebba, not knowing exactly what I was reassuring the guy about. "Look, I'm back. I'm on it."

"Sure, you're alright. What about the rest of us? I remember her coming to my pool party."

"Oh. Right."

"She seemed to be on something, to me. High. But her pimp wouldn't care."

"Watch it, Yellburton. Loeb is a big boy and will get over this."

"Over it? Will we? Sure, the suck-ups will be fine, in their corner offices." He pushed past me onto the elevator, which closed behind him.

That was the first conversation I'd ever really had with the guy, come to think of it. I rarely exchanged nods with him in the hallways. Fucking bully. What was going on?

Ruth had disappeared, but I didn't want to see her anyway. Down the hall, past the conference rooms, it seemed most of the support cubicles were empty, and, in fact, every warm body I intercepted was heading for the elevators as far as I could tell. Around a corner, Dalton Harpe bumped into my chest.

"I can't believe it," he said.

"Well. . . ." I was starting to feel uneasy.

"Where have you been? Couldn't you have . . . stopped this? Prohibited it rather than . . . ?"

"I already stopped it. Or, it's not going to happen, anyway."

"It's deception, Bent. Can we trust that it doesn't go through the whole organization? Like a cancer!"

Then Dalton began to dance step, wobble, and curse, and I saw Heidi behind him, the bottle-red, high-piled hair at about our belt level. She bumped him at ankle height with her Hoveround. They cursed each other momentarily, but it wasn't Dalton who interested her.

"If he's going to be doing something this stupid, he should do it with me!" She directed this at myself, and fiercely.

Dalton flailed at her, then walked towards the elevator. "We all regret the stupid things we haven't done with you, Heidi."

"Like you'd know anything about it." She squared her device in front of me, blocked the hallway. "She has nothing. Literally. She hasn't got a pot or the piss to put in it."

"I suppose," I said. "But look: I'm going to talk to her, and everything will be alright."

"What were you thinking? You're all morons, and this just proves it more. Loeb and I could have pooled our resources. We'd have a dynasty."

I bent low. "If you think so, you shouldn't worry. Maybe you yet shall reign."

"The only answer is this." Her arm shot out and she clenched my crotch, fortunately encased in enough denim to keep her surprisingly strong grip from crushing my *cojones*. "This is what all of you use for thinking. You don't consider the kind of portfolio you need to get along in the world."

I scraped her off, pried her away finger by finger while I worked around the chair, but she turned as I orbited.

"Shit! Heidi!"

"Except for some of you, who aren't worth a damn in the first place. How long have you been her go-between with Loeb?"

I loosened her dry claw, finally, backed quickly down the hall, but she pursued.

"I'm handling it. Hearts get broken."

"This whole firm is screwed!" she said.

I knew she'd be on top of me if I stopped at my office door and had to grapple with the card key besides, so I circled the staff room once and got some distance on her.

Occasionally, I cut across the rat's maze of cubicle partitions to throw her off. It seemed that the whole floor had emptied out. Nobody clacked their keyboards. The AC nearly roared on the otherwise silent floor. Heidi cursed when I made a quick corner around a storage component, and she rattled one of the temporary walls, grazed it in her follow-through of a hairpin turn. I leaned into the occasional cubicle, took up some trash cans, dumped them into the aisle behind me to slow her progress, but she came on: delayed, not halted. Bump. Crash.

Out of her line of sight, I ducked into a cubicle—some junior staff stuck in a tiny eight-by-eight configuration—and crouched. I held my breath and pushed under the desk as far as I could go while Heidi went past. She cursed ever louder over the hum of her personal mobility vehicle. On this desk was a picture of a young boy, a stapler, a banjo music CD, and a two-year-service award (cheapo plastic clock). Might be Jim or Romana's space, though I couldn't be sure. I waited a few beats, watched until I was certain she'd gone past, then crawled out and retraced my steps. I made a right at the aquarium and heard her over my shoulder—outraged. Heidi had spied my deceitful maneuver. "Halt!" But she was at the wrong end of the cubicles by then, and I made it to the flickering (still!) fluorescent bulb, the light around me spastic and weird as I caught my breath. After some immediate clicks and whirs, I pushed into my office only moments before Heidi arrived. The Hoveround's bumper slammed the door behind me with a jolt.

I felt that by achieving my office I'd actually entered a new life: a period of change. I'd put behind me my time of lacklusterness, of laziness, of "just getting by." I'd shut down all of that, and opened another era that now lay before me. Things were going to be different for Bent and Chloe. And— *Hey, let's not get ahead of ourselves*, I thought, but for a millisecond there I could imagine a way. I could leave my loveless marriage and get into something else, with someone else. I could have the things that people with good lives had: closeness, trust, passion . . . sitting together on the sofa and watching dumb TV shows together. I could be part of a couple. What a great couple we'd make, too. It would be hard, rough going, but

Henry wasn't so little any more. Couldn't I provide him all the help he needed now? Did I actually require an entire family of Filipinos to take care of my own son? Yvonne could help me out with this. That would be the first step. I'd tell Yvonne my plans, and—together—we could start to work the problem.

With my back pressed against the door, I felt the pop of Heidi's bumper as she rammed into it with fair force. The impact jostled me out of my new future. I reached to flick on the light switch.

Inside my office, everything was gone.

As in, everything mine: the books, the papers, the pictures of Henry, the framed shot of my family at the crocodile cage, and even the empty wine bottle. I moved after a few moments, while Heidi continued her tirade outside. I went to pull open a desk drawer, but it was locked. I never knew the desk could be locked. I breathed in deep. Good Lord, the gym-locker smell had been removed. There was no computer to check, just the phone on the desk. I turned in a complete circle, confused. It wasn't the wrong office.

A trick.

I opened the blinds and looked down on the city. In the hallway, a shift in the sound led me to believe Heidi had begun to harangue someone else. Then came a light knock at the door.

I leaned against the back of my chair . . . or somebody's chair. "Go away."

Whir, click, the door pushed open, and Loeb stuck his head into the office.

"Hey, Bent. God, Bent. What a mess. Right?"

I was silent.

He stepped in, closed the door behind him, and checked his watch. Loeb rubbed his forehead and along his dark eyebrows. "Wow. She's crazy, right? I can't get over it."

"Whom do you mean?"

"What's that?" He looked over my head, out at the skyline.

"I'm going to need to know what happened," I said.

"Oh! This? Don't worry, it's all been moved to a corner office upstairs."

"A corner office is not what I'm talking about, and you know it." I paused. "But, before I do get to what I'm talking about, what is this about a corner office?"

"Yeah, Ruth said you were here. I'm surprised. You've been moved upstairs."

"I have?" I nudged my pleasure aside with difficulty.

"Equity partner. Congratulations."

I sat.

"I think you deserve it, after all you've done. But, Bent, why are you here now? Shouldn't you be in Mexico?"

"What have I done?"

"The Road to Nowhere. It's a finished deal. Maggie's signed off on it."

Something was profoundly wrong. "I don't care about the road. The real question is: why are you so happy?"

"You deserve it. Oh, the other thing."

"Yes. The marriage. Chloe."

He shrugged, moved away from the door. "I mean, what can I do about it?"

I nodded. "That's a healthy, if somewhat bizarre, attitude. What about her, then? Is she alright?"

"Upstairs. Big window." Again he watched the skyline. "But, yeah, of course. We need to be on the same page about Chloe."

"It's not about pages."

Loeb moved his hand vaguely inside his coat pockets while his eyes met every object in the room but me, and there weren't many other objects in there. I was definitely the only horizontally orange-striped one. "Well . . . what is it about? Also, I need to get to Bold Springs."

"What?"

"Uh-oh. I wasn't supposed to tell you that." He shook his head, either not believing he'd let that information slip, or trying to give the impression he'd told me something he shouldn't have. It was always so hard to tell with him. "Look, Bent. It's love. People living and dying for it, right? You know how it is."

"Really."

"And there's no reason to make it any more complicated than that, although people will. But it's everybody."

"So you're not hurt?"

"It's not going to be so bad. How did you even find out about it? Kebba?"

"I talked to her."

"Oh, right, I heard that," said Loeb. "Crazy kid. She was getting cold feet. Why should I be hurt? It's just going to be weird. Look, I need to get going . . . somewhere."

"Why do I keep hearing about that place?"

He looked stricken. "I'm sorry, what did you ask me?"

"Bold Springs."

"I'm really sorry. Please forgive me."

"No, it's okay." There I was, forgiving him again. I tugged on the drawer handles a few times more, to no purpose, then eyed my paper bag. I'd only been there a few minutes, but already needed something to take the edge off the Davison, Kohlhoeffer & Loeb experience.

"Now I'm worried," Loeb said. "You're not thinking about going are you?"

"Going?" I noticed then that the phone readout was blinking sixty-eight messages. Oh, man.

"The thing is, people are angry, Bent."

"Are they?"

"They're making assumptions. That are unwarranted, true, but you know how they can be."

I activated the voice mail. The phone apparatus was still under my passcode. "Bent," said a voice on the first message. "Bent, this is your mother."

Sure enough, it was from a few days back. While I'd been gone she'd left the hospital, checked out with her new hip and a fancy walker that "folds up into practically nothing, goes right in the trunk." She said Blanca had been with her, but, "Wouldn't you know, Blanca's house burned down! Burned down while I was at the hospital. I think her cat's behind it." Mom always projected evil onto pets. "All those cats of hers!" (There were two.)

"Oh, no. That's awful," said Loeb.

"It's fine. Is that where everybody is going this early in the day?" A terrible fear began to seize me. "To Bold Springs?"

"I told her someday one would brush against a candle,"

Mom said. "Can you come? Come and see me? There are a few things I need you to pick up because Blanca's so busy. . . ."

"Oh my God," said Loeb. "Maybe you should go check on her."

"Where is this famous Bold Springs, anyway?"

He was taken aback. "It's not famous. I grew up there. It's where we live."

"We?"

"Well, the Loebs," he said. "Since grandfather."

"Alright, Mr. Bent." A different voice on the answering machine, but sounding familiar. "This is Vijay Rangarajan speaking to you."

I dropped my forehead onto the desk.

"Okay. Yes, we know that there are some problems," said Vijay, "but we are working through them, and I don't think you are a good lawyer, or even a passing fair one, and my anger at you persists, but . . . because you know us so well . . . maybe know us better than anyone . . . we are hoping, maybe . . . maybe you can help us with the TXBC."

Another voice in the background broke in—a woman. "TXBRA."

"Yes, TXBRA"

"Texas Bicycle Racing Association," explained the background voice. It was Amy, I was sure of it, now. "They won't let me register for time trials for the series at Bear Creek, Mr. Bent."

"As in, you know. . . ." said Vijay.

"Won't let me register as a woman. Can you help?"

"Can you help us, Mr. Bent? Uhm. We have some other problems, too."

Rangarajan left a call-back number, thanked me, and hung up. I was astonished.

"I didn't know he had it in him," I said to Loeb.

"Register as a woman? You do get into the weirdest stuff, Bent."

You can pick your nose, but not your clients, you judgy piece of shit. Then:

"Are you lost?" asked the next voice on the next message, which I took momentarily to be Mom again, maybe calling back after the space of a few hours, but my mind shifted audio memory slots and then I identified the sound. "Do you need guidance and/or directions? Were you unable to find your way back to room 304?"

Alice went on in this fashion, and explained—in her manner—how odd it was that I should become lost, as she herself had found her way without problem. "Such a fascinating hillside, Bent. So interesting to run down . . . at midnight . . . topless."

"That doesn't sound like fun for that woman, Bent," Loeb said.

"She had a vinyl jacket."

"Do I know that voice from somewhere?" Then he rose, made to leave.

"You're not going anywhere."

"I can't stay."

"You need to understand," I said. "She'll never be your wife."

"My what?"

Mom was becoming ever more put out with Blanca in the messages that followed. "Who else would just go burn her house down? Now when I need her most. She's got to go out and replace all her furniture, today."

Then Alice ("Alice Dowling?" asked Loeb. "From Bracewhite? Again?"), who insisted by her third or fourth message that I wasn't an attorney at all. "You are a *teacher*, Bent. Look what you've taught me. About myself. That I am ugly. That I am small. You have taught me that I am a waste of your time."

Then Vijay and Amy Rangarajan called back again, left their number, apparently reconciled—somehow—and needing help with their immigration status, but, more immediately, with discrimination from the governing body of two-wheel oval track competition.

Then: old Mr. Duc, who, ironically enough, asked much the same thing Alice had. "Are you lost? Did you overdose in the gutter, you son of a bitch?"

"It's kind of all out of control, isn't it?" Loeb asked.

"I don't care what I have to do to stop this."

"But you've got something wrong. Chloe's not my wife; she's my mom. You do know she married my dad last night, right?"

"Of course I forgive you," Alice said in the phone's final recorded message. "But this is the last time. Also, I'm pregnant."

ii.

"She didn't think you'd approve," said Loeb as we walked the tunnel to the parking garage. "That's why she sent you to Mexico."

It was early afternoon. Ruth was gone now, and the switchboard shut down because the whole place had been given time off to go to Bold Springs for a reception celebrating the nuptials of the not-at-all-even-remotely-favored paralegal of Davison, Kohlhoeffer & Loeb's naturalization and immigration division—who might be something, but it was certainly not a bore—and the wealthy founding partner with the big personality, the long ponytail and the sixty-six years of life on planet earth: Thomas Loeb. The binding act itself, Loeb explained, had taken place in a twenty-minute ceremony, a JP at one of his father's favorite small claims courts presiding.

By the time we got to the garage, it was pretty much as empty as the office. I told Loeb we'd take his car and, oh, shit—that's right: he had a Hummer.

"Let me move some of this stuff so you can sit down." He unlocked his door, climbed up into the thing, relocked it quickly before I could react, started the engine, and threw the massive square box into reverse.

Man, these people did not want me at their party.

I jumped on the hood.

I believe there is something about a Hummer's great height that actually makes it easier to get on top of it—you can kind of put your elbows into the project. Another point: everything is rugged on those suckers. The windshield-wiper arms were downright stout, and I clung to those, whipped a little across the hood as he backed out, turned hard, then crunched the gears into forward. I looked at him through the windshield and shook my head. I screamed through the glass. "I'm not crazy!"

He drove forward, attempting to navigate out of the parking lot, me moving my head to block his vision every time he tried to look around me.

"You're fucking up everything," he called through the windshield.

"Not even close!" I held the wiper blades and he decided to take a hard left, attempt a tight circle, to throw me off the hood. This must be easier to do in movies than real life, or he didn't have room to build speed and inertia.

"Please leave me alone!" he hollered.

He turned on the windshield wipers, then, and, man, those arms really are built sturdily: my hand-holds started whipping—*floppety frappety*—back and forth, making it, yes, difficult to hang on, but not so difficult as all that, and I pulled myself up as far as I could, mainly with my right arm, as my left shoulder was such junk, up and onto the windshield to try to block his vision completely while I whooshed my body from side to side. All fun and games until someone finds a concrete support pillar. I looked over my shoulder to try to ascertain if it was a possibility.

This is a very good idea, I thought.

As everyone had left for the day, there was little for Loeb to run into, yet he managed to find a concrete curb divider. The Hummer leapt over it, which made me first careen off of then slap back down onto the very solid hood. When he tried to back up, the curb stopped him. He couldn't seem to get traction.

If you can't climb a curb in a Hummer, just shut up.

I felt like I'd taken a beating but slid off the high front of the thing, knocked on his window with my fist clenched, though I trembled. "Open up!"

"I'm sorry, I wasn't listening. Why don't you tell me in your Russian accent?"

Funny. "That was a joke, Loeb, and I got you out of it," I said. "I covered for you and no lives were ruined."

"His life isn't ruined. He does what he wants. Now go away."

"I thought he wouldn't leave the other one until his daughters were grown."

This seemed to loosen something in him: the mention of his half-siblings. Loeb opened the door. When he climbed down from the leather seat, he looked like he wanted to run. Then he ran. Loeb took off towards a nearby stairwell, but I caught him, not so easy in huaraches, but he was slow and I didn't really need to catch him so much as catch up with him, then shove him from behind. He tripped forward, cratered without resistance, like back in the day, pushing those smaller kids onto their faces in the playground. Loeb smacked the concrete wall with his arm, sprawled on the oily pavement.

"Why don't you take care of your mother!" he screamed. "Go smooth over . . . whatever the fuck you did with that Bracewright woman."

"I'll drive," I said.

I popped over the curb like nothing. I mean, it *had* four-wheel drive, shithead.

iii.

I sweated the whole drive up I-45 North, no matter how high I cranked the Hummer's air conditioning. In October.

"Such a reckless girl," from Loeb.

"How can you say that?"

He shrugged. "She rides a motorcycle with no helmet."

"She doesn't have a motorcycle."

"Dad does. She loves it."

"Jeebus." I couldn't believe she hadn't told me any of this. "She was always talking about you."

"It was a secret. You have to be careful when you're an important man."

As opposed to those other, less important, less careful types, I supposed. "But you followed her, drove her around."

"He's always being watched. People have an interest in the firm, don't like the way he lives. It's a pain."

"You were his beard?"

"We were. You and I. I mean, people always knew you and Chloe were close."

What did Loeb know about me and Chloe? And what did Big Loeb, the *real Loeb*, know? Whatever it was, it seemed to have turned—in Chloe's hands—into my equity partnership and corner office. Still. "I've never met your father. How the hell could I be his pimp?"

"You two would get along."

"How does she even know the guy?" I remembered her on the phone: her mention of "Tom" when I'd called from the Ruiz compound and raised the possibility Maggie was being manipulated by her family with the help of Davidson, Kohlhoeffer & Loeb. *"That's awful. Tom wouldn't do that."* I couldn't imagine them traveling in the same circles. "Night before last, she told me. . . ."

"They got together at the pool. Galveston. The night you were fooled into breaking the window."

"The night who was fooled?"

"At that hotel. I'm talking about the perception, Bent. That it was you who fell for that. He got drinks for everyone after you skulked up to bed."

"I pretended to skulk to save you some wicked embarrassment."

"That you caused me. But they sat out all evening. On the beach. I guess they got to know each other."

Great.

"I think mainly they talked about you and that boneheaded move you made, going out the window."

I shook my head. I would have buried my face in my hands if I hadn't been driving that expensive behemoth. They might never have met at all, except for me.

"So every time I've been with her, and she's been texting 'Loeb'. . . ."

"She's really gotten him hooked on smartphones. They do pictures, too. Who can explain love? I think he wanted her on his lap for that picture the next day, but he put her on my lap instead."

"What? I did that."

Loeb hummed a little. "He let you do that."

"He wasn't even there."

"That you noticed he wasn't there underscores his omnipresence."

"Oh, for Christ's sake." He was fat enough to claim omnipresence, but otherwise. . . .

"Anyway, since then, yeah, I've sort of been covering for him."

So I had been only a few hundred feet away while Thomas Loeb—that nasty old man in desperate need of a tummy tuck—had been stealing the love of my life. Probably it had happened while I had my face down on the Hotel San Domingo pillow, thrashing and cursing the lonely night. I thought of the two of them kissing on the beach. Or anywhere. It was unimaginable.

"Wait . . . what do you mean he's 'everywhere'? Has he been having me followed?"

"Jesus, Bent, you're as egotistical as Chloe says you are."

"She says that?"

"Why would anyone want to follow you?"

Loeb seemed nearly cheerful now. After all, why shouldn't Bent go to the reception? What's done is done. If I'd had some help I would have thrown him out of the vehicle as we trucked along at seventy miles per hour on the freeway. At that moment I could have snuffed out his life with no remorse, but it would be hard to accomplish single-handed. That's the problem. In life there are friends you can count on when you need help, and other friends—better ones—you can count on when you need help burying something, but I had neither. It was sad. I began to understand why I'd spent so many dollars on street-corner panhandlers: so I could recognize in their voices the resonance of their great worth, especially compared to people like Loeb.

"I need to talk to her. I can't figure out why she had me call her. Why she said she'd made a mistake."

"The Leudeckes really want that road, Bent. Not Maggie, but the rest of them. Chloe's land grant research could have totally thrown a wrench in all that."

I thought of the girl with the wrench tattoo. "You mean. . . ."

"They had some hopes you'd really screw that up, and then—so typical. You had to go and not let them down."

"My bad."

"At the hearing, yes. That was classic Bent. But that old Leudecke grant." Here Loeb, in that maddening way he had, reached to touch my shoulder, to underscore, I suppose, his profound sincerity in this actual physical connection, and emphasize the importance of his next words: "Little gold digger really plowed up a snake."

I searched the off-ramps ahead, finally found a likely exit where tall, primary-colored signs of several major oil company gas stations stood in abundance. I put on the Hummer's blinker. I wasn't totally sure what I would do with him once I got off the freeway.

"And you say the Loeb properties are in Bold Springs? Where the freeway is going?"

"Dad really had to twist her arm not to mention it to Maggie. And of course, we've got all that property out at Bold Springs, too."

"Yeah. But it's the Regional Center that's the real problem, right?"

"Bent, nearly sixty investors sunk half a million to a million each out there."

"And got visas for doing so. But if there's no road. . . ."

"Or at least the option for a road, well . . . hello Securities and Exchange Commission."

I tried to sort it out. "This has to be a major conflict of interest."

"That's why real estate and project finance couldn't fight the road."

"Rich Jefferson."

"He's an officer of the Regional Center. They needed a department with some distance, to show due diligence. Limited liability. And, preferably, a department that couldn't deliver."

"Immigration and naturalization. And good old Harrison Bent."

"Thanks for nothing."

I felt physically ill. Gee, I'm sure I could have fucked it up if they hadn't given me such a competent (if slutty) paralegal.

I thought I saw a likely exit ahead. "Was this your idea by any chance?"

"Why?"

"Because your ideas never work. I'm pretty sure, as you say, that the Securities and Exchange Commission will agree with me on that." I remembered something Tony had hinted at. "The money from those investors: it's already been spent, hasn't it?"

"Oh, like you've never done it."

"Those were loans, and for a few thousand!" I shrieked like a little girl. "EB-5 processes are a million dollars apiece! That's . . . stealing!"

"Only if somebody tells. And, Bent, you're an equity partner, now. With a corner office. And it's eminent domain. There was going to be a road no matter what."

"Until Chloe found a way to stop it."

I pulled into an Exxon on the feeder road, stopped the vehicle, removed Loeb's Blackberry and his wallet from his jacket by reaching in his pocket and taking them while he remained motionless and clueless.

"What are you going to do?" he asked.

"What do you care?"

"Look, I'm not happy about any of this either. What exactly is my 'mom' going to be bringing into the family, anyway? Plus my stepmom is distraught. But the old man rarely does anything that makes sense. I guess that's part of his appeal."

I walked to the passenger side, opened the high door, grabbed Loeb by the arm, and pulled him out. He offered no resistance, which seemed about right.

"He shouldn't be doing business with someone who has less to lose than he does," Loeb said.

I manhandled him beside a windshield squeegee and paper-towel trash-bin station under an awning. He'd be out of the sun.

"She can't even spell."

I drove. Somewhere past the North Belt I tossed his phone and wallet out the window.

iv.

The Hummer featured a large-screened, buxom-voiced GPS box that got me easily from the freeway to Bold Springs, a place that consisted of not much more than some low storefronts around two intersections, both blessed with stoplights for some reason. There was little traffic at first, but soon I found the rear of a procession of cars, quite a few Audis and BMWs among them. A good portion of the legal profession of the greater metropolitan area, and, I assumed, all of Chloe's friends and family, too, passed that afternoon through the "business district" of Bold Springs (indicated by a city limits sign: POPULATION 420). There was a "country" gift shop; a restaurant resembling Maggie's steakhouse ranch; and a bed and breakfast in a tall and rangy mansion that reminded me of the house in *Psycho*, except it was right on the road and had plenty of parking—this being the place I thought we were headed at first, but the procession passed it by. There was a small Action Savings and Loan, and I remembered Tony's anger about a bank, and "that joker out there" who'd tried to buy everybody out. After this scatter of commercial buildings, on either side of the two-lane came a few blocks of wood-frame houses with fallen porches and weathered paint, all hunkered behind mud yards under leafless oaks. These I supposed to be Tony Ruiz's clients, hopeful that a loop could alter their fortunes. I was nearly fifty miles from the Leudecke Ranch, yet Maggie's anti-capitalist influence spread its powerful pall . . . or could, were it allowed to flex its Republic of Texas pedigree from the 1830s.

Soon this residential area ended and the pavement narrowed to a single lane that curved left, upwards towards a visible hilltop home. The line of cars rose so slowly and steadily up this road that a bystander might have thought "funeral." Finally, guys with flags and green jackets appeared to direct cars onto a grass lawn at the foot of a hill. The Hummer and I seemed to be the last arrivals, and when I couldn't get the thing into the space pointed out for me, I bore on a bit farther, hung a left, and just put it in a culvert under some chinaberry trees. Shit, it could climb back out, right?

I went up to a sidewalk with everyone else, although I was decidedly more poorly dressed. The group of us climbed in a trudge towards a white tent awning beside a good-sized mansion at the very top of the hill. That was one long sidewalk, and I started to feel winded. At first I supposed that the Loeb family plot was also situated on the grounds—the old family homestead—because we passed an iron rail with leafy swirls, hooked designs, and several aged monuments and stones behind it. There were faceless angels, crosses, and cracked tablets. Creepy. Many were old, viny, and separated from more contemporary arrivals by low stone fences. What had Loeb the Lesser said: he'd grown up here? Well, there was a nice old graveyard in the backyard to play in.

Good times.

I attempted to educate myself concerning the generations of Loebs: but no—glancing through the markers—some of those most effaced by the elements going back to the nineteenth century—the names indicated the present occupants were recent additions. There were plenty of Buchanans and Fullers. I saw two Kuykendahls, a common settler family of German extraction in the region. In the corners of some of the walled enclosures stood smaller markers with first names only (Tobias, Deacon), each with the carved title *Trusted Servant*. There'd apparently been lots of servants on that hill over the years, and lots of trust. I looked at the white awning flapping in the breeze. Chloe was going to be somebody up there.

But I knew she was somebody. I was the one who always knew.

It appeared we were approaching the House of Loeb from the rear, the awning centered in a large lawn carpeted in lush St. Augustine, so green it looked to have been painted.

Hell, maybe it had been painted. Along with bird baths and feeders, sculptured juniper animals ringed the perimeter. There were two bushy poodles and nearer the tent—naturally—a giraffe. The space under the tent was narrow and—odd for a reception—longer than it was wide, with the bride and groom seated already on folded chairs atop a raised platform along one of the long sides, while a woman with shoulder-to-ankle-length-wing-like sleeves moved around them and talked into a headphone mike, like the kind rock stars sported onstage. Thomas Loeb sat in a tuxedo on this elevated perch with both fists on his knees, and grinned big (he had really big teeth). He flipped his ponytail occasionally and pointed at people in the crowded space, recognizing and validating them with a smile and a nod of his head. And Chloe was there beside him, a white blur that I glimpsed only for an instant through the crowd.

I didn't really want to see her, though. Not yet.

The tent was packed and chaotic. The woman in the winged sleeves was some kind of mistress of ceremonies, and it didn't take too long to contextualize her as she kept explaining who she was: Chloe's sister Claire. Claire reminisced over the PA system in a high voice similar to Chloe's. She toasted, and called up others whose names appeared on a sheet of lined paper to similarly reminisce and toast and—shit. Chloe's sister was actually kind of hot, her hair longer and darker than Chloe's, her features more chiseled: high cheekbones and a dancer-like slinkiness broadcasting itself even under all the fabric. But to see the two of them side by side also made it clear that Claire was, compared to Chloe, kind of . . . usual. Wait on a street corner in any large city and you will see twenty—yes, very attractive yet very ordinary—skinny brunette Claires go past for every Chloe. Her voice did have, unlike Chloe's, an annoying, digging quality. Or: possibly all mistresses of ceremonies at wedding receptions project such a tone.

The crowd could be identified much along the lines of the couple on the raised platform: the old, wealthy, and bloated mingled in one group, while the young, middle-class (or below), and glowing-with-health-and-energy likewise mixed in their own section nearer the canapé and punchbowl table. There were few representatives of any category in between.

The bride's friends were definitely more multicultural. I found myself near a group of emotional, sniffling young ladies—Chloe's school chums? "She is so beautiful," said one of these to the group. I moved as stealthily as a man in a smelly orange-striped guayabera shirt could move to peer through the heads and see just how beautiful she might be. Chloe held not flowers but a green spray of some kind. And the dress was modern, but classy: long, trim, sleeveless, and white—but something seemed wrong. That was Chloe, yet it wasn't. Like the line of cars going through Bold Springs, there was a funereal impression inside the tent, too, but mostly it was the bride. Rather than saying she looked "beautiful," I might have said "natural," as she was much more put together than I'd ever seen her, yet also dryer, less mobile. Chloe's coloring was off: her skin sallow, near gray, and almost powdery in texture. In profile—for she'd turned to a particular corner of the room to interact with some people there—she seemed a Madame Tussauds version of herself. Her hair was a great deal more involved than any style I'd ever seen her use in real life. This was some kind of weird, grown-up Chloe.

Claire, in the flowing dress, moved and talked, though she was difficult to hear at the back of the tent where I decided to lurk. Something about the sister's weirdly draped dress, the crowd, the synthesized music from small speakers up in the rafters of the tent: it gave the impression of a New-Age, time-share, hotel ballroom investment seminar. Unlike most of those, however, many in the room sobbed, apparently from something heartfelt coming from Claire.

I do not do well with sobbing. Young men—quite a few of them—sat teary-eyed in ill-fitting suits, and, like I said, a number of women Chloe's age or younger formed recognizable clumps in the audience, huddled together. In fact, the one who'd spoken about her beauty eyed me carefully. She had an olive complexion, and smelled of clean soap.

"Hi," I said.

"Who are you?" she asked.

"Enemy of the bride."

This made her laugh. "Another one? Because she's so great?"

"And I'm so old and shitty in comparison? Yes."

"And *fat*," said the girl, passing a palm down her own torso, indicating, I suppose, that the bride made her feel chunky in comparison.

"What bullshit!" She looked fine. Something about her was of the "beefy nurse" mode, but that's a perfectly good mode. I looked towards the canapé table. "Can I buy you a drink?"

"What if someone thinks I came with the guy in the guayabera shirt?"

Really? A clever person, then, though young, and probably inexperienced, and I wondered if she was from the law school, or from Chloe's undergrad days. Did she ever get into town? She wiped at her eyes. "Sorry," she said. In spite of her chipper mood, it was clear she'd been crying.

"There's no better time to cry than at weddings and funerals. I mean, well . . . the whole absurdity of life comes bubbling up at those times, don't you think? Without filtration."

She smiled again, worked at getting her eyeliner off her cheek with the corner of a Kleenex. "I think I'm just overpowered by the vodka coming off your breath."

"It's rum. Do you like Hummers?"

"Those suck."

"But do you know how hard? Stay here, I'll find us something."

So this might be alright. I moved towards the punchbowl and imagined that this girl had problems. If she were Chloe's age, she no doubt had problems, including the whole issue of having a friend ripped from the single world, and what that meant. You can't end up unescorted (no one appeared to be associated with her, and her fingers revealed no wedding or engagement ring) and alone on the back row of a tent reception for a twenty-six-year-old friend who was marrying an incredibly wealthy, though grotesque, old fuck without having problems. And I could listen to those. Women love to have people listen to them; that's always the main thing. Maybe we could go someplace when this was all over, have a drink. Talk about the mysterious world of . . . what?

Chloe was lost to me, but life would go on.

I found the open bar nearly hidden behind its line of booze seekers, so went to stand in that line, sniffed at myself a little, tried to keep some distance from others, but as I waited, the line snaked past a table with a green felt covering where several photographs of Chloe and Loeb—*Loeb the Elder*—leaned in frames, each of which broke my heart. There was Big Loeb, grinning in black on his Harley, a noticeably darker tint to his ponytail. There again: shirtless, with his gut protruding, Thomas Loeb grinning big, holding out—as if to serve on an altar—a beastly, huge, dripping tarpon, behind him the deep sea, Pacific blue. I touched the table with my fingers to stay in the world of matter. I felt dirty from my travels, and so, so poor. Did equity partners make more? How much more? That seemed like something a real lawyer would have asked. To get it I would have to accept the title and corner office. I could use the money. It was closing in on November. How would I pay for Henry's special school the following month otherwise? Otherwise what? Find a desperate Malaysian storeowner somewhere willing to bankroll it? Maybe with enough left over to file the paperwork for the desperate Vietnamese restaurant impresario before he ordered me chopped, peppered, and deep fried? I tugged at the scratchy collar of my cheap shirt.

On the table, I came across a photo of an adolescent girl, maybe middle-school age. It wasn't Chloe . . . no, it was. And she was such a butterball. It was the little fat Chloe I'd heard so much about, the one who no doubt lived on—insecurities intact—inside the triathlete who sat in the white gown on the raised dais. This used-to-be Chloe had a space between her teeth, too: there must have been braces involved at some point. It was the fat child Chloe had—through biking, running, working out—carved herself into the trim young woman I knew . . . with somewhat chubby ankles.

"This is starting to make sense now," Tony Ruiz said at my elbow.

"Fuck me. What?"

"Hey man, I was invited." He fingered the sleeve of my shirt. "Who are you kidding?"

"Asking questions you know the answer to again." I looked around for the olive-skinned girl. Where was she?

"I hear you're the one who gets the big man his women."

Tony pointed at the raised platform and the waxy-faced girl in the wedding dress. "Nice work."

"I don't even know him"

"Really? I play golf with him. In fact, I have this inside driving range. He comes sometimes." Tony shrugged. "Well, you gotta do what you gotta do for The Man." He indicated the photos. "I was thinking odd couple, till I saw these. Do you think the little fat girl in her cries out for the chub-fuck that is Thomas Loeb?"

"You're always so kind to one and all."

"I mean, Thomas Loeb, Esquire. But he did it, I'll give him that."

"Really. You think this is it?"

"I mean his road." Tony nodded down the hill. "Be going right through the petunia garden."

"I thought there wouldn't be a road."

"If it were to ever be built, that's where it *would* go. Yeah, Maggie's on board, didn't you know? But, hey, I'm happy."

"And the nice people of Bold Springs?"

"Could be ripped off any minute, but I'll look out for them. And they won't be robbed by some crazy witch! Nice work all around, Bent." He slapped my shoulder, and it hurt. "Come sit with me."

"Don't you want to know about Eladio Trejo?"

"What difference does he make now?"

"Right. Some dead Mexican. Who gives a shit?"

Ruiz looked around to any who might be listening, then spoke histrionically: "I have never seen this man before in my life. But hey, did Alice ever find you in Mexico?"

I was stunned.

"I take it that's a yes?" He glanced around. "Is she here?"

"You."

"Well, she was worried about you."

"How could you do that to me?"

"What? I wasn't supposed to talk to her? Besides, she already knew. She just pumped me for details."

"But how could you tell her about Chloe?"

"Who the fuck is Chloe? Wait, you mean . . . ?" He looked towards the raised platform. "Oh . . . hey, how you doing, man?"

He reached past my shoulder to grip a hand, and I feared Thomas Loeb, Tony's indoor golf partner, had descended from that platform to have a word with his friend and the uninvited interloper, but no: it was Alan from New Hampshire.

"I expected a bigger tent. Hey, Bent."

These were two people I thought I knew, and who I thought knew—and possibly even liked and respected—me. Yet they had both been invited to this soiree while I hadn't. In fact, I hadn't even been told about it. And I was one of the bride's best friends.

Wasn't I?

"Looks like you did get south of the border." Alan examined my shirt. "I'm surprised you're here. I hear you're *persona non grata* with the bride's family."

"Latin," said Tony. "So big time."

"At least, that's what the bride's family is saying."

"Why is all this happening?" I asked.

"Hey," said Alan. "Alice ever catch up with you?"

I rubbed my forehead with the back of my hand.

"Did you tell her how bad this guy had it for Chloe?" Tony asked. "Because I know I didn't. I've never seen the chick before today."

"I did know that," said Alan. "He told me all about it in a drunken telephone call."

"Oh shit, Bent," said Tony. "You need to start drunk dialing me if it's going to be that good."

"It was all new to Alice, though. Did you bring her along?"

"No." I fumed. "I'm expecting her at any moment, of course. Why in hell would you tell Alice that?"

"She was worried about you!"

"I told him the same thing!" said Tony. "Hell, I thought Bent was just setting this Chloe up with the Big Guy."

"No I wasn't."

"That's not what everyone's saying around here," said Alan.

Tony pulled Alan aside. "You know, I might have something for you to do for me up in Connecticut."

"New Hampshire."

"Same, same."

Big Loeb had stepped down from the podium by that time and worked his way through the crowd. Claire hovered above the now solo Chloe. "I prepared an homage for this one," said the sister. "Oh yes. A five-page tract." The crowd laughed. "On aspects of cause and effect, how actions produce other actions, which then go on to form other actions. And then others."

Frankly this woman seemed a bit drunk herself, and Chloe might have thought so, too, as she shook her head and grinned.

"But I want you to know," said flowing, nearly sobbing, white Claire, "that all of this. All of it. . . ." And here she swept her wing in a way that gave the impression she didn't mean only the crowd under the tent, but the lawn, the carved topiary animals, the hillside beyond the awning: possibly the woods, graves, cities, and universes beyond that. "It is preparation only. Preparation for a very good thing."

"Yes," said some of the people in the crowd. "That's right." Several young men, football players by their stance and mannerisms, raised fluted glasses towards the stage.

"Some much more creative, good thing to come. You and Thomas will create a reality for yourselves. Reality as it can be, at its most wonderful. Its most improbable."

"Its most expensive," I said.

Too loud, too loud.

Claire searched the crowd for the source of the statement, but soldiered on while my ears burned. I needed to get a drink, find the olive-skinned girl (what was her name?), and calm down.

"Yes, I dare say," said sister Claire, "that it is going to be downright unbelievable . . . in general." She became suddenly coy. "Some of you may know—oh, Thomas must know this for sure, wink, wink—that Chloe has a tattoo."

A mixed murmur from the crowd, and Chloe looked downward, framed her hand over her face to cover her eyes, but seemed in good humor about this inevitability.

At the canapé table, Thomas Loeb guffawed. His mouth showed teeth, crumbs, and sturgeon eggs.

"And I won't necessarily say where this tattoo is." Claire

touched the small of her own back, just above the buttocks, pressed a palm against her own winged gown.

"Tramp stamp!" said one of the football players, and received snickers and high fives.

"I will tell you that this is a tattoo of an A." She sounded nearly mystified. "I always wondered what that A stood for, and I always meant to ask." She grew suddenly, almost eerily somber—a shade of memory drawn over her mirth. I hate those kinds of hyper-dramatic drama chicks. I imagined the dark, snarky girl at the back of the tent rolling her eyes.

"Today . . ." Claire went on. "Today, seeing you with Thomas, and thinking about the life you have before you, I know what that A stands for after all," Claire said. She nodded to herself. "Oh yes. You have an A on your butt, Chloe,"—laughter general from all directions—"because . . . you are *AWESOME*." And she began to daub at her eyes with the fringes of her oversized sleeves.

This mistress of ceremonies clutched her list—a sheet obviously torn from a spiral notebook—and used this to call more people up from the crowd, offering each a rolling-pin-sized wireless microphone to make similar testimonials. The first few to speak were young women who took the hand microphone from Claire to express their admiration for their "best friend." It was, in fact, quite a lot of best friends.

But most around me weren't listening by then, and, in fact, by that time—still not having made it to the head of the drink line—I found myself among a group of my co-workers. Or it's possible that they had arranged themselves around me, surrounded me to make sure I didn't cause any trouble. But I wasn't there to cause trouble. It's just that the line to the open bar was moving so slowly, and I wanted to know a few things. I wondered if there were any way—if I hung around long enough—that I could get just a few words with Chloe.

I remembered her phone call to me. I halfway seriously still felt I needed to get her out of this mess.

"I doubt it stands for *awesome*," said Kebba. "I mean, I'm not saying she's not awesome. She wasn't totally great in the sack, but it's probably something else."

"You don't think she was that good a lay?" asked Alan from the edge of this group.

"She looks A-1, it's true," said Tony. "Firm, young tits and everything."

"She wasn't very inventive," said Alan.

"I'll still say the tattoo stands for A-1, though," from Tony.

"Invention," said Kebba, his voice deep, "can be annoying."

"I'm going to kill all of you," I said.

Right in front of me, already established in the line, was a matronly, aunt-like type, probably not used to the champagne that she'd already used to toast the happy couple. "She's so active. Do you think the tattoo stands for *active?*"

"I'm beginning to think so, yes ma'am."

She touched my chest, as if she'd just gotten an inspiration. "How about *always on the go?*"

"Also appropriate."

I tried to remember what the "A" stood for. Chloe had told me one time. Possibly more than once. At the coffee shop the week before I hadn't even recalled that it was an "A," but had thought it was a dragonfly. No. There must have been a dragonfly tramp stamp somewhere among some of my other friends or relations. Then, as the aunt turned away from me, I did remember why there was an "A."

Claire gave the microphone to a small boy, Ricardo, who was maybe seven or eight. He stared out into the audience, frozen upon realizing the size of the group he'd be speaking in front of. After a few silent moments, he began to cry, which elicited a sustained "Awwww" from those assembled. "I love you," he managed to get out, finally, and Chloe leaned from her perch to give him a hug. I didn't catch the relation: nephew or child of a friend, or something. I noticed a frizzy beehive hairdo colored that red-found-nowhere-in-nature hovercrafting it through the crowd, and so moved to hide myself from Heidi.

"*Accessible?*" said Harrell, the naturalization and immigration head. "I mean, from what I've heard."

Dalton murmured. "Yes, heard."

"*Agreeable,*" said Alan. "Until she's not."

"I can't believe you fucking people," I said. "What's wrong with you?"

"I can't believe you put any store in her," said Alan.

"No," from Kebba. "He was right to do that."

"She certainly sounds *acquiescent*," tried Dalton, and he squealed a bit with the silliness of his own attempt.

"*Aquatic*," tried the old aunt again. "Such a good swimmer."

The woman depressed me with her happiness at this event, her pleasure in the tattoo-guessing game, her assumption, whoever she was, that she was part of things. That she was taking part in life. This woman, obviously, didn't realize how much of the world had simply passed her by, and done so in a way that would never happen, obviously, to the two sisters up on the stage, timeless in their youth, with their moist cheeks, their "firm young tits," and their diaphanous gowns.

In my trouser pocket, I rolled the pill bottles with my fingers.

"Bent," said Alan. He raised his chin, pointed it into a corner of the tent. "See those guys? Who look like firefighters?"

"I thought they looked like a football team."

"That's Station 11 in the Heights. It's behind her apartment building. They call Chloe 'The Moped' there. I thought maybe she used one to get around the neighborhood, but two of them told me it was because she was good for a ride, but you wouldn't want to be seen on her."

For the second time that day, I had an attorney on the ground. I tried to shake him, or throttle him, my one good friend who'd left for New Hampshire, or threaten him, even, but words wouldn't come. Up on the raised dais the little boy, Ricardo, wouldn't let go of the wireless mike until he managed to squeak out "I love you *very much, Chloe*," before giving it up finally, to great applause and more "Awwwww"'s.

Kebba, Tony, Harlan, and Dalton pulled Alan and myself to our feet.

"Oh, slipped and fell," said Tony.

"They're fine," boomed Kebba, though no one really seemed to ask about us.

Yellburton, that fuck with the swimming pool, grinned, swigged some champagne, and wandered away.

"Knock it off, Bent," said Tony. "Come with me. I told you these people aren't worth a shit."

"Like you'd know," said Dalton.

"You," I said to Alan. "I went to Mexico because of you."

"What?" from Tony. "You went because of me."

"She told me to do it." Alan nodded at the raised dais. "Her!"

"Doubtful."

"Then ask."

I left the bar line, shook away from my "colleagues." The powerful-looking young men of Station 11 began to look different to me: an evil gang, like the one that had fallen on me in the Calle Mesones a few nights before, rather than comrades on a team of emergency responders. I felt like I needed to go somewhere for a long nap, or at least find a place to sit down, hang my head, close my eyes.

I thought, for some reason, about Yucatán Bob, and whether or not he was conscious when the plaster started to fill his tub, and what that would feel like. I looked around for the dark-skinned girl. Yellburton had gone to stand near his whole family, an arm around his wife's shoulder, protective. The friends and acquaintances of Chloe filed up onto the stage to wish her well, but nobody from Davison, Kohlhoeffer & Loeb took a turn.

"*Able*," said someone in the crowd. They were still mulling over the tramp stamp. "Or *alert*. Or maybe *always smart*."

Jesus. I noticed there was no ALIENATED, or ANGRY, or ANNOYING among the tattoo conjectures, any of which would also fit her, from my experience, but I noticed also that the mood on Chloe had shifted among the lawyers in the crowd— or I translated that mood more accurately. She wasn't harmless any more, and I could smell the resentment. I definitely wished this whole line of "tattoo guessing" had never begun, however, because I couldn't help myself, and I even knew I couldn't.

"*Asylum*," I said. "It's an Asylum logo."

"*Shhh!*" Ruth was there, suddenly, and she hissed at me, but a quiet break in the overall tattoo conversation and the shout-outs from the platform had made my input and her response ring louder than they would have otherwise. Many turned to look at us.

"You know," I said to them. "The band? The Bad Boys of Grunge Rock from Seattle? It's an 'A' for 'Asylum' with wings around it. She snuck out on the sly in high school to see the band when her parents told her not to, and then rubbed it in their faces with the tattoo." I looked around at all of them. "I actually know her, see."

"Her parents are behind you," said Ruth.

I turned slowly to find a red-faced, middle-aged couple. The man appeared to be chewing on something distasteful while the woman had her lips to his ear. Both glared at me. Neither looked particularly like Chloe.

I went back to Ruth. "What is it everyone has against me, anyway?"

"You and her both. She's skinny. She's a whore."

"Well, that's just two things, then. And keep it down— her parents are behind us."

"She doesn't have to be alone." Tears rimmed Ruth's bottom lids, which were heavy and reddening. "My husband has remarried," she said.

"Okay."

"When I came to work? With a shiner? My wrist bandaged in gauze?"

I tried to remember.

"You said I shouldn't put up with that any more, and that I could do better."

I couldn't place it, but shit. "Of course you can. You're better off alone."

"No one is."

Was everyone insane? Maybe I had advised her to leave her husband, but was I sober when I did so? Why on earth would anyone take advice from me?

It wasn't worth arguing with her. I put on my most gloom-filled expression, and prepared to eat shit for yet another tragedy.

"I'm sorry."

"That you are even pretending to care is pathetic, but I've still come to tell you," and she took me by an elbow, "they are about to throw you out of here."

"And you're giving me this warning because. . . ."

"Because I hope you'll just go. I'll go, too, how's that? I can't take much more of this anyway. Please, Bent."

The right thing was to leave, accept my equity partnership, head for the big door of the awning, and go back and find Loeb's Hummer. It would be easier on everyone, including Ruth, who'd been kind enough to warn me. I shouldn't put her through any more of this. And I was sick of every fucking person under that big white awning . . . well, maybe not the black-haired chick with the olive skin. And there were some waiters who seemed alright. But I nodded. I resigned myself. In fact, I got nearly out into the sunshine with Ruth on my arm before I realized I hadn't said anything to Chloe at all.

v.

"A man in the preoperative stage of a sex change procedure to become a woman," I said, "enters a triathlon . . . as a female. You're into those, right? Triathlons, I mean, not females. What do you do? Do you let her, or him, compete?"

"What a surprise," Chloe said. "Except it's not."

The surprise, I suppose, referred to the fact that I had stepped up onto the platform and taken the chair beside her—the chair still warm from Thomas Loeb's aged, enormous, and pungent ass—and I had done this as the winged creature, Claire, continued to work through her list of well-wishers. Individuals rose to take the wireless microphone and say a few kind words to their beloved Chloe, who grinned and nodded at each. I remained beside her, my legs crossed, and also nodded at the kind well-wishers.

"Came to express my congratulations," I said. "And sympathies. But, do you have an opinion? On my example?"

"In my opinion, you've been drinking." Somehow she managed to make the statement into a lilting song. "Having fun?"

"Can't remember a better time in my life. What about my cyclist?"

"Ban her . . . or him," Chloe said. "She or whatever . . . it could damage the sport." She spoke from the corner of her mouth, still smiling at Stuart's not overly thin fiancé, who had arrived with many cheerful platitudes (though seemed a bit frantic as she sought out Loeb everywhere: "I thought I saw his Hummer in a ditch."). "And you knew this could happen, by the way."

"You've got to be kidding."

"I told you. And told you. You were the person I confided in the most."

"You didn't tell me it was this Loeb."

"I didn't tell you it wasn't."

"You also didn't tell me you'd fucked the entire labor and immigration department."

She grinned then and took the hand of a young woman in a mini-skirt who had finished her testimonial about "the best camp counselor ever." The camper glared at me just as Chloe's parents had.

I pondered it. She had always been all: *Loeb is so THIS,* and *Loeb has all THAT.* Crap. Was it possible she had been telling me the whole time?

"Not fair," I said.

"And you are?" Claire asked. She levitated her big microphone towards me, perhaps thinking I'd placed myself "on deck" to make a general comment of congratulations— someone "off list," but acceptable.

Chloe moved quickly to push the microphone away with her forearm. "Don't mind him."

"I could say a few words."

"No!"

Claire returned to her list and her fluttering. "She seems a bit crazed," I noted.

"That's another nice thing to say. Look, Bent, he's really funny."

"I've heard he is. Not having ever had the pleasure of meeting him, of course. . . ."

"A pleasure you won't get today either, unless he comes with the security guards. Please leave. Ruth was supposed to escort you out of here. Oh: he's a great kisser also."

I closed my eyes. "I can't picture it."

"Smells good."

"Rich people do. Always a turn-on."

"You know it's not about that."

"Except maybe a little."

"Don't."

Another young woman had taken up the microphone, someone from a group of athletic women Chloe hung out with; they'd encouraged each other through several endurance events. "In fact," said this woman, "I was supposed to run eighteen miles this morning, but I knew Chloe was too busy to talk me through it on my cell"—she held up her cell phone—"so I made *five* miles, went home, and ate ice cream."

Hahahahaha. I slapped my knee.

"His eyes are so kind, Bent. Even in a picture. I *like* him. You wouldn't want to hurt him, would you? After all he's done for you?"

"Like what?"

"Do you even have to ask?"

I considered it. Obviously, she meant the ongoing kindness Thomas Loeb had bestowed upon me by continuously—and for quite an extended period—not firing me.

"What do you have in common? He's not exactly an Iron Man."

"He supports my athletic endeavors."

"Did you really sleep with all of these people?"

"Of course not!"

"Most?"

She squinted into the crowd. "Well. . . ."

"Stupid." I leaned forward, made to leave. "To think I was . . . *whatevah.*"

She pushed me back into the chair. "You are."

"The phone call. *Bent, I've made a mistake.*"

"I needed you then. I really did. I wasn't sure." She wrinkled her face in that unattractive way she needed to be on the lookout for in the future. Or: maybe she didn't have to worry about her looks any more. Maybe she could revert to the child-chub Chloe and forget the running, the biking, and the working out.

"Make sure to leave time for your child to come out and play," said the triathlon girl. She also didn't seem to be too happy to find me there beside her running partner. "Push yourself to invent new ways to do and be."

"I thought I could talk to you about it," she whispered, still out of the side of her mouth. "I always talk to you. But you take things too seriously."

"*Bent, I need you* . . . you said."

"Look, when he told me. . . ." She began to whisper.

". . . how badly Maggie was going to hurt his own interests."

"Do you have any idea how unethical that is? The whole firm could go down if Maggie had a mind to press it." It was unbelievable. "So you didn't inform her about the land grant."

"In the end it wouldn't have given her any advantage."

"That's for her to decide."

"You still don't get it about her, do you? Look, it was confusing. What to do, ethically. I called you to help me figure this out."

"Glad to. Inform Maggie about the Treaty of Guadalupe Hidalgo and don't go through with this marriage."

"It's done!"

"A technicality. My God, you're one of those sneaky Loebs now."

"There was never any way she was going to stop that road, and it's not even going to be built, and she's getting what she really wants."

"She is? She wants her ranch. Doesn't she?"

"Plus the poor people will get some cash."

My head felt as if it were unevenly attached to my neck. Wobbly. "Ah, the poor. Yes. While the Loebs and the Leudeckes all get a little richer in the meantime." I glanced at the trees along the hillside of the estate. "If I'm such a problem for all you high-minded officers of the court. . . ."

"Don't start."

"I'll leave the firm. That might give you more room to operate. You won't have to be so sneaky in the future."

"Don't do anything on my account."

"What does that mean?"

"Finally," said Claire. "We'll hear from Chloe's boss at the law firm where she's been interning. Her special mentor. He has written a poem that he will now recite."

"I've written a poem?" I looked at Chloe.

"Plus, he's also her new son!" There was laughter all around. "Stuart Loeb!"

I saw Kebba, who stood a head taller than the rest of the crowd, slowly bring his hands together. Even his applause was languorous and ironic.

Naturally Little Stuart didn't appear, as he stood, at that

moment, under an awning at an Exxon station some fifteen miles away, unless he'd managed some other kind of transport. So Claire spoke on, stalled, pointed out how this person, and the time he took to write the verse he would soon recite, bespoke of how important, and how highly in its regard the law firm held their professional staff colleague, and the Loebs their newest family member. "Stuart Loeb?" she tried again, but got no response, nor did the elder Loeb stir from where he was speaking with Yellburton at the canapé table, a cracker between his greasy Loeb-lips. He stared hard at Chloe, who, I could see, caught his eye and then shook her head.

She was holding off the troops.

"So, immigration fraud selling visas before there's anything to sell, insider information hoarded for personal gain, withholding pertinent—no, vital—advice from a client: all that's fine, but if some sweet little t-girl wants to ride her bicycle, fulfill her dream. . . ."

"Bent, why don't you tell me what you need? If you'd like, I can drop by your office now and then. We can have lunch."

"Is that something you want to do?"

"If it will help you, it won't be a bother. Or, I can stay away completely, if that's better for you. I mean, you'll be on the thirty-third floor anyway."

"So, either way is fine."

"Look, I didn't bother sending anyone else off to Mexico."

I thought about it. "You didn't?"

"You believed in me. And you're my friend."

I came pretty close to accepting it. Also, however, pretty close to saying something like: "Just come with me now."

No. I mean it. I was close. I was close to taking her hand. Tugging on it. Pulling her to her feet. I could get her off that platform before anyone thought too much of it, I figured. I might even make it past the canapé table, and past her new husband. "Won't be a sec," I'd say to Thomas Loeb—the first words I'd have ever spoken to him, although I'd worked for him more than a decade and a half—and the last words he'd ever hear from me. It would be the last he'd ever see of the two of us, as well, because . . . out that big, gaping flap in the big white tent we'd go, into the sunlight and onto the green lawn. "Look at me," I'd say, and I'd tug on her slightly damp fingers. "Let's run!"

"No," she'd say. She'd be shy.

"Let's skip, then. C'mon."

The two of us would have gone down that hillside, skipping towards the sunset. I'd leave Marisel. I'd leave my autistic son. I'd done worse things (hadn't I?). Besides—hadn't they both left me? They started it! Chloe and I would gather speed as we stiff-legged it down that sidewalk that descended the hill, swooshed past the cemetery, whooped it up. We'd laugh and taunt the dead people. All those *dead people*. Dead people can't run out of weddings (or even receptions), but we could: together, start a life, go to a new city, find new jobs . . . we could drive her new son's new Hummer to Austin, Dallas, Phoenix, Jackson, Seattle, Schenectady, Providence, *yes*. And as I drove the Hummer up and out of the ditch, I'd have her on my lap. I'd have my hand on her tummy and my lips on the back of her pretty neck.

I came close.

I came near to pulling off a kiss, too, before I made my spiel, my offer, and told her of my plan—our plan—of escape, and would have, too, up on that raised dais. It would have been the sort of kiss that might have made a difference, although probably a difference that would have lasted only as long as it took Big Loeb to arrive with those two guys in the green jackets—hired to deal with the parking, but suitable for security detail as well. Heidi had me, too, suddenly, by the knee. Then two more guys in green.

"Get your shit together," Heidi said.

"Dear?" asked Thomas Loeb.

"You're all worthless and you know why," said Heidi. She went for my crotch again. Pretty soon I was on my feet, held up between four of the green jackets, who also fended off Heidi. We were all a bit unsteady.

"You're a danger to my sport," I said to Chloe.

"Get him out of here." She turned her face from me.

Oh, she was acting. Pretending to be disgusted with me. For Big Loeb's benefit. Clever girl.

I think.

They lifted me and took me feet first out of the tent, and I saw the girl with the olive skin outside, drinking champagne with some of her friends.

"I'll call you," I said.

She looked at the four men, who swung me between them, each holding an appendage. She laughed. She was really something.

"But will you, my love?"

She was right, I never did, but something nagged at me as I was lugged down the hill. What had Chloe said? About Maggie? That she'd gotten what she really wanted?

Which was?

Part VI.

Incantation

i.

It was hella hot: one of those record-breaker days in a record-breaker summer, when the temperatures in the north of the state went triple digits for weeks at a time, and I sat up in the shiny, skin-scorcher aluminum stands along the third-base line of a softball diamond in a sun-blasted Dennison, Texas, afternoon. Around me stretched prairie flatland. A few school and office buildings in the distance rippled in the heat. Driving in we'd passed a Jamaican dance club, whitewashed so bright it hurt the eye, and from the stands, I could see that white building easily—like a welder's arc that flashed along the road. There was no breeze. Nothing moved but the players, mainly the pitcher, who targeted one towards home plate, then—*thud* of ball on bat, oh please, one more run, it's all we need.

I wanted it to end, yes, but I also wanted to see that last run along the baseline, the foot planted firmly at home (it was always a question in that league: did the foot land on the base?), the coach (who turned out to be a surprise) running over to home plate to yell and motion the runner in by scooping his big hands, to try nearly to draw the runner home by creating a vacuum with all the hand scooping. "Run! Run!" Would he make it?

It happened! It was the winning run, and, jacked up, the North Houston Scorpions emptied their dugout, some uncertain of where everyone was going, but all of them running out anyway, most with arms spread wide in a Victory V. Best of all, the foot that touched home was Henry Wallace Bent's—*him*, my Little Bent who scored the winning run in the Southwest Young Adult Developmentally Delayed Slow Pitch Softball Special Olympics.

With the game tied, he had doubled at the bottom of

the seventh (there were only seven innings in Young Adult Developmentally Delayed Slow Pitch Softball Special Olympic regulations). Then the slugger kid came to bat, the one whose dad was a Navy recruiter: the kid with forearms like Popeye's. I'm not claiming that this was because of the Navy connection, but they did look like Popeye's forearms. He stepped up, *thoink*, and it was Henry's day.

Amazing.

Henry had not played, or even seen, softball before this season. Ever. He had not struck bat to ball. But Marisel, who stood beside me in the rickety stands, stayed close to him after she dropped tennis and tennis friends, after she started spending more time at home. "It's time for *training*," she would say, and hand Henry his glove, which had once been my glove, and which, after a few months, he began to put on his left hand by himself. Every day in the backyard while I was at work, at first before and then after school, then—as we couldn't afford private summer school any more, or private anything, really—several hours more every day through May and June, Marisel and Henry were out there. They threw. They caught. They swung bats and ran imaginary bases. After Henry's run on this day in Dennison, Marisel and myself did not exchange glances, did not share a cold smile, but without thinking, fell instead into a clench, clung to each other, tongues in each other's mouths, our faces slick with sweat. I levitated her as I squeezed, raised her up from the hot aluminum, her arms around me, and when we kissed, her lips felt dry and unusual, the lips of a stranger.

Those kinds of lips are always exciting.

"I can't believe it," I said.

"Henry," she said, almost squealing in pleasure.

The end of my employment at D, K & L had saved my marriage—or the thing that served as my marriage—after all. Knowing exactly why would probably require a combination of explanations having to do with pity, sentimentality, and pragmatism. Oh, and there had been that apology of mine, too. Cheso had been right about that part: never underestimate the power of saying you are sorry, especially when spoken with sincerity.

Or spoken with the impression of sincerity.

There was, then, after the fashion of sportsmanship in any league, a lineup: the long walk of "us" (North Houston Scorpions) past "them" (Sweetwater Blue Devils) with manly handshakes all around: "Good game" and the like. But man, the Blue Devils were very blue. Sweetwater, in far West Texas, was, to my understanding, nothing like its name. It was a dry pit. It was more depressingly hot and arid even than Dennison on a hot summer afternoon. The West Texans seemed not quite able to process how they'd come so far only to fall so short, and appeared baffled by a requirement of sportsmanlike gestures at this point in the process. They were losers who knew they were losers, as opposed to the other, more common kind.

Well, poor Devils. We were victorious.

A lady next to me, Glen's mother—who arrived at every game I'd attended with a soft side cooler box, an umbrella, and a truly wide ass that pretty much wiped out the possibility of anybody sitting behind her—demonstrated her expertise at coming up with new and exciting ways of saying "Good job!" to the Scorpions while she clapped and made screechy finger-in-mouth whistle exclamations. That's good because there is only so much "Good job" any boy can take, but I knew everything she said came from a list, one of those "positive feedback reinforcement" charts, which is what these parents did love to do: consult resources. It was almost like she'd studied the list just before arrival at the ball field. "That's the way!" "You've got it right!" "Splendid."

I stood with my arm around Marisel's shoulder, and the sun beat down on my Lumpy's baseball cap, and it was as if I had a window seat overlooking myself, especially my relationship with Henry, especially all that I hadn't helped him with. I saw the lists I hadn't memorized. Games and practices missed. School meetings. Flash cards. Once I'd tried, unsuccessfully, for nearly twenty minutes, to teach him how to blow his nose. I had tried to get across the concept of forcing out the air and snot rather than sucking it in. No go. Otherwise, I had not been there for any of it. Parents like Glen's flabby mom, the (surprising) coach, the Navy recruiter, even Marisel were full of these resources, and were always willing to share them.

The sun continued to beat down on my cap. The view from the window closed. I knew I would not change.

But today was the day of the tournament and the Scorpions' win, an "away game," a "field trip," that had required travel of nearly five hundred miles up into the far reaches of North Texas. And that the winning run came from Henry Bent: all this made for a very, very good job. The game had run long, and put me off schedule, and I checked my watch (a cheap digital model). I needed to be somewhere in six hours, before sundown, or matters were going to be difficult. "I've got to go," I told Marisel, "or Ruiz is going to shit a cow."

"Ruiz." She felt ever since I began to work at ABOGADOS Y MÁS, and began to bring home miniscule paychecks at irregular times, that I wasn't really working at all: that all I did was frequent topless bars with The Latino Guy, but that was untrue, except some Fridays when we weren't busy. Lately we had far too much business for that kind of crap. In fact, Ruiz and I had teamed up, at his suggestion, to represent the Rangarajan family (or "family") pro bono. "Shit, Bent—those people will take us to the Supreme Court. Twice! Guy's a pain in the ass, but he is pretty brown."

I had taken care of two other things quickly after arriving at ABOGADOS Y MÁS, one with Tony's help. My first week on the job, I phoned the La' Mai II and reached Mr. Duc.

"You're calling me, you asshole? What explains your delay?"

"That's for me to know, and you to . . . oh, never mind."

"You need to watch your shit. You don't know who you're talking to."

I didn't feel like getting into it with him. "I've got your visa processed. Or your nephew's," I said. "We'll schedule his interview. Sorry for the . . . hang-up."

"You're kidding."

I gave him the address on Navigation Street where he could send his nephew for some paperwork. It was a work visa Tony had arranged already but that had never been claimed. Or so he said.

"Three things," I said to Mr. Duc. "First, that is the sorriest Asian gang I have ever seen." So, yeah, maybe I was getting into it with him a little, but he surprised me and laughed hard.

"Gang? They're waiters. Got ya, right? Right?" He laughed with his high-pitched, nasal buzz.

"No." I thought I'd test one other theory. "Two. Please call off the giant with the single eyebrow. Now."

There was a long pause. "What is that, some kind of peckerwood proverb? Translation please?"

"Never mind."

"What's the third thing?"

"Your nephew. If anyone asks during his interview, he's an expert in C++ programming."

"Mr. Bent," said Ngo Dinh Duc, "I never doubted you."

The second call I made upon beginning my work for Tony was to Channel Four, where I asked for Isaac Mintor, *Eyewitness Probe*. After a few hours, he got back to me.

"It's the new loop being built . . . or supposedly being built in the Northwest counties," I said, then proceeded to explain, as best I could, the Regional Center created by the offices of Davison, Kohlhoeffer & Loeb, how the firm had been working hard to get the road approved, but how efforts to stop the loop had also been taken up by D, K & L.

"That sounds illegal," Isaac Mintor said. "Or really, really dumb."

"There's more. Fire up the white van, and check with the Securities and Exchange Commission." I hung up, returned to the issue of a man's attempt at asylum for his Salvadoran daughter who had unwisely dated two men. More unwisely, one worked for a pro-government death squad, the other an anti-government death squad.

Some people have real problems.

I had never worked so hard as I did at ABOGADOS Y MÁS. Marisel, however, was right to have suspicions, because, really, I didn't have to go back to work just then, on that same afternoon following the softball finals. I didn't have to be back in Ruiz's office for two more days, in fact.

I needed to be somewhere else.

Marisel and I stood by the dugout and I waved at Henry. He was still on the field, where he high-fived his teammates with a stolid expression, his fingers spread wide. I waved and hollered, but he didn't notice, much the same as when I would return home from work. "Splendid," I called to him. "Good job." It was alright. I was proud of him. Possibly more than I thought I'd ever be.

I wondered how long that feeling would last.

"You have to leave now?" asked Marisel. She'd come up with the team in the van with some other parents, her new entourage. She needed to have an entourage, no matter what. There was talk of pizza and celebration. Her hands were on her hips and she no longer wore the museum display of rings, only her wedding band.

"I was here, wasn't I? For the big game?"

She nearly smiled at me, I think, before I gave her a last peck, said good-bye to some parents, and turned away.

I made my way across the sun-blasted parking lot. I didn't know if Henry really saw me there in the stands, or saw me wave good-bye. For that matter, I didn't know if he ever saw me, or knew who I was, or if every morning when I told him "Say good-bye to daddy" and he said "Goory Darry" and "Dee di daddy dino-saur" if he ever really got the concept behind it. I turned back and Marisel was beside my son, looking pretty good in those shorts as she shielded her eyes with her ringless hand and talked to one of the mothers, smiling. She seemed, what?

Happy?

Let's not go crazy.

And the coach . . . I mean, that guy was a really good guy. He was a really, really kind, patient, saintly sort of guy I couldn't stand, and who I'd met before, or at least seen before. It turned out to be Miguel Perez, the "good son" with the immigration issue, the fanged reptile tats, the eighties marijuana conviction and the screaming mom. Perez had turned out to be pretty impressive after all, but I always felt like I needed a bit of a buzz after spending an afternoon with him, and I'd go and achieve that this afternoon, too, if I hadn't quit drinking. I'd also quit the pills. I'd quit everything. I didn't even drink with Ruiz when we went to topless bars, or the Cantina Henderson, places that were some of his favorites for discussing business away from business. But I'd been around the coach more than once since first seeing him with Monica (that was the name of his attorney—I knew everyone's name now). I'd certainly heard him talking to the softball parents about their kids. He looked fierce with his glowering, his ink, the sloppy basketball shorts, but he'd say things like, "Oh, Chris. Chris, he'll go after everything. Chris's got the *never quit*." And "I'm paid just by the smiles. The smiles on the faces is all the pay I need." The fact that he'd sold all of us these Scorpion uniforms, caps, and T-shirts from his graphics and design company didn't matter. At that moment, several parents worked to roll up the GO OLYMPIC SCORPIONS banner we had chipped in and gotten, too, to bring to Dennison for tournament play, and that pricy banner had also came from his shop. No, he would not be retiring on T-shirts and a banner, and yes, he'd gotten into Developmentally Delayed Slow Pitch Softball Special Olympics because of his son—his kid who'd had a disability that actually proved fatal at age thirteen. Yes, Miguel Perez was great, a great man, an undeniably big-hearted human and a definite asset to our community who deserved his green card and more. But, shit. His tone. It really got to me.

"I wish professional sports figures could just have the same attitude these kids have," Miguel said to me one time. "That's what it's really about."

Yeah, I get it.

Sadly, some parents were bringing their little screaming Blue Devils into the parking lot, getting down to eye level with them, promising them French fries, promising them popsicles, trying to explain that you can't win everything. The poor Devils looked devastated.

And so I got to the very weathered and pockmarked Elantra (there was some kind of sappy tree in the gravel lot behind ABOGADOS Y MÁS where I parked in the daytime, and it dripped onto the car, then the dirt got into the sap—kind of pointless to wash it by this point), and it was a *hot* motherfucker in that Elantra, and very humid. Some seal problem in the trunk lid had caused the spare tire well to fill with water every time it rained. It had been basting for seven

Special Olympic Softball innings on a North Texas prairie, and I was pretty sure Marisel knew that I wasn't heading back to work at all, and I would not be manning my desk there at the back of the big room at ABOGADOS Y MÁS today, or taking up my role as designated gringo.

I put on sunglasses. I drove my un-air-conditioned Hyundai across the cracking dead grass.

I wondered if my candle in the trunk had melted.

I headed south, through the Dallas metroplex, and then into that part of the state that is so boring: everything the same on the same stretch of highway. I dropped down I-45 through those towns that are also all the same: Corsicana, Fairfield, and Buffalo. I stopped for fast-food tacos south of Centerville, but didn't much register them in my mouth. When I got back on the freeway, I somehow became confused, and had trouble holding that last taco and steering, too. I thought the feeder road was two-way when it was only one-way, as a sheriff explained to me when he pulled me over. "Man, I screwed that up," I said. "I'm so sorry." (Shithead.)

"Shame. It's a $500 fine. Could cause a head-on."

"Oh, man. My fault (fascist turd). Totally my fault (living goatfucking turd.)"

"Okay, move on."

"Don't blame yourself," the self-help gurus advise.

Hah!

Just before I got to the on-ramp, I noticed a convenience store.

So fine. It had been seven, possibly eight months since I'd had a drink of any kind, back on the day of Chloe's funeral—I mean wedding reception—but I'd just saved myself a $500 fine. A celebration was in order, and in order again for Henry and his good day. Such a fine job somebody was doing with that boy, even though Alexandria and Cheso had to find other positions because of our reduced circumstances. At least I had gotten them visas. Wait: let's celebrate that, too. And I even thought about Chloe and thought again that this was the day to break with my no drinking tradition, because, after all, it was our anniversary.

So I bought and sipped from one can—just one—of that weak, can-flavored beer convenience stores south of Centerville sold from tub-sized ice chests near the checkout counter. I didn't feel like I was putting that in my mouth either. Nothing registered any more. When I stopped at a Madisonville convenience store a half hour later, I got a six-pack and checked the trunk. Bizarrely, the candle didn't look much worse for the extreme heat. It was one of those candles that are really decorated glass tubes filled with wax. The decorations—herbage, leaves, distinctive flowers of some kind, fat with drooping petals—were etched into the glass, which was damp from the closed space's humidity and the rust-red pond that sloshed in the spare tire well. I brought the candle up front with me. I sipped beer, watched for sheriffs, and glanced at my candle occasionally as I got back on the freeway. I headed towards Huntsville and beyond that—once again—Bold Springs.

ii.

I'd gotten the candle from Maggie Leudecke the month before. Just a few days after my departure from D, K & L, the financial pages had reported how she'd relented and officially given over some of her low-lying prairie for the Road to Nowhere, but there was no sign of freeway construction to my eye as I arrived at the ranch. All seemed as Tony predicted. After a few months, the legal entanglements holding back the new loop had fizzled to nothing, or next to nothing, yet the project had not moved forward, but merely simmered down: the road, the easement, the parcels that bordered it had all been converted into "packages"—commodities meant to be bought and sold, not actually constructed. It had been one of those chimerical deals the whole time, with money and rights changing hands, futures more important than the present: a side bet made on pieces of reality with the ante raised, traded, then bet and raised again. If Isaac Mintor ever found anything wrong with the road and its finances, it must have been too complicated for him to crowbar into a ninety-second news spot. The deal did not lend itself to simple explanation or flashy headlines: just small, corrupt fortunes.

"Maggie's mistake," said Tony one morning at The Kettle, "was to consider this an actual threat to someone with a firm and shapely ass as wealthy as hers. See? I know these things."

But he didn't. Maggie hadn't made a mistake at all.

After a few months I called her, and went to see her. When I drove past the stone wall—covered now with summer vines on a rampage—and pulled into her compound, the thought of detonated hillsides and earth movers as big as houses disturbing that isolated place did indeed seem absurd, but the scenery had been altered completely anyway. Only the sunken wrecker truck remained as before. The lumber of the barn had been dismantled and removed; the chickens were nowhere to be found. All of the trash, cardboard, and rain-warped furniture had been cleared from the porch, and three guys labored in her dusty front yard, lashing boxes and crates onto a long-bed trailer that had been attached to Maggie's towering black pickup. Thick ropes that looped through the handles of the two scorched caldrons held them in place in the bed of the truck.

"My sister and I are going out of state," Maggie Leudecke said. We were once again at the kitchen dinette while around us workmen and movers stomped and called to each other through the halls of the log cabin mansion. Paperwork, forms, and what appeared to be slickly produced promotional materials featuring enticing landscapes covered the oilcloth surface of the table. Presenting mainly snowcapped mountains and cloudless blue skies, they did not appear to be scenes from anywhere nearby. At first I just considered these part of the general chaos—a spring-cleaning spree at the Leudecke ranch. I'd hoped we'd be in the room with the sofa, where I'd watched the piece of flint. Also, once again, I was offered no coffee.

"I didn't know you had a sister," I said. "Is she a witch, too?"

"Camellia. She's a year younger. No. She's into these ridiculous sweat lodges. Not that there's anything wrong with them," she added quickly

I paused, recalling my experience at Lumpy's with the coyote and the Sparrow Lodge.

"I'd say I'd love to meet her," I said, "but think I'll pass. Does she also wear a red ribbon around her wrist?"

"She used to. She took it off."

"And your ribbon is gone. From around your wrist."

"Yes. Yes it is."

"Because. . . ."

"I removed it."

Not a person for pleasantries. "So, you don't want to be here when the road comes through? Because Tony really thinks that's not going to happen."

"I'm leaving permanently, Mr. Bent. I've sold the ranch."

I had been rubbing my nose as she spoke, so stopped with my fist covering my mouth. Because of this, when I asked: "You sold the ranch you hired us to save?"—it sounded more ominous through my clenched fingers than I'd really intended.

"Or traded it. It's Daddy's problem, now."

"Wait. . . ." I hadn't come to see her about the Road to Nowhere at all, but this sounded powerfully off-kilter. "You mean, the ranch owned by Leudeckes since Spanish land grant days? The spiritual home of true-blood Texas aristocracy? You sold? Or traded? For. . . ?"

"Well. . . ." She leaned forward. Her low, sultry voice— that modulation that had staggered me more than once—now sounded muted, and raised almost an octave in tone. The voice of a younger and more excitable girl. She seemed nearly breathless. "My sister and I are going to Aspen, Mr. Bent." She grinned. Beamed. Maggie indicated the brochures spread before us on the oilcloth. "To the Beartooth Ridge Resort and Corporate Center."

I examined the illustrated materials as she handed them over one by one. The Beartooth Ridge Resort encompassed forty "panoramic" acres of Colorado countryside, contained 26,000 square feet of meeting and "event space" in six Bauhaus-inspired buildings, each of which included state-of-the-art audio-visual capabilities, twenty-four-hour business centers, guest suites, and first-class resort amenities, including fine cuisine using "sustainable regional ingredients."

"You're moving to a resort in Colorado?"

"Camellia and I are going to run the resort, Mr. Bent. It belongs to us now. Daddy's transferred it to our names."

Indeed, in the fine print at the bottom of the Beartooth Ridge Resort brochures, alongside contact information and disclaimers, was the Leudecke International Inc. imprint. And now it was Maggie's? And . . . uhm, Camellia's? This was a hell of a trade: no way less than forty acres of heat-blasted— albeit historically important—Texas prairie equaled forty "panoramic" acres of Greater Aspen. "I'm sorry . . . you're not going to be a witch any more?"

She smiled. "Of course I am. I'm expanding. I'm moving into large group self-improvement awareness training, Mr.

Bent." She barely glanced at me as she spoke, fixated on the mountainous terrain of the pictures. "We'll host companies, organizations, community and governmental groups . . . law firms." She smiled. It was the most seductive smile I'd ever gotten from Maggie Leudecke.

"You're letting lawyers in?"

"Some. Camellia is installing a wood-frame, domed sweat lodge here by the lake." She touched one of the documents with her hard, bony finger. "Also of Bauhaus-inspired design, and climate-controlled."

"A climate-controlled sweat lodge? I thought. . . ."

"We're converting the campus into a spiritual retreat. Top leaders can meet with practitioners of Wicca, First Nations spiritualists, shamans, kahunas, innovators in the field of personal and professional development, multi-level marketers . . . working with us at Beartooth Ridge, they'll develop solutions."

"Hang on. You're saying this thing was already your father's?"

"Innovative solutions, at that."

Maggie continued her spiel, dealing out pseudo-spiritual-psycho-babble similar to that featured in the promotional materials. Obviously this had been in the works awhile. The "interior path" and "vision quest" were emphasized, as were spiritual wisdom, life lessons, symmetrical and harmonic money management, and the fact that all fees were nonrefundable. I tried to process it.

"Stop," I said. I didn't even want to get into how difficult it was for me to see this person as the controlling force behind an exclusive resort-institute. I mean, she couldn't spell "hooky." But there was something more incongruous. "Wait. Because, see . . . you're a *Leudecke*!" I held out my hands. "You can't just quit the ranch to go to . . . *Aspen*! That's . . . that's. . . ."

"Mr. Bent, have you ever been sitting around in the evening, some pleasant evening, and heard someone say, 'Why, it's so nice tonight, it's almost like we're not in Texas at all'?"

"Of course, but. . . ."

"This Leudecke is tired of waiting for pleasant hours. I'm going to go find them."

I rubbed my forehead. "Back up." I began to piece

it together. "Your father wouldn't give this to you, would he? That was it. He wouldn't hand this over, until you had something he wanted."

She shrugged. "The ranch by itself isn't worth much."

"Right." The Leudeckes had, perhaps, started their empire on that parcel deeded by Spain, but that didn't really translate to real-world real estate dollars. "Unless it's got a highway and easement parcels running through it. But that's still not enough for this." I indicated the luxury resort photographs. "But if you stop it *all* from happening . . . how many other Leudecke properties were you holding hostage with your save-the-ranch lawsuit?"

She raised a finger. "I believe the term is leveraging. And when that crazy little hell bitch you had working for you . . . what's her name . . . found that exemption . . . Jesus. It all turned out alright in the end, and scared the crap out of Daddy, but thank the universal laws of cause and effect that you two didn't pull that off or the land would be worthless." She snorted. "And Mr. Kohlhoeffer assured me you were the one man who would never stop that road."

Fuck me. The Leudecke case had been a nest of hidden—and competing—agendas, and I'd almost managed to derail nearly all of them, and totally failed to learn the fate of the Trejo brothers in the bargain. I'd let down not only my client, but my client's opponents, and even the law firm that had handled—apparently—both sides of these jockeying interests. And I'd accomplished it all by failing to live up to their collective perception of my complete ineptitude. Tony's clients and others like them, who thought they were battling greed, racism, and corruption, had mainly been struggling under the shadow of two sisters' desire to leave the heat and play resort in a Rocky Mountain wonderland.

I felt small, as if surrounded by a dark shell, and stood to leave. "You needed to stop the road, but . . . not to the extent that it stopped the road."

"Well put."

"Enjoy Colorado." I rose and turned for the front door.

"I'm sorry, I thought you knew all this. I mean, why are you here otherwise?"

I stopped. I eyed the prices she'd be charging in Aspen for spirit quests, personal transformation, and teambuilding. "I don't think I can afford your nonrefundable advice any more."

"Well, I do have a lot of packing to do." She made as if to raise herself from the dinette.

"Okay, *fine*," I blurted out. I actually touched her. I put my hand on her shoulder, and nudged her back into the chair, then sat down myself. "It's Chloe. I've come about Chloe."

Maggie Leudecke narrowed her eyes. "Chloe."

"The . . . my assistant. Or paralegal." She still didn't register recognition. "Little hell bitch?"

"What does *she* need?"

"No, it's . . . a few months back, last time I was here, as you'll recall. I was in love with her."

Maggie Leudecke's face revealed nothing.

"Maggie," I said, feeling no compulsion to be formal or professional around her. "She got married. To someone not me." I began to feel a bit teary-eyed.

"Oh, right. You hooked up with her, didn't you?"

"Yes, yes. Me and everyone else I know."

"Bizarre. So your heart is broken." Maggie sounded as emotional as people who speak of famine in distant nations on distant continents. Terrible: but what can I do about it?

"I came back because I thought you were the person I needed," I said. "To help me."

"With?"

"Her."

Maggie cocked her head. "Sounds like she's . . . spoken for?" She spread her palms to either side on top of her resort brochures. "Married. That's pretty hopeless, Mr. Bent."

"Yes," I agreed. "*Pretty* hopeless."

And then I asked her to tell me about Roy.

She was surprised at first, I could tell, but smiled. Maggie Leudecke grew distant, looked off over the sink, across the prairie, into a stand of oaks along that little creek—a creek that would, no doubt, kill all those oaks with overflow from the septic systems of suburban tract homes someday. I was fairly sure her prairie would be another treeless, blasted inferno covered with winding streets and claustrophobically huddled single-family dwellings by the time Henry was my age.

"Roy," she said. "My guy. It's funny you should ask."

Roy, it appeared, had a drug habit "back in the day," but had kicked it. He had been with her for many years, and they had been so happy together. "We traveled all over Mexico, all over the Southwest together in his pickup truck."

"So he had a lot of vacation time?"

She stared. "He wasn't employed in the classic sense. Fine. But he wasn't a bum. You are starting to sound like Tony Ruiz, Mr. Bent."

"Just Bent." I saw no reason why Tony or I couldn't feel superior to someone who "wasn't employed in the classic sense." Then again, who was I to tell anyone about objects of affection? She was no doubt right to think fondly of him. At that moment I knew there would never be anyone who would crawl into a sleeping bag with me in the back of a pickup truck.

Maggie seemed slow on the uptake that day. Actually, she seemed a little stoned. I wondered how she'd ever possessed so much power over me.

I can't help but admit it: I also wondered if maybe her sister was hotter.

"Roy kicked this habit, until some old friends of his came by and gave him a taste of what he used to love."

"It sounds like chocolate, when you put it that way."

"He was forty-five," Maggie said. "A stupid waste. Amazingly, this very friend who brought him the dangerous and fatal substance died a few months back." She looked away from me. "In a canoe accident."

It was broad daylight in a well-lit country kitchen, complete with box of baking soda on the metal sink, stacks of Colorado brochures on the dinette, and legal documents spread across the oilskin tablecloth. My skin crawled. Maggie Leudecke, without her ribbon, seemed somehow crooked, angular. A manipulator. A leverager.

A witch.

"Holy fuck."

She shrugged. "Eladio passed himself off to some

Dutch construction company as somebody who knew me, could influence me. He showed up here one day."

"He caused Roy's death."

"Roy's overdose. Eladio was always into me, even though he'd married one of my best friends."

"Janet," I said, trying to remember what Lieutenant Montez had called her. "Or Jane."

"Jamie, yes. He showed up here, and we went down to the tank in the evening. We had some wine."

I paused for a long while. "I distinctly remember," I said, "you telling me how getting rid of someone . . . using spells or powers to do so . . . it's what no sane person would ever try."

"True. No ordinary person should ever attempt it. Without understanding the consequences, that is."

"You said it would turn back on you. Not be pretty."

She leaned close. "Oh, it has to be worth it. And, no, it isn't pretty, Mr. Bent. Then, after Eladio drowned, Jamie came to visit me. It was a few months later in a place I owned down in Mexico."

"In San Judas Tadeo," I said. I noted she'd used the word *owned*. Past tense. Lieutenant Montez had told me about the Leudecke's liquidation of assets in San Judas, so it sounded like that had happened. To fund the High Country Mega-Dollar Witch Resort? "What kind of accident did she have?"

Maggie Leudecke laughed. Or possibly cackled. She rested her chin in her hands, her voice low and confidential. I felt there was no one around. Possibly no one for miles. Yes, I could hear the workmen in the yard outside, and others moving furniture in some distant part of the structure. Still, there was the oddest sensation of isolation, and an ominous feeling, like what she told me would mean I would never be allowed to see the world outside her house again.

"You know, she might have ended up getting herself injured one way or another, but . . . something happened. She came, on this visit, and cried about Eladio, and I sat with her and cried about Roy. And we talked about how we would always love our boys."

"Uh-huh." So loveable, the heroin dealer Eladio and the jobless, dead junky Roy.

"The most mysterious part of all was that I had placed a candle in the bathroom when Jamie came over, a particular kind of candle. And I had made an incantation over this spiritual tool."

"Tool?"

"Every candle is a bright peephole into the spirit world, Mr. Bent. And as we were talking about our boys, that candle smashed into a million pieces."

So, by this time, this Maggie Leudecke, who I'd had such a strong reaction to—who I'd picked up such a strong vibe from—well, except for that vibe that, as it turned out, I'd picked up from her sister—she was just starting to creep the shit out of me. "First off," I said, "it's kind of weird to use a word like 'smashed,' don't you think? Do you mean something like 'shattered?'"

"It was sitting in the bathroom where Roy himself had departed for the next world. The visitation happened while we were talking about him."

"Second of all, you're talking about all this love, these vibrations, living off the land in a pickup like a gypsy . . . but the whole time you've been manipulating your father, the State Transportation Board, DeVries Construction, and even me to negotiate a resort takeover." I closed my eyes. "So you're saying it was Roy smashing the candle?"

"That's right."

"His ghost? Good old dead boyfriend Roy? You mean, like . . . wait, he died on the pot or something? That's why it had to be there?"

She crossed her arms and turned from me. I really had blown Maggie Leudecke up into something huge in my mind, I think, and here she was using words incorrectly, being all . . . *capitalist real estate mogulish,* and talking about this great boyfriend of hers who sounded like a non-starter to me. I mean, what sort of a life career does a guy have, exactly, that allows him to drive all over Mexico, all over the Southwest, at age forty-five, strum a few instruments, and snuggle in sleeping bags under the stars?

Helping out people with their I-94s, F-1s . . . helping people in trouble navigate the H-1B program at a factory ABOGADO shop . . . it was more "up and coming" than that. Hell, she'd probably been into him because she could manhandle the powerless little twerp like a hand puppet.

"What you're telling me is that this unemployed dude had been there shooting up in the bathroom . . . and OD'd on the john, and so you drown the guy that gave him the heroin. . . ."

"I certainly did not."

"Drowned Eladio Trejo right here on this property, and a few months later, a candle explodes in Mexico and. . . ."

I was myself losing the train of logic in all this.

"Roy saved her life, I think," said Maggie. "Saved from, as you say, a terrible accident."

"Uh huh."

"Because he was sending me a message. He was telling me how his death was necessary to our relationship. As great change sometimes is. You see, Mr. Bent, if you want the love part, and the possession—of a person, or a ranch, or anything—you have to live with the pain part."

"Like I don't know that. But I think I need to be going now."

"I see no indication that you do know it." Then Maggie grabbed me. She grabbed me hard. She took my arm in that leathery claw of hers—and squeezed.

"Ow!" I said.

She spoke, and at any point where she would come to some word of emphasis, she gave my arm a hard, clampdown pinch, and said she was telling me, now, about the sort of pain that cannot be stopped: something so good that when it was gone, it was a gone kind of gone, a loss so intense you wouldn't wish it on a hostile enemy, you wouldn't seek to use it for the worst sort of vengeance, and, "Those are the stakes of love, Mr. Bent. You might want to ask yourself if it's worth it to have a love so strong if it comes with a hurt so strong."

"You're kind of hurting me right now."

"Has anyone ever held a street parade for you, Mr. Bent?"

"Of course not."

"Have you been put on a stage in an auditorium, given an award? With the president in attendance?"

"Of the United States?"

"With ballet dancers also performing for you? And a children's choir, a party with orchestra, plus avant-garde jazz ensemble, and actors hired to play your life—your life, which makes the crowd go wild?"

"Roy did all that?" He must have been one of those layabouts with inherited money, too. Disgusting.

"No, I'm asking you to imagine how you would feel. Here, let's customize it, just for you." Maggie held one palm over her eyes momentarily. "Okay. The woman playing piano in the jazz ensemble, she actually leans up over the top of the instrument, plucks at the strings like playing a harp."

I could feel beads of sweat on my forehead. "In a long, flowing gown?"

"Oh, yes."

I don't know. It was the description, or the dry witchy tone of her now once again low, low voice, but I was getting a hard-on, an intense one. Really, I couldn't remember getting an erection like that . . . nearly painfully stiff, gravity-defying . . . in quite a while. Yes. It hadn't happened Viagra-free since I don't know when. And something in those squeezes she was putting so rhythmically on my forearm was connected to it. It was Maggie herself, more than anything she said. Until she added: "And this pianist is Asian."

"No!"

"In her gown, plucking her Bergendorfer with long, elegant fingers, while you're eating *migas* overlooking a river from a trellised Spanish balcony."

I smelled around me the damp and moldy vinyl-floored kitchens of my childhood, then gripped the dinette as the shudder moved through me. My spine rattled. My vertebrae nearly loosened, and I gasped.

"But then . . . well, really it's not even that it ends," she went on. "It's not that it stops. Or it's been ruined. But it's gone, Mr. Bent." She released my arm suddenly, the way one of those body-rub artists of the "cum and done" variety let go of your cock—the ones who don't mess around after the happy ending has been reached. My hard-on had disappeared. Gone! As if she knew, she reached over and—maddening!—

patted my lap like it was a pathetic puppy that had begged to come in from some rainy back porch.

I was pissed. "Is this like one of your high-priced life lessons for teambuilding when you get to the Rockies?"

"As always. In the moment of it being there, it already isn't. Because you know that however good, at some point it will . . . it will just go, won't it?" She leaned away, pulled a paper towel from the upright dispenser, wiped at her fingers with something like disgust, as if she really had just jerked me off. Truly, I had to glance down at my crotch to make sure she hadn't. "It will not have time for you. It will be sleeping with someone else, or want yoga lessons instead of you, or God will tell it *this is wrong*, it can't happen any more. Or it will go out of town with you on a trip to a luxury hotel where all they have available are rooms with double beds, and it will take the other bed."

"Shit."

"Right, Mr. Bent? Those are the instants that are built into every one of your other instants."

She didn't look at me, which was fine. Maggie Leudecke had gone from sexy witch to frumpy, post-coital, sun-damaged chairman of the board in a matter of seconds.

"We were at the tank, and I told him I had no intention of allowing that road on my land, and he got a bit drunk on the wine. He went out on the canoe, to impress me, I suppose, and stood up on it, and when the canoe slipped out from under him, the bow caught him on the chin. He went under the water."

Sweating and shaky, I could barely say through my anger: "And you didn't go in after him."

"He went under the water."

I thought about the way the floor had gone out from under me the first time I'd met . . . well, I guess it had been Camilla Leudecke—how the bedroom floor had failed to support me just listening to Maggie's voice on an internet stream. If I'd been in a canoe. . . .

If I'd been in a bathtub. . . .

"But his brother. Yucatán Bob."

"Yucatán Bob gave Eladio the heroin that destroyed my

Roy." She wadded up the paper towel, stepped on the foot pedal of a nearby trashcan to raise its lid, and tossed the wad inside. The lid closed with a smack. "Is there anything else?"

I stood, rubbed my arm, pulled off some of the paper towels myself. "What kind of candle are we talking here?" I asked.

She happened to have one left, and let me have it—along with handwritten instructions for the proper incantation—for thirty dollars.

At the door, I stopped. "It was you. Both of them. It was you."

Maggie Leudecke shrugged. "They were fine. The last I saw of them."

iii.

Those people who say it's a bad idea to even get started on anything once you've given up everything—they have a point. It was obviously a point Roy should have attended to. Too late for him, but too late for me, too, because there I was. I leaned back, listened to Steve Earle on the MP3 player, spun the steering wheel of the crapped-out Elantra with one finger. Seven beers in, I saw a package store outside Madisonville, and . . . I might have been starting to lose a bit of my courage, was the thing. I also might have been losing a bit of my good feeling towards humanity, which I didn't have that much of anyway. So, at this package store, I looked and, sure enough, they were stocked with real liquor, including rum. At first I couldn't find anybody in the place. I poked around nearly ten minutes, but then this big guy ran in from the back, like he was in a hurry, and stood behind the counter. I asked, "You wouldn't happen to have any of the actual syrup, the syrup that's used in those soft-drink dispensers like you have over there?"

The clerk was poorly dressed: a tall but fat, rangy-looking, redneck guy. We went together into the back room. A screen door let some air come into the close space, but it hadn't stopped the flies. It smelled kind of gamey back there, like many cats had made it a home for a while. There was a metal table that had probably once been a workbench, as it had a vice at one end—no handle—and beneath it several rows of dusty syrup canisters. One of them, according to its sticker, was diet cola. Also back there: one cage. And in the cage was a coyote.

"Oh fuck no," I said.

I was much more buzzed than the last time this had

happened to me. Plus the cage was smaller, the coyote larger, his space much more limited. This wasn't the same wild dog I saw in Bastrop, surely! But who knew? It would be bigger than the one I'd seen eight months before, if it were eight months older. At any rate, the panic I'd seen in that pup's eyes from before was drained out of this creature. This was one defeated canine: morose, depressed, and still. It lay flattened on the damp floor of the rusted cage. Flies walked across its dry brown nose.

I looked at the counter guy. Let's put it this way: he had no name badge. He'd also, possibly, never tucked in his shirt in his life, or encountered a dental hygienist. He was tall, yes, but looked totally out of shape. Obviously a meat-eater, his stomach was huge and hung over his belt—like the impressively proportioned Thomas Loeb—and he had an irregular beard, some spots on his cheeks still baby smooth.

"You want the syrup?" he asked.

"How much for syrup and coyote?"

"Buy the syrup or move on."

I could take this guy, couldn't I? How embarrassing, though, if I tried and found I couldn't.

I felt old.

I looked around, saw something I did want. It was a hose connected to one of the other syrup canisters that ended in a plastic, pushbutton spigot.

"Okay, these items, and the rum. Got any cups?"

I noticed, then, the guy's unibrow.

"Hey," he said, and raised something that looked like a TV remote. "Look." He pointed the device over my shoulder, out the back screen door.

In the gravel yard behind the store, a dirty white truck sitting in front of a low garage burst into flame.

"No," I said.

I moved to the door, mesmerized. It wasn't nearly as high-impact as watching a BMW burn in the night, but the little truck's cab soon filled with roiling smoke, and pillow-like lozenges of fire burst up from below the chassis, then from the grille, and around the seal of the hood. Then I'm pretty sure the gas tank exploded—independently of the fire in the front—and the truck *popped* loudly; then, like a cat getting comfortable, settled into the gravel on its rear, as first the driver's side tires, then the passenger's side tires, caught and burned.

"Impossible."

But the counter man had peeled off his filthy, sleeveless T-shirt. He loosened some dark straps that had been hidden under it. A padded appendage—his gross stomach—dropped onto the floor with a thud and revealed an impressive six-pack beneath this apparatus. Shirtless, his arms—though visible the whole time—now looked powerful and solid, and he started to peel at the scraggly beard, flicking it off his fingers onto the workbench.

"You."

"Bent."

I had no real idea what this guy was capable of, and knew that the best thing would be to play it safe, say something that would pacify the situation.

"I've been missing you, asshole," I said. "Have you found someone else to fuck with, or did you actually have to go get a real job?"

"So predictable." With his hands on his hips, he leaned down towards me and took a big sniff along both sides of my head. "Drinking again."

"What's it to you?" I wobbled a bit from all the beer after such a dry spell. Outside, the truck crackled and snapped. "Tell you what, I'm going to skip the most obvious *Who the fuck are you?* line of inquiry and go right to *Why the fuck are you doing this?* How did you get here? Hey, this Road to Nowhere deal is solved."

"So?"

"Ngo Dinh Duc is a happy fuck," I tried.

"So?"

"Who do you work for, then? Is it the Leudeckes?"

"Of course not."

"Uhm . . . Satan?"

"I'm Agent Reynolds."

This meant so little to me that in my state I chuckled. "Agent of what? Irritation? Why are you chasing and . . .

annoying the shit out of me, Agent Reynolds?" I felt in my beery haze that possibly the best thing would be to run out that back screen door, try to beat him around the building to the Hyundai, as he was definitely blocking the way back into the front of the store. I needed to get the hell away from there. But that seemed like just asking for a slow-motion nightmare: a game of tag that wouldn't really get me anywhere.

"FBI. Dallas office."

Oh, shit.

"Alton?"

He grinned. Not pleasantly.

"You're fucking Alton?"

He seemed taken aback. "Why not?"

"I just expected somebody. . . ." I wasn't sure what to tell him. Somebody good-looking, for one. Somebody hot. This was the cockmeister? This was the guy who did it for Alice? The serving-boy with the menu of sexual delights? I kicked a bit at his "gut" on the floor. "She just always described you as a fancy dresser."

"Obviously not all the time, Mr. Bent."

"Obviously." Although buff and very tall, his skin wasn't good. His cheeks were pockmarked and lined. He vaguely resembled horror movie butlers that come down creaking stairs in haunted mansion pictures. "How the fuck did you find me here?"

"I knew you'd stop. This is the only package store between here and Huntsville."

"No, no. How did you find me *here*? Why do you know I'm even on I-45 on a Saturday in July?"

"Special Olympics today in Dennison," he said. "It's easy. You're pretty much the only one who doesn't know where you're going."

"That's a nice thing to say."

"Plus the tracking device."

"No."

"Since the day you tried to give me a dollar, cheap motherfucker." He leaned towards me again, bared his teeth, and I saw it in him: the homeless guy with the attitude problem who'd nearly smacked Chloe—my little Chloe—in the face with some dripping produce back in October.

Fucking October.

"You are so sued, Agent Alton."

"Can't sue a governmental agency."

"That's a myth." Wasn't it? I pointed out the back door. "And I'm suing you, not the feds. What's with the auto infernos?"

He shrugged. "Getting your attention."

"Getting my attention to what end? Look, Alice and I are *not on*, okay?" I waved my hands, crossed my arms in front of me. I X'd her out in the scorecard of the air. "I mean, she was trying to get to me through my mother for a few weeks, but she's met the son of a natural gas tycoon."

"I know."

"Go haunt that guy, you crazy fucking ghost." I went to move around him, get back to the front, escape—forget the rum, the diet cola. The coyote seemed nearly dead: motionless, and didn't even bother to follow us with his eyes. "She tried to convince me she was pregnant for a while. She's so full of shit."

Then he had me, brought my shirt up around my throat with his powerful fingers.

"Not that she isn't great."

"Too good for you."

Authority figures. You've got to respect them, or they'll definitely fuck you over.

"Way too good for me," I agreed. "Yes, you're right." I could barely breathe as he clamped down on my collar. "Although, that thinning hair."

He narrowed his eyes. "You think you're smart. You're not."

"I think I'm something, but smart isn't. . . ."

"I'd hoped that little Indian guy might shoot you when he found you in his wife's apartment."

"Mr. Rangarajan *has* a name," I croaked. So, he'd placed that call. Followed my every move, since . . . Austin? What else had he done? I tried to mentally tick off the inexplicabilities that had befallen me in the last few months. It would be good, at least, to have those loose ends wrapped up before I was asphyxiated. Let's see: burning car. Homeless psycho. Panjamalangabang's telephone tip-off. The "woman" in the poncho. For a second, I had a mental image of a sculptor/

drug dealer encased in plaster but then remembered—no, I think I know who's responsible for that one.

He squeezed tighter. I felt I might piss myself before I died. It was time to make nice.

"You took my picture of Eladio Trejo," I managed to say. "Thief."

He shrugged. "Who turned out to be a drug dealer. Couldn't really do anything with that." He loosened his grip around my throat then.

"You might have told me."

"No."

I pointed at the cage. "So, what's with the coyote?"

"Coyote?" He looked confused. Really, he didn't seem so smart himself. "Who gives a shit about a fucking coyote?" He let me go.

I leaned over, fought off nausea, tried to keep all the beer in my stomach. I held my knees and breathed in deep. Poor coyote. "Fine. But look, Alice isn't innocent in all of this. If you haven't figured that out. . . ."

"It doesn't matter. You needed the punishment."

I cringed as I imagined him saying that to Alice—her in an outfit resembling a rope hammock, him in a tie-dyed loincloth—in the midst of one of their dungeon-and-slave-girl routines. "For?"

"Your emotional unavailability."

"Really. Really?"

He nodded.

"So shoot me."

The light in this back room was low. Alton was grim, monster-like, shirtless, the flecks of the fake beard still patching his jawline. "You're right. She's finished with you. It's over. So I'm leaving you, too," he said. "Here. Alone."

It was weird, because—maybe it was the tone—that did sound kind of bad. "I'm leaving you," like the way a lover would say it. It was a solemn and forlorn statement.

"You mean, tied upside down with my throat slit?"

He shook his massive head. "As you are. All by yourself."

"We're breaking up? You can't be my psycho nemesis any more?"

"Something like that."

I laughed, but it wasn't a real laugh. I felt cold inside.

"You're a sad, sad person, Bent. Alice deserves better."

Weird, but he was getting to me with that. I guess we'd spent so much time together, he and I, even if I hadn't really known it, that I started to feel that bizarre pull and push I got from Alice herself. In fact, I pretty much got it from everybody.

Low and dark, he added: "And you're not worth putting out of your misery."

I looked up at him from my crouched position. I stared into his pale, dull eyes.

"Yes I am."

Quick, just as he'd darted down the side alley, up over the metal wall—like the way his fist with the crushed orange had come so close to cracking Chloe's skull, then stopped just in time—in one motion he had an actual pistol, a small revolver, aimed at my head.

I shouldn't even say "aimed" because that implies if he pulled the trigger he could miss. The details of what happened afterwards are confused and tinged with the cold round hardness I associate with the sensation of having that chilly gun barrel touching the skin right between my eyebrows, in that space where he was so bizarrely hirsute. Try it sometime and you'll agree—it's memorable. Alton muttered a few more things about what an unredeemably bad person I was—I think. I mentioned how Alice had said he wasn't popular in high school. "I can't imagine why." So he told me if I were smart, I would be quiet, and I said that didn't look like an FBI gun to me, not the kind you see on FBI shows on TV anyway—"Are you sure you're in the FBI?" and so on. Finally, he cracked me over the head with the pistol, but I squirmed, so it was a glancing blow.

I was on the floor as he walked away. I could see his crappy Doc Martins beating an exit (some fancy dresser). The front door of the package store slammed shut.

I held my head for a while. I whined. After a few moments, I got up on an elbow. The floor in that place was filthy. "Don't come back!" I mumbled, then something dropped from my chest and rattled onto the sticky tiles.

My Rolex.

I thought of the dragon on the *jardín* in San Judas, clapping its hands. Fucking Alton.

I heard a lurching, a heavy pressing, a moan, and I thought the coyote had come to life, but no. He still looked existentially sad in his far-too-small cage. It was like he knew he wasn't part of this plot, and Alton's saying so had been the last straw. Stumbling, I made my way stiffly to the front room, leaned on the checkout counter—with one eye still on the lookout for Alton (asshole), in case he was hiding or meaning to return. I wondered, in fact, how he'd gotten there in the first place: I had to assume it wasn't via the truck presently toasting in the back lot. Then, behind that counter, I found the source of all the sighing and moaning: a man I assumed to be the actual clerk—shirtless himself, nearly toothless, with smudged green tattoos on his biceps and his massive belly plopped onto the filthy tiles as he lay on his side. He snored vigorously though serenely. He'd been knocked out with an FBI tranquilizer dart, or debilitated by a secret grip, or maybe just conked on the head by that jerk. Poor redneck. His hands were behind his back, wrapped in duct tape. He was a tired little barrel-gutted angel with his wings clipped.

"Hope that's not your truck, Bubs."

I left my cheap digital watch on the redneck's wrist and fastened my Rolex to mine. I collected the items I'd tried to buy from Alton the *faux* clerk and carried them to the car. Had I wet myself? No. Win! I seat-belted the syrup canister into the passenger side like a family member, connected the hose that made a scary hissing when I attached it but seemed to seal. I might need easy access on the road. Back inside, I located the freezer and pulled out a ninety-nine-cent bag of ice, and threw forty dollars onto the passed-out redneck clerk. Before getting started, I ran my hand along the headboard, the driver's seat, dash, and headrest. I found nothing, but then, on top of the car, my fingers picked up on a raised bubble. It was like a round-cornered square piece of tape, colored the same as my Elantra, and covered now with specs of sap from the ABOGADOS Y MÁS parking lot. When I peeled it off—with difficulty—underneath, embedded in its little pad, I found a

complex city map grid of solid-state circuitry. It was evidence, but what was I really going to do with it? Maggie Leudecke had, apparently, murdered two men. Had I gone to the police?

I'd bought a candle from her.

I rolled the tracking device like a used Band-Aid and ground it into the parking lot with my heel.

In the car, I mixed a fabulous Cuba Tiránica in a red plastic cup: ice, rum, and diet cola syrup. I tossed a whole plastic sack with forty-nine other red plastic cups into the back seat, and put the big bag of melting ice back there, too. I was about to peel out of the parking lot, but I couldn't.

"No."

I drove behind the place in the hard afternoon sun, to where the now singed marshmallow-colored truck sent chunks of black cloud upwards in a long, thick, segmented sky worm. I needed to get out of there, but instead I walked towards the back screen door. I pictured myself as if through a long lens—the way Clint Eastwood is seen when outlaws notice him on the ridge. Naturally, the screen door was unlatched, so I walked in, lifted the coyote, cage and all, by a wire handle someone had twisted onto the top of it—a real jury-rigged operation there.

The thing was heavy. Though it had been morose, still, once I lifted it, the coyote began to scramble on the uneven floor of its filthy cage, and although silent except for its long nails clicking against the metal, it seemed to get some of its spunk back. My back and shoulder ached. I really needed to return to my workout regime. Well, the one from a few decades back, anyway. I wondered if Tony Ruiz would let me use his sons' facility in off hours.

That's just how drunk I was.

I took one last look at the smoldering truck. What had Maggie Leudecke said about the stakes of love? "You might want to ask if it's worth it to have a love so strong if it comes with a hurt so strong."

Alton—fucker—obviously thought that payoff made sense. I was about to find out.

"You," I said to the coyote in the rear-view as I drove out of the parking lot. "Trickster. Border crosser. I wouldn't pay a dime for you."

iv.

And what would Yvonne have said to me, if she were there? Which I would not have been able to afford, by the way. If I were an equity partner at Davidson, Kohlhoeffer & Loeb, I probably could have had her make house calls. Maybe I could have even gotten mobile advice: had her ride in a town car with me while I went from important meeting to important meeting. Well, no, that was bullshit. Equity partners at a place the size of D, K & L didn't make *that* kind of scratch. Also—what did I need her for? It's not like I didn't know what she'd tell me already. "Perfect, Bent. Throwing ourselves a big old pity party, aren't we?"

"Oh, really?" I said to the imaginary Yvonne I carried in my head, now that I couldn't afford the real one. I rolled down all of the windows, tried not to breathe too deeply the coyote's gamey though somewhat cabbage-like musk. "Really, Yvonne, is that all you've got?" Imaginary Yvonne, ironically, was often far less imaginative than the actual Yvonne. So—"Yes," I said. "I am doing that. Notice it's also a journey."

I arrived in Bold Springs as the sun set behind the pines. The boarded-up businesses, the red-brick Savings and Loan: it was all the same. No one seemed to be cashing in on their new fake wealth as of yet, but maybe it happened behind the scenes. I searched the horizon for the hilltop cemetery and was pretty sure I'd located the road we'd traveled by convoy a year earlier. I drove up the single lane and soon situated myself.

As for me, I was not really that drunk. Would someone who was completely snockered even be able to find that place? Especially as night was falling? I found it: the field where we had parked on the day of the reception, which meant the house must be . . . right . . . up . . . there. I turned

off the ignition. That coyote smelled damn odd, but didn't
fidget. He accepted his fate, I supposed. But the path to the
house was shut off—a gate had been pulled closed across the
weird sidewalk pavement that went up to the rear of the Loeb
mansion. It was not just an ornamental gate, either: the thing
was padlocked with a chain. A high security fence drew off
into the dense woods at either side of it. I didn't remember
any of this stuff being there before.

I pondered this obstacle. Who the fuck would put up
barriers to keep people out of their hilltop mansion?

"It might help you," said imaginary Yvonne, "to reflect
on what she meant to you. Did she represent 'Love,' or
'Desire,' as concepts? That is: rather than realities? Did she
represent a continuation of who you used to be: not old and
decrepit, but youthful, like before Kelly, for example?"

"Shut it," I told imaginary Yvonne. "I'll ask her when
I see her."

"Or did she remind you of someone from your
boyhood?"

I started by trying to go between the slats of this gate,
but those were very close, and my chest wedged and stuck
before I got very far. The gate was actually rickety—corrugated
tin or something like that—and I felt wobbly myself, but to
climb over seemed the only choice, though a chore. I looked
around for a flashlight in the back seat, to no avail. "You wait
here," I told the coyote. He had started to make the Hyundai
smell God-awful. He looked so depressed. I thought maybe
he should have some kind of water or something in that cage,
but all I had was ice and red plastic cups, and I didn't see a
good way to open the cage without opening it all the way.
Then he'd be gone. Naturally, gone was what he should have
been, but I wasn't thinking clearly. In my mind, I had to deal
with Chloe first, release Mr. Coyote into nature later.

Oh, nature.

I rolled up the windows and locked the car door so he'd
be all safe and sound.

I climbed the gate, not so much cutting my palm when I
went over the metal slats as creasing it really badly. Fortunately,
I had placed my Cuba Tiránica through the openings in the

gate, and could stoop to retrieve it once safely on the other side. I swallowed some of the pasty liquid to relieve the pain and sucked on my hand as I tried to stumble up the sidewalk in the dark.

Oh, fuck. Forgot the candle.

So I struggled back over the damn gate, then found some way to stick the key in the door lock, because it was getting really dark, and when I finally had checked on the so-depressed coyote that watched me now without moving ("You okay in here?") and retrieved the candle, it was dark indeed, and truly stifling in that car. Son of a bitch, why had I rolled up those windows? I could have suffocated the poor beast in all the heat. I was horrified. I pictured the coyote's carcass, its lolled tongue, its clouded, accusatory eyes. I started to cry. "Emotional unavailability *my ass!*" I screamed. (That's how bad it had gotten.) What to do?

Wait a minute.

Why didn't I deal with both of these issues simultaneously? Why didn't I release the coyote in Loeb's yard? It was a very nice yard. (I remembered the soft grass, the sculpted junipers.) What a great place for him! So I wedged the candle tight into my back pocket with some difficulty, then hefted the cage out of the back seat by its wire handle, which felt none too good on my creased palm, either. Again there were no complaints save the occasional snick of his nails on the crusty floor of the cage.

I put the glass candle through the slats as securely as I had my drink before, then perched, once again, precariously up on that gate, only this time I also had to balance the cage. My shoulder *skreeked* under the strain. This was all taking a lot longer than I'd planned, and it had gotten so dark. I glanced up at what was left of the still faintly purple sky and. . . .

It was a sky full of spiders.

I had one of those "Is this something big and far away, or something small and very close?" moments that froze me atop the gate. A complicated web hung between several trees and branches directly above me, and I would conservatively say twenty or thirty spiders dangled from it: silhouettes in the gloom. One really did seem to be huge: a grand-momma spider of some kind, suspended from the middle of a group of variously sized other arachnids, this one, however, spinning slowly. It seemed big enough that spider steak might be carved from its bulbous abdomen.

I made a few incoherent statements appropriate to the occasion and fell from the gate onto my side on the sidewalk. The cage rattled and thumped when it hit the concrete. At first I scrambled, afraid the cage's door had come open, and that the beast had escaped. Maybe it would turn on me! Maybe it would bite me with its angry canine fangs—but the cage was sound. The animal was as morose and silent as ever. He raised his dull eyes to examine me when I leaned over him.

I let the adrenaline charge drain from my chest. "Don't give me that look."

I rested a few moments. I flipped onto my back on the pavement, stuck my legs out straight to make sure my hip hadn't broken, and felt the still warm concrete against the back of my calves, but then I accidentally kicked my drink into the dirt. As I tried to right it before everything spilled, I knocked the candle into some underbrush by the walkway. I had to kick around in that for a while trying to locate the candle, as I saw no future in thrusting my hand into underbrush in such a spidery region. I ducked my head low, not sure how far into the road that web dipped.

"It's not good out here," I said to the coyote in his overturned cage. I could hear crickets and night insects. I felt suddenly alone and vulnerable.

Finally I did connect with my candle.

I replayed these horrors in my mind as I struggled to lug the cage up the hillside in the dark. Left foot. Right foot. I feared I was approaching the hilltop house from the wrong direction, or even had the wrong hill, as nothing seemed familiar. Or else the sweet, sweet rum and syrup had worked confusion on my mind. Or the scary spiders had disoriented me. I stepped with care when the road ended and I saw iron fencing and aged gravestones—relieved, really, to locate those landmarks nearby—and I lit the candle with my butane lighter so I could have a chance at avoiding any yard ornaments. I had only a vague sense that I'd find the house right up at the tippy-most top of the hill, as there was no white-tented awning any more to give away the location in the darkness. The breeze made the oaks and pines emit strange creaking noises I didn't much like, and when I looked up, there seemed to be a vapor trail overhead—like a jet had just gone past at low altitude. I was beyond the "lightness of the brain" zone of drunkenness, heading into the "heaviness of the mind" region and becoming sad. But I held my candle, and peered around, and finally saw a sliver of brightness very near. It was a window on the mansion. It had to be. Light came through the space between some curtains. I was close.

I patted my pockets. Where was the paper with the incantation on it? The incantation that—together with the candle, would insure my connection . . . my reconnection to Chloe, so that I could communicate with her across those spaces that divided us, the void between myself and that distant world she now occupied. I needed that incantation to initiate the magic that had worked so well to connect Maggie and Roy in the bathroom of death.

I realized, in fact, I had no idea where I'd even last seen that paper with the incantation on it.

"Oh, fuck."

It was too much. Going back down to the car to search for it wasn't going to happen. I would just have to try it on my own.

I brought both candle and cage as near as possible as I could to the sliver of light. Within the house, I could make out a short, empty hallway, a polished wooden floor, a pile of clothes against a wall. I noticed a feminine-looking mauve sock on top of this pile, barely ankle-length with a fringe, and something that looked like sweat pants wadded into a ball. I must have been looking into the laundry room. I stepped back a few paces and surveyed the rest of the house in the gloom, but could see no other vantage point. I'd really imagined something else. I thought I'd spy on her as she moved about in a stately dining room, perhaps, or sat by a glowing fireplace, reading. This was not the ideal spot for my first attempt at being a spiritual peeping tom.

It would have to do. I began my personal incantation.

V.

Hi. Not what you expected.

Damp out here. I'm drunk enough that I don't feel, or don't care, about the dampness. Mind if I put this candle on this flowerbed? It's a candle. Hole into another world or something.

It's not pretty is it? I don't mean the candle.

The candle's okay. Flickers. As they do. I'd hoped to avoid all this darkness by coming earlier.

So, it's July 7. And I guess you were bummed or something. Having a bad day? But I'm glad you called. Called me. And I've tried everything to remember . . . everything. I do know it was your idea. It was! Not just mine. It was your phone call.

You said, "I'm saying that I need some help with something at the office. But what I really need is to meet you. Do you understand? The two of us?"

And I looked right at Marisel, and said into the phone: "It needs to be taken care of."

So, anyway. I'm here.

Mom's fine. Alice was trying to get to her for a few weeks, but now she—Alice, that is—has met some rich fuck. Thank God. And then there's Alton.

Never mind Alton.

Man, it's crazy, actually going to deportation hearings. And then appearing in court. Court! Plus, I'm such a freak. Yeah, I'm a palooka at ABOGADOS Y MÁS, but it's mainly just that careers usually start out there, and it looks like mine is going to end up there.

So. I'm letting this coyote go in your yard. I think it'll be fine. Shit. Okay. Latch on this thing, the only piece of quality workmanship on this . . . cage . . . there. Alright. There ya go.

Complicated latch.

Go. Go, man.

You!

I told you not to look at me like that, motherfucker.

Well, he'll sit in there awhile. Then he'll go. He'll be fine.

And everything is high-risk, Chloe. Working with Ruiz. Everything happens fast. The people won't talk to me, sometimes. They hide shit. They're afraid. I'm afraid.

I'm thinking now, just looking overhead, that those things I thought were clouds before, they're not. Oooh. Give a guy goose bumps. That's not a vapor trail; it's the Milky Way. Like silver paint on a black ceiling. Whirled patterns. Not sure I can really make out constellations. Well, sure. The rich have better skies, even. Better twinkle twinkles.

You! Coyote!

I guess those people buried behind the shrubs back there—the pioneers and their trusted servants—get this view every night.

What was it? What didn't work? I have this voice in my head—I won't say whose—and it asks: "Was it exciting to be picked by her? Even though you weren't even close to being the only one?" Or: "Why do you think you needed her acceptance? Her praise or love? Did you feel special in her company? If you can boil it down to something concrete it might help."

Fucking voice in my head.

Only thing concrete I see now is an ankle sock with a fringe. Sweatpants.

I'm dizzy.

You there?

So: I remember finding you in your car in the Super 8 parking lot with your baseball cap turned backwards. You sat in the car while I arranged the reservation. When I got back, we kind of slunked over to the room. The two of us, walking into that *skak* hotel in broad daylight. Oh, and the key for the room was one of those cheapo plastic cards. There was an ad for pizza delivery on one side.

Yeah. The door opened when I used that plastic card with the pizza ad on it, and we walked together through the open door. Happy July 7.

Maybe if I touch the window, I can reach you better.
I'll start over.
Hi. Not what you expected.
Oh.
Fine.
That's just fine
Really? Lights AND sirens?
That does it. We are through.
You.
Trickster. Border crosser.
Up!
I say go.
Go!
Go!

ACKNOWLEDGMENTS

I am grateful to many who helped in the writing of *Pretty Enough for You*. Angie Cruz and my seminar-mates in the Spring 2012 Fiction Workshop at Texas A&M University aided in transforming the initial manuscript from rant to narrative. David Samuel Levinson's encouragement, friendship, and feedback have been a great influence, for which I'm thankful. Several friends and colleagues offered invaluable advice over the course of many drafts, including (alphabetically) James Cortese, Michael Dunican, Miriam Kassouni, Lana Myers, David Parsons, Kelly Patton, Jay Rohfritch, Cassie Tomchik, and Randall Watson. I first began thinking about eminent domain because of Jan Reid's *Texas Monthly* article "Showdown at the Maverick Ranch," and poet/attorney Daniel Rice helped me greatly in pondering aspects of this topic. I gleaned important and helpful insight into the Houston legal scene and the vagaries of immigration law from attorney Jacob M. Monty. Another of the city's immigration lawyers *par excellence*, Carolina Ortuzar-Diaz, thoughtfully examined the manuscript for glaring impossibilities ("Why is he seeking a waiver of unlawful entry when it's obvious he needs a waiver of unlawful presence?")—however, all remaining egregious errors of law or believability belong to the author, not the aforementioned consummate professionals. Thanks to Paul Ruffin at Texas Review Press for his support, and Nancy Parsons at Graphic Design Group for the book design. I could not have finished this work without the melodious grownup heartbreak music of Richard Thompson. Finally, all I write is influenced by "Stern's Laws," and the ever-sounding-in-my-brain counsel of my teacher, Daniel Stern (1928-2007).

AUTHOR BIOGRAPHY

Cliff Hudder flunked out of law school in 1981, but received an MFA in fiction writing from the University of Houston in 1995. He has been an archaeological laborer, a film and video editor, a photographer, air compressor mechanic, electrical lineman, and educator. In addition to articles on regional and American literature, his short stories have appeared in several journals, including *Alaska Quarterly Review*, *The Kenyon Review*, and *The Missouri Review*. His work has received the Barthelme and Michener Awards, the Peden Prize, and the Short Story Award from the Texas Institute of Letters. His novella, *Splinterville*, won the 2007 Texas Review Fiction Award. He teaches English at Lone Star College-Montgomery in Conroe, Texas, and is presently at work on a PhD in English at Texas A&M University.